Into the Inferno

Book Eleven of Rise of the Republic

By

James Rosone and Miranda Watson

****

Illustration © Tom Edwards
Tom EdwardsDesign.com

****

Published in conjunction with Front Line Publishing, Inc.

Manuscript Copyright Notice

ISBN: 978-1-961748-67-5
Sun City Center, Florida, United States of America
Library of Congress Control Number: 2024919541

Table of Contents

Additional Content

We have spent quite a bit of time and money creating artwork for this series. If you would like to see images of our ships, the different alien races, and scenes from various battles, please visit the "Members Only" section of our website at the following link, https://frontlinepublishinginc.com/members-only/
and sign up with your email. It is completely free. We hope you enjoy it—now on to the book!

Chapter One

Early May 2114
Eridu Spaceport
Sha'ab District, Zidara
Gurista Prime

Karnix Joltar hated babysitting duties, but the higher-ups had decided that since the construction of the space elevator was nearly complete, it was important to up the security level. Besides, even though he would rather be engaged in active combat any day of the week, Zodark soldiers simply did not say no when issued an order.

Twenty Zodarks and a company of two hundred and sixty Gurista Defense Force soldiers seemed a bit excessive to Karnix. He wondered if the powers that be had some inside intel that would require such a large presence at this time. He hadn't been informed of a credible threat, but intelligence didn't always flow downward the same way it did upward among the Zodark ranks.

Bang!

A piece of metal paneling struck another during the construction process, causing Karnix to startle. Something about the apparent overkill in security had made him jumpy. He looked around to make sure no one had seen him flinch. The coast was clear.

Boom, boom, BOOM!

Karnix checked himself. Those noises he had just heard were definitely explosions, not the sounds of building materials clanging together. He ran to the nearest window. Plumes of black smoke were rising from several locations around the city.

He keyed his mic. "NOS Tarvox," said Karnix, "I heard several blasts and can see evidence of the capital under attack."

"Raka!" cursed Tarvox. "This must be that insurgent group I was briefed on yesterday. We knew they were fomenting dissent, but we didn't expect them to attack. I want you to call in the exact locations where the disturbances are taking place. Stay vigilant—we may be on the move soon."

"Yes, NOS," Karnix replied. He started to calculate the exact location of each plume of smoke when he had a sudden realization.

"NOS Tarvox," he said, keying his mic again, "the palace is under attack!"

The guttural roar that followed over the comms caused Karnix's chest cavity to vibrate. After a brief silence, Tarvox responded, "There is no time for my rage. There is only time to attack. I am headed to your location now."

A few minutes later, NOS Tarvox had selected three Zodark soldiers and thirty Gurista Defense Force soldiers to stay behind and guard the space elevator. The rest of the force—seventeen Zodark soldiers and two hundred and thirty GDF—were told to head to the palace and see what was going on.

"Keep alert!" ordered NOS Tarvox as he signaled for their makeshift reaction force to advance. "If anyone sees anything suspicious, I want to know about it immediately."
****

Outside the Capitol Palace
Zidara, Gurista Prime

Staff Sergeant Anders Johansson's pulse was pounding, and he could feel all the muscles in his body tense. He took a deep breath and let it out slowly. The heightened state of awareness was justified given the fact that they had just overthrown all of the Zodark overlords on Gurista Prime, but if he didn't calm down his fight-or-flight instinct, it was going to get in the way of him doing his job.

There were two groups of six Republic Delta soldiers guarding the perimeter of the palace, and each team of Deltas was working with a group of twelve insurgents they had trained up over the last several months. Although they had a lot of history working together, there was a huge difference between training drills and dealing with actual potential live combat.

Isolated pockets of Guristas battled it out with some of the other units that had been stationed throughout Zidara to keep order; the noises of combat, although seemingly isolated and contained, were unnerving.

Staff Sergeant Johansson had expected to have *some* trouble. It was impossible, given the situation, that there would be zero Guristas who decided that they had an allegiance to the Zodarks. But Johansson was hopeful the number would be small, especially given the shock and awe campaign they had carried out—the show of force had hopefully been sufficient to scare many of their potential attackers away. However, he knew that if things went sideways, their group of thirty-six guarding the perimeter could turn into a speed bump. It would be up to Drew and his Kites to manage getting Tammuz to the bunker.

One of the drone operators responsible for providing overwatch waved his arm to signal for Johansson to come over and look at something he had found. "Boss, looks like we have company," he announced.

Johansson's stomach dropped downward until it felt like it was reaching his knees. Coming from the direction of the spaceport that had been under construction was a large group of inbound Zodark and Gurista Defense Force soldiers, and they looked like they were in a hurry.

"Send it out to everyone," Johansson ordered.

After clicking a few keys, the drone operator pulled the overlay of known enemy combatants and sent it to the HUDs of those guarding the perimeter of the palace. Sergeant Johansson heard several soldiers curse beneath their breath as they realized what was headed toward them.

Before anyone had a chance to panic, however, a Zodark Zeek swooped in, seemingly from nowhere, and started raking through their ranks.

Zip, zip, zip, zip!

"Take cover!" yelled Johansson.

Several of the insurgents Johansson had spent the last several months training were mowed down almost instantly. If Johansson hadn't narrowly missed the same fate himself by jumping behind one of the large decorative columns that surrounded the palace, he would have mourned their deaths. They were good men and women. However, at that moment, Johansson was just grateful that whatever concrete-like substance they used in their construction on Gurista Prime had apparently been sufficient to keep him from getting sliced in half.

After two passes, the Zeek had managed to kill at least fifteen of Johansson's soldiers. Johansson realized that if he didn't want to find out firsthand what really happened in the afterlife, they had to get a move on.

"Fall back to the palace!" he roared. He knew that the best thing they could do at this point was to make sure that Tammuz got moved to the bunker, especially as the Zodark and GDF forces closed in. He beat his fist against his chest and psyched himself up for a fight to the death.

"If I'm going down, I'll take as many of those blue bastards with me as I can!" he yelled.

Several of his comrades in arms yelled with him as they sprinted to the palace. The Zeek took another pass at them, killing several more soldiers. However, just as Johansson reached the nearest doorway, he heard a new sound from the air. He turned in time to see an F-11 Gripen swoop in from nowhere and lay into the Zeek.

Boom!

The deadly alien craft exploded and tumbled from the sky— right toward the entrance to the palace where Johansson stood.

"Run!" he screamed.

****

Inside the Capitol Palace
Zidara, Gurista Prime

"Tammuz, would you like to accept the offer of support from the Republic and our alliance?" asked Dobbs.

"Yes, we would most graciously accept whatever kind of support and assistance your force can provide to aid in our quest to remain a free—"

Boom!

Something loud had occurred near the palace, but it wasn't clear what just yet. Tammuz could feel his palms getting sweaty.

What the hell is happening out there? he wondered.

He heard the voices of several Gurista insurgents yelling near the northern entrance to the palace, followed by a much louder and closer explosion-like boom. Something had slammed into the building—that much was certain.

The connection to Dobbs had been lost, but that was now the least of Tammuz's concerns. He found himself being guided by the man he simply knew as "David" toward a side entrance he hadn't noticed before.

"We've got to get you to the bunker!" Drew bellowed. "It's not safe here right now."

David had them racing down a hallway until they reached a room with a stairwell that led to another hallway, then it turned and led to the entrance of an elevator shaft.

Two other men, and two women, had quickly joined them.

"We need you to start the biometric sequence," David directed.

It was like reality struck Tammuz in the face and he realized why everyone was standing around and staring at him.

Thank goodness we reprogrammed the palace accesses as soon as we took over, thought Tammuz as he placed his hand on the fingerprint reader. A line of blue light scanned his eyes, capturing the images of his retinas. A second later, the door to the elevator opened with a hiss.

Tammuz walked onto the elevator with Drew, David, and his crew and turned around. Several Deltas and Gurista insurgents were running toward them.

"Should we hold the elevator?" Tammuz asked Drew.

"No," Drew replied flatly. "They're here to make sure that none of our enemies get close to you."

Tammuz took a deep breath and let it out. He looked at the men and women one last time as the doors to the elevator closed, realizing that the next time he saw them, he would likely be speaking at their memorial service.

****

Tammuz was sullen. Sitting in the bunker, he felt helpless. As a man of action for most of his life, this left him despondent. He skulked his way into a corner and rested with his head in his hands.

After a minute, he grumbled, "Are we just going to wait here until we die?"

"No, sir," Drew replied. "We do have a plan."

Tammuz's ears perked up. "Oh?"

"Yes. You see, this bunker has another exit," Drew began.

"It does?" asked Tammuz, bewildered.

"The powers that be on Gurista Prime apparently decided long ago that having their leader isolated and unable to escape was a bad thing. So in their wisdom, they created a tunnel that goes out about one hundred meters and then branches out in three different directions."

Tammuz sat up much straighter now. "Where do these paths lead?" he asked.

"Well, I have good news, and I have bad news," Drew explained. "We've sent drones out to map the tunnels and see if there are any enemy forces we need to be aware of. So far, we know that one tunnel goes to the Mukhabarat headquarters, which is not exactly the best location for us to show up, as you can imagine. Another tunnel goes to the closest military base—"

"Excuse me, but what was the good news?" interrupted Tammuz.

"Well, so far, the tunnels themselves are clear, and the military base closest to the Capitol Palace was absolutely decimated, so I'm sure that my team could handle whatever is left there."

"All right…and where does this third exit go?" asked Tammuz, not certain exactly what his odds of surviving this day were looking like.

"Still waiting to find that one out," said Drew. "It's a long tunnel. I hope you have your walking shoes on."

Tammuz looked down at his feet. He was wearing business shoes, but they were comfortable enough. The idea of being in a tunnel for such a long time made him nervous, though. With only six defenders, he would be in a very vulnerable position.

Still, if I didn't know about these tunnels, how many Zodarks or GDF out there knew about them? Tammuz wondered. *And of those, how many survived and have the ability to do anything about it?*

These thoughts gave him solace. Even if there were some enemy forces out there with such knowledge, with all the attacks that had taken place, it was unlikely that they would be in a position to act on that information.

Five minutes later, Drew approached Tammuz again. "Are you ready to move?" he asked.

"Where are we going?"

"To the Enuma Archives," Drew replied.

A wave of relief washed over Tammuz. He had never been so happy at the thought of ancient historical texts and scrolls in all of his life. He wondered why the designers of these tunnels would have chosen such a benign, non-hardened location as an exit, and then it hit him. *It's because it's boring*, he realized. *No one would expect it.*

All these years, he had thought that the ground floor of the Enuma Archives had been turned into a vault to protect historical documents and keep them preserved. Now he understood the truth.

Chapter Two

Early May 2114
Task Force Lightning
RNS *Maximus*
Gurista Prime, Orinda System

Brigadier General Brian Royce stood at the holographic map table, his gaze fixed on the spinning image of Gurista Prime's capital, Zidara. The command center buzzed with the frenetic energy of precombat operations. The massive orbital assault ship, RNS *Maximus*, was descending into the planet's lower orbit. Squadrons of F-97 Orions and B-99 Raiders were being prepped for launch, made ready to intercept any Zodark Vultures or Zeeks that might rise to meet them.

With a wave of his hand, Royce shifted the holographic display to show the descending *Maximus* and its formidable escort: the battle cruiser RNS *Invincible*, flanked by the heavy cruisers *Vortex* and *Dominion*, with the *Maximus*'s sister ships, *MacArthur* and *Eisenhower*, trailing. A pair of frigates formed the rear guard. It was an impressive invasion force, but Royce knew they were far behind enemy lines. If things went wrong out here, they were on their own.

An ensign approached, stumbling over his words. "Um, excuse me, General, um—"

Royce turned, his expression patient. "At ease, Ensign Horn, right? Take a breath and start over. I'm a person like you. I put my pants on one leg at a time. Now, what's the message you have for me?"

Horn nodded, swallowing hard. "Sir, we received a message from *MacArthur*—General Berg is asking to speak to you on the secure comms."

Royce gave a reassuring smile. "See, that wasn't so hard, was it? Confidence, Ensign, you can do this. Now link the call to my station." His words were not just a command but a reminder of the crucial role confidence plays in the military.

As Royce walked to his workstation, he couldn't help but hope that this wasn't another instance of the "Good Idea Fairy" striking at the worst possible moment, bringing with it the chaos of unexpected changes. When he activated the secure comms, the image of Major General Jørgen Berg—JB—flickered into view.

"Brian, good to see you. I wanted to catch you before the landings start. I've been thinking about what you said regarding the Serpentis campaign and how your SOF task force is best used as a scalpel, not a broadsword. I've decided to change your orders per your recommendations."

Royce raised an eyebrow, intrigued. Berg continued, "I'm sending a FRAGO to the *Maximus*, reassigning Colonel Hiro's regiment back to your task force. You're right; you'll be more effective in achieving our mission objectives this way. I know VC has a bit of a reputation as a hardnosed hard-ass. I'd like to think I'm at least smart enough to know when a better plan is presented. For the good of the soldiers I lead, I should place my ego aside and embrace the better plan. If your force needs additional support, don't hesitate to ask. Do you have any final questions before everything kicks off?"

Royce felt a surge of relief on hearing the humility expressed by JB as the overall ground force commander. Royce's SOF task force was at JB's mercy in how he wanted to use them to support his overall mission—reasserting Free Gurista control over their home world and the five colony worlds they controlled.

Leaning forward, bringing his face closer to the camera, Royce said, "Just one question, JB. I've got the palace as our primary objective. But what about the spaceport? That was a Ranger objective, Colonel Hiro's. Is that still one of your targets or transferred to mine now that the Rangers are back under my control?"

Berg thought about that for a second, then shook his head. "Eh, that's a good point, Royce. Tell you what, I'll handle the Eridu Spaceport with the other two Ranger regiments staying with my force. You focus on your other objectives for now. Once we have our initial goals met, we'll reconvene to assess what else needs a military response versus a civilian-led effort. For better or worse, we're the muscle for the new regime—at least until we can get a proper Gurista force to replace us. Like I said earlier, if you need support, just ask."

"Thanks, JB. I appreciate your willingness to listen. We Deltas can make a big impact if we're used in a way that maximizes our special abilities."

Berg smiled at his reply. "I'm going to like working with you, Brian. Good luck. Berg out."

Royce leaned back in his chair, staring at the blank screen for a moment, satisfied with how the conversation had just gone. Now that he had Hiro's regiment back, his options had expanded. Glancing at the clock, he saw they had forty-nine minutes until deployment.

Better round up the troops and brief them on the change of plans.

He stood and made his way back to the holographic map table, a renewed sense of purpose driving him forward.

****

Echo Company, 2nd Regiment, 4th Ranger Division
RNS *Maximus*
Gurista Prime, Orinda System

Captain Paul "Pauli" Smith stood before the Rangers of Echo Company, his eyes scanning the faces of the men and women under his command. The brightly lit hangar of the RNS *Maximus* hummed with the sound of final preparations as ground crews ran through last-minute system checks and the pilots hastily finished their preflight checklists. Pauli stepped onto a container box to address his troops, his voice steady and commanding as he spoke.

"Listen up, Echo Company! For those of you who are new to Echo, this might be your first jump, your first real taste of combat. For many of us, this mission is just another of many jumps we've made during this war and the last. But this mission, this jump, is special. Previously, our jumps were to invade an enemy planet, liberate an allied planet, or defend our own. Today is different—today we're coming to the aid of a planet that has thrown off the shackles of bondage previously held by the Zodarks. Unlike previous missions, we are not liberating an alien race. We are liberating a fellow *human* society, a group of humans once from Earth but stolen from our planet to be bred like cattle to fight on behalf of the Zodark Empire. Well, we've come to put a stop to that," Pauli declared, his tone infused with a mix of seriousness and determination. "In a few minutes, we're going to board our battle taxis and Uber our way into destiny."

Laughter and snide comments rippled through the ranks, breaking some of the tension.

"All joking aside," Pauli continued, "in a few moments, we're going to board our ATACs and head into battle. When we win, we will liberate the Gurista people—freeing a society of hundreds of millions not just here on Gurista Prime but on five other colony planets in this system and the one next door. These people have been under Zodark rule for centuries, forced into servitude. Rangers, today, we change that."

The Rangers nodded along in agreement, their expressions more serious.

"In a coordinated effort, the Gurista government was overthrown by the Free Gurista movement. This was accomplished with the help of Republic Intelligence and Delta Special Forces units, which had infiltrated the planet and Gurista society more than a year earlier. While some Gurista military commanders, their units, and many local law enforcement units hastily recognized the new government—some did not," Pauli explained, recounting details from the Commander's Brief he'd attended an hour earlier.

"This is a fluid situation, Rangers. We have limited intelligence and likely will not have more until we're on the ground and can begin to collect it ourselves. What we do know is this—some Zodark units garrisoned outside the city have managed to rally some local military and security personnel who had yet to switch sides and remained loyal to local Zodark units. At least one of these forces has launched an attack against the spaceport while a separate force attacked the palace, where the new leader is currently under siege. Now, here's the fun part," Pauli explained, a crooked smile forming along the edges of his mouth. "Our company has been detached from the regiment and assigned to support the JSOC unit being led by Brigadier General Brian Royce himself in a direct assault against the palace."

Several of the Rangers whistled softly at the mention of being assigned to work with the Joint Special Operation Command again and General Royce in particular. The Delta soldier was a hero within the SOF community and revered like a living legend.

"As everyone knows, we're still short on officers and noncoms. I'm going to continue leading First Platoon," Pauli said, then looked at Yogi. "Lieutenant Sanders, you're in charge of Second and Third Platoons. Lieutenant Yassin, you have Fourth and Fifth Platoons. I know this isn't exactly the ideal situation. We just have to make do with what we have, and remember—our job, once on the surface, is to support JSOC in any manner they deem necessary. Hooah?"

"Hooah!"

Pauli stood there a moment longer, his eyes searching their faces. He could see the determination in their eyes, a burning fire within. They were ready for him to cut them loose. Just then, the cadre of JSOC soldiers walked into the hangar deck, making their way toward them. Pauli looked on in admiration of these gods of war, these harbingers of death that walked among them.

The Rangers of Echo Company parted like the Red Sea as these augmented supersoldiers walked through their ranks to waiting ATACs. Then Pauli saw a soldier breaking off from his comrades to walk directly toward Pauli as he stood on his crate. As the figure approached, Pauli saw the nametape on the front of the Dragon Skin exosuit—BG Royce.

Pauli extended a hand to the approaching soldier, who accepted and joined him atop the crate as the Delta soldiers loaded into four of the waiting ATACs. "I'm Captain Paul Smith, Commander, Echo Company—everyone calls me Pauli," he quickly introduced himself.

With a firm handshake, Royce answered, "It's a pleasure to see you again, Pauli. I see they pulled you from the NCO ranks to make you an officer, eh?"

Pauli bunched his eyebrows in confusion. Then it dawned on him they had met many years prior during the Intus campaign—on the RNS *Mercy*. They had both been wounded during one of the battles, and their paths had crossed aboard the hospital ship.

"Ah, took me a moment to place where we had met—the *Mercy*. You had given me some advice about Special Forces as my enlistment was coming up. But, yeah, made master sergeant, then shortly afterward was given a battlefield commission. Either way, sir, Echo Company stands ready for orders," Pauli commented, gesturing toward his Rangers.

Royce nodded approvingly, then faced the Rangers to address them briefly. "Listen up, Rangers! I'm Brigadier General Brian Royce, and for better or worse, Echo Company will be joining with JSOC as we jump into history—a history that you and I will create through our shared victory as we bring death and destruction to the enemies of our nation, the Zodarks."

Royce spoke in an animated way that inspired the Rangers to do more than they thought they could. Pauli admired the command he immediately had of the group.

"Our mission is simply this: we are to counterassault the Zodark and Gurista loyalist forces in and around the palace, where a contingent of Deltas and Republic Intelligence have been held up since the start of the siege," Royce continued. "We must break this siege, restore order across the capital, and then expand that order across the remainder of the planet—bringing stability for the new regime to establish itself and bring the Gurista people in league with the rest of our alliance.

"Echo's objective is simple. You are to kill Zodarks and anyone who fires upon you. Clear the perimeter around the palace and ensure the enemy has no room to retreat, reorganize, or counterattack. In a few minutes, you'll be forwarded a digital map with an overlay of the city and the palace. You will see a parade ground to the northeast of the palace, maybe a kilometer in distance. When the parade ground has been secured, Scarabs will ferry in a few dozen Bobcats, courtesy of the RA, to give us some wheels and rapid mobility.

"If and when the skies are deemed secured, some Starlifters will land at the parade ground, offloading our standard DN-12 Cougars, Linebacker APCs, and some Puma light tanks for direct fire support. You have a big task ahead of you, Echo, and we are counting on you. Do not let us down, do not leave us hanging—you got me, Echo?"

As the soldiers shouted "Hooah!" in response, Royce pointed to the waiting ATACs, gesturing for them to board their wings of destiny.

"Good luck, Pauli. I'll see you on the other side," Royce said before hopping off the crate and jogging toward his waiting ATAC.
****

Echo Company
2nd Ranger Regiment

Inside the ATAC, a more heavily armored Osprey Charlie model, Pauli took his seat in the troop bay as the crew chief signaled they were ready. As the rear hatch closed, the bright lights of the hangar deck steadily disappeared. They were replaced with the overhead lighting as it cast a dim blue glow inside. Then came the sound of the engines, the pilots starting them up as they prepared to disembark.

As Pauli glanced around, noting the mixture of seasoned veterans and fresh faces he was still learning to put names to, he felt a reassuring calm. He watched the more experienced soldiers from the Serpentis campaign helping the newer members of their unit to make last-minute adjustments and fixes to their gear or weapons. It was at small moments like this when the light touch of a veteran carried more weight to a new soldier than a civilian could comprehend. Something about going into battle, to fight for one's life and the lives of those around one, had a mysterious way of maturing and unifying people that those who never served rarely understood.

We've got this...we'll do fine, Pauli thought to himself before closing his own eyes, refocusing his mind on the task at hand until a nagging thought returned—how he'd found himself in command of Echo Company.

During the Great Demobilization effort after the end of the Zodark War, it had been decided that the Rangers no longer needed two active-duty divisions. One division would remain on active duty, the other would transfer to the reserve, with one regiment of the latter remaining active but assigned to the Army's training and doctrine command or TRADOC. Their job was to recruit, train, and prepare soldiers to become Space Rangers and manage the officer and NCO academies.

A few years ago, Pauli had reluctantly agreed to accept the promotion to master sergeant, a decision that haunted him to this day. The only reason he had agreed was that his friend Yogi had talked him into it. He'd bragged about how they could even attend the training at the same time, and Lord knew he'd been a staff sergeant for nearly a decade—he was overdue to be promoted. He knew if he kept turning down the promotion, they'd eventually boot him out of the Rangers and demote him to a line unit—infantry, regular Army. The thought of losing the prestigious tan beret he had worked so hard to achieve was eventually enough of an incentive to accept the promotion.

Looking back on things, he should have listened to his wife and just left the Army. He'd gone on to become a millionaire multiple times over, so he didn't need the retirement. He already had a chest full of medals and awards from the First Zodark War, and he had done his bit, his service to God and country. But like many reservists, he enjoyed the camaraderie, and the two weeks of training each quarter was a nice change of pace and reprieve from the daily grind.

Opening his eyes as he looked down at his rifle, he felt every ounce of the weight of command that bore down on him, threatening to crush him the longer this war dragged on. That was when he noticed the slight tremor in his hand as he tightened his grip around his rifle. It seemed to happen on the eve of every battle. At least, that was when he observed it.

It's just stress, he told himself. *Nothing to be alarmed about.*

Still, the loss of soldiers under his command during these past couple of years was beginning to take its toll on him. The losses had become so severe and so frequent that they had necessitated the reorganization and, in some cases, disbandment of entire companies and even regiments, at least until enough replacements could arrive to bring them back. With nearly twenty years of service in the Army, he felt it was his duty to lead them, regardless of the losses they sustained, regardless of the physical toll it was having on his mind, body, and soul—he owed it to them.

"We're off, sir. Finally getting into the action," commented one of the new Rangers—Rosales, a private first class who had joined them fresh from Camp Darby a week before shipping out.

"Don't worry, PFC, this war is far from over. There will be plenty of action in the coming years," Pauli assured him, the sound of the engines growing louder as they lifted off the flight deck.

"We're on the move, Rangers! Remember your training and keep your heads on a swivel. Stay frosty—stay alive," Master Sergeant Drew Tinker shouted to the platoon.

Just then, the ATAC must have left the ship as the feeling of weightlessness took over, causing anything that hadn't been properly secured to float free for all to see. It didn't take long for the pilots to begin their descent, their mad dash to the surface before returning to the ship to rinse and repeat.

Pauli had just linked his HUD to the ATAC's forward camera when a DM from the pilot appeared. Opening the message, he felt his stomach tighten as he read the words.

Hang tight back there—fighters inbound.

"Aw, crap, they had to send fighters," Pauli mumbled to himself.

"Whoa, back up there, Captain—did you just say we've got fighters inbound?" Pauli's platoon sergeant asked. Not sure at first how the man had heard his musings, he checked his comms setting and realized the DM he'd meant to forward to Lieutenants Sanders and Yassin had inadvertently been sent to his entire company.

Damn it, the cat's out of the bag now, he lamented privately.

"Yup, they sure are," he responded.

Chapter Three

Carrier Strike Wing 16
Strike Fighter Squadron 30, "Red Rippers"
Gurista Prime, Orinda System

Captain Ethan Hunt gripped the controls of his Gripen starfighter as he led his flight of four beneath the hull of the RNS *Maximus*. The ship was a beast of futuristic engineering, a heavy orbital assault ship that could carry up to 6,200 soldiers into battle. It was these ships and many others that brought the fight to the enemy, and it was his fighters' job to make sure their assault transports made it to the surface unmolested.

He was leveling his fighter once they passed beneath the giant ship when he caught his first glimpse of the orbital assault as it began. He saw waves of ATACs and older Osprey models descending into the atmosphere, followed by several of the Scarab heavy assault transports right behind them.

Ethan's eyes scanned the tactical display on his HUD. The sleek fighters of the Red Rippers flew in a tight formation around him. The Rippers were the squadron he had flown with the most since taking command of Carrier Strike Wing 16. They were the squadron he felt comfortable flying with.

When the RNS *Freedom* had been forced to return to a Gallentine shipyard to finalize repairs the human and Altairian shipyards couldn't handle, many of the pilots were temporarily reassigned to fill squadron billets on the three newly completed star carriers joining the Fleet. Not all, but many of the pilots that comprised CSW 16 had flown with him aboard the *Freedom*. It helped make the transition from the Gallentine Hellcats back to the Gripens a bit easier, knowing everyone was going through the same readjustments.

Just then, his radio crackled, and his heart raced in excitement. "Paladin, Hen House. Be advised we have foxes approaching the chicks. Red Ripper and Warhawk are directed to engage hostiles and clear a path for the assault shuttles. How copy?"

A glance at his tactical display showed dozens of hostiles rising from the planet's surface in the vicinity of Zidara and another city he didn't know the name of. The tactical feed from the *Aquila* indicated the contacts were Vultures—Zodark starfighters.

"Hen House, Paladin. Good copy. Will engage hostiles with Red Ripper and Warhawk. Out," he confirmed before switching channels to his squadron commanders. "Ripper One, Hawk One, this is Paladin. Looks like we have some foxes looking to pick off some chicks. Hen House wants us to engage before they can get in range."

"Hot dog! I told y'all we'd get to see some action, Ghost. You owe me a hundred credits," Ripper One hooted in excitement at the news.

"Hey, simmer down, guys, I'm not done yet," Paladin chided. "Ghost, I want you to take your Hawks and hug tight to our chicks. You cannot allow those Vultures to break through and start downing transports—you got me?"

"Roger that. You can count on us, Paladin," Hawk One confirmed. He dropped out of the channel to start issuing orders to his squadron.

"Viper, I want you to take Rippers Nine through Sixteen and flank that rear element of Vultures lagging behind the main force," Ethan continued. "I'm going to take Rippers Two through Eight with me. We're going to swoop down on them from over top that flight of Scarabs that just left the *Maximus* and engage 'em with our JATM missiles. This should cause them to scatter. That's when I want your flight to engage them with your missiles. If we do this right, Viper, we'll throw their attack into disarray and pick off whatever the missiles leave us."

"I like it, Paladin. Let's do it!" Ripper One replied gleefully, switching back to the Ripper squadron channel to start issuing orders.

Like a well-oiled machine, the squadrons of Strike Group 20 began moving their F-11 Gripen starfighters with skilled determination, honed from years of combat and thousands of hours in the cockpit. With the Warhawks flying tight as a tick, the distances between the Vultures and the Osprey ATACs continue to close rapidly. Meanwhile, Paladin's other two squadrons, the Vigilantes and the Rattlers, continued to maintain a tight combat patrol around the remaining ships of Task Force Lightning—the ground contingent of OP Gurista Freedom-14.

Paladin opened a comms channel. "Rippers Two through Eight, this is Paladin. As you can see, we have multiple squadrons of Zodark Vultures rising from the planet to engage our transports. I don't have to tell you how important it is that we protect them at all costs. I want you

22

to stay in a tight formation and prepare to engage with four of your six JATM missiles. Save your final pair for after we break this attack up and they look to scatter."

The comms buzzed with acknowledgments from seven of the Gripens in his formation. As Ethan gave the engines more power, he watched as his speed accelerated, his sleek killing machine closing the distance to the flight of Scarabs they were going to overfly to swoop down on the Vultures still approaching the assault force.

Ethan kept a steady eye on his squadrons as his fighters continued to move into their attack or defensive positions. This part of any orbital assault was always tricky—balancing how many fighters to have on offense while not leaving the larger capital ships underdefended. With three strike groups within the wing, he tried to balance the timing, deploying each one so as to provide proper coverage while also making sure his squadrons had the time to rearm and refuel between fights.

"Paladin, Aquila Three." His radio activated, the carrier's Ops center hailing him.

"Aquila Three, go for Paladin," he responded, waiting to hear what else was about to join the funtivities.

"Paladin, we're detecting multiple ground radars activating from the surface. Be advised of imminent ground fire," warned the Ops center just as alarms began to sound. He relayed the warning to his squadron commanders, who by now were already reacting to the intermittent flashes of light from the surface.

From what Ethan could tell, it looked like the gunners on the surface were firing at the larger warships, not the waves of assault transports and fighters escorting them. If they hadn't been closing in on the Vultures, he might have spared a minute or two to look and see if the ground fire was hitting anything. He hadn't seen any friendly ships taking damage yet, so he wasn't sure what those gunners were doing.

"Paladin, Viper. We're nearly in position. When do you want us to attack?" asked Ripper One.

Ethan glanced in his direction, spotting his flight of eight Gripens racing past a Republic corvette descending into the planet's lower orbit. He watched briefly as the corvette's weapons fired several times at the surface.

It's about time they got someone to start shooting at those ground targets, he thought.

23

"Viper, Paladin. Stand by to engage. We're approaching our optimal engagement envelope. Once the Vultures react to our missiles—begin your attack. Paladin out," he replied hastily.

Activating another comms channel to the Gripens he was leading, he said, "Listen up, Rippers. When we engage these Vultures, I want you to use no more than two missiles. We don't know what else they might throw at us, and I want everyone to have a few missiles ready should we need them. Use your guns on the remaining fighters, and let's end this fight. Watch your sixes and your wingmen. Gripens Two through Eight—you are weapons free. Engage at will."

****

Echo Company
2nd Ranger Regiment

"Wow! Did you see that!?" PFC Martin Rosales shouted. Pauli and the others looked out the rear hatch at the ongoing aerial battle as they approached the jump zone.

"All jumpers—prepare to jump!" came a loud shout from the pilot up front.

Pauli jumped to his feet, issuing orders like he was still a platoon sergeant. He joined his NCOs in getting their soldiers ready to run and jump off the rear ramp into the battle below.

Following their descent into the planet's atmosphere, the squadrons of ATACs and older-variant Ospreys and Scarabs began separating toward their drop zones. For Echo Company, that meant heading toward the capital city of Zidara and the palace grounds. On the final approach toward the capital, the airspace swirling above the city had become a veritable hornet's nest around the ATACs that ferried Echo Company to their objective. As if Zodark Vultures weren't bad enough, the more dangerous Zeeks and some sort of indigenous Gurista interceptors tried to overwhelm the F-97 Orion escorts and the more venerable F-11 Gripens.

From the moment the crew chief had lowered the rear ramp as they neared the drop zone, the Rangers were given a front-row seat to the aerial battle taking place around them. After witnessing flashes of light and hearing thunderous explosions from nearby misses, the Rangers wanted off this ride and back to the familiar territory of ground combat, where they dominated.

Pauli stood near the ramp; he felt his adrenaline surge, knowing the order to jump would come at any moment. He fiddled with his rifle while checking his gear one more time. When he looked at the Rangers around him, he saw a group that was eager to fight, their war faces on.

"Remember your objectives," he told them. "Once we hit the ground, stick to your training and watch each other's backs. We've got this."

Just then, the red jump light above the ramp flashed, signaling the final countdown. Pauli took a deep breath, his mind sharpening as the moment of truth approached, his heartbeat quickening. The light turned green, and everything became a momentary blur of action.

"Go, go, go!" shouted Master Sergeant Tinker, leading the way as he jumped out of the Osprey into the chaos of battle below.

Pauli followed quickly behind him, amid flashes of movement as the soldiers to his right and behind him followed him off the ramp. This was the part he enjoyed the most: the rush of wind all around him, the sight of his fellow Rangers descending toward the surface, the ground rushing up to meet them. The air around him wasn't filled with laser bolts trying to kill him before he reached the ground this time like it had been on so many other occasions. He cursed loudly when he spotted a Zeek peeling off its attack on an Osprey to train its guns on the falling soldiers as they descended.

He reached for his M-111 Slayer to fire at the Zeek when a warning on his HUD captured his attention. It flashed the seconds until his exosuit's drag chute would deploy and the rockets affixed to the sides of his boots would fire to slow his descent as he approached the ground.

Looking below, Pauli saw the ground rapidly approaching. The drag chute deployed with a hard jerk, abruptly ending his rapid free fall. Preparing his legs, he watched the countdown reach zero, and then the rockets affixed to his jump boots ignited, the remaining speed bleeding off as the ground continued to grow closer. Second later, his feet touched the ground, and he moved his rifle to the ready position, looking for targets to engage.

"Master Sergeant Tinker, get me a head count. Squad leaders, rally your soldiers and move to your objectives. Let's roll, Rangers!" ordered Pauli, having cleared his immediate surroundings. He listened to the radio chatter as his platoon leaders reported in, breathing a sigh of relief once he'd heard that the Zeek shooting at them had only managed to injure one of his soldiers. Two others had gotten hurt during the jump, but otherwise, his company was in good shape.

With the morning sun up, it wasn't long before the city awoke to the sight of alien soldiers walking amongst them. Pauli had ordered his soldiers to clear their masks, turning the one-way mirrored finish off so their faces and eyes could be easily seen by the locals. He wanted to make sure they knew they were human, just like them.

With the remaining fighting concentrated around the palace, the Rangers had gotten to work securing the stadium, nearby bridges, road intersections, and other strategic positions as directed. It wasn't long before waves of Scarabs and Starlifters began ferrying vehicles and more soldiers to the surface. Whatever resistance there had been prior to their arrival had either concentrated itself around the palace or melted away into the civilian populace. For now, that wasn't Echo's problem—it was an issue for another day.

Chapter Four

Kilanzi Military Base
About One Hour Outside Zidara, Gurista Prime

Turok Vilzar of the Dochuta tribe was letting off some steam after finishing his shift in the northern guard tower. He and several of his fellow Zodark soldiers had a raucous game of chance going in the designated gathering room for the "grunts." The officers had their fancy furniture and free Eudarian wine, but Turok and his friends took turns emptying each other's pockets in noisy rounds of Nappangi.

It was Turok's turn. While his compatriots hissed and hollered to distract him, he reached into his pouch and took the set of bones, which had been whittled into perfectly cylindrical dice with markings on them, tossing them on the table, where they landed in a scattered pattern. His set had come from the hand of a Tully, which was a bit more uncommon, but he found them to be a better set than the bones of a human, Primord, or Gallentine. Each of the Zodarks had to earn these bones on the battlefield, and the most coveted sets came from the rare instances of hand-to-hand combat with Altairians. With his left lower hand, Turok pulled out a wrist bone, calculating the angle of his throw as he called out the final score he anticipated. The group placed their bets accordingly.

"Victory!" Turok bellowed as his throw rang true, yielding the exact score. He slapped his upper and lower arms together with a loud clap, celebrating his win as his fellow soldiers reluctantly pushed their money toward him, grumbling loudly.

Suddenly, one of the officers burst into the room, interrupting their fun. "Pack it up!" NOS Jorun Tylkar barked. "Something huge is going down on Gurista Prime right now—multiple bases have activated their emergency signals. We don't know exactly what it is yet, but I guarantee you, we are next. Activate all countermeasures and grab your weapons!" he ordered.

"Yes, NOS!" the group replied.

Turok dared not fiddle with the game pieces while an NOS was in their midst. However, despite the impending danger, as soon as the coast was clear, Turok took the two seconds to collect his Tully bones before he retrieved his armor, blasters, and swords.

27

He raced back to the northern guard tower, bounding with every stride. The soldier he had relieved less than an hour ago, Raxim Voltak, seemed very confused to see Turok there, but Turok didn't pause to explain the situation. Instead, he grabbed for the external communication device and attempted to contact one of the Zodark ships in orbit.

Nothing, he realized after a few frazzled seconds.

"There's something jamming our signal," Turok said aloud. "Time to turn on our own jammers," he directed.

Raxim picked up on the heightened tension, even if he didn't yet understand the reasons for it, and quickly complied.

Turok's training kicked in, and he started to execute his countermeasures with automaticity. Atop the Zodark guard towers and administrative buildings, there were antidrone microwave systems and separate signal disruptors. He flipped them both on. These were designed to jam any remotely controlled UAVs and fry any nearby enemy electronics.

No sooner had he done this than he noticed a strange black cloud approaching.

"What in Lindow's name is that?" asked Raxim, pointing to the strangely swirling mass.

Are those birds? Turok wondered. He picked up a nearby magnifying scope and zeroed in on the mysterious haze. All at once, the situation became clear.

"Those are drones!" he roared. "Get to the lasers!"

Just below the guard tower was a pair of short-barrel laser autocannons, which could be used to independently target and engage threats to the base perimeter. They raced to take their seats. Turok was beginning to panic, thinking that perhaps he hadn't fully engaged the microwave systems or signal disruptors, but then the approaching swarm of drones suddenly thinned out as several dropped abruptly from the sky and fell harmlessly to the ground.

Apparently, not all of the UAVs racing toward them were equally affected by the Zodarks' countermeasures, so Turok took aim at one of the surviving drones and blasted it from the sky.

"There's still so many of them!" Raxim yelled.

"Just keep shooting!" Turok roared.

As the swirling cloud of death approached, the countermeasures became more effective. More and more of the drones dropped to the ground without any effort on Turok and Raxim's part, but there were still plenty for them to fire their lasers at.

Turok's pulse quickened and his muscles tightened. He zoned in on drone after drone, removing them from the threat board.

Bang!

A sound between an explosion and one of those human magrail slugs hitting a surface rang out, followed by the howls of some of their Zodark compatriots. Turok forced himself not to immediately look to see what had happened. He narrowed his eyes and focused on taking out more drones.

Bang, bang, BANG!

More blasts struck within the borders of the base. Gurista as well as Zodark screams followed. The cloud of UAVs had thinned out considerably, but Turok kept firing until he realized that there were no more drones left to shoot.

"Clear!" Turok roared.

"Clear!" Raxim confirmed.

The two of them went back up into the main part of the guard tower and surveyed the scene below. At least a dozen of their fellow Zodark soldiers were dead or seriously wounded. However these drones worked, they seemed to go for the heads. Bluish blood and bits of brain matter were sprayed about. A few of the Gurista Defense Force soldiers had been a bit too close to his Zodark brothers, and they had become collateral damage.

The same NOS that had interrupted his winnings at Nappangi keyed into the guard tower intercom system. "Insurgents have attacked the capital," NOS Jorun informed them. "Load up in the vehicles—we will avenge our dead!"

All throughout the base, Turok and his fellow Zodarks let loose their war cry. The GDF on base, enraged by their own losses, hooted and yelled along with them. Soon, fueled by adrenaline and a desire for revenge, the whole group of around one hundred Zodark advisors and six hundred GDF had mobilized.

They were about an hour's travel time from the palace at Zidara, and they still didn't know what they were dealing with. Initially, Turok was angry and hot to get into combat, but as they continued along, he wondered what they were facing. Whatever it was, they had managed to carry out multiple attacks, almost simultaneously. As columns of smoke became visible, rising into the sky above where other military bases had once been, he wondered how many of his fellow Zodarks, if any, had survived the attacks.

As they neared the city, the group approached a rather large Zodark-Gurista base, which had obviously been heavily damaged. Char marks, rising smoke, and damaged border walls told a story of their own. NOS Jorun ordered everyone to pull over so they could render aid and consolidate forces.

Most of the Zodarks at this location had been killed. The few that had survived were trying to get the Guristas mobilized to counter whatever had attacked them. When Jorun learned that the head NOS there had been killed, he announced that he was assuming command.

Turok marveled at how NOS Jorun rallied everyone behind him. He wondered if he might one day be such a strong leader. In no time, all able-bodied survivors, both Zodark and Gurista, were willingly accompanying them as they deployed to the city. Jorun stirred the entire group into such a fever pitch, Turok felt that they were all salivating to put down whatever this rebellion was.

After they had been driving for about ten minutes, NOS Jorun apparently got some intelligence that the spaceport was in trouble, so he chose one of the soldiers to lead about a third of their forces to reinforce their position. The rest of them continued on toward the capital.

Boom!

One of the lead vehicles was thrown over by the concussive force of an IED.

Lindow, preserve us! Turok thought. He and the other soldiers in his vehicle immediately piled out, blasters and swords at the ready, searching for any threats nearby.

Zip, zap.

A rebel soldier on one of the roofs took shots at Turok and his men, who moved as quickly as they could to get behind some form of cover. The Zodark soldiers immediately returned fire, causing their attacker to duck below the ridge of the roof above. A moment later, the same rebel fired at them again—this time, Turok managed to get the man in his sights. He pulled the trigger, ending the threat.

They continued on, more vigilant this time. Turok became concerned about crossing the bridges. The Sha'ab River bisected the capital city, and there were only eight bridges that connected the eastern and western sides of Zidara. In order to get to the Capitol Palace, they would have to pass through these potential kill boxes.

Chapter Five

Echo Company, 2nd Ranger Regiment
Al-Sha'ab Combat Support Base
Amil District, Zidara, Gurista Prime

The darkness of the predawn would have given way to a beautiful sunrise and morning if it hadn't been disrupted by the sounds of battle still raging in parts of the city. Angry shouts and guttural howls of Zodark warriors intermixed with periodic explosions, and the rapid fire of Zodark and Republic battle rifles continued to echo throughout the city.

Shortly after Pauli's unit had landed, they'd moved rapidly to secure the Al-Sha'ab stadium, establishing a perimeter for what had quickly become the regimental combat support base or CSB. Once they reported they had the perimeter secured, two waves of six Scarabs descended through the clouds to land in the center of the stadium. During the next two hours, they watched as four of the much larger T-92 Starlifters descended into the stadium.

While the Scarabs had landed troops, the Starlifters had brought much of the gear. The first pair delivered sixteen of their DN-12 Cougar infantry fighting vehicles the Deltas and Rangers primarily used. The IFVs were swiftly put into action, establishing checkpoints across the city and reinforcing squads and platoons that were holding down critical pieces of infrastructure, preventing them from being captured or destroyed by the enemy.

Flying overhead in periodic aerial battles, Pauli saw more than one aerial duel between F-97 Orions and the occasional Zeek as it attempted to engage the waves of transports and shuttles delivering soldiers and gear to the surface. Even with the skies not fully secured, the Fleet had released the squadrons of AS-90 Reapers—a remotely piloted dedicated close-air support vehicle. If troops were in contact with the enemy or on the verge of being overrun, the Reapers would swoop down from the skies, their guns firing, their bombs falling, and their missiles finishing the job.

I can't even remember the number of times a Reaper saved my ass, Pauli thought.

As the sun climbed into the morning sky, the fighting around the palace had mercifully come to an end. Unfortunately for the Rangers, their fighting continued to intensify. Ordering the company ISR drones into the air, Pauli watched over the shoulder of the operator as the drone caught sight of a problem. Entering the city from the north and northeast were several convoys carrying small bands of Zodarks leading a much larger formation of local GDF units—Gurista Defense Forces the Zodarks had trained and cultivated to fight alongside them.

"Damn, that doesn't look good," Master Sergeant Drew Tinker commented.

"Whoa, that's not a small force either," Lieutenant Yogi Sanders joined in. "Pauli, that's going to be more than Staff Sergeant Hill's squad can handle—even with the help of their Cougar. Sir, I'm requesting permission to reinforce his checkpoint with the remainder of my platoon."

"Hold on a second," Pauli countered as he pulled up a digital map of the city. Using his thumb and index fingers, he moved the map around until he found what he was looking for. Zooming in, he pointed. "Yogi, this spot right here—it's a high point just opposite the Sha'ab River that runs through the city. I want you to take the remainder of your platoon and establish positions that'll cover these three bridges.

"We don't have enough troops to properly block or engage a force that large," Pauli acknowledged. "We also can't adequately cover down on all eight of the bridges crossing the river. So instead of spreading our forces across each of them, here's what we're going to do."

Pauli moved his index finger along the Sha'ab River that cut through the northern part of the city until it emptied into the Sea of Assaf. "We can't fight them toe-to-toe without flattening dozens of city blocks. What we *can* do is funnel the enemy into predetermined kill boxes. I'm going to see if we can get the Fleet to drop the other five bridges, leaving them with just these three—the ones your platoon will cover."

Yogi smiled as he listened. "I like it. Just make sure the Fleet keeps the CAS coming. So long as we can call on those Reapers, we'll be fine. But I'm going to need to be reinforced eventually. While two of those bridges can be covered from that point you mentioned, that third bridge—it's a kilometer and a half south. That's a lot of ground to have four squads trying to hold down—even with four Cougars," Yogi explained, making sure Pauli knew they couldn't hold the bridges indefinitely.

With a flick of Pauli's wrist, the map disappeared and he turned to Yogi. "I know, Yogi. You're right. I just need you to buy us some time. I have to relay this situation to Regiment and see if they can detail off another unit to cover down on the stadium. We're stretched too thin trying to maintain a security perimeter with just three platoons and a fourth as QRF. That regiment those Scarabs brought took off twenty minutes ago to reinforce Colonel Shinzo and the rest of our regiment at the spaceport. Apparently, that fight's turned into a hot mess. We've got three companies of Rangers and two Delta ODAs slugging it out with a force that appears to be a lot larger than those intel weenies briefed us on. Colonel Shinzo said it's imperative for us to keep the CSB running as long as—"

Boom!

Hearing the sound of the explosion, Pauli and Yogi turned to look in the direction of the stadium. With their eyes wide, their mouths agape, they watched in shocked horror as fiery debris rained down across the rooftops of homes near the stadium.

Emerging from the smoke and blackened clouds, the second Starlifter emerged, its giant frame racing to get out of danger and land inside the protective walls of the stadium. Like a switch had been flipped, the onboard antimissile countermeasures fired bursts of blazing hot flares in half-circular arcs behind and in front of the giant cargo vessel. Even amidst the noise and chaos, the roaring of engines was incredibly loud— almost overwhelming. The pilots gave the engines more power, the lumbering cargo hauler deftly shifting to the right as the belly turret fired rapidly at a missile heading for them.

Bam!

A hailstorm of blaster bolts zipped around the missile until it exploded.

"Holy crap! Did you see that?" a voice shouted somewhere behind Pauli.

"That's insane, Captain Smith!" another Ranger commented.

Pauli turned to see who it was.

Ah, there's Salinas, he realized.

"Yeah, it is," Pauli replied.

He turned to Yogi. "You know what to do—get your platoon to those bridges." Pauli pointed to a row of Linebacker APCs and Bobcats—the Army's light tactical vehicles or LTVs. "Take a pair of Linebackers and four of those Bobcats. Their weapons should help you defend the bridges and provide some drone defense."

As Yogi took off for the vehicles with his platoon, he told Sergeant Major Tinker to have the platoon leaders from Third, Fourth, and Fifth Platoons pick a squad they could do without and send them to his position. Then he told Tinker to find some crews to man a couple of Puma light tanks and at least two Yeti heavy tanks. If they were going to hold the bridges, they would need some firepower.

While the vehicles were being handled, Pauli made contact with the Fleet, relaying his request to drop the bridges and establish a continuous loop of close-air support or CAS rotation near the stadium. It was highly likely they would be relying on CAS missions to save their butts until more units were brought to the surface.
****

75 Minutes Later
1st Platoon, Echo Company
Sinak Bridge

Pauli inhaled and held—three, two, one—then exhaled and held—three, two, one. His breathing calmed, his heart no longer beat out of control. He stood with his back against the outer wall next to the window.

When Sergeant Major Tanner had linked up with the rest of First Platoon near the Sinak Bridge, Staff Sergeant Hill, the platoon sergeant, called to them, asking them to join his fire team on the sixth floor and to bring the platoon's pair of A9 Hydras with them. The A9 Hydras had recently replaced the M12 multipurpose launchers as the go-to weapon of choice for the infantry when something of value had to be blown up. What made the Hydra missiles leaps and bounds better than the MPLs they were replacing was their programmable warheads. The operator could quickly designate the warhead to disperse smoke or choose from among the high-explosive, high-explosive antitank, high-shrapnel burst, starburst, thermobaric or fuel-air explosive options. The A9s had become the infantry's Swiss Army knife.

After grabbing a pair of launchers and ammo packs from the Linebacker armored personnel carrier in which they'd ridden over, they raced up five flights of stairs with gear in tow and extra ammo and energy packs for the M90 and M91 gunners. As Pauli tried to catch his breath, the only thought running through his mind was *How did I let my cardio get this bad?*

Pauli saw Corporal Salinas smile as he approached him. "Thanks for bringing us more ammo and power packs," Salinas offered as he reached down for one of the A9 Hydras. "Me and Jose will take these off your hands. We're heading up to the roof, just above the twelfth floor. If they try to rush some of those trucks or armored vehicles across the bridge again, we'll be ready for it." Salinas smiled again as he patted the side of the launcher.

"Hey, if you guys need more ammo…there's four additional packs in the rear of the vehicle. Make sure to let the vehicle commander know you're coming for it so he can leave the rear hatch unlocked for you," explained Pauli.

As Pauli leaned against the side of the wall, his eyes surveyed the highway spanning the bridge. What caught his attention was the number of charred and burning vehicles scattered about the bridge. When vehicles exited the bridge, there were roughly two hundred meters of open space before buildings like the one he was in began lining both sides of the six-lane highway.

"I got movement on the bridge—looks like infantry," announced Staff Sergeant Hill. "Sir, do you think you might have a bead on them from your position?"

Smiling, Pauli commented, "Let me check it out. I'll see if I got a shot." The window was fortunately already shattered, which made lining up his battle rifle through the window a lot easier.

As he peered through his rifle's targeting scope, he spotted the soldiers Hill had identified. Sure enough, he watched as teams of three to four soldiers methodically advanced from one destroyed vehicle to another. It was a textbook infantry tactic called bounding overwatch. One group would cover the other as they bounded forward to the next covered position. Once the bounding group had reached cover, the overwatch group would switch positions, bounding past the first group until they had reached the next covered position.

"I see them—I've got a shot. Stand by," Pauli announced as he zeroed in on the soldiers preparing to move. *Breathe in...breathe out and hold...*

Crack!

The first soldier went down, the left side of his head exploding into a red mist. As the man's body fell to the ground, the other soldiers took off in a sprint toward their next position.

Ting, ting, thwap...

"Watch out, sir, they know we're shooting at them from this building," warned Staff Sergeant Hill as the sound of blaster shots hitting the face of their building continued.

"Echo One-One, Echo One-Seven. We're taking heavy fire from the units advancing across the bridge," Staff Sergeant Hill replied before continuing. "One-One, see if your LMG can respond. Break, break. One-Three, One-Seven. Get the Hydras ready to engage. If you can spot a cluster of troops or an armored vehicle worth a missile, hit it. How copy, One-One, One-Three?"

"One-Three—good copy. Will engage targets of opportunity."

"One-One—that's a good copy. Repositioning our LMG, stand by."

Pauli looked on in the direction of the advancing infantry when his eyes saw multiple red tracer rounds tear through the partially destroyed vehicles the Zodarks and soldiers from the local Gurista Defense Forces had been using for cover. Moments after he watched the tracer rounds and penetrator slugs tearing through the vehicles, his ears began to register the sonic booms of the .338 projectiles being hurled down the barrel of this rapid-fire magnetic railgun.

"Oh, crap. I think I'm seeing a targeting laser zeroing in on Alpha Team—One-One," exclaimed Staff Sergeant Hill in an urgent voice. "Sir, see if your rifle's targeting system might help you pinpoint the location of the enemy targeting laser. If you can spot them, shoot them before they can shoot us."

Pauli gave him a curt nod as he began looking through his rifle's target scope.

"Echo-One-One, One-Seven. We just spotted what looks to be a targeting laser searching for your position. You need to evacuate and get out of the building now!" Hill warned his fire team leader.

Suddenly, Pauli spotted it—he saw the targeting laser and began to follow it back, unsure of what he was going to find. His mouth fell agape as his eyes grew wide as saucers. Lurking in the shadows near the edge of a darkened alleyway, he spotted what looked like a barrel— a barrel similar to those of the Puma's 50mm cannon or the Yeti's 140mm.

Bang...BOOM!

The cannon fired, and a thunderclap sounded as a bright blue energy bolt shot out of the barrel, crossing the distance from the tank to the apartment his soldiers were shooting from. As Pauli turned to look at the apartment, multiple floors of the building exploded outward, debris falling to the highway below.

Holy crap! Half the building is gone, Pauli realized in horror.

"Oh, God, no, no, no!" cried out Staff Sergeant Hill. "The entire fire team was wiped out!"

Swoosh...Bam!

Pauli turned in the direction of the explosion, a plume of black smoke rising where he had last seen the tank that fired on them. Lifting his rifle to his shoulder to peer through his optics, he confirmed the tank was ablaze, a burning wreck. That was when he remembered Salinas and another soldier had taken a pair of A9 Hydras up to the roof.

They must have taken it out...

"Captain, I suggest we move to a new location. The enemy knows we're here, and God help us if another one of those tanks or whatever that was fires on us," warned Sergeant Major Tanner, a look of concern on his face.

"Yeah, good call. Let's get out of here," Pauli agreed, and everyone started grabbing their gear before heading for the stairs. As they descended the stairs, he saw the back of Corporal Digger's uniform, his name stenciled on the back of his helmet. "Corporal Digger, we're going to need some air support if we're going to stop that group forming up to bum-rush the bridge. Get on the net and see what assets we've got and vector them in."

"Roger that, sir. I'm on it," replied Corporal Thomas Digger. He was the Echo Company's CAC or combat air coordinator.

The CACs were a new position within SOF. They became the primary points of contact between the Fleet operation center and the units on the ground requesting support. During limited testing of the CAC concept within selective Delta units, the CACs had decreased the time between when a call was made for close-air support and when that support arrived. They had also greatly improved the battle damage assessments, with their units scoring more hits on targets than units without CACs.

When Pauli reached the exit to the building, he stared across the street for a moment, taking in the damage caused by whatever that tank had fired at it. Most of the first floor and even parts of the second showed light damage to their facade. The four floors above them were thoroughly destroyed, with broken water pipes leaking water between floors and shredded electrical wires sparking as the wind blew exposed wires into each other.

"Captain Smith, I just spoke to the squadron commander for FAS-225," Corporal Digger announced. "They have four Reapers on station. They're vectoring them to our location now. I also spoke to the *Vega*—Flight Ops. They're sending a flight of Valkyries and Gripens. They're also relaying our situation to the *Maximus*—we should have reinforcements arriving within the hour."

"Wow, outstanding, Corporal," praised Sergeant Major Tanner before walking up to Pauli. "Sir, there's nothing we can change about what happened to our guys over there." He nodded in the direction of the destroyed building across the street. "We've got reinforcements and a lot of airpower on the way. Right now, we need to relocate to a new position and hold these bridges until those reinforcements arrive. Come on, sir, we've got a fight to finish."

Pauli knew Tanner was right. He was just tired of losing soldiers. "You're right, Sergeant Major. Let's finish this."
****

A Few Hours Later
Tunnel Below Enuma Archives
Zidara, Gurista Prime

The walk through the labyrinthine tunnel had taken longer than Tammuz had anticipated. There had been one hairy part of the journey where they'd encountered a few surviving Mukhabarat trying to escape through the underground network, but their attempt to hide and fight another day was quickly thwarted by some deadly drones that one of

Tammuz's temporary bodyguards, a man named Somchai, had employed. Still, the whole experience had set them all on edge. They took longer than they needed to, double- and triple-checking each turn and utilizing all available methods to monitor potential threats.

During the long trudge from the palace, David and the other guardians had been in constant contact with the forces above ground. Soldiers on the surface swept through the city with shock and awe—had there been any remaining Mukhabarat in the headquarters, they would have been eliminated. Confirmation came in that the military bases had been secured. Things were definitely looking up.

Word came that the RNS *Aquila* had established air dominance over Gurista Prime. The star carrier's Gripens, Reapers and Valkyries had picked apart any Zeeks that had managed to take flight, and the skies were firmly under Republic control. The noises of battle, which had been loud enough to be heard even from their underground route of egress, had now dwindled.

Other than the blister on his left heel that was growing with each passing step, Tammuz felt pretty optimistic by the time he reached the ladder that led up to the basement of the Enuma Archives.

A biometric pad accepted Tammuz's fingerprints and activated a retina scanner, just as had happened before they'd entered the bunker. He realized that the two systems were obviously tied, so his access to the palace also worked there.

The heavy door hissed. With a significant amount of effort, they were able to pull the thick metal barrier open and reveal a room that was a bunker in its own right. Tammuz marveled at the collection of weaponry and the stocks of survival rations.

It looks like I could stay down here for months, he realized. He was grateful his time here hopefully wouldn't test the facility's limits.

Tammuz realized that hours had gone by since they'd left the bunker underneath the palace...he had completely lost track of time. He turned to David.

"Is it safe now? Can we really leave?" he asked.

"From all reports, I believe you should be fine to exit the archives, sir," David replied. "After the *Aquila* established air dominance, the Republic made short work of the remaining Zodarks and their loyalists. There was a major battle at the bridges over the Sha'ab River, but ultimately, our people prevailed. I believe the only major fighting that's still ongoing is at the spaceport. Of course, there are sporadic battles with very small groups of insurgents, but they're quickly being hunted down. Overall, the capital has been secured, and the Republic is in the middle of deploying an entire division's worth of soldiers to Zidara as we speak."

Tammuz nodded, then cautiously opened the other heavy door to exit the bunker, revealing a false bookshelf that held what appeared to be ancient manuscripts behind glass panels. He wondered if they were actually real or simply well-made replicas to throw off any suspicion.

Some of these scrolls are real, thought Tammuz as he examined the tables before them. Airlock-encased work surfaces had robotic arms inside, along with various potential tools that could be used by their historians to restore the rare ancient texts.

They made their way through the special work areas and shelves and passed one more biometric entrance that led up to the main floor of the Enuma Archives. Somchai released several drones into the library to scout out the location before they emerged. The building was empty except for the staff who regularly worked there. Anyone else who would have normally come there that day had sheltered either at the university, at their places of work, or in their homes.

As Tammuz and his guardians entered the library, he was struck by the beauty and majesty of his surroundings. It had been a while since his time as a student, and he had forgotten how high the ceilings were and how immense the mass of knowledge that was contained in these shelves. He was grateful that the building had been untouched by the fighting.

One of the librarians spotted him and her jaw dropped. "It's Tammuz!" she shouted, a very uncharacteristic thing for someone in the archives to do.

Several of the other librarians reacted to her call, and one of them grabbed her tablet and began recording.

"Hey!" David exclaimed, hand held out in a stop motion, apparently hoping to keep her from filming.

Tammuz reached over and pulled David's arm down. "If she's live-streaming, the people who are following the Enuma Archives will already have seen me here," he explained calmly. "If you say it is safe, just let them have this moment to celebrate."

David grunted, but he let it go.

The archives were so expansive that it took them a few more minutes to meander through the hallways of shelves. By the time they exited the front door of this important landmark, several people were leaving their nearby homes, coming to see their new fearless leader.

"I guess you went viral," David commented.

"My people are known to love a good gossip story," Tammuz replied, his smile betraying a mischievous streak.

Spontaneous applause erupted. The crowd grew. Tammuz could tell that his guardians didn't like so many people to be around him, but he waved off their concern. A moment like this was not to be squashed. Even if he was potentially in more danger, Tammuz felt he had no choice but to act in a way that an inspiring leader should.

Someone in the crowd began singing a song that pulled Tammuz all the way back to his childhood. This soulful melody was one of the tunes that his mother used to sing to him when he was a young boy. Another voice joined in, and then another—it was as though they were choosing a new anthem for themselves, one that was uniquely Gurista.

As Tammuz approached the crowd, several larger men came forward and lifted him up, carrying him as if he were sitting on a seat elevated above them. He caught David's eye and gave him a look that told him to back off. David tilted his head in a slight nod, and the five guardians integrated with the crowd, staying near Tammuz but not stopping any of the festivities.

An instinctual parade of sorts naturally grew. People were dancing and singing. Some had brought instruments from their home and played music with the crowd. The Guristas were clearly excited to be liberated from the control of the Zodarks, and they viewed Tammuz as the face of that victory.

Tammuz smiled and waved at the people. He was excited as well, but the weight of what to do going forward secretly pressed on him.

Do we create our own government, just for the Guristas? Or do we fold in with the existing human societies and officially join the Republic? he wondered.

That problem would take time to solve, but at the moment, Tammuz realized, it was time to dance.

Chapter Six

Office of the Viceroy
Alliance City, New Eden
Rhea System

Viceroy Miles Hunt stared at his longtime friend Gunther Haas, the man who had been a friend to him during tough times at the Space Academy and the person he'd placed in charge of running the firm Void Scientific Research. In the world of espionage, it was called a cutout—a legitimate company, but one that held a dark secret. Following the end of the First Zodark War, some loose ends needed to be tied up, secrets buried, and weapons kept in a dark place just in case they were one day needed. When they needed someplace safe, someplace secure, someplace they could bury their biological weapons program—they'd created VSR.

When the Altairians had invited the Republic to join their alliance, the Republic had to agree to a series of rules that governed how this interstellar war was fought. In spite of the vastness of space, habitable planets were still considered rare—rare enough to be vehemently fought over, and rare enough that even adversaries agreed to a series of rules to determine how battles within these worlds should be fought. Namely, weapons designed with the intent to harm or destroy the habitability of a planet were strictly forbidden.

A clear example of forbidden weapons were variations of nuclear fission or fusion warheads laced with cobalt—however, any weapon specifically designed to irradiate a planet or prevent a planet's use via a persistent chemical or biological weapon was prohibited in the strongest possible terms. The use of these kinds of weapons within the atmosphere of a planet was strictly forbidden. Failure to adhere to what the alliances called the Intergalactic Rules of War (IRW) was punishable by the leaders of the Collective and their proxy alliance, the Dominion, or the Gallentine Emperor and his proxy alliance, the Galactic Empire. The fact that the Republic had created a biological weapons program, let alone a viable, functional, and deployable virus, meant it was already in direct and persistent violation of this most basic rule of armed conflict.

Gunther placed the yellow-striped tablet down on Miles's desk, having finished reading the classified Gallentine intelligence report

Miles had given him to read. "It's an interesting report, but it doesn't directly imply a biological weapon had been used."

Miles snorted in response. "The Gallentines aren't idiots, Gunther. Anyone with half a brain will eventually piece together the timeline of events and notice the obvious—"

"And what is it that's so obvious, Miles? What has your panties in a wad?" Gunther interrupted.

"Seriously? You can't see it?" Miles scoffed, his annoyance beginning to boil over. When Gunther didn't respond, Miles explained, "The Zodarks started experiencing their initial symptoms within the incubation period we had designed for the Zeta Respiratory Inhibitor. It won't take long for the Gallentines to piece together that whatever it is that's affecting the Zodarks began to occur shortly after our reconnaissance forces arrived in the Gravaxia system. It's a hell of a coincidence, don't you think?"

"What do you want me to say? 'I'm sorry'? I think we're a little past that point, Miles." Gunther looked incredulous as he waited for him to respond.

Miles breathed in deeply, then exhaled. "I don't get it. I trusted you with this—you really let me down, Gunther, and placed me in a really tough spot. I mean, thank God that the virus wasn't as effective as you anticipated, or we'd really be up a creek without a paddle."

"Miles, when the Zodarks attacked Earth, I lost everything. I lost my wife. I lost my kids and my grandkids. I should have died with them, and God, how I wish I had. But I didn't. For a long time, I asked myself why. Why was I spared? One day, it occurred to me why. Inside the facility I worked in was the answer. I alone could bring our families justice. The kind of justice I'm afraid your position doesn't allow you to deal out. When my nephew shared some of the horrors of war he had seen on the battlefield against those blue beasts, I asked him, 'What if there was a way to eradicate them, to wipe them out, but it was an illegal weapon, a weapon against the laws of armed conflict?' Do you know what he told me, Miles? 'If you aren't cheating, you aren't trying hard enough.'"

Miles scoffed at the comment. He'd heard it a million times before. Hell, he'd used the phrase himself.

"The point is, Miles, people want revenge. They want justice. I couldn't just sit on ZRI knowing my nephew could surreptitiously release it on one of his upcoming missions. I told him if he did this—he was done. His military career would be over, and he'd likely be facing charges," Gunther explained, then brushed aside a tear racing down his cheek. "You should have seen him, Miles. I was so proud of him. He didn't hesitate for a second. He said if that was the price for ending the threat to humanity—a threat to his wife and kids, to his fellow Deltas and the soldiers under his command—it was a price he was willing to pay, even if it meant becoming a traitor. Doomed to a life of breaking rocks in a penal colony, he would pay the price."

Miles tried to be angry with his friend, but as he listened, he found his resolve weakening, his anger abating. *How could I have let my people down so badly that they would be willing to take actions such as this on their own...?*

"Gunther, I don't know what to do. I never should have placed our people in this kind of situation. No amount of words or actions will ever be able to convey how awful, how terrible, I feel about what happened to our people, to Earth. Every day I wake up, I wish I had done something differently, something to prevent what happened. I'm the one who lives with the knowledge that I'm responsible for why your family is dead—why a billion of our people are dead. I understand wanting revenge. I just don't know what to do right now. If I wait to tell the Emperor, wait for him to find out on his own"—Miles shook his head, his expression becoming dour—"humanity may not survive if I'm replaced. If we find ourselves on our own, we'll be in trouble," he confided, sharing more than he dared with virtually anyone.

Gunther hung his head. There really wasn't any response that would have sufficed, given the circumstances.

Miles felt a knot in his stomach. *I'm going to have to eat a lot of crow*, he thought.

****

Two Days Later
Chancellery Building
New Cambria, New Eden

"Miles, what are your thoughts on what President Gudea mentioned, establishing an outpost or colony—a return to the Milky Way?" Chancellor Aimes Morgan asked, sipping on his tea.

Miles didn't respond right away. He sat back in his chair, his mind racing with all the implications the reemergence of the Humtars would or could have for both the Republic and their Gallentine patrons.

"From a personal perspective, I welcome it. I think it's an opportunity for us to reconnect with our ancestors—our real ancestors. In my capacity as the Viceroy and in service to Emperor Tibus SuVee, this could present a serious problem—"

"How so?" interrupted the Chancellor, placing his tea down on the table between them.

"Hmm. OK, let me try to explain this differently," Miles replied. "The Gallentines have been a spacefaring species for more than a thousand years. In that time, they explored the galaxy together with their ally the Amoor before their transition into the Collective until they stumbled upon the stargate network. From that day forward, the Gallentines have overseen a tremendous expansion of their territory, eventually discovering the Humtar home world and learning more about this ancient race that created the stargates.

"For all intents and purposes, Aimes, the majority of the Gallentine Empire has been built on the ruins of Humtar worlds and colonies. Most of their advanced propulsion, shipbuilding, weapons, etc., came from rediscovering Humtar technology and recreating it. Now ask yourself this. If the ancient civilization that you built most of your current empire upon suddenly returned, do you think your emperor might be concerned that this poses a possible threat to his empire?"

"Ah, I see what you mean," Aimes slowly replied. Then his face lit up as he offered an idea. "You bring up a good point about the Gallentines being nervous about the return of the Humtars to the Milky Way. What if we try to help alleviate that concern by offering to provide the Humtars with a place to establish a colony of their own inside *our* territory? This way they don't infringe on existing Gallentine space, and it could also provide for some major security guarantees as the Humtars will want to protect their colony, which will be enmeshed within our own territories, necessitating their protecting our colonies as their own."

Miles smiled warmly at the idea. "Aimes, that was exactly what I was going to suggest. I also think there's a way to leverage this to help solve another problem, a bigger problem that's actually the real reason for my visit today."

"Oh? All right, Miles. Why don't you explain what's going on and how you think we might be able to leverage this into solving another problem?"

Miles took a deep breath as he began to explain the true nature of Void Scientific Research and the dirty little secret it hid.

****

Four Days Later
Security Council Chamber, Tiberius Hall
Alliance City, New Eden

Viceroy Miles Hunt remained seated as the assembled commanders took their places around the circular table in the Security Council Chamber. The table itself symbolized unity—no head, no visible rank—but Hunt's chair sat two inches higher, a subtle reminder of his role. His eyes scanned the faces of those around him. Gallentines, Primords, Altairians, and the Republic were all represented, each bringing their expertise and forces to bear in the final push against the Dominion Alliance. Behind them, additional seats and tables held aides, strategists, and advisors, all ready to observe or assist.

Admiral Wiyrkomi, Hunt's friend and confidant, sat directly across from him, his gaze steady, offering silent support. To his left, Captain Nebularia of the House TharVex, a naval advisor, whispered quietly with Commander Mivon FenTal, the Gallentine Special Forces commander. On the other side of the table, Primord Minister of Defense Eydis Starweaver exchanged glances with General Ragnulf Cosmokar. In contrast, Admiral Vargr Asgardsson and the other Primord leaders sat in resolute silence. The Altairians—King Grigdolly, Admiral Pandolly, and Zudolly from the Schendolly—observed with their usual calculating demeanor, their three heads bobbing slightly as they whispered in their unique language.

Hunt's mind churned as he watched them all, his thoughts turning to the two-pronged assault they were about to commit. Vice Admiral Willie Rosentreter and Lieutenant General Jayden Hopper would lead the primary thrust, while Vice Admiral Ripley Lee and LTG Vernon "VC" Crow would command the second prong. The Primords and Altairians were embedded within the Republic forces, fighting as one cohesive unit, their military pooling together in this final stand.

The tension in the room was a living thing, swirling around the commanders as they waited for Hunt to speak. He felt the weight of their expectations like a heavy mantle on his shoulders. The battle plan he was about to unveil would commit millions of soldiers, their lives hinging on his decisions. There was no turning back now, and he knew what this would cost them—hundreds of thousands of lives. And yet, the path ahead was clear—he had to make the hard call, regardless of how it hollowed him inside.

His voice, calm but unyielding, cut through the tension as he finally broke the silence. "Gentlemen, ladies," he began, his eyes sweeping across the table, "what I present to you today is the final phase of this war—the end game. A little more than a year ago, we launched our invasion of Orbot space. Thanks to the incredible intelligence work of the Aurion Shadows," Miles gave a nod to Commander Mivon FenTal. "We discovered an incredible vulnerability we were able to use against the Cyborgs that rapidly dismantle their will and ability to fight. This rapid collapse of what we had originally viewed as the stronger member of the Dominion meant we were able to accelerate our plans significantly.

"While we continued to isolate the two remaining members of the Dominion. It was a covert operation run by Republic intelligence, Special Forces, and some advisory help from our Gallentine friends. We were able to successfully infiltrate the Guristas—a hidden society of humans the Zodarks had established a few hundred years earlier from the humans on the planet Sumer. We have since learned from our friends in the Schendolly," Miles nodded this time to Zudolly, the Altairian intelligence operative who seemed to be everywhere and nowhere at the same time. "The Zodark, the insidious beast they are. Had a unique plan and purpose for the Guristas.

"After cultivating a god-like caretaker relationship with the Guristas, a relationship that saw the Zodarks encouraging and rewarding women for having large families and many children. This had grown their society into the low hundreds of millions before they began to unveil their long-term plan for our fellow humans—our ancestors even. They were being bred and conditioned to be replaceable soldiers, spacers…cannon fodder to further Zodark expansion and conquest. Well, we ended that—"

Miles paused when some claps and cheers began. *Let them clap…it's well earned,* his mind reasoned before he resumed.

"While Operation Gurista Freedom was a success as we liberated an entire society from the clutches of the Zodark Empire and its Janissary designs, the battle to liberate the Ry'lian system—Lyrius, from the Pharaonis, proved to be a costly challenge. It paved the way for us to gain access into the Pharaonis Hive—Pyrallis and Zanthea systems. The battle to end the threat of continued Pharaonis border wars is still ongoing as Vice Admiral Rosentreter and Admiral Pandolly prepare to invade Pyrallis and Zanthea.

"I know there are some who question why the Alliance is devoting resources and manpower to a pair of Pharaonis systems and not pivoting our forces to invade Zodark space. I'll tell you why—because once we have eliminated the Zodarks as an ongoing threat to our people, our alliance will experience something is hasn't known in hundreds of years—peace," explained Miles. "When the fighting ends...when the last Zodark ship and garrison has surrendered, we will not celebrate our victory and begin to enjoy the fruits of peace while leaving a member of the Dominion to lick its wounds and plot its revenue. The time to end these threats to our people is now while we have the ships and the soldiers to win."

Nods of heads and murmurs of affirmation permeated the room as Miles lifted a glass of water to his lips.

He turned to face Admiral Lee. "Ripley, your Task Force did a hell of a job causing havoc and running amuck with your cross-border raids into the Gravixia system. It forced the Zodarks into keeping a larger force in Tueblets and prevented them from attempting to recapture the Orinda system from Admiral Dobbs. For the time being, her force is the only thing preventing the Zodarks from reenslaving the Gurista people.

"When I spoke with the Primord Minister of Defense, Eydis Starweaver, and Admiral Bjork Stavanger, they believe Pfeinstgard should be the launch point from which to invade Zodark territory—starting with returning to the Gravixia system, this time to stay. From there, we invade Tueblets, the logistical hub and heart of the Zodark Empire. Whoever controls Tueblets controls the Empire," Miles explained before turning to face Admiral Rosentreter. "Willie, this is where things turn to you. Following the destruction of the Pharaonis, your fleet will be bridged into the Orinda system, where your fleet will link up with Admiral Dobbs fleet and consolidate into a unified fleet.

"While Admiral Lee and the Primords will be pressing Tueblets from the Gravixia system, your combined fleet will move to seize the Shwani system—the home system to the Groff and around forty percent of Zodark ship production. Shwani is also next door to Tueblets. As we press the Zodarks from both sides, one of them will break. That will be the moment when we throw everything we have at them until we overwhelm them and capture Tueblets or Shwani. In either case, the Zodarks will crumble under the combined weight of our converging fleets. Make no mistake, gentlemen, ladies, this is the end state—the final moves on the chessboard."

Chapter Seven

Shooters Lounge
11th Spartacus Armor Regiment
RNS *Callisto*

The rec hall reverberated with the sound of pool balls and the loud, excited chatter of soldiers. They had just returned from a company award ceremony, wearing their medals proudly on their uniforms.

Within the haze of cigar smoke, Staff Sergeant Peter Kennedy leaned over the felt-covered table, cue stick ready to strike. Conversation and laughter from the bar faded into the background as he focused on the cue ball. He took a deep breath to steady his nerves, then sized up the angle and calculated the trajectory.

In the next moment, a memory hit him like a punch to the face. He was back in his Yeti tank. A beautiful valley stretched out before him. Explosions rocked the ground. Plumes of dirt and debris flew into the air. To his right, a tank erupted in a ball of flame. The force of the blast slammed his side into his own vehicle. He gripped the controls tighter, his knuckles turning white.

"Loader, HEAT round, now!" he ordered.

The loader pushed the round into the breach. Kennedy swung the turret, searching for the target that had just blown up the vehicle next to him.

To his left, a Bobcat light tactical vehicle disintegrated in a fiery eruption. The warped metal hailed down on the valley floor. The once green and bright grass and colorful flowers covering the area now sat charred on the earth. The smell of burning rubber and fuel filled Kennedy's nostrils, making his eyes water.

"Target, two o'clock!" his gunner said.

Kennedy swiveled the turret. Enemy Pharaonis came into view. "Fire!"

The Yeti shuddered as the round left the barrel. The shell streaked toward the cluster of Pharaonis warriors. It struck true, the high-explosive round exploding in their midst. Limbs and gore flew in every direction as body parts flipped end over end in the air.

There was no time to celebrate. More blasts rocked the valley. The ground trembled beneath the treads of his tank.

"Hard left! Get us out of this kill zone!" Kennedy yelled.

He scanned the battlefield in search of the next threat. The entire valley was marred by the ugly wounds of combat.

"Yo, Kennedy, are you all right? Are you there, man?"

The voice snapped him back to the present. Kennedy blinked. *How long have I been staring at the cue ball?* he wondered.

Staff Sergeant Joe Wilson stood beside him, his fingers in mid-snap next to Kennedy's ear.

Kennedy straightened and forced a smile. "Yeah, I'm good. Just… just thinking about my shot. In fact, you got me off my rhythm."

Wilson scrunched his brow. "Your rhythm usually doesn't take two minutes to strike the ball, my friend."

"I know, and I understand," Kennedy replied, "you get mad when my lining up takes longer than you take in bed, but…"

"Oh, ha… ha." Joe folded his arms over his chest. "You can't think of better jokes than that?"

Kennedy shrugged. "What, man? I'm just saying what your lady friend tells—"

"Cut the chatter. You gonna hit the dang ball, Kennedy, or what?" interrupted Captain Michael Martin, their Alpha Company commander, who stood on the other side of the pool table. He held a pool stick in his hand as he waited, no doubt hoping Kennedy would miss his next shot.

Kennedy rolled his eyes. "Yes, sir. Hold on."

As Kennedy bent down to make his shot, he could see in Wilson's gaze that he was still concerned by his momentary blackout. Trying to shrug it off, he returned his focus to the cue ball and did his best to push the memories back into the recesses of his mind. Nonetheless, they lingered, like a bad taste in his mouth he couldn't get rid of.

With his cue stick gliding between his fingers, he lined up his shot. The four ball sat at the edge of the corner pocket. It was an easy shot for someone with Kennedy's skills. He drew the cue stick back and then pushed it forward. The cue ball cracked against the four ball with a sharp snap.

The sound startled him. He flinched. He felt his heart race as he straightened up. For a moment, he was back on Serenea. The sound of gunfire and explosions rang in his ears. He took a deep breath to calm himself.

Wilson tilted his head. "Hey, man, seriously. Are you all right? Maybe you should go check out that combat stress clinic down on deck four. They have some good counselors and even psychiatrists."

Kennedy forced a laugh. "Nah, I'm good. I don't need to see some headshrinker. I'm just a little jumpy, that's all. Besides, aren't you the one who needs a shrink, Wilson? I saw you talking to that vending machine earlier today like it was your best friend."

Wilson grinned. "Hey, that vending machine and I have a special relationship. It always gives me an extra candy bar when I ask nicely."

Captain Martin chuckled at them. "I'm surprised the general hasn't court-martialed you both for bad jokes—these are worse than dad jokes."

They all laughed. Then Kennedy looked at Captain Martin. "Sir, speaking of the general, that Silver Star was well deserved. If your tanks hadn't breached that final enemy line, I don't think we could have taken down those ion cannons. Lord knows we could still be on that damn planet for who knows how long." Truth be told, Kennedy was eternally grateful to be off that rock of a moon. He hadn't been sure how much longer his nerves were going to last before he snapped or did something stupid and got himself and his friends killed.

Martin threw his hands out wide as a smile appeared on his face. "Ah shucks, Staff Sergeant, I'm just trying to spread some of my awesomeness around to the rest of you pukes." He waved off his own feigned arrogance. "All kidding aside, it wasn't me who broke through the enemy line. It was my team. It was NCOs like you who took command of a platoon when your lieutenant was killed and you kept going. You knew the objectives, just like the officers, and when yours was lost, you stepped into that breach, and you led! I couldn't be prouder to serve alongside soldiers like you. Anyway, thanks, Kennedy."

Kennedy nodded. His gaze flicked to the Bronze Star with Valor device pinned above his own left breast pocket. Even the idea of receiving this medal still felt uncomfortable. In the midst of combat, he'd acted on impulse. His training had taken over as he'd moved his tank into a position to provide fire for the pinned-down infantry squad. At the time, he'd simply been doing his duty and made the split-second decisions necessary to protect his brothers- and sisters-in-arms. They'd deemed his actions exceptional. Odd—he'd do it anyway, without the hope of anyone giving him an award.

When he eyed the next shot, he broke his rhythm as he caught soldiers playing ping-pong at a nearby table out of the corner of his eye. He stood, shook it off, then watched a group of people battling it out on arcade games. He rolled his neck to loosen up, his gaze falling on a few men and women troopers sitting at the bar. They sipped drinks and chatted amongst themselves.

Martin chalked the tip of his cue stick. "All right, Kennedy, enough stalling. Take your shot and miss so I can show you how it's really done."

"Ha, don't pretend you're good. I've seen you play. Just don't cry when I run the table on you," replied Kennedy with a smirk on his face.

Wilson snorted. "Run the table? More like run your mouth."

Kennedy turned to Wilson. "Hey, don't get me started on you. I've seen better shots from a Stormtrooper."

Martin shook his head. A smile tugged at the corners of his mouth at the old *Star Wars* reference. It was bad enough that Disney had ruined that multigenerational franchise, but now they just kept making more and more spin-offs of it that few people watched, especially since interplanetary travel was now a reality and not some neat scene in a sci-fi movie.

"Kennedy, if you don't shoot, I'm gonna go get a drink and find myself some other friends to enjoy the evening with. Your choice, but the clock's ticking, my friend."

"Understood." Kennedy eyeballed the line, his cue stick secure for another shot. He noticed the green felt beneath the ball was worn and faded. He shot and the cue ball careened toward a solid. The blue two ball dropped into the corner pocket.

Clunk.

"Nice shot, Pete," Wilson said. "So what, now you're on fire?"

Kennedy winked. "Nah, sometimes luck helps the best of us."

Captain Martin rolled his shoulders, awaiting his turn. "That's some impressive marksmanship. Honestly, once you've completed your enlistment, you ought to consider going pro on the pool circuit. I've witnessed you pull off shots like that countless times, and you make it look routine."

"Yeah, maybe. Dreams are free." Kennedy squared up his next approach, a tricky combo requiring pinpoint accuracy. The cue ball hit its mark, but the angle was off by a hair and the eight ball missed the pocket by mere millimeters. "Ahh, damn, sir, you jinxed me."

Captain Martin pushed out his lower lip. "Ah, did I do that? Ah shucks."

With a cross face, Kennedy straightened in his posture. As he did so, a sudden movement in his peripheral vision caught his eye. He flinched. His heart raced and he froze. However, it was just a crewman walking by. For a split second, Kennedy had been back on the battlefield and inside his tank as enemy fire rained down around him.

Wilson frowned again. "Seriously, are you OK, Peter?"

"Yeah, just annoyed I missed the shot," Kennedy lied, feeling his cheeks flush.

"You sure?" Wilson pressed. "You've been really jumpy since we left orbit."

"I'm fine," Kennedy said with a bit more heat to his tone than he meant.

Deep down, though, he knew it was a lie. The memories of the war were beginning to consume him. They were always there, always just beneath the surface. The close calls, the friends he'd lost... it was enough to rattle even the strongest soldier. He knew he needed help, but admitting it, even to himself, that felt like admitting weakness—and you never show weakness in front of your enemies. That's when they'll pounce.

"OK." Wilson shoved his hands in his pocket, not knowing what else to do with them in this moment. "Fair enough, Kennedy. But if I witness you trying to salute the mess hall's rubber ducky again, I'll throw you into therapy myself. And you know how nuts I am, so that's saying something."

"Whenever you two stop bantering, it'll be great. 'Cause it's time to witness me sinking this ball right here. Watch and learn, gentlemen." Captain Martin took his shot and sank a stripe with ease into a side pocket.

"Well," Kennedy said, "nice shot, sir. A little lucky, but well done."

"Lucky?" Wilson snorted. "I'm surprised he can even hit the ball after the way he missed his shot with that girl on New Eden." He shifted his gaze to Captain Martin. "What was her name again, sir? The one at the Starlight Bar?"

Kennedy chuckled, happy for the change of subject. "You mean the one who tossed her drink on him?"

"That's the one!" Wilson threw a fist in the air. "Greatest day of my life. I thought she was going to slap him into next week."

Captain Martin blushed. "Hey, now. Can't blame a guy for trying. We were getting ready to ship out. Besides, I thought you guys volunteered to be my wingmen at that dive joint."

"Yeah, well, we did warn you, sir. Leaving officer country to hang out with the NCOs is bound to get you in trouble. Maybe next time you should take some pointers from Pete here," Wilson said, jerking his thumb in Kennedy's direction. "He never seems to have any trouble with the ladies."

Kennedy laughed, holding his hands up in mock surrender. "Don't look at me anymore. I'm trying to stay the hell away from ladies these days. I'm nothing but trouble with them."

"Sure, just keep talking, you guys," replied Captain Michael as he sighted his next shot, then struck the ball against a stripe ball at an awkward angle. It bounced off the cushion, missing the pocket by a wide margin.

"Ouch. Tough luck, sir," Kennedy said. He then stepped up to the table. "My turn. Now watch and weep, gentlemen. The master is about to show you how it's done."

Wilson rested his shoulder against the wall, sipping a beer a server had just given him. "Guys, can you believe it? I mean, we've got two whole weeks of R&R. It feels like a dang dream."

Captain Martin nodded. "After the hell we've been through, we deserve it. I don't even want to think about the next campaign."

At the mention of the upcoming mission, Kennedy felt a tightness in his chest. "Shh, you two. I'm trying to concentrate." He tried to push the feeling aside as he scoped his position on the pool table and gauged his approach. After studying his shot, he struck the cue ball cleanly. The eight ball rolled straight into the corner pocket.

"Nice one, Pete!" Wilson said. "You're unstoppable."

Kennedy grinned. "Thanks. And, I agree, I'm glad we've got some time off to relax."

Captain Martin racked his cue stick. "So, Kennedy, whatever happened to your kids on New Eden?"

"What do you mean?" replied Kennedy.

Martin lifted his shoulders and then let them sag a second later. "I don't know. You don't talk about them much anymore. Are they doing OK? Everything fine back home?"

"Actually, I think about them all the time. I guess I haven't talked about it much since we left." Kennedy's expression turned wistful. "But, yeah, I can't wait to see little Evan and Olivia. It's been way too long."

"That's cool. How are things with the missus?" There was caution in Wilson's voice as he stepped closer to the pool table. "You think there might be a chance of reconciling?"

Kennedy shook his head. "Nah, man. That boat has sailed. It's just too hard for her with me gone sometimes for years on a campaign. You gotta remember, this is my third campaign. I've been gone way too much. If I could change things—you know, a dirtside assignment—I mean, maybe we could, but..." His voice trailed off.

"Anyways, she's with another guy now," Kennedy said with a shrug. "With her filing for divorce, I don't see us being able to get back together. I can't say I blame her." He'd been numb to the fact of their coming divorce for a year now. Getting married and having children had seemed like a good idea at the time, but a soldier's life these days didn't bode well for marriages working out.

Captain Martin clapped him on the shoulder. "Hey, at least you're out here helping humanity—you're keeping your kids safe. It's a tough life we live. At the end of the day, though, if it's not us who goes to fight, then who? If it's not you, then who? We do this soldiering thing not for glory, and you certainly won't get rich off it. But we do this so our society, our people, can be safe. Never will we allow what happened in Sol to happen again. This is why we fight."

"I can't add to that, sir." Kennedy gave them both high fives. "Good game, fellas. I think I'm going to call it a night. Both of you, start practicing, and I'll be here tomorrow to whip your butts again and maybe show you a few moves."

"We'll take you up on that." Wilson raised his beer. "Cheers, my friend."

"Cheers."

Kennedy bade Wilson goodnight and gave a casual salute to Captain Martin as he turned to walk toward the exit. The low hum of conversation and clinking of glasses faded behind him as he entered into one of *Callisto*'s many corridors. He passed several soldiers he recognized—Jenkins regaled Hawkins with an embellished tale, no doubt. Stephens slouched against the bulkhead. He closed his eyes as he tried to catch a few moments of rest.

Instead of making his way back to the bunk room, Kennedy's boots carried him toward the stern of the ship and down to deck four, where the combat stress clinic was located. As he passed the armory checkpoint, he nodded to the familiar faces of Sergeants Ramirez and Kimura, the unlucky bastards who had drawn CQ duty the first night of their R&R.

As he stepped off the lift onto deck four, the corridor almost appeared to stretch longer with each step. The memories of the last seven months replayed in his mind. He hated it—the smoke, the deafening blast of enemy fire, the screams of the wounded, all the blood—it never left. For the life of him, he couldn't figure out why.

I didn't have these problems during the other campaigns, thought Kennedy. *So why now? In the past, I used to push the bad memories into a box. Now? That just isn't working.*

Kennedy quickened his pace until he stood before the psychiatric services facility's door. He drew a steady breath and walked in. The nightmares and flashbacks had been intensifying. He knew he needed to talk to someone.

Chapter Eight

Early July 2114
Titan Training Facility
Sol System

Admiral Ripley Lee leaned back in his chair, his eyes glued to the holodisplay floating above his desk. Beside him, XO Noriko Sato sat with her back straight, her expression one of concentration. The schematics of the RNS star carrier *Vega* rotated slowly before them. Its massive form dwarfed everything they'd seen before.

Lee whistled softly, his fingers tracing the outline of the ship in the air. "Three thousand, two hundred meters. Makes our old cruiser look like a rowboat, doesn't it?"

Sato nodded. She scanned the specs, scrolling alongside the hologram. "Bronkis5 armor belt. That's top-of-the-line stuff, Admiral. This ship could take a beating."

"And dish out one hell of a punch too," Lee said, pointing to the weapons array. "Twenty-four twin-barreled antiship turbo lasers, twenty twin-barreled twenty-four-inch magrail turrets. It's enough firepower to level a small moon."

Sato's eyebrows shot up as she read the missile specs. "Two hundred fifty antiship missiles in five pods of fifty each. Sixty point-defense guns, twenty pods of fifty antifighter missiles. It's a flying fortress."

Lee's gaze shifted to the fighter complement. "Two full wings, each with three groups of four squadrons. Sixteen fighters per squadron." He did the mental math. "That's…"

"Three hundred eighty-four fighters and bombers, sir," Sato finished for him.

"XO, I never thought I'd see the day when we'd command a vessel of this magnitude," said Lee. "The *Vega* is truly a marvel."

"It's like they took every captain's wish list and made it a reality, sir," Sato agreed. "And they're giving it to us."

Lee chuckled. "I half expect to find a swimming pool and a bowling alley somewhere in here, given the size of this beast."

"Who knows? I wouldn't put it past them to try and squeeze those in," she laughed.

Lee leaned forward, zooming in on the bridge section. They'd arrived on the ship recently and dropped off a few supplies in Lee's quarters but had yet to walk to the bridge to view it in person. Instead, they'd decided to stay put in Lee's quarters to pull up the ship's schematics and talk in private. "Look at the size of that command center. We could fit our entire old bridge crew in there and still have room for a party."

Sato snorted, quickly covering it with a cough. "I'm not sure Fleet Command would approve of bridge parties, sir."

"Killjoys," he said but inwardly acknowledged his reluctance to join such festivities anyway.

"The crew..." Sato pulled up a file on her data pad. "I've been reviewing the personnel assignments. We've got some of the best and brightest in the Fleet coming aboard."

Lee rubbed his chin, resting his back against his chair. "I'm looking forward to meeting them all." He paused, a mischievous glint in his eye. "Think we should greet them in formal uniforms or flight suits?"

"Formal uniforms, of course, sir. We need to set the tone from day one."

"Always by the book, aren't you, XO?" Lee laughed, knowing he was by the book most times as well. "All right, formal uniforms it is. But I reserve the right to switch to flight suits if things get too stuffy."

"Noted, sir. Shall we review the rest of the specs?" asked Sato.

Lee turned his attention back to the holodisplay. "We've got a lot to learn before we take command of this beautiful behemoth."

"With you, Admiral, all will go fine. Your tactical prowess during the Zodark attack on Alfheim was nothing short of brilliant. The brass noticed."

"Flattery will get you everywhere, Sato, but that was a long time ago. I've learned a lot more since then. Still, let's not forget your contributions—all you've done for me and our crew throughout the years. That maneuver you pulled in the Rass system. Textbook stuff. No way we could have survived without your quick thinking."

"Just following your lead, sir." She hesitated for a moment, and her expression sobered. "I... received a letter from my brother yesterday."

"Everything all right?"

"His best friend..." Sato swallowed hard. "KIA. Zodark warrior took him out, apparently. All he said was it was gruesome, and he can't get it out of his mind."

Lee's jaw tightened. "Damn. I'm sorry. That's... rough." During the long years Lee had commanded ships, crew members, and pilots, it never got any easier to accept the loss of people under his command. The sacrifices they made for him, their brothers and sisters in combat, and for the Republic. Heck, for humanity. He'd seen things he *still* couldn't get out of his head, even with all the therapy he'd received since.

Sato's eyes looked distant. "It was difficult to read. He described the aftermath... it wasn't pretty, especially for his unit."

"What unit is he in?"

"3rd Ranger Regiment, 1st Division."

"War's brutal, ugly. Like your brother and those who died beside him, we fight so others don't have to."

"Yes, sir," Sato said.

The mood in the room shifted, tension settling over them like a heavy blanket. Lee rested his elbows on his desk, his expression serious. "We have a few months to prepare before we embark to the Pfeinstgard system. We have a lot of people to train. You rested up?"

"Aye, Admiral." Sato tapped the tablet in her hands. "What are your thoughts on that latest intel report from Space Command? It sounds like the Zodarks have been busily fortifying Gravixia should we decide to pay it another visit."

"Not surprising. Our previous incursion caught them with their pants down. We achieved total surprise. The Primords and Space Command confirmed it rattled their cage. The little bits of intel the Gallentines have gathered suggest the Zodarks have bolstered their early-warning systems and QRF protocols. We won't penetrate their system undetected this time. Expect heavy interceptors the moment we cross the line."

"Sir, do you have any concerns about this multipronged approach to encircling the Zodarks before going after Tueblets?" Sato asked, pulling up a classified file on her data pad.

"I have my thoughts, but something is clearly on your mind, so why don't you share your concerns?" said Lee.

"It's a multipronged assault. It splits our forces," Sato explained. "We'll be leading the main thrust, but there are at least *three other* battle groups involved. I understand the logic. I wonder why we just don't consolidate our efforts and just push through Gravixia into Tueblets directly."

"Yeah, the logistics alone are a nightmare," Lee acknowledged. "We'll be operating deep in enemy territory, far from our supply lines, once we cross into Tueblets. If anything goes wrong..."

"We'll be on our own, I get it," Sato finished. "Getting back to business. I'll start working on training schedules and simulation scenarios immediately, sir."

"Did you comm Captain Blake Cooper?"

"Affirmative, sir. He's on his—"

A sharp knock at the door interrupted their conversation. Lee glanced at Sato, then called out, "Enter."

The door slid open and revealed Blake "Coop" Cooper. He stepped in, his back straight, and snapped a crisp salute. "Captain Cooper reporting as ordered, sir."

Lee returned the salute. "At ease, Captain."

Coop relaxed his posture, shifting to parade rest. His eyes darted between Lee and Sato.

Lee gestured to a chair. "Have a seat, Coop."

Coop hesitated for a heartbeat before settling into the offered chair. His posture remained alert, hands resting on his knees.

Lee interlocked his fingers, setting his hands on his desktop. "I'm expanding your command, Coop. In addition to commanding Carrier Strike Wing 14, you'll be the lead wing commander aboard *Vega*. Captain Mason Lewis is commanding CSW 15, but he'll fall under your overall command. It's a significant step up. Are you prepared to take on this added responsibility?"

Coop squared his shoulders. "You can count on me, Admiral. I'll give it everything I've got and then some."

"Good, 'cause it looks like our strike wings are going to be flying those newly upgraded Gripen IIs. That means I'll need you to oversee their integration into the squadrons. We've got a short window to get the squadrons and the ship ready to deploy within eight weeks. It's not much time, I know, but we have to work with what we're given."

Coop remained expressionless as he listened. "Huh, eight weeks is a tight timeline, sir. We'll figure it out and make it happen, but back to these new Gripens. We've been hearing about them for some time. Have you been shown the specs yet?"

Lee nodded, then typed on his data pad, bringing up a holographic display of the fighter. "Top of the line, Coop. Improved maneuverability, enhanced armor casing around the critical system, and an upgraded EW and defensive weapons package will make it that much harder for a Zodark to gain a lock and engage. Sato will send the update over to your data pad shortly so you can spend some time looking it over. Oh, something else I need to share with you. That request you made to run the wings through the Pilot Adaptive Combat Training—I pulled a few strings and called in a few favors. We got it, but only for a strike group. My suggestion, for what it's worth, is to consider having your least experienced pilots go through it. They'll be the ones to gain the most from it."

Sato chimed in. "With the pilots from the *Freedom* returning to the Fleet, we'll be receiving a mix of highly experienced pilots and a lot of junior pilots either fresh from flight school or finishing their first assessments. We'll let you and Captain Lewis decide how you want to divvy up the pilots, but one thing we want the two of you to figure out is what sort of new tactics and strategies we should employ given the number of squadrons the *Vega* can field."

Lee stared at Coop. "I also want you and Lewis to work with Commander Rhom from Tactical to develop strategies that take full advantage of our fighter complement and the ship's weapons. Let's see if there's a better way for us to utilize the tools given to us."

Coop nodded in agreement. "Absolutely, sir. I must admit, though, I'm still in shock you secured enough training time at PACT to run an entire strike group through it. This will really improve the pilots we send. Once I've had a chance to look over the official specs of these new Gripen IIs and what we encountered during our last incursion into Zodark space, I'll have our training officers focus on how our new capabilities can be leveraged against what we encountered during our last battle with the Zodarks. If we're going to seize Zodark territory, then I'm going to focus some of our training on atmospheric flight and providing close-air support.

"I think what surprised us during those attacks against the mining facilities in the Gravaxia system was the vast improvement in the Zodarks' integrated defense system. They made serious upgrades to their electronic warfare units and point-defense guns. We're going to need to place a higher emphasis on suppression and destruction of enemy air defenses if we're going to clear a path for our orbital assault transports and close-air support units. I may even dedicate a squadron or two for just this purpose," Coop explained as he shared his ideas on how to get his pilots ready for the battles to come.

Lee grinned as he listened. "That's why I'm putting you in charge, Coop. You've got the experience and the drive to make this happen."

Coop raised his chin. "Thank you, sir. We'll have the best damn space wings in the fleet."

"It's going to be a lot of work, Captain," Sato said. "Long hours, tough decisions. Are you ready for that?"

"Born ready," Coop replied confidently.

"Good," Lee said, "because we start tomorrow—0800 hours, in the ready room. I'll brief you on the full scope of Operation Starburst and our role in it. This should be the turning point of the war." He paused, studying Cooper for any sign of hesitation or doubt. He found nothing— no nervous tic, no uncertain gesture, no telling expression. "All right, Coop, let's get into the nitty-gritty. I want a rotating schedule for all squadrons. Three shifts, eight hours each. That means round-the-clock training and maintenance."

Cooper's posture exuded unwavering confidence. "Understood, sir. We'll keep those pilots singing day and night."

"Good. Now, for the training regimens," Lee continued. "I want a mix of standard and advanced maneuvers. Start with the basics— formation flying, evasive tactics, target acquisition. Then we ramp it up and add whatever new tactics you and Lewis come up with. Speaking about training, you've heard of the Thrasher Run?"

Coop's eyes narrowed a little. "Sir, I'm all gung-ho for tough training, but that's not exactly a walk in the park. It's got a reputation for chewing up pilots and spitting them out."

"Exactly," Lee shifted in his chair. "I want our pilots to eat it for breakfast. By the time we're done, they should be able to fly it blindfolded."

Coop grunted at his optimism. "Aye, sir. We'll make sure everyone gets a chance at it."

"With the *Vega*'s improved weapons, we're going to implement a new strategy we're calling the Hammer and Anvil," Sato then added as she read off her data pad. "Your fighters will be the hammer, Coop. I'll explain more in the coming days, but it'll involve coordinating your squadrons with our capital ships to create a series of kill boxes."

"Kill boxes? I like the sound of that," Coop exclaimed.

"Precisely," Lee added. "We'll use our larger ships—you know, battle cruisers, battleships, heavy cruisers—to herd enemy fighters into predetermined zones. That's where your squadrons come in. I want precision strikes and the use of overwhelming firepower. We're not looking to just win dogfights; we want to obliterate the enemy's ability to fight back."

"Understood, Admiral." Coop folded his hands on his lap. "Captain Lewis and I will make it happen. Anything else?"

"Incorporate basic training into their routine. They need to build endurance for various aspects of their lives, especially to improve their physical fitness." Lee stood to signal the end of the meeting. "That's all for now, Captain. I have full confidence in your abilities. Dismissed."

Rising from his chair, Coop snapped to attention and offered a salute. He turned sharply on his heel and strode out of the office. The door hissed shut behind him.

Sato watched as the door closed. "Sir, do you remember when Coop was just a rookie pilot? He made so many mistakes back then."

"Indeed. He was an arrogant son of a... there was a time I considered recommending him for administrative separation. But he's come a long way since then, proving himself to be one of our finest aviators."

"Remember that incident with the landing gear?" Sato shook her head.

Lee groaned and pinched the bridge of his nose. "How could I forget? The deck crew was scrubbing skid marks off the flight deck for days."

"And that time he accidentally jettisoned his payload during a routine patrol?"

"Don't remind me," Lee sighed. "I thought Admiral Oldendorf was going to have an aneurysm when he saw the report."

Sato's lips twitched. "To be fair, sir, the safety protocols were a bit confusing on those old Orions."

"True. But most pilots didn't manage to dump their entire missile complement into an asteroid field."

A smile played on the sides of Sato's lips. "He certainly kept things... interesting."

"You know, Noriko, I think those mishaps were exactly what Coop needed. They taught him humility, forced him to focus."

"I agree, sir," Sato said. "It's been remarkable to watch his transformation. He's gone from a cocky hotshot to a leader who truly cares for his pilots."

"That's why I pushed for his promotion. He's got the perfect blend of skill and experience. Plus, he's been there. He knows what it's like to screw up, to feel like you're not cut out for this life, and to overcome that feeling."

"It makes him an excellent mentor as well."

"Exactly, and I've noticed he can spot potential in pilots others might overlook. Gives them a chance to prove themselves, just like he had to."

Lee received an alert that an urgent message was coming in from the Primord system Pfeinstgard, and he held up a hand to Sato as he pulled up the report. As he read, a smile spread across his lips.

"What is it, boss?" Sato asked.

"After we left, the Zodarks apparently thought the Pfeinstgard system would be ripe for the plucking and staged an attack. However, the Primords report that they utterly smashed them—only a very few Zodark ships managed to limp away with their tails between their legs."

He laughed at the overconfidence of the blue brutes. Lee was proud of his Primord friends-in-arms. Of course, there was still more work to be done, but he couldn't help but feel that the tide was shifting and that he was on the side that was bringing more good into the universe.

Chapter Nine

Office of the Viceroy
Alliance City, New Eden

The leader of the Humtars, President Gudea, graciously took his seat on one of the chairs in the library room. It was connected to Miles's official office and presented a relaxed, intimate environment, suitable for the kinds of discussions they were about to have.

"This is a beautiful room you have, Miles," admired President Gudea, his eyes delighting in the walls of bookshelves filled with real, honest-to-goodness books. "It is not very often these days that we come across physical books where I am from—and these bronze statues, and what are those...oil paintings? Incredible. I feel as if I have walked back in time—to a period we have long lost. It's like reconnecting with one's ancestors, if I may be so bold."

Miles felt his cheeks flush as he smiled warmly at Gudea's compliment.

"Thank you, Mr. President—"

"No, none of that, Miles," interrupted the Humtar leader. "Please, we are in private, and I would like to think the two of us are steadily becoming friends with each visit. Just call me Gudea. Our culture is rather similar to that of the people I believe you call Sumerians. From the planet Sumer, correct?"

Miles nodded. "Ah, OK, I can do that. Since you mentioned the Sumerians, I would be remiss if I didn't mention that we have discovered over time that the people who populated the planet Sumer originally came from Earth. They were relocated there by the Altairians when they believed a cataclysmic event would lead to the demise of humans on Earth.

"Obviously, they were wrong about us, but unfortunately, the Sumerians were dealt a different fate from our own. Their planet eventually fell under the control of the Zodark Empire after the Altairians lost a series of battles. Since then, large numbers of their people were steadily transplanted to repopulate a series of planets held deep within their territory," Miles explained.

"Ah, yes. I seem to recall that bit of information you shared with me during our last visit," responded Gudea as he leaned forward. "In fact, Miles, that is a big part of what I would like to address in our discussion about our return to the Milky Way."

Speaking for the first time since the meeting had begun, Chancellor Aimes Morgan leaned forward. "So you will return?" he pressed. "Your people were pleased with our offer?"

The Humtar leader turned to the Chancellor. "Yes, Aimes. Our governing body, those who advise and assist me in leading our people, spent a good bit of time evaluating the proposals and options you enclosed."

Gudea then turned to Miles. "You also brought up some good points about potential conflicts and unease with the Gallentines and Altairians that our return might cause. We have been absent—gone from this galaxy and theirs for many millennia. While our people believe we are justified in demanding the return of some of our core worlds, we acknowledge, sadly, that they had lain in ruin for untold hundreds or even thousands of years before being rediscovered and populated once again. It would serve no purpose or greater good to displace those societies and people now sitting upon the sites of our once expansive empire. At the height of our power, our empire covered multiple galaxies, before the events we call the Great Fall forced us to isolate as many of our people as could be saved.

"In terms of your offer, Aimes"—Gudea turned to face the Chancellor—"I tasked our historians and keepers of time to search into the histories from before the Great Fall. I directed them to collect as much information as possible about our knowledge of Sol, Rhea, and Alpha Centauri—what explorations of these systems had taken place and where colonies might have been settled. I must say, it was an exhaustive search that yielded very little beyond the acknowledgment of these three systems, the planets within them, and approved proposals to populate them.

"In all three of these systems, a colony had been established, but only the Rhea system had been connected to our Stellar Conduit Network, or 'stargates' as your people call them. The data we have on these settlements is minimal at best. Still, our settlement on Earth was the largest of them at the time of the Great Fall," Gudea explained.

"In regard to our colony on Earth, we managed to find the name of the settlement and some details your historians and keepers of time may find helpful in reconstructing the histories of your planet and *your* origins. For example, the first Humtars to arrive on Earth had established a colonial outpost called Kerma, settled in a location near what you call the third cataract of the Nile River. I believe the Republic calls this region the State of Northeast Africa."

Miles remembered a course in ancient human history he had taken where he learned that evidence of human civilization in that region went back to before 5000 BC. It was fascinating to think that his people and the Humtars were connected from the very beginning of Earth.

"There are several religious cultures on Earth that place the origins of mankind in that region, Gudea," Miles explained. "It's not necessarily congruent with all the data from our archaeologists, but the link certainly sparks my curiosity."

Gudea nodded. "In view of this information, we would like a place for us to establish a colony or outpost so we may reconnect with our ancestors and the history of our people. You see, regardless of how you may view yourselves in contrast to us, in the eyes of the Humtar people, you *are* Humtar. You are direct descendants of our ancestors. For our people, discovering you has rekindled a desire to connect with our past—to learn from its triumphs and mistakes, to become better Humtars for future generations. With this in mind, and if the Republic is still open to it, we would like very much to resettle where our ancestors first had— this region you now call the State of Northeast Africa."

Aimes responded quickly, "Yes, of course, our offer still stands for the Humtar people. However, as I explained earlier, this is a particularly heavily damaged area. We still have many people living in temporary shelters while we continue to work to rebuild."

Gudea waved his concerns away with a swipe of his hand. "You need not worry about that, Aimes. Once I return to our world, I will direct the appropriate resources to aid in your rebuilding efforts and prepare locations for our future cities and spaceports. You are Humtar. You are us, and we are you—one people separated only by time. We will help you rebuild, and together we are going to create an incredible future for generations to come."
****

Three Days Later
Office of the Viceroy
Alliance City, New Eden

"You both know the Gallentines. What do you think they'll say once we tell them about the Zeta Respiratory Inhibitor virus?" the Chancellor asked nervously. He had only briefly met the Emperor once and the other two Gallentine advisors a couple of times since becoming Chancellor.

Admiral Bailey shrugged, then reached for his glass of brandy.

"Chester, you may want to slow-walk that until after they get here, or after the meeting is done," Miles commented as the admiral downed the contents of his glass.

Grunting at the suggestion, Bailey countered, "I'll be fine, Miles. It helps calm my nerves, and right now, that's what I need."

Miles shook his head as Bailey refilled his glass, then turned to the Chancellor. "I'm not sure what to expect, Aimes. Maybe this is a big deal and they'll enforce these rules on us, or maybe it's not that big a deal and it'll get swept under the rug so long as it can stay silent. In either case, after our meeting the other day with Gudea, I feel a lot better about our current position in this matter."

Bailey bunched his eyebrows in confusion. "Um, wait, I thought our meeting with the Humtar President was tomorrow—before we met with the Emperor? Did I miss something while I was gone?" Admiral Bailey had just returned from a meeting with Admiral Rosentreter as his forces now planned the final campaign against the Pharaonis.

Miles was about to tell him about their earlier meeting with Gudea when his secretary announced the arrival of their guests.

When the door leading into his office opened, Admirals Helixar and Wiyrkomi, followed by Second General Orionis, entered the room. Their presence was imposing, each step exuding authority and command as they walked towards them.

"Welcome, Admirals, General. Please, if you'll follow me to the study, we'll have our discussion there," Miles greeted them warmly, offering firm handshakes as he guided everyone to the adjacent study with its more comfortable setting.

Admiral Helixar nodded curtly, then followed Miles's lead, walking into the study. "Viceroy Hunt, Chancellor Morgan, Admiral Bailey, we received your message requesting an urgent meeting. We are here. What are the matters you wish to discuss before you meet with the Emperor?"

Chancellor Morgan adjusted his tie with a sense of unease. "Admiral Helixar, Admiral Wiyrkomi, General Orionis, as the leader of the Republic, I must regrettably bring to your attention an incident that has transpired in the Gravaxia system. This information has only recently come to our knowledge—"

"Does this have anything to do with the strange illness that seems to be plaguing Zodark warriors and civilians alike on the occupied planets and moons in the system?" interrupted Admiral Helixar, his eyes narrowing, his facial expression becoming hard.

"Yes, it does," Morgan answered flatly.

Helixar made a grunting noise at the Chancellor's response. "Ah, I see. Chancellor, we have our own ways of collecting intelligence and analyzing what's happening based on a variety of factors and probabilities. Given the way this strange illness has spread, the most likely culprit seems to be the use of some sort of biological of chemical agent—but these kinds of weapons are forbidden, are they not?"

"They are, Admiral Helixar." Miles stepped in for the Chancellor. "This is why we asked to discuss an urgent matter with you prior to our meeting with the Emperor. As you have suspected, a biological agent is the reason why the Zodarks are becoming ill. We…*I* am admitting that this was an unauthorized use of a banned weapon. I, as Viceroy, became increasingly concerned about the threat that the Zodarks posed to us humans as a species. In a period of weakness, I authorized a research project to delve into possible ways to exploit any weaknesses they have—and I took the gloves off. No limitations."

Miles took a deep breath and let it out slowly. On the one hand, it felt like a weight was being lifted off his chest. On the other, the anticipation of what might happen due to the confession he had just made caused his stomach to curl up in knots.

"I realized the error of my ways, and I had the project pulled. However, the main scientist who had been in charge of the project…well, in the attacks on Earth, his entire immediate family, including his grandchildren, were murdered in cold blood by the Zodarks. His mind focused in on revenge and it got hold of him like a parasite. He enlisted one of his few surviving family members, a nephew, who happened to serve in the Republic Army, and had it released."

The three Gallentines exchanged glances with each other, likely using their neurolinks. While Miles shared the same type of neurolink device the Gallentines used, he was unable to figure out how to listen in or join their conversation.

Miles continued. "I want to assure you that this incident is not going without consequence on our end, and obviously, we are now implementing safeguards to ensure nothing like this ever happens again. I cannot undo what has been done, though I wish with everything in me that were possible.

"Now my concern turns to my people. I wanted to meet with you before we speak with the Emperor because we need to have some kind of idea of what sort of response or punishment we may face. What will the implications of this violation be? How will this affect the alliance?"

After nearly a minute had passed without comment from the Gallentines, Miles breathed a sigh of relief when Admiral Wiyrkomi, his trusted advisor and friend of the past fifteen years, leaned forward to speak. Wiyrkomi's gaze was intense as he looked at Miles before turning to face the Chancellor. "Chancellor Morgan, and my good friend Miles, what you have just confirmed constitutes not just a serious violation of agreed-upon rules for how we wage war, it is a grievous violation of trust—trust the Emperor had placed in you, Miles. The use of a biological agent in warfare is not tolerated within the alliance.

"Before we would consider speaking to the Emperor on your behalf regarding this violation of trust, we will want more details as to what the Republic has done to address this breach, and what you will do to ensure something of this nature never happens again."

When Wiyrkomi had finished speaking, Admiral Bailey placed his glass down. "You're right, Admiral Wiyrkomi. This never should have happened. The moment we learned about it, we began a thorough investigation to determine how it happened. We are prepared to turn over to you the remaining stockpiles of the biological weapon that was used and allow your people to inspect the facility it was stored in and to assure the Emperor we have fully divested from this program."

Admiral Helixar's eyes narrowed as he glared at his human host. "I would like to remind the three of you that the Gallentine Empire has provided the Republic with immeasurable help in technology, military support, and advisors. The Emperor even went so far as to replace the Altairians as the leaders and caretakers of the Milky Way alliance. King Grigdolly lost his title as viceroy, and it transferred to you, Miles.

"In spite of this multigenerational war our people have been waging with the Collective and Legion, the Emperor has shown great benevolence to the Republic. With this benevolence come expectations, and perhaps the most important of these is your complete and unwavering obedience and compliance with the rules we have given you. I will not lie or mislead you—this breach of the Emperor's trust…it could have severe consequences."

Admiral Wiyrkomi then added, "I cannot say how the Emperor will respond once he is briefed on your error. What I can say is that I will remind the Emperor of the achievements and exemplary service the Republic has and continues to provide in service to His Majesty. It is my position that you should be shown leniency. There is no denying that the Republic's leadership, tenacity, and creativity are why the war with the Dominion is nearly over. As Viceroy, Miles, you have achieved what the Altairians and former Viceroy Grigdolly could not—victories across the star systems of the Milky Way. This means that the alliance may soon be able to join the Emperor's forces in the war against the Collective."

Miles nodded solemnly. "Thank you for your candor, Wiyrkomi. I would just like to assure you once again that I did *not* authorize this virus to be released. It was an action taken by two men who had suffered mightily at the hands of these blue beasts."

General Orionis sat back in his chair as he crossed his arms, his expression stern. "Viceroy, the mere fact that you developed these weapons, despite knowing they were banned, does not speak well of your leadership. Why should I or the Emperor believe you won't start another illegal program like the first?"

Miles felt ashamed, but he knew the general had a point. "General Orionis, you are right. I allowed fear to rule my decision-making. I thought I had enough safeguards in place to stop something like this from happening, but I was wrong. I deeply regret this incident and will do what has to be done to earn the Emperor's trust again."

Admiral Helixar exchanged a glance with Wiyrkomi and Orionis. "Very well. If the Republic turns over the weapon and provides all information regarding its development and unauthorized use, then, at least from our end of things, we will consider this breach to have been addressed. The Emperor may agree with our assessment, or he may make his own. I cannot speak to what he may choose, but I can assure you of this—any future violations will have swift consequences."

Miles breathed a sigh of relief. "You have my word, Admiral. We will comply immediately."

Admiral Wiyrkomi's gaze then softened slightly as he sought to change the topic to other important issues that had to be dealt with. "Let us move forward from this and discuss the meetings you have had with the Humtars. The Emperor is most keen on knowing what their intentions are now that they have revealed themselves to us."

Miles nodded, happy to move on from the illegal weapons issue. "Admirals, General, we spoke with President Gudea a few days ago specifically about their intentions and plans now that the gate between their galaxy and ours has been unlocked. It was a productive discussion, and I can assure you, they come in peace."

Admiral Helixar's eyes narrowed. "The Humtars' return could shift the balance of power significantly. Why do you believe their intentions are peaceful?"

Miles smiled disarmingly as he explained, "The Humtars have expressed a desire to reconnect with their descendants—us. Earth, New Eden, and Alpha Centauri were once Humtar colonies. After confirming via DNA testing, we can confidently say we are their direct descendants. Armed with this knowledge, they wish to establish a colony in a heavily damaged part of Earth and help us restore the planet after the Zodark invasion."

Admiral Wiyrkomi leaned forward. "And what assurances do we have that they will not seek to reclaim their former territories now under Gallentine, Altairian, Tully, or Primord control?"

Miles smiled reassuringly. "I relayed the Emperor's concern to President Gudea. The Humtars understand the current political landscape. They have no intention of reclaiming their former territories. They are aware that the territory of their ancient empire now belongs to many other empires and races, and they will respect that. Their primary goal is to reconnect with their descendants and assist in our rebuilding."

Chancellor Morgan then added, "President Gudea has made it clear that their interest lies in the regions that were once their colonies that now reside within the Republic—namely Earth. They believe that everything that has happened must have been for a reason. When Gudea and his people learned of the damage the Zodarks had done to the Earth and the loss of life they inflicted, they came to believe they must help us, and in doing so, they believe they are helping their ancestors—atoning for their abandonment of their people during what they call the Great Fall. They have offered to establish a colony in a heavily damaged region of northeast Africa and provide substantial resources for the restoration efforts."

General Orionis's stern expression softened slightly the more he heard. "So they wish to integrate, not to dominate?"

Miles nodded, expressing understanding. "Indeed. They are willing to contribute to the defense of Earth and support its security. Their technology and resources could prove to be invaluable assets. Importantly, they have assured us of their commitment to respecting the Emperor's authority and the existing power structures of the alliance."

Admiral Helixar exchanged glances with Wiyrkomi and Orionis. "If the Humtars' intentions are true, as you say, then maybe this could be beneficial. However, we must proceed with caution. They could also be laying the groundwork to establish a forward base in the Milky Way to reclaim it."

Admiral Wiyrkomi, sensing the need to reassure his Gallentine counterparts, spoke up. "I can vouch for Miles and the Republic's commitment. Over the past fifteen years, I have seen their dedication and loyalty to the Emperor. The Republic has consistently worked towards the goals he has set forth. The assistance of the Humtars could accelerate our progress in the Milky Way."

Miles agreed and then added, "With a Humtar colony on Earth, we can count on them to aid in its defense. Additionally, the Humtars may prove invaluable allies in the Emperor's war against the Collective and Legion. They seem to possess detailed information about the Collective that could aid the Emperor in this ongoing conflict."

Admiral Helixar nodded thoughtfully. "Very well. We will proceed with caution and monitor the situation closely. The Humtars' reappearance could indeed be an opportunity, provided their intentions remain as stated."

General Orionis's expression finally relaxed. "If their intentions are genuine, this alliance could be beneficial for all parties involved. We will support this initiative and ensure it aligns with the Emperor's goals."

Miles felt a wave of relief washing over him. "Thank you, Admirals, General. We will continue to work closely with the Gallentine Empire to ensure transparency and cooperation in all our endeavors."

Admiral Wiyrkomi gave a nod of approval. "Let us move forward with unity and strength. Together, we will achieve great things."

Chapter Ten

RNS *Vega*
Carrier Strike Wing 14 (CSW-14)
Titan Training Facility, Sol System

The RNS *Vega* was an impressive vessel, the Republic Navy's latest and most advanced star carrier. It spanned thirty-two hundred meters from bow to stern. Its Bronkis5 armor belt provided exceptional protection against enemy fire, while its array of weaponry ensured it could hold its own in any engagement. Its vast array of weapons gave *Vega* a formidable punch.

To Captain Blake "Coop" Cooper, this ship was just another amazing example of ingenuity in a series of exceptionally advanced military vessels the Republic had been creating over the past several years.

As he walked alone down one of *Vega*'s corridors, holowindows displayed the Titan Training Facility outside where the ship was currently docked. A breathtaking view of the Proving Grounds—the facility's nickname—glared back at him. This training location was massive as it floated along in the Sol system.

The Proving Grounds was an impressive sight—a sprawling network of structures and modules connected by tunnels. Here, the Republic Army and Navy conducted their most rigorous drills, where they pushed their personnel to their limits.

For the Navy, this served as the home of their elite pilot training program that had been formed after the end of the First Zodark War. In the aftermath of the disastrous losses the pilot corps had suffered during the transition from the drone fighter program to manned fighters, the Republic had realized that if they didn't refocus their pilot training on technical precision, team tactics, and pilot leadership programs, they might not win the next war. That was when Rear Admiral Aaron Blade and Captain Ethan Hunt, the son of Viceroy Miles Hunt, had formed what had eventually become the Fleet Advance Fighter Tactics School or Top Gun. To make selection for squadron command, you now had to be a graduate of the school, making it a sought-after course to attend.

Coop had gone through the program years ago, under the tutelage of Ethan Hunt, the famed Paladin, while he was still an instructor. Coop could still remember the long hours in the simulators, the punishing physical training, and the relentless pressure to perform under simulated combat scenarios while in the cockpit of a Gripen.

The Navy also used the facility to practice orbital bombardments, where they dropped ground forces from orbit and coordinated complex fleet formations and attacks in support of landing operations. New warships commissioning into the Republic Fleet had to pass through the Titan Training Facility during their shakedown cruise and fleet certification.

Coop halted for a moment and watched as a group of soldiers in heavy armor conducted a zero-g combat drill in space.

That's cool, but I have no time to watch, Coop thought to himself as he got moving again toward his new office quarters.

Earlier, he had gone over *Vega*'s flight deck reports and composition summary regarding the new space wing under his command. His wing consisted of the new Gripen II starfighters and the venerable Valkyrie bombers. Three fighter groups in total, comprising 192 Gripens and Valkyries—a daunting responsibility for any commander.

Rounding a corner, Coop strode into his new office aboard the *Vega*. The door slid shut behind him as he took in his upgraded surroundings.

What do I have here? he thought.

The office was spacious—way bigger than the last cubby-hole he'd worked in. A large viewport offered a stunning view of the starfield beyond. An oak desk dominated the center of the room. Data tablets covered the desktop along with a few personal items Coop had brought from his previous posting, dropped off here by an assistant.

This, in fact, was the first time he had stepped into this room. And, boy, was it a magnificent sight.

He settled into the luxurious chair behind the desk. The leather creaked slightly as he leaned back. He stretched his arms above his head. It had been a long day of meetings and introductions, one even with Admiral Lee himself, and he was eager to dive into the files of the pilots under his command.

As a newly promoted captain and commander of a much larger space wing than he had led on the RNS *Cassiopeia*, Coop had his work cut out for him.

He picked up the data tablet and began scrolling through the pilot files. He recognized a few names from his time on the *Cassi*, but most were unfamiliar. As he read through their service records and performance evaluations, he made mental notes about each pilot's strengths and weaknesses.

One file in particular caught his attention—a young lieutenant named Jace Harding, call sign Badger. He had an impressive record in the flight simulator but limited real-space and real-combat experience. Coop straightened his lips tightly as he considered the pilot's potential. On one hand, Badger's raw talent was undeniable. On the other, throwing an untested pilot into the thick of combat could be a recipe for disaster. He'd push this guy to misery to make him the best pilot possible. Otherwise, he'd have a dead pilot on his hands during the young man's first engagement in combat.

As Coop delved deeper into the young lieutenant's file, he saw that Badger's scores in the flight simulator were off the charts. He consistently outperformed his peers in every scenario, from dogfighting to bombing runs. His instructors praised his lightning-fast reflexes, his uncanny ability to anticipate enemy movements, and his fearless approach to combat.

There were also notes of concern. Badger had a reputation for being a maverick. He often broke formation to pursue his own targets. He was known for taking risks, pushing his fighter to its limits and beyond. While his impressive kill count in the simulators turned heads, whispers circulated that he cared more about personal glory than mission success.

Not good.

As Coop read through the reports, he saw his younger self in Badger. He had once been a rebel, a maverick in his own right. Back on New Eden, when he was just a young lieutenant, Coop had been assigned to a firebase tasked with defending the planet from Zodark troop transports, bombers, and starfighters.

In those earlier years as a drone pilot flying the F-97 Orions, Coop had been more interested in racking up kills than in protecting his wingmen. He had broken formation countless times, leaving his fellow pilots exposed as he chased after Zodark Vultures. His actions had resulted in the shoot-down of an Osprey and several Orions.

It was a mistake that had nearly cost him his career, haunting him for years. He'd vowed never to repeat that mistake. As he looked at Badger's file, he concluded that the lieutenant was headed down the same path. If Badger wasn't reined in soon, the kid could end up causing even more damage than Coop had.

The thought sent ice through Coop's veins. *Not on my watch and not with my wing.*

He reached for the comm panel on his desk and keyed in the code for the flight operations center. A moment later, a voice came over the speaker. "Flight Ops, Lieutenant Commander Sandoval speaking."

"Commander Sandoval, this is Captain Cooper. I need you to locate Lieutenant Jace Harding and send him to my office immediately."

"Yes, sir," Sandoval replied. "I'll have him report to you ASAP."

"Thank you, Commander." Coop cut the connection.

Badger was a talented pilot, and the Navy needed every advantage it could get in the war. Talent alone wasn't enough, though. A pilot needed discipline, teamwork, and a willingness to put the mission above all else.

He set the data tablet down and rubbed his eyes. As commander of such a large force, every decision he made could have far-reaching consequences. He would need to carefully balance the need for aggressive action with the safety and well-being of his pilots.

With eight fighter squadrons and four bomber squadrons under his belt, Coop would need to develop strategies for deploying his forces effectively in a variety of combat scenarios, just like Admiral Lee wanted. He was to be the iron fist of the carrier—the haymaker to bring down its enemies.

For now, there was still much work to be done. Coop yawned, feeling his energy beginning to fade. Sleep hadn't come for twenty-four hours. Duty called, though, and he picked up the data tablet once more and resumed his review of the pilots, determined to familiarize himself with every member of his command.

Ten minutes later, a knock sounded on Coop's office door.

"Come," Coop said.

When the door opened, Coop looked up from his data pad. A young man stood in the doorway. The pilot was tall and lean, with short-cropped dark hair and piercing blue eyes. He wore a flight suit with the sleeves rolled up, revealing a tattoo of a Gripen starfighter on his forearm.

"Lieutenant Harding, reporting as ordered, sir," Badger said, full of bravado.

Coop motioned at a seat across from him. "Sit."

Badger stepped into the office. He crossed the room in a few long strides and sat. "Sir, I wanted to say it's an honor to be assigned to your command. You're a legend in the fighter world."

Coop grunted at the flattery as he gave the flier a once-over. "An honor, you say. Give it a few months, and we'll see if you still feel that way. So, getting down to brass tacks, Lieutenant," Coop said, beginning his interview, "why don't you tell me about your experience flying a Gripen?"

Coop knew it was a silly question, but Badger's answer would tell him a lot about the kind of man and pilot he was.

Badger's eyes lit up at the question, and a smile tugged at the corners of his mouth. "The Gripen—it's an incredible machine, sir," he said, his voice full of enthusiasm. "The way it handles, the speed and acceleration are incredible. But the way it moves, how it reacts to the commands of the pilot, and its maneuverability… it's like nothing I've ever flown or seen before. Well, maybe those Gallentine Hellcats, but you get the picture."

Good, he has passion—but I need to see if he can balance that enthusiasm with tactical awareness.

"It's a great starfighter, Badger," Coop agreed. "You probably haven't heard this just yet, but the *Vega* is going to be fielding the new Gripen IIs—an upgrade on what's already a superb starfighter. But let's put that aside and acknowledge it's not just about the machines we fly. It's the pilots who fly them that make them deadly, isn't it?"

Coop watched Badger's enthusiastic expression fade. *He didn't like me taking his fire and his fervor away,* Coop observed. *He seems easily discouraged. Let's see if he tries to overcompensate by telling me what I want to hear…*

"Yes, sir. That's true. A machine is only as good as its operator or, in our case, its pilot."

OK, a little better than expected, Coop thought before continuing with his questions. "Lieutenant, let me tell you something." Coop lifted a tablet off the desk. "I've been looking over your fitness

81

reports and comments from past instructors and commanders. They speak highly of your natural skill as a pilot. You know, in my early years, I was a lot like you, Badger. I also thought I was invincible, that I could take on the whole Zodark fleet by myself if people would just get out of my way. But you know what? I learned the hard way that being a maverick can get you killed... and it can get your wingman killed, too."

Badger shifted in his seat, his expression uncomfortable. "I understand, sir."

"Do you?" pressed Coop.

"Aye, sir."

Coop fixed him with a steady gaze. "Because from what I've read in your FITREPs—you have a serious problem. You've developed a habit of breaking formation, going off on your own, and disregarding orders. So here's the deal, Badger. You're in the Fleet now. That kind of crap and attitude isn't going to cut it in any of my squadrons. You got me?"

Badger swallowed hard, his expression going flat. "Yes, sir, loud and clear. I mean no disrespect if that's how I've come across." His tone suggested that he differed with his FITREPs and the comments of his commanders.

Oh damn, this guy's going to be trouble, Coop realized quickly. His cavalier attitude bordered on unprofessionalism. It was the kind of liability that could endanger the entire wing during a critical mission. *I'm going to push this guy harder than anyone else. If he quits, so be it. Probably for the better...*

Coop stared him down. "Lieutenant, what I need you to understand is when you're out there in your Gripen, you're not just flying for yourself. You're an integral part of a larger team. A team that must function with unity of purpose and obey orders. Your wingman, your squadron, they have to trust you. They have to know you will have their backs and you won't abandon them to pursue some personal glory. I'm going to keep saying this over and over until it sticks in your brain and becomes second nature."

"Understood, sir," Badger replied, his cheeks flushing.

"Badger, this means you *will* respect the chain of command, your flight leader and squadron commander."

Badger nodded solemnly. "Aye, sir."

Good, he looks a little shaken up. Coop then realized this might be the first time someone had spoken to him like this.

"Good, Lieutenant, because I need you to be a team player. There are no second chances, no do-overs in combat. If you screw up, people die. My pilots die. So, put aside any personal scores. Forget about simulator kill counts. I need you to watch your wingman's back and to cover each other's sixes when they need it. I need you to be there for them," Coop explained, then paused. "You know what? Here's what I'm going to have you do for a few of the pilots in your new squadron. From now on, each day, you'll be put on schedule to make a pilot's bed for them. And they'll make your bed for you."

"Sir?" Badger had a look of confusion on his face.

"Look, this isn't about making beds. It's about helping your squadron mates without question and learning that sometimes you have to swallow your pride and do things you don't like for the sake of the team and the mission."

Coop saw the skin around Badger's nose twitch a little. He hadn't been expecting this turn of events. "Yes, sir," he responded quickly.

"Badger, I need you to develop trust in the pilots around you. When you're out there in the thick of it, that's all you've got. Just you and them. Dismissed, get out of here."

Chapter Eleven

Zon Private Study
High Council Building
Drokanis, Zinconia
Zodark Home World

Zon Otro sat in one of the chairs near the fireplace as he read the Groff's latest report from the Orinda system. The more he read, the hotter the anger burned within him, like the coal embers in the fire glowing white. The latest report he'd received from the Malvari and the Groff regarding the Orinda system had made it clear their once firm grip on the Gurista people was now lost—likely permanently.

Otro clenched the edge of the report, the words blurring before his eyes as his rage simmered just beneath the surface. Not only had the Republic thwarted the Malvari's attempt to reenter the Orinda system—beating back their second attempt to break the blockade and resecure the system—but the longer the system stayed under the control of the Republic, the more likely it was they would succeed in unifying the Gurista people with their own. The thought of the Republic bolstering its ranks with yet another human faction—one that the Zodarks had controlled for over two centuries—was almost unbearable. It had been bad enough losing control of the Qatana system and the Sumerians. The loss of the Guristas would be a devastating blow.

Finishing the report, Otro placed the tablet on the table as he reached for a drink, working up the courage to read the other tablet with the Groff's report. He downed the glass, then poured another before accessing the report. NOS Vorun Talvex, his trusted advisor, had already warned him this was not a happy, feel-good report. He shook his head dismissively, then began to read.

He didn't have to read long before it was clear the Groff's intelligence had confirmed the worst of his fears. The Republic was preparing the Gurista people to join their military, turning them into yet another weapon to be used against the Empire. He growled to himself. He knew this would turn out like Sumer—the Republic integrating them into their people, their government, and their military. It made the Malvari's defeat in the Orinda system all the more poignant. The Guristas' unity and resolve to side with the Republic over the Zodarks

84

would only grow stronger with each passing day, fueled by a shared purpose and the promise of freedom from Zodark rule. The people who had once been loyal subjects and soon-to-be foot soldiers for the Empire now constituted a rising threat. A dagger pointed at the heart of the Zodark Empire.

Otro leaned back in his chair, staring into the fire as the pair of Malvari and Groff reports played over in his mind. Their recent defeat had exposed a weakness in their strategy, an inability to exert enough force to overwhelm them. If there was one thing he had learned from battling the Republic, it was that they were extremely efficient at capitalizing on any mistakes his people made.

He brushed aside the toxic thoughts polluting his mind, souring his mood, and turned his attention to another brewing problem. The increased military buildup in the Primord system, Pfeinstgard, another looming danger he had to deal with. Based on the reports from the Malvari and the Groff, the two of them seemed to have found something they could agree on—an attack was coming. The Republic was positioning itself for a direct assault on the Gravaxia system, and the Malvari's forces there had barely held the line during the Republic's last attempt to seize control of the system.

The virus that had plagued the Gravaxia system during that last attempt had finally burned itself out due to the quarantine, but the damage to the system's defenses and infrastructure had been done. The Malvari were reinforcing their positions, sending additional ground forces, fighter squadrons, bombers, and warships to defend them. At the same time, engineers and slaves worked tirelessly to rebuild some of the system-wide defensive platforms, particularly in the asteroid belts. But as Otro reviewed the Malvari's numbers, his concern only deepened. His years of military service and his own time as Mavkah of the Malvari told him the reinforcements sent wouldn't be enough. The Republic and Primord forces were growing stronger by the day, and their momentum was terrifyingly effective when backed by the Altairians and their more advanced warships.

Otro's thoughts drifted to the battle damage reports from the Sol campaign. The losses of soldiers weren't what had hurt the Malvari—it was the loss of the *Nefantar* and the squadrons of battleships and heavy cruisers. More than a dracma[1] had passed since that humiliating defeat, yet their fleets were still devoid of their primary combat power—battleships. Despite devoting their entire economy, every factory and industrial center, in support of the unprecedented construction of new battleships, the shipyards of Tueblets, Zinconia, and Shwani struggled to replace the losses as the Republic and their allies nipped at the edges of the Empire.

When the Groff had reported that the allies had turned their focus first to the Orbots, then to the Pharaonis, Otro had hoped the allies would struggle against them and become bogged down in a war of attrition. Instead, they had struck like lightning at the Orbots, destroying their Collector ships and consciousness repositories. The Orbots' hubris in believing they had conquered death and cheated their way into immortality had ultimately become their undoing. Now, the Groff's intelligence and the Malvari's military assessments of how the Pharaonis were faring in their struggle against the alliance painted a grim picture— one that left little room for error. He hoped that the Pharaonis wouldn't fall apart like the Orbots had. For every month the Pharaonis could keep the Republic bogged down on Eurysa, the Zodark shipyards would be able to complete another four heavy battleships.

"Cursed these damn humans to Hark!"[2] He stood up, pacing the length of his study, the weight of his position pressing down on him like never before.

Otro stopped in front of the large window overlooking the capital city of Drokanis. The city had stood for centuries as a symbol of Zodark power and dominance. But now, with the Republic closing in and their enemies gathering strength, that dominance was being challenged in ways he had never imagined. The future of the Empire was at stake, and he would need to summon all his cunning, all his strength, and the wisdom of Lindow if he was to turn the tide in their favor.

With a determined look, Otro returned to his desk, the flames of the fireplace casting a flickering light over the room. He knew what needed to be done. The time for half measures and cautious strategies was over. The Zodark Empire would not fall on his watch, not as long as he had breath in his lungs.

---

[1] Zodark term for a year.
[2] Hark is the Zodark word for Hell.

He activated his comm panel, his voice cold and resolute as he spoke. "NOS Vorun, summon the High Council. It's time we discussed the next phase of our strategy. We must prepare the Empire to receive our enemy—to receive the Republic and its allies."

The message was sent, and while he waited for the Council to assemble, Otro couldn't shake the feeling that the days ahead would define the very future of his people. But whatever the cost, whatever the sacrifice, he was prepared to make it. The Zodark Empire would survive, even if it meant dragging the galaxy into the abyss with them.

Chapter Twelve

August 2114
Imperial Palace
Cobalt Prime

Emperor Tibus SuVee felt antsy about this meeting. A lot would ride on how his viceroy responded to questioning, in his opinion. He wasn't sure yet if his trust in Miles Hunt had been misplaced or if his gut instincts had been correct all along, but there was only one way to find out. A holographic call would not suffice in this case—he needed to look the man in the eye.

When Viceroy Miles Hunt entered the room, he didn't walk as tall as he usually did. He kept his eyes on the ground as he approached the Emperor to kiss his ring, then he took the seat that a Gallentine guard held for him.

"Emperor, before we begin…I have something I must confess to you," Miles choked out.

"Oh?" asked Tibus, trying hard not to sound sarcastic.

"You see, before the battle on Alfheim put a pause in the hostilities, there was a genuine concern among members of the Republic that we might be wiped out, exterminated from existence."

"Hmm," said Tibus, waiting to see where Miles would take this.

"Emperor…I'm ashamed to admit that I authorized research into a biological weapon that could be used against the Zodarks. We did develop a virus that could target their unique lungs, that would be incredibly deadly to them and *only* to them. But I did subsequently realize the danger of such a project and shelved the whole thing."

Miles wrung his hands, pausing. Tibus had never seen him this nervous.

"The lead scientist on the project decided to go rogue, Emperor," Miles confessed. "After the attack on Earth, his entire family—his wife, children, and grandchildren—were all butchered by Zodarks, and he sought revenge. He had a nephew in the military, and the two of them conspired and released some of this virus…" His voice trailed off. "I am so terribly sorry. This should never have happened."

Emperor Tibus took a deep breath. "I knew," he stated plainly. "Even before you came clean to Wiyrkomi."

"What?" Miles blurted out, clearly shocked by this revelation.

"Did you think that we, the Gallentines, do not have our own intelligence apparatus?" asked Tibus. He laughed, which seemed to make Miles very uncomfortable. "Although I do appreciate you coming clean without my having to probe you like an interrogator. My problem is that this is a very serious violation...a *very* serious violation. I have been weighing what to do with you, with the Republic."

"What have you decided, Emperor Tibus?" Miles dared to ask.

"The fact that you confessed your transgression openly without trying to make excuses for yourself has done a lot to restore my trust in you, Viceroy. You demonstrate that you are willing to face your consequences and take responsibility. The thing is...I do not want word to get out amongst the other members of the Galactic Empire. Should the Altairians find out about this, they would surely want you to be harshly and very publicly punished, and that would lead to actions on the part of the Collective, which I absolutely do not want."

Miles let out a slow breath, apparently realizing he was not about to be publicly executed. Emperor Tibus had thought about kicking the Republic out of the Galactic Empire, but especially with the Humtars now rejoining this part of the universe, he felt that it would be better not to test Preident Gudea's allegiances. This was not the time to have two new adversaries.

"But this *is* an extremely serious offense, Miles," Tibus emphasized. "These treaties have been put in place for a reason. Even the Zodarks, as horrible, savage and bloodthirsty as they are...they have not violated these treaties. So this crime cannot go unpunished, even if it is to be kept quiet."

Miles nodded slightly, acquiescing to the Emperor's power in these matters.

"Miles, your people are about to be put on a leash," announced Tibus. "I have put together a team of about one hundred scientists who will report directly to our head of intelligence. They will be given access by you to your various military research facilities, and they will perform periodic inspections."

Miles held up one hand. "Emperor, while I deeply appreciate your mercy in one respect, I am concerned that this will impede the Republic's ability to carry out its own intelligence operations."

Emperor Tibus clenched his jaw. "Miles, you are not wrong," he affirmed. "However, I believe your people have lost the right to complete autonomy at this point. Frankly, this was one of the least punitive of all my options. Even if I believe that I can still trust you, your people are the ones that made this mistake, and it absolutely cannot happen again."

The Viceroy hung his head for a moment, silent. Finally, he nodded, acknowledging that this was an acceptable outcome.

"There is something else I must speak to you about," said Tibus.

"What is it, O Emperor?"

"I have reservations about these Humtar people and their return to the Milky Way," Tibus explained.

"I believe President Gudea when he says that his people have no desire for new conquest," Miles explained. "Although they could come in and attempt to reclaim any planet that the Humtars had once occupied, you will find that they make no overtures towards aggressive actions of any kind."

"You can see what my concerns are, though, can you not?" asked Tibus. "What if their motives for returning are to ally themselves with your people and then to attempt a coup?"

Miles shook his head. "Emperor, they genuinely have as much of a personal vendetta as we do when it comes to the Collective. Rising up against the might of the Gallentines would not serve their purposes."

Tibus stroked his fingers through his hair. What Miles said about the Humtars did make logical sense. However, a part of him remained skeptical.

He stood, and Miles followed him in standing. "I suppose for now, you have convinced me of their motives. Just know that I remain cautious about them going forward."

"Yes, Emperor," Miles responded, sounding very relieved. Tibus contained his urge to smirk—that would not have been very becoming of an emperor.

When Miles had left, Tibus reflected on their conversation. He had stared into his viceroy's soul, and he knew that Miles was not being deceptive. However, he was still leery of these new Humtars. President Gudea did not seem dishonest, per se, but this whole scenario presented a fair bit of risk for the Gallentines.

Chapter Thirteen

July 2114
Capitol Palace Building
Zidara, Gurista Prime

Sitting at the giant desk in the presidential office, Tammuz checked the time until his biweekly meeting with his growing staff of advisors and ministers of newly formed departments along with Admiral Dobbs and her staff. Tammuz had known it would be difficult trying to cleave the Gurista society from the Zodarks, but the practicality of it was proving even harder than he had imagined.

When Ashurina and her colleagues had shown Tammuz the videos of the final days and weeks before the Zodarks had lost control of Sumer, it had shocked him. The coldheartedness, along with the absolute brutality and their grisly disregard for life—it was more than even he could stomach. Yet, for whatever reason, some people couldn't accept what was portrayed in those videos as truth. When the few survivors began arriving on Gurista Prime and Moraga, the stories of those who were capable of speaking about the atrocities they'd witnessed were harrowing and overwhelming. Yet people continued to dismiss the accounts, attributing them to bitterness at having to relocate to a new planet because theirs was about to fall to the Republic and their alliance.

In the weeks following the arrival of Admiral Dobbs's force in the Orinda system and the rapid defeat of the Zodark garrison force, the confidence of the social elite and the clan elders in the invincibility of the Zodarks had been rocked. The life the Gurista people had lived for generations under the benevolent hand of the Zodarks had abruptly ended in the span of hours. This sudden and immediate loss of status, clan ranking, and societal hierarchy had plunged his people into a short period of utter chaos. With the help of the Republic Army, however, Tammuz had been able to quickly restore order and stamp out any potential foolish secession ideas such as some of the clan elders on the other planets had considered.

Knock, knock. His outer door creaked open to reveal Hamad, his head of security. "Excuse me, Mr. President. You asked to be notified when the admiral and her staff arrived. They are being escorted into the conference room as requested."

Tammuz smiled at the interruption. "Excellent, Hamad. Come, let's greet our guests," he replied.

As the two of them approached the conference room, he spotted his newly appointed Minister of War, Minister of Economy, Minister of Trade, and lastly, his Minister of Finance as they walked in ahead of him.

When Tammuz entered the room, the Republic representatives stood out of respect—followed by everyone else. Tammuz waved his hand about as he made his way toward his seat, encouraging everyone to sit. He was still uncomfortable with the protocol of being president.

"Good morning, President Tammuz, and thank you once again for taking time from your busy schedule to meet with us," offered Admiral Dobbs, ever the diplomat.

"You are too generous, Admiral. I am just a humble man, grateful for the help and assistance the Republic has offered," Tammuz said. He truly was grateful for all they had done and whatever assistance they were willing to provide in the future.

"We are one people, separated by time and happenstance, Tammuz," Dobbs continued. "Freeing the Gurista people is akin to freeing a distant cousin. Once these Zodarks have been destroyed, the threat against humanity will at last come to an end." The other Republic representatives nodded in agreement. "And speaking of the Zodarks, I've received a message from Viceroy Hunt, the leader of our alliance."

Tammuz tilted his head forward in acquiescence. Whatever he could do to support the destruction or defeat of the Zodark Empire, he would surely do. Unless the Zodarks were dealt with, his people's newfound freedom might be short-lived.

Admiral Dobbs leaned forward in her chair. "Tammuz, the orders I've received from the Viceroy are to ask that you and the Gurista people support us in this final push, this coming campaign to finish the Zodarks once and for all," she explained.

Tammuz had suspected this request would eventually come. He cleared his throat and made eye contact with each of his newly appointed ministers and Republic counterparts before he responded. "Admiral, the Gurista people are free because of the actions of your people—and the Republic. You have fought for decades against the Zodarks, these blue beasts who have dominated the Sumerians and tricked our people into believing they are a good people when in reality they have been grooming us to become their foot soldiers, their 'cannon fodder,' as one of your people once said.

"I stand here as an ally in this war between humanity and the Zodarks. As the President and leader of the Gurista people, I stand with the Republic—we will answer the call to service, the call to defeat these bastards once and for all," Tammuz loudly proclaimed. His ministers banged their right hands on the table in support.

"Thank you, Tammuz. We're honored to have your support and help in this endeavor," Dobbs replied. "There's much work to be done. The final campaign to end the war, to invade Zodark territory, is moving forward as we speak. With the support of the Gurista people, one of the invasion points into Zodark space will start from the Orinda system. In the near future, convoys of supplies will begin to arrive in the system. Gurista Prime will become a critical supply hub as our forces penetrate deeper into Zodark space."

Dobbs turned to her ground force commander, Major General Ward Custer. "General, I'll hand things over to you now."

"Thank you, Admiral. Mr. President, Ministers, as Admiral Dobbs said, I am the commander of the Republic Army XIV Corps," said Custer. "I have just under seventy-five thousand soldiers in my command."

The Army general motioned with his hand to the man next to him. "This is Brigadier General Brian Royce," Custer explained. "He commands the Special Forces units that are part of this task force. Royce's task force is going to assist in training up four divisions of Gurista infantry soldiers. Many of the Guristas had already been conscripted to serve in the military previously, but now that they have joined the Republic, they need to learn how *we* fight: our tactics, our rank structures, our weapons, etcetera.

"When Admiral Rosentreter and his forces finish the Pharaonis campaign, they'll head here, to the Orinda system, where they'll undergo a rest and refit period before opening a second front against the Zodarks. It's imperative that we begin this task at once. When the Army units from the Pharaonis campaign arrive, their ranks will likely be depleted and will need to be replenished. The soldiers that Royce's task force train will take care of any replacements that will be necessary before we filter the Gurista soldiers into our regular Army units," Custer concluded.

Tammuz took it all in. He hoped his new Minister of Defense would prove to be helpful in making all these plans come to fruition.

For the next several hours, Tammuz and his ministers worked with Admiral Dobbs and her staff to prepare Gurista Prime for its role as a major logistical supply node and the eventual arrival of the supply convoys. Toward the end of the meeting, Admiral Dobbs asked to speak privately with him in a couple of days. He agreed. This time they would meet aboard the *Aquila*, the Republic star carrier in orbit above.
****

Three Days Later
RNS *Aquila*
In Orbit of Gurista Prime

Admiral Dobbs watched Tammuz as he stared out the window in her office—his planet, his home, a bluish-green marble against a backdrop of pure blackness. She took a deep breath.

It's time, she thought. *The Viceroy and the Chancellor need an answer.*

"Tammuz, thank you again for agreeing to meet with me on the *Aquila*," she began, then turned to look at the other two people she had asked to join this meeting. "And thank you, Ashurina and Dakkuri, for agreeing to meet with us as we discuss the future of the Gurista people."

Drew Kanter then added, "I hope you understand why we requested to hold this meeting on the *Aquila* and not in the palace or someplace else on the surface."

Dakkuri, the consummate spy, flashed a half-crooked smile. "It is no problem, Drew. Hosting the meeting on the *Aquila* has given us the opportunity to see the newest, most powerful, and most beautiful warship your people have built. I am impressed, truly—the capabilities of this vessel must be incredible. But we all know why we are meeting here and not on the surface."

"Oh, perhaps you could enlighten an old man such as myself," countered Tammuz as he turned first to Dakkuri, then to his daughter and now senior advisor, Ashurina.

"What Dakkuri means, Mr. President, is that aboard the *Aquila*, the chances of this conversation being overheard are slim at best," Ashurina interjected before Dakkuri could respond. The relationship between Tammuz and Dakkuri was tenuous. Tammuz was still angry with Dakkuri for having withheld the fact that his daughter was alive and not dead, as he had allowed her father to believe.

Admiral Dobbs caught on to the tension between the two men and proceeded to press on with the reason for their meeting. She cleared her throat, "Mr. President—"

"Please, Admiral, we are in private among friends and family," interrupted Tammuz. "Honor me by addressing me as Tammuz and not by the honorific of my station."

Dobbs felt her cheeks flush. "Yes, as I was saying, Tammuz, a series of events have taken place in Sol—events that have created ripple effects even now being felt by the members of the alliance. In particular, recent discoveries have resulted in the unraveling of the mystery of the Humtars: who they were, if they were still alive, and if it was possible to reconnect with them."

Tammuz's eyes lit up. When she'd shared their reappearance after Republic scientists had found the keys to unlocking the very stargate they had used to seal themselves off from the rest of the universe, he had been like a kid in a candy store as he'd read every report, every discovery this group of scientists and archaeologists had made and written about over the years.

"Yes, I can only imagine what kind of excitement their discovery has caused across the alliance—learning that we humans are the descendants of the Humtars and that there is a far more advanced society than even the Gallentines must have come as a shock," Tammuz offered.

Dobbs smiled at his enthusiasm. "Their appearance has certainly changed the dynamics of the alliance," she acknowledged with a chuckle. "Some of the technology transfers are going to provide the Republic with advantages we haven't had in the past. The Humtars seem genuine in their desire to reconnect with us, and they have asked if they could be given some territory to govern within the Republic. The Chancellor has agreed. They'll be overseeing a heavily damaged section of Earth called the State of Northeast Africa, and they will govern and control it as they see fit.

"The Humtars have offered to construct several new stargates that would further connect the territories of the Republic. For instance, Sol would be turned into a Conduit Nexus—meaning it would have several stargates connecting it to New Eden, the Qatana system, the Great Wilds, Alpha Centauri, and the Intus system. This would dramatically increase the free flow of goods, people, and transit across the Republic like never before.

"This all brings us back to a question I posed to you a while back—would the Gurista people like to join the Republic? If you do, the Humtars will build a stargate in the Orinda system, connecting it directly to Sol," explained Admiral Dobbs, relaying the information she had been told to provide.

"Is this true, Father? The Republic has extended an offer for our people to join them?" asked Ashurina, surprise evident in her voice.

"They have," Tammuz acknowledged. "I have been weighing the considerations for and against our joining. If we were to unite with them, there would be obvious benefits to our people—a large standing military and the industrial capacity to maintain it and grow it. The Republic has an established interplanetary and interstellar economy, trade routes, and industrial and economic hubs. I can only imagine that the expansion of this Stellar Conduit Network would further economic growth within the Republic and enable the movement of people so that they can further spread out within their territory."

Dakkuri shifted his weight from one foot to the other before commenting. "And the price for becoming a member of their Republic is…?"

Tammuz snorted at the way Dakkuri had phrased his question. "There is always a price," Tammuz replied. "We have just won our freedom and autonomy from the Zodarks. If we accept this deal, then we are giving up this newfound independence—the freedom for our people to choose our destiny, our way forward as we forge a new path."

"It's a tough decision, Tammuz, and one I'm glad isn't mine to make," Drew offered as he shared a glance with Admiral Dobbs. There was an unspoken concern between them. They would respect the decision Tammuz made for his people; they just hoped it was in favor of joining the Republic.

Ashurina walked over to her father and placed her hand on his shoulder. She spoke softly. "When I first traveled to Sol, while I was still an operative for the Mukhabarat, I was surprised when I arrived on Earth. I had never seen so many people walking around freely, unafraid of the Zodarks. It took me some time to understand why they had no fear of them—it was because they had lived a life without them. I saw that, and I was jealous of it. I asked myself why they were spared from being subjugated by them and we were not.

"This decision you have to make is a decision that will impact the future of our people," she continued. "If we go it alone, perhaps we can make it—create a future like what I saw the first time I arrived on Earth. However, *if* we go it alone, challenges will arise that we have not considered. We cannot anticipate an unknown unknown. And we would be forced to deal with those trials on our own. Our people's entire future could be destroyed if our leaders make a critical error, and we are not used to governing ourselves. We haven't had to make hard decisions yet—the Zodarks used to do that for us."

Tammuz grunted. Ashurina had a valid point.

"Joining the Republic won't remove that kind of risk, but it will spread it out. Our new brothers in the Republic will support us logistically and militarily because we will be *one*. I think this greatly reduces our chance of self-destruction as a nation. Our people won't go running back into the arms of the Zodarks, hoping to serve their old 'benevolent masters.' If we become part of the Republic, we join our people with theirs and we forge a future *together*, united for the first time since the Humtars left. I say we join," Ashurina finished.

Tammuz looked to Dakkuri. "What say you?"

Dakkuri held Tammuz's gaze for a moment. "Our people will have a better, more prosperous future if we join the Republic than if we choose to stay independent," he asserted.

Tammuz took the information in as he weighed his options. Turning to look at Admiral Dobbs, he finally said, "This decision may be difficult for our people to understand and support. I will do my best to win them over with the benefits of being part of this Republic. You may tell your Chancellor and Viceroy that the Gurista people will join you."

Chapter Fourteen

11th Spartacus Armor Regiment
RNS *Callisto*

The faces of his little ones flashed in Staff Sergeant Peter Kennedy's mind—their bright smiles, their innocent laughter echoing in his memories. He just wished he could scoop them up in his arms again and reassure them that Daddy still loved them more than anything in this galaxy, no matter how broken things had become.

For the last two years, he'd watched them on holovids and spoken with them over the communication channels. Still, the war had kept him away from them and that killed him inside—knowing he couldn't be there when they fell and skinned their knee and just needed a reassuring hug and to be told that it would be OK. Hell, his kids only knew him as the man who spoke to them on a holovid when the Fleet would allow grunts like him to use the coveted interstellar comms network.

Four years ago, like many young, dumb soldiers, he'd fallen in love. He'd further compounded his situation by asking her to marry him. Sol hadn't been invaded yet, and the Zodark War had ended five years earlier. Kennedy had felt it was a good time to try and actually settle down. A few months into marital bliss, she had announced she was pregnant. Later that week, they'd found out it was twins. He was elated. Twins! Not only was he going to become a dad, he would was going to have a daughter *and* a son. He felt like he had won the lottery.

Then the Zodarks had invaded Sol, devastating the planet. They'd wiped out entire megacities from space with orbital bombardments. The Orbots had followed with a second wave of attacks. Kennedy felt lucky they hadn't invaded New Eden, but so many of his fellow soldiers had lost their entire families during the invasion. Everyone *he* knew or loved was on New Eden.

With war thrust upon them, it wasn't long before his unit was shipping out. They were part of the first wave—the first combat element to hit the enemy back. They were determined to hit twice as hard.

Kennedy tried to convey to his wife the challenges that awaited her should his unit join a campaign—he would be gone a long time. With the astronomical distances between stargates, it took months to reach the next destination (unless, of course, their Altairian allies created a bridge that allowed them to cross dozens of light-years at a time). But as the months dragged on past the one-year mark since he'd been gone, Kennedy could see in his wife's eyes that she missed him, and she was lonely. She had the twins, of course, but she didn't have *him*.

When twelve months had turned into twenty-two months, she was done. She'd broken down in a holovid and said she couldn't bear the idea of him being dead for weeks or months before she ever learned of his fate. The calls from him were few and far between while the holovids she sent to him continued to stack up, unanswered. He hadn't blamed her when she'd hit him with divorce papers. Hell, if he was married to himself, he'd file for divorce too.

In an attempt to seek solace, or at the very least clarity, Kennedy hoped a therapy session or two would provide some help from the hell plaguing his thoughts.

He approached the door of Dr. Samantha Wallace's office, knocked twice, loudly, and waited for a response.

"Come on in. Door's unlocked," he heard Dr. Wallace call to him.

Kennedy opened the door and stepped in. When he entered Dr. Wallace's office, he could tell she had done her best to make this place look as "normal" as possible. He almost forgot for a second that they were aboard a transport. Instead of the grayish off-white paint scheme that lined the walls of so many of the rooms aboard this freakishly big ship, her walls were beige, with actual pictures, not holovids. He spotted a comfortable-looking couch that sat across the room with a couple of equally comfortable-looking chairs. He smiled when he saw a picture on the wall of the young doctor receiving a medal from an admiral. In it, her blond hair was pulled back in a tight bun. Her blue eyes shined with pride.

Damn, she's gorgeous, Kennedy thought when his eyes found her staring at him.

"Are those real books? Like with paper?" he asked before even introducing himself.

She smiled at him. "They are indeed, but I must say they're becoming harder and harder to find these days, what with everything being digital. Most of them are self-help books." She gestured to the corner. "Those, of course, are my few plants to remind me of home.

Somehow, despite them being aboard a ship like this, I've managed to keep them alive—with the help of a few grow lights, of course."

Kennedy returned his gaze to Dr. Wallace. "I like it. It reminds me of home."

"Well, come in. My name is Dr. Samantha Wallace. Please, feel free to sit on the chair or the couch, or lie down if it makes you feel relaxed." She gestured towards the chairs and couch. "I've done my best to make this place a peaceful haven for soldiers like yourself," she explained as she sat in one of the plush armchairs.

Kennedy stumbled at first. "I, um, I'm sorry I didn't introduce myself. I'm Staff Sergeant Peter Kennedy," he finally managed to say as he walked closer to the chairs and couch, unsure which one to take.

He wasn't normally this clumsy around women, but for some reason, he felt crazily attracted to her. The way her blond hair cascaded to her shoulders and the way she wore a simple gray blazer over a white blouse and black slacks—it was the picture of professionalism. The only women Kennedy had seen since coming aboard were spacers and his fellow grunts. She looked stunning.

Of course, there was a reason why a pair of security guards stood outside her door. It was common practice just in case a patient turned violent during one of their sessions. When unpacking the kind of trauma most soldiers went through, it was a good idea to keep some muscle around, with tasers and tranquilizer darts. For some reason, just knowing they were outside that door made him feel calm, made him feel safe.

"Well, it's nice to meet you, Staff Sergeant Peter Kennedy. Please, have a seat," Samantha repeated. She gestured to the couch since he seemed to be closest to it.

"Just to make sure it's really you and not one of your buddies trying to get you out of seeing me, can you give me your last four and your date of birth, Staff Sergeant?"

He sat on the couch, then answered, "Yes, ma'am. My last four is 4-3-2-6. Date of birth 04/02/2079." He rattled off his ID number like he had so many other times during the eighteen years he'd spent in the Army.

"Excellent, thank you for verifying that for me. Just another piece of administrative information I need to pass along before we begin." She calmly lifted her blazer just enough to reveal the stun gun she concealed carried with her. "It should go without saying this is more for my protection than it is yours. I do my best to make sure you feel safe and secure when we're in session. Should a patient decide to get a little carried away…well, you've got Bruno and Max standing outside the door. They're Fleeter master-at-arms types. I think you guys call them MPs in the Army."

He laughed. "Yeah, MPs is the nicer thing to call them. We usually just refer to them as Mud Puppies. MPs—get it?"

Samantha smiled at the reference. "I hadn't heard that one before. Your record shows you talked with one of the counselors a few days ago, and he referred you to me. So, let's talk. What brings you here today?"

Kennedy hesitated as his gaze fell to the floor. "I… guess… well, I miss my kids?"

"Is that a question or a statement?"

He shifted uncomfortably in his seat. "A statement, ma'am. I haven't seen them in person in over two years, and with the divorce…" He trailed off, his eyes trailing off.

Samantha nodded, her expression sympathetic. "It's understandable to feel that way, especially given the circumstances. I'm sorry to hear about the divorce, and we don't have to talk about that if you don't want to. Why don't you tell me a little more about your children?"

"I've got twins." A small smile grew on Kennedy's lips. "Evan's a few minutes older, and he's three. Olivia is obviously the same age. They're…" He cleared his throat to stop himself from choking up. "They're amazing—smart, funny, always getting into trouble." His smile faded. "I hate being away from them for so long. I feel like I'm missing out on everything—and I am. Life moves on whether I'm there or not."

She sat straighter in her chair. "That must be incredibly difficult. And you mentioned a divorce. How long have you been separated from your wife?"

"Ex-wife," Kennedy corrected. "Sorry, I keep forgetting. Not my ex-wife yet. We were still working through things the first year I was gone. It was the start of this second year when things began to go south between us. That's when she filed for separation while she decided if she wanted a divorce or not. A few months ago, she sent me a holovid explaining it all with the divorce papers attached for me to sign."

Samantha grabbed a tablet from a side table and scribbled something. "I'm sure this must be tough. How has it affected you?"

Kennedy shrugged. "It sucks. I mean, I get it. I'm never around, always off on some training exercise and then the invasion. With VI Corps stationed on New Eden and not Earth, we're one of the few major Army formations to have survived. What was I going to say? 'I can't deploy because my wife needs me here?' Do you know how many others are in the same boat as me? We're soldiers. They give us orders and we execute. What I really feel bad about is that none of this is fair to her or the kids. But... you know..." He swallowed hard. "It still hurts.

"Did I make the right decisions?" he asked aloud. "Should I have gotten out of the military somehow? Should I still?" He shrugged his shoulders as his body sank into the couch cushion. "I hate leaving them without a father, but I swore an oath to the Republic. No one forced me to join, and no one said I had to reenlist after I reached fifteen years of service. I guess what I'm saying is I intend to honor my oath to the Republic and at least finish the terms of this enlistment. I just hope my kids will understand when they get older—when they start to ask why their daddy only appears on a holovid and not in real life."

"That's a lot to unpack, but there's something you need to know. Your kids, they do have a father. I'm looking right at him." She leaned forward, her eyes on his. "A divorce is never easy, especially when children are involved. It's important to remember that it's not your fault entirely. You're doing an incredibly important job, fighting for the safety and future of humanity. At the same time, like you said, you have children to look after. So, what do you do? How do you separate the two?"

After a pause, she continued. "Can you quit the military? Maybe that depends on the terms of your contract or medical. Would that be easy? Not a chance. And from looking at you, my guess is that you're not going to go in that direction either. This means we need to figure out some compromises not only with you and your children but with you and yourself. I can tell you from years of experience that the first step is going to be hard because the first thing you need to do is learn to forgive yourself before you can forgive anyone else."

"Huh. What do you mean—forgive myself before I can forgive others?"

"It's about guilt," she said. "I can see it in your eyes. You're guilt-ridden. That's fine. It's also very understandable. Your government has placed you in a position to do what most people wouldn't—putting your life on the line to make life safer not only for every human out there, but for your kids, too.

"But it's not just about putting your life on the line, is it?" she continued. "It's also the taking of life. And, sure, we say and do a lot to demonize the Zodarks, the Pharaonis, or the Orbots, but at the end of the day—it's still a life you're taking. That's not something that's natural to us humans. Can we be trained to do so? Of course, look around us. We're aboard a transport with an entire division worth of soldiers of trained killers. But the difference is we don't kill for sport. We don't kill out of innate desire, or at least the majority of us don't. The act of killing is tough on the mind, especially if we don't know how to process it." She leaned her back against the chair. "Let me ask you something else—how many times a week do you chat with your kids?"

He grunted at the question. "Once a month."

She hesitated, then asked, "Why only once a month?"

Kennedy sighed loudly. "Lately, it's all that their mother allows."

"I see." She thought for a moment. "If I can coach you on what to say to her, how would you like to speak with your children twice a week whenever it's possible?"

"Doc, when in combat, it's not possible, ma'am. The BattleNet isn't for personal calls."

"True, but when it's possible, does twice a week work?"

Kennedy's heart filled at her words. "Yes, ma'am, that really would be great."

"OK, we'll get it done, all right?" she said. "Now, let's get to those funny things we call feelings."

If she wasn't so attractive, Kennedy might have snorted. He did his best to hold back his laughter. With her last words, she sounded like a puppet on a kid's cartoon holochannel. "OK."

She winked. "I saw you hold that back." She grinned. "Next time, laugh, all right?"

"Yes, ma'am."

"It'll help you open up. So, let's get a little deeper. Why do you feel guilty, other than the surface reasons we know?"

Kennedy nodded, but his expression turned troubled. "I told you, ma'am. I just feel like I'm letting them down. Like I'm not there when they need me."

Samantha's eyes became intense. "Sergeant, listen to me. You are not letting your children down. You are fighting for them, for their future. And even though you can't be with them physically, you're always with them in their hearts. And the more you speak with them on a regular basis, the more they'll know this."

"I hope so."

"There's something deeper, something else bothering you, something beyond the separation from your family. Can you tell me about it?"

Kennedy was starting to dislike this line of questioning. He hesitated, his hands clenching and unclenching in his lap. "I... I've been having these nightmares. Flashbacks, I guess. Of the things I've seen out there. The people I've lost."

"I see. I can tell you this much—you are not alone in dealing with this. When you think about it, the mind can only handle so much trauma before it begins to shut down or vent its anger and frustration at others," Samantha said in a calm, reassuring tone.

"Huh, so a lot of others are going through the same thing as me?" asked Kennedy.

"Yes, exactly. In clinical terms, we call this post-traumatic stress injury or PTSI. It's nothing to be ashamed of, and it's certainly not a stigma you should concern yourself with. Why don't you tell me more about these flashbacks? When did they start?" she pressed.

"I don't know."

Her expression softened. "What's the first thing that comes to mind?"

Kennedy closed his eyes for a moment. His mind drifted back to that fateful day many years ago. "OK, Doc. I'm on a routine patrol on Intus during the First Zodark War," he said, feeling himself back in that moment. "An eerie quiet hangs in the air. The tank rumbles beneath me, and the easy banter of my squadmates fills the cramped space. Corporal Jackson is at the wheel, his eyes fixed on the road ahead, and Private Nguyen is on comms. And then...in an instant, everything changes.

"A large explosion hits our tank—we're careening off the road into a ditch. The heat of the flames washes over me. There's a smell...smoke and burning flesh. It completely fills my nostrils. My head slams against the side of the vehicle, and then everything goes black.

"I come to. I don't know how long I've been out, but the world is on fire. The tank is a gnarled wreck, and a blaze licks at the metal hull. Jackson and Nguyen are gone—their bodies were consumed by that inferno before they could get out. But Private Torres..."

Kennedy squeezed his eyes shut even tighter. He tried to block out the memory, only to feel compelled to speak. "Torres, his body is broken, bleeding. I look in my friend's eyes, and they're wide with fear. I have to get him out of the line of fire.

"I realize our patrol had been caught in an ambush by a Zodark squad. Good God, those bloody war cries send shivers down my spine. Still, I manage to get up, and then I half carry, half drag Torres toward a nearby forest, away from the burning tank and the blaster fire happening around me. Torres is in severe pain. He cries out in agony with every step, his breath coming in short, shallow gasps. When we reach the tree line, I manage to call for help on the comms."

"Peter?" Samantha's voice cut through the haze of his memory. It brought Kennedy back to the present. "Can you tell me more about what happened that day?"

Kennedy shook his head, his jaw clenched. "I... I don't... I'm fine, ma'am. What day?"

"The day you're remembering." Samantha leaned forward again. "I know it's difficult, but talking about it can help. It's important to process these memories. To work through the trauma."

Kennedy couldn't. The words stuck in his throat. The images were too vivid and too raw. "Things went wrong. That's what happened."

Samantha tapped her stylus against her tablet. "Peter, I understand your reluctance. But bottling up these emotions, these memories—"

"Ma'am," Kennedy interrupted her. "Listen, I'm..." He grasped the bottom of his shirt and twisted the fabric, then buried his face in his hands as he began speaking. "'Hold on, Torres,' I say. 'Just hold on, we'll get you out of here.'

"Torres is always the realist in the crew. He shakes his head and whispers to me, 'I don't think...I'll make—'

"But I cut him off, telling him to stay with me, I've got a medevac on the way. I refuse to accept that Torres might die. I never give up on a friend.

"'Stay with me,' I say. 'You're gonna be OK, you hear me? You're gonna be just fine.'

"Torres looks up at me, his eyes glassy with pain. 'Tell my mom...,' he starts, his voice breaking. 'Tell her I love her. And my sister...tell her I'm sorry I won't be there for her graduation. For her future...kids. For...everything.' He coughs and cringes. Blood drips past his lips.

"My heart shatters into a million, billion pieces. I say, 'You can tell them yourself, Torres. You're gonna go home and hug your mom and watch your sister graduate. Watch her kids grow old. All of that.'

"Torres smiles a sad, resigned grin. For an instant, it seems like all of his pain goes away. 'It's OK, Sarge,' he says. 'It's OK. I'm not afraid.' He points a shaky finger. 'Do you see her?' he asks.

"I look up, but I only see foliage between two trees. 'See what, Torres?' I press.

"'The angel, sir,' says Torres. 'The angel. She's so beautiful.'

"'There's nothing there, Private,' I tell him. 'You're going to be fine. The emergency team is on their way. They'll be here any minute...Private?' Everything stands still, even the nature around me. 'Private?' I ask again.

"But Torres is gone. His eyes stare sightlessly at the plants between the trees. I gather his body into my arms, and tears stream down my face. I rock back and forth, whispering apologies and promises to Torres I know I'll never be able to keep."

"Peter?" Samantha's tone burst through Kennedy's memory.

Kennedy lowered his eyes. "Not today. Not now. I can't talk. I'm sorry."

"Peter, I understand your fears. You can take all the time you want."

What does that mean? "I don't need to talk about it. I just... I just need to move on. I came in to talk about my kids. Not this."

Samantha set the tablet beside her and cupped her hands in her lap. "I know you did. And that love, that connection with your kids, it's what will help you through this. And that memory you just had—it's what will give you the strength to keep fighting, even on the darkest of days."

"I didn't have a memory," Kennedy fibbed.

She squinted at him, no doubt seeing through his lie. "Are you sure?"

"Positive." Kennedy stood. "Thank you, Dr. Wallace. I think you helped." He stepped toward the door.

"Peter, wait, please." She stood and walked to her desk. "I'm glad if I could help, but something in me tells me I didn't. Now, before you go, I want to give you some techniques to help manage your PTSI symptoms. They won't make the memories go away, but they can help you cope with them in a healthy way."

"I'm OK."

"I know you are. And if you come in again, we can eventually get through some tough trauma." She smiled. "You'll feel a lot better once you do."

He went to turn the doorknob to exit.

Samantha stopped him. "Can I please gift this to you?"

Kennedy bit his bottom lip, wanting to just leave. "Sure."

"Thank you." She handed him a small pamphlet, filled with breathing exercises and mindfulness techniques. "Try these whenever you feel overwhelmed or triggered. And remember, you're not alone in this. There are people who care about you, who want to help you through this, including me. I'm here for you, Peter."

Kennedy took the pamphlet and tucked it into his pocket. "Thank you."

As Kennedy stepped out into the corridor, he felt the crinkle of the pamphlet in his hands. Breathing exercises, mindfulness techniques…they were such small things in the face of his trauma. He had to start somewhere, though.

He thought of Evan and Olivia. He longed to talk to them, to hear their voices.

Kennedy ran a hand through his hair. He didn't know if he'd ever go back to see Dr. Wallace, if he'd ever find the courage to speak the unspeakable. There were countless memories, not just one.

How many will I have to tackle?

He understood he couldn't let the past consume him. He had to find a way to move forward, to keep fighting for the future he believed in. For his children, for humanity, for the chance to build better worlds.

He'd take the good doctor up on getting more calls with his children.

Kennedy squared his shoulders. He would take things one day at a time. One step after the other. And maybe, just maybe, he would find the strength to face his demons and emerge stronger on the other side.

Chapter Fifteen

Carrier Strike Group 17 (CSG-17)
Titan Training Facility, Sol System

Commander Jake "Lax" Riggs stood at attention in the hangar bay. His broad shoulders squared as his green eyes scanned the assembled pilots. At six foot four, he towered over most of the men and women in the room. His muscular frame was honed by years of rigorous training—running, weight lifting, calisthenics. At the age of thirty-five, he had short dark hair that was flecked with gray at the temples, bearing witness to the stress of his demanding jobs throughout his career, and now as Coop's second-in-command.

The hangar bay was enormous. Its high ceiling, supported by massive steel beams, stood at a little over a hundred meters in height. Gripen IIs were lined up in rows close to the walls. Their aerodynamic shapes, accompanied by their powerful engines, were designed for speed and agility in the black expanse of space. Next to them, Valkyrie bombers presented themselves like giant armored beasts. Their heavy armor and electronic warfare pods made them hard to intercept before they released their payloads of plasma torpedoes or cruise missiles.

The bright lights of the Proving Grounds reflected off the polished metal surfaces of the ship's open hangar bay doors. They cast a harsh glare, making Riggs squint in front of his pilots. The anticipation of the assembled pilots was palpable in the air as they waited for Coop to arrive.

Riggs glanced at his chrono, noting the time. Coop was due any moment, and Riggs knew the captain would expect nothing less than perfection from his pilots. With the exception of a few new pilots, the ones present had trained hard throughout their careers to be assigned to one of the few star carriers in the Republic. Now came the time to put their talents to the test and learn to work together as a team.

As Coop's second-in-command, Commander Riggs held the responsibility of ensuring the space wing's combat readiness. Captain Coop placed unwavering trust in Riggs, and for good reason. Their paths had first crossed midway through Coop's first assignment with the Republic Navy, and they'd been thick as thieves ever since, almost as if the solar winds themselves had destined their alliance. To Coop, there was no better pilot than Riggs. A man by the books, a talent forged by the angels, a fierceness crafted by lions. A man who would stick with his wingman through the deepest pits of hell.

For a year, they'd been assigned to different ships, but when Coop had received his new command aboard this behemoth, he'd immediately put in a request for Riggs as his number one. The brass had initially balked, but thankfully, Admiral Ripley Lee understood the wisdom of pairing these veteran spacers. With a stroke of his stylus on a data pad, Lee had authorized the transfer, uniting the formidable duo aboard the same vessel once more.

****

When the doors to the hangar bay slid open, Captain Blake "Coop" Cooper strode in, his boots clicking on the polished metal floor as he walked. He approached the assembled pilots, who snapped to attention, their eyes fixed on their commanding officer as he made his way to the front of the formation.

Standing in front the crowd, Coop felt déjà vu wash over him as he surveyed their faces. He remembered being in their shoes not so long ago, standing at attention and waiting to hear what his new commanding officer had in store for him. The uncertainty, the anticipation, the desire to prove himself—it all came flooding back in a rush.

He set his jaw like flint. "Listen up," he said. His voice resounded off the hangar bay's walls. "Most of you are here because you're the best of the best. The cream of the crop. The elite. But let's be honest: some of you are cherries, and this is your first real assignment, and that's OK. You're here because you're filling the slot of a pilot who paid the ultimate price—a replacement. Everyone is a replacement at some point in their career; you are no different, and you will be honed and trained until you are a precise tool and weapon to serve our Republic."

Coop watched the faces of his pilots as he spoke. They thrived on such praise. In reality, Coop's statement stretched the truth, a fact of which he was well aware. However, he had indeed been assigned some of the most skilled aviators ever to serve under the Republic's banner. So, he'd exploit his words and effusive compliments for maximum effect, savoring every ounce of their impact.

110

He kept his mouth shut for a moment, letting his words sink in before continuing. "Those of you who have served with me know that being the best isn't enough. Not here. Not now. You will be pushed, and pushed hard—so hard some of you will want to quit, and I want you to quit if that's how you feel. I will not have quitters in *my* wing! Is that understood?!" Coop shouted with force.

"Yes, sir!" the pilots shouted in near unison.

"Good, now listen up. What I'm about to share with you does not leave the *Vega*. Our flagship, the RNS *Freedom*, was forced to return to a Gallentine shipyard to finish the remaining critical repairs after the damage it sustained during the second invasion of Sol," Coop explained. He heard some groans from the pilots at the news that the Republic would be losing its most powerful warship for a while longer.

Raising his voice, Coop shouted, "At ease!" silencing the murmurs.

"As I was saying, the pilots from the *Freedom* bring a wealth of experience with them. They truly are the elite of the fighter corps. However, they're used to flying Hellcats and Devastators. This means we have the opportunity to learn from some of the best pilots in the Fleet as they familiarize themselves with our Gripen IIs and Valkyries.

"I fully intend to capitalize on this opportunity for our wings to fly and compete against each other. There's an old saying that goes something like this—iron sharpens iron. I will sharpen you against the best we've got. In the days, weeks, and months ahead of us, you will be tested in ways you never thought possible. And you will come out the other side stronger, faster, and more capable than you ever dreamed."

Coop's gaze swept over the assembled pilots, taking in their expressions. As he looked them over, he saw Badger standing at the end of one of the lines, shifting his stance like he was uncomfortable. It was enough to tell Coop that Badger didn't want to feel the coming pain of hard training. "I expect nothing less than your absolute best from each of you. You will give one hundred percent every day you're part of *my* wing. No excuses, no exceptions. I want to see you eat, sleep, and breathe these ships, this training, as you build the bonds of service and combat with your brothers and sisters. You are each responsible for yourselves and each other. If a member of the team fails, the team fails. You are one! When it comes to your ships, I want you to know them inside and out, backward and forward. I want you to be able to fly them with your eyes closed and your hands tied behind your backs. Am I making myself clear?"

"Yes, sir!" the pilots chorused.

Coop nodded, satisfied. "Good. Because the mission we have ahead of us is not for the faint of heart. It will require every ounce of skill, every shred of courage, and every bit of determination you possess. But I know that you're up to the challenge. I know that you won't let me down. Am I right?"

"Yes, sir!"

I love to hear those words.

Coop turned toward the ships. "These ships, the Gripens and Valkyries, are more than just machines. They're your steeds, ready to carry you into the heart of battle when the time comes. You will learn to trust them, to rely on them. Because when you're out there in the void of space, with nothing but your ship and your wits to keep you alive, you'll understand what I mean. You'll feel the power thrumming through the engines, the responsiveness of the controls, the sheer exhilaration of flying on the edge of what's possible."

Coop twisted around and locked on a few pilots—a woman, call sign Lucky, and the men beside her, Shrike and Nomad. He'd flown with them before and considered them three of the Navy's finest. "And when the enemy comes, when the lasers start flying and the missiles start launching, you'll be ready, more so than ever before. You'll be the tip of the spear, the first line of defense against those who would threaten our way of life. You'll be the ones who stand between the innocent and those who would do them harm."

His voice dropped to a low, intense growl. "And you will not fail. You will fight with every ounce of skill and courage you possess, and you will emerge victorious. That is what we do. That is who we are."

One of the Gripens roared to life, its engines blaring through the hangar bay with a deafening rumble. Some of the pilots flinched in surprise at the craft's raw power.

Coop remained unfazed, a slight smile crossing his face as he watched the ship come to life. He had anticipated this moment—a planned demonstration of the incredible force these pilots had commanded and would soon command again.

As the Gripen's engines settled down, Coop paced as he shouted above the noise, "This is just a taste of what you've experienced many times and what you'll soon experience repeatedly. I expect every one of you to maintain your readiness and situational awareness at all times. When the time comes, there will be no room for hesitation, no margin for error. Ever! I love training. I love the challenge of pushing myself, of discovering just how far I can go. You will embrace that challenge with the same zeal, the same determination that I do."

When he stopped pacing, he stared at them for a moment. "You will continue to prove yourselves worthy of the title of a Republic Navy pilot. Laziness will not be tolerated. I have faith in each one of you. I know that you will not let me down, that you will give your all and then some. And together, we will forge a legacy that will be remembered for generations to come."

As he fell silent, the hangar was utterly still, the only sound the faint thunder of the Gripen's engines. "All right, pilots, assume standard running formation!"

The men and women before him sprang into action. They quickly organized themselves into the prescribed arrangement. As he watched, one pilot in particular caught his eye: Lucky. The young woman moved with grace, her movements confident as she took her place at the head of the formation. She barked out orders to her fellow pilots as she directed them into position.

A natural leader, thought Coop. *She's grown since I last saw her.*

Coop looked over at Riggs, who stood beside him with his arms crossed over his chest.

"She's got potential," Riggs said with a nod in her direction.

Coop agreed. "Indeed. You saw it too?"

"It's hard to miss when a voice can take charge of a bunch of fighter jocks with just a few words," commented Riggs.

Coop smiled, nodding in agreement. With a final command, he stepped forward, his voice booming out across the room. "Pilots, on my mark, you will begin running." Lines marked the boundaries of the hangar. "You will run on those lines, and you will not deviate more than two meters in either direction. Failure to stay on the lines will only prolong your run. You will not stop until I give the order." He hesitated for a second. "Now, go! Go!"

As one, the pilots surged forward. Their feet pounded against the floor as they ran. Coop's heart swelled as he saw the grit etched on their faces.

"Hooyah!" he shouted to them.

His pilots chanted "Hooyah!" in return.

Coop edged closer to Riggs as they ran. "By day two, they better hate me."

"Yes, and I hope they throw up when they see my face by the end of each day," added Riggs. "But when the fighting begins, they'll thank the discipline we trained into them."

"Exactly." Coop tapped Riggs's shoulder to get his attention. "Did you see Badger?"

"Negative, sir."

"He ran three meters beyond the line." Cooper strode toward the runners. "Listen up, everyone! You've got a pilot outside the boundary, which means your run time just got extended. You can thank Badger when you're finished!"

Chapter Sixteen

Early August 2114
Carrier Strike Wing 14
Pilot Adaptive Combat Training
Range 100, Titan Training Facility, Sol System

Coop watched as the last of the pilots filed in, their faces etched with exhaustion. Riggs paced in front of the line, his stern gaze sweeping over them. Despite their rigid attention, he could see many of their eyes looking about the vast expanse of Range 100. It wasn't often pilots were afforded the opportunity to train here. Range 100 was a sought-after training facility, and despite the evident fatigue of his pilots, he could see they were impressed and maybe intimidated by what they saw. While Coop stood behind Riggs, who was giving the range briefing, he began to pace, his hands clasped behind his back, continuing to observe their reactions to what many a pilot would claim was unnecessary training.

Pilots liked to train in flight simulators or the cockpit. What Coop needed these young pups to understand was there was more to flying than just being able to handle yourself in a fighter. You needed the ability to think fast, to think under pressure. You also had to know how to survive should you need to eject. The Republic's manned fighter program was still relatively new, having come into being in the latter years of the First Zodark War. For decades, they'd had a remotely piloted force, opting for unmanned platforms instead of manned ones. That had all changed when they'd begun to encounter the Orbot, the Cyborg race that had threatened to turn the Republic's remotely piloted fighters and bombers against them.

"Today begins your training at Range 100—the first part of the Pilot Adaptive Combat Training," Coop heard Riggs announce as he started his brief.

The Pilot Adaptive Combat Training, or PACT, took place on a complex series of training facilities and ranges that Space Command had spent nearly a decade building. Nestled beneath Titan's surface, the range boasted an artificial gravity system and a breathable atmosphere, essential for realistic combat training. Spanning two thousand, one hundred meters in length, two hundred meters in height, and four hundred meters in width, the PACT was designed to push soldiers and spacers to their limits in a variety of simulated scenarios.

When Riggs had finished the safety briefing, everyone put on their eye and hearing protection. Coop fiddled briefly with his own noise safety device before he realized just how incredible this seemingly simple gadget was. These new state-of-the-art audio dampeners filtered out harmful noise levels while allowing for clear communication. Unlike the cumbersome ear protection of the past, these high-tech earmuffs utilized bone conduction and selective audio processing, enabling normal conversation and the perception of essential sounds without risking hearing damage from the weaponry.

When Coop had his protective gear ready, he resumed observing his pilots, noting the dark circles under their eyes from lack of sleep, particularly Badger's. Despite their fatigue, he could see many of them were excited to begin this next training evolution.

"OK, the boring administrative stuff is done. At ease. It's time to begin the fun stuff," commented Riggs, now assuming a more casual demeanor.

The pilots immediately relaxed, their shoulders slumping as they shifted their weight. The shooting range stretched before them, a vast expanse equipped with advanced targeting systems and reinforced barriers designed to withstand the full brunt of their weapons. Dim lighting from targeting computer screens and the faint, pulsing glow of energy barriers illuminated the space.

At the far end of the range, holographic targets flickered to life, controlled by sophisticated training algorithms. These targets varied from simple geometric shapes to detailed simulations of enemy soldiers, drones, and vehicles, each designed to challenge the soldiers' reaction times, accuracy, and tactical decision-making.

The range's versatility was its most impressive feature. It could mimic urban warfare, open-field engagements, and countless other combat scenarios, all within the safety of the underground facility. Soldiers practiced coordinated attacks, defensive maneuvers, and precision strikes, adapting to the ever-changing conditions presented by the range's dynamic systems.

"Now before we start the funtivities, the Wing King wants to say a few words—listen to his words, learn from his experiences and those of your instructors. It may mean the difference between life and death," exclaimed Riggs as he turned to face Coop. "They're all yours, sir."

Coop nodded, accepting the handoff as he stepped forward to remind them why they were here. Standing before his assembled pilots, he felt every bit of the burden of command now resting on his shoulders, the weight of his responsibility evident in his steely gaze. As he took a breath, he could feel the air was thick with anticipation, the pilots' eyes fixed on him, their wing commander. He needed them to know this wasn't just another training exercise; it was a crucible meant to forge them into the warrior pilots the Republic needed.

"If you want to survive this war, you'll listen to what I'm about to say," Coop began, his voice carrying the authority of countless battles fought and won. "You may think being a good pilot is all about time in the cockpit. You may even think flying a simulator makes you a better pilot. Well, let me set you straight. There's more to being a pilot than just pulling g's and executing maneuvers."

Now, he paced in front of them, the intensity in his eyes piercing through their fatigued expressions. "When you're out there dogfighting, you need to think fast. You need to think under pressure. But what happens when the enemy is firing all around you—when alarms are blaring, and your fighter shakes as it's hit—systems fail, and you realize you're not going to make it? That's when you punch out, or worse, your AI does it for you and ejects you fractions of a second before your fighter explodes. While you descend to the ground, ripped from the comfort of your cockpit, you're now behind enemy lines. What do you do now? What happens once you're on the ground and you see a Zodark patrol looking for you—hunting you? This isn't just about flying; it's about surviving."

Coop's voice grew harsher, each word a verbal slap to the face. "This training isn't for my benefit; it's for yours. The Republic's manned fighter program is still young. We need to accumulate veteran pilots, and that doesn't just mean flying missions. It means knowing how to stay alive when it all hits the fan. It means knowing how to fight alongside the Army if you have to. You're not just pilots; you're officers of the Republic. Act like it."

He paused, letting his words sink in. The pilots shifted uncomfortably, but their eyes never left Coop. "I don't give a damn how many flight hours you've logged or how many kills you have in a sim.

Out there, it's different. The Zodarks don't give a damn about your score. They'll gut you without a second thought. You need to be ready for anything."

Coop's gaze swept over the pilots, his voice lowering but no less intense. "You're here to become better pilots, but more importantly, you're here to become survivors. The Republic is depending on you, and so am I. Don't let us down."

He took a step back, the silence heavy in the air. "Grab your gear. It's time to show me you've got what it takes."

The pilots straightened, the weight of Coop's words settling over them. They understood now. This wasn't just training; it was a test of their resolve and their ability to adapt and survive. As they moved to the weapon racks, Coop watched, knowing that the crucible of Range 100 would either break them or bring them out the other side stronger and prepared for battle.

Chapter Seventeen

Carrier Strike Wing 14
Pilot Adaptive Combat Training
Range 100, Titan Training Facility, Sol System

The Titan Training Facility's expansive layout housed an assortment of specialized training areas, from the thunderous artillery ranges to the sprawling vehicle maneuver course, from the vacuum combat chamber to the disorienting zero-g adaptation zone. Spacers could hone their skills in the aquatic warfare simulator, while the Army could train at the extreme environment endurance center. However, it was the crown jewel of the facility that truly captivated the imagination: the holographic engagement arena. It spanned an area equivalent to four football fields. This colossal chamber could transform into any battlefield scenario. Today, it buzzed with activity as pilots, weapons at the ready, prepared to face off against holographic enemy combatants in a realistic jungle environment. As the participants positioned themselves, the line between simulation and reality blurred.

Coop stood in the viewing room, Riggs by his side. Monitors before them displayed the simulated tropical woodland environment below. Control panels pressed against the walls around them, their holodisplays' illumination lighting the room. The screens both Coop and Riggs watched showed six pilots from their squadron: Lucky, Badger, Spark, Nomad, Shrike, and Hawk. Each pilot's face looked like they'd had quite a long day. After two weeks so far into this training regimen, they were exhausted.

The pilots stood in the middle of a dense holographic jungle that looked real. They each held a standard-issue M1 battle rifle as they prepared to start the next training evolution. One of them pointed to some alien bugs as they skittered across the ground, their chitinous exoskeletons brightening in neon yellows and greens in the fake moonlight that filtered through the thick canopy above. Hanging from some of the branches were giant caterpillar-like creatures. Their segmented bodies pulsed with a viscous goo that dripped onto the forest floor, pooling wider with every drop.

"This looks too real," Badger said under his breath.

"Don't get too excited, sport. Might not be real, but it'll sure as hell feel like it," Nomad replied.

Roots and vines created a tangled mess on the jungle floor, the soil rich with the decay of countless generations of holo plant life. The trees stood high above the pilots with leaves of many colors, from deep, verdant greens to vivid shades of blue and purple.

Coop and Riggs finally took a seat as they got ready to start things. Coop pressed the intercom button to reiterate their instructions for this simulated event. "Just a friendly reminder as you prepare to begin this next training evolution. Your squadron was tasked with a DEAD mission—destruction of enemy air defense—in preparation for an allied bombing campaign set to begin shortly after the start of your mission. Should you find yourselves shot down, you're to proceed to rally point Alpha. In the event RP-Alpha is not a viable option, you are to proceed to RP-Bravo. You have approximately forty-five minutes to reach one of the two RPs for extraction. If you fail to reach the RPs on time, you will have to wait until Fleet Ops can identify another RP and timeline for when you need to be there. Failure to reach the second RP on time will result in a failure to accomplish the mission.

"Remember, nothing in this simulation is real, no matter how authentic it may look. This simulation is going to test your abilities to work as a team following being shot down while participating in a large-scale mission on a Zodark-controlled planet. Remember your training and be aware of everything around you and you'll do fine. Now stand by and prepare to begin," Coop explained as he started the simulation.

The pilots collectively nodded with grim expressions, thankful they would begin the simulation already grouped together. Armed with nothing more than a simulated M87 assault rifle, a handheld emergency radio and earbuds, a small patrol pack with basic necessities and a canteen of water, the pilots stood by, waiting for the clock to start.

When the simulation around them came to life, among the first things they noticed was how their boots sank into the soft, spongy ground—followed by the humidity of the air inside the facility, a slight breeze hitting them, the smell of the jungle wafting around them.

When Coop had programmed the simulation, he'd wanted this fictional world to mimic some of the worst-smelling places imaginable. As a result, the place reeked with an overwhelming stench. It was a cross between rotting food, dirty baby diapers, and burnt flesh.

"OK, the clock is ticking. Let's move," Lucky announced, immediately taking charge of the situation.

As they moved deeper into the woods, they began to see the most unusual pulsating pods dangling from tree branches. They were translucent, each pod's interior full of a swirling yellow liquid. Every one of them appeared to be alive, as if they grew some type of creature within.

One of the pods burst open and spilled its contents onto the ground in a noxious, steaming puddle. The pilots jumped back, their weapons raised as they studied the muck. An alien snake of some sort slithered away through the underbrush.

Lucky aimed her weapon at it. "That thing's huge."

"That's what she said," replied Hawk with a snicker.

"Cute, real cute, Hawk." Lucky poked him with the butt of her rifle.

"Hey, keep your eyes peeled, Lucky. You're supposed to look for enemy movement, not weird critters," commented Spark.

Lucky shot him a disapproving glare. "My eyes are wide open, Spark. These Zodarks blend in like chameleons on steroids."

Hawk slowed, though he trudged just behind her. "You're right about that, Lucky. I've got a bad feeling about this stretch of jungle."

"Cut the chatter, you two," Badger said, taking up the rear. "We're making too much noise. Talk only if it's important."

Shrike pushed aside a large fern leaf as he rounded the plant. "Agreed. Let's focus on the mission—getting to the rally point before the enemy gets us."

"Hold." In the middle of the pack, Hawk raised his fist to stop everyone. "Movement, four o'clock. Could be nothing, but stay frosty."

Everyone froze, looking around as they kept still, their eyes listening for what their eyes might miss.

"Nothing's ever 'nothing' in this godforsaken simulator," Spark said. "Don't know what Coop has in store for us, so keep your weapons hot, people."

"Spark, cool it," Lucky said. "We don't want to give away our position if it's just simulated wildlife."

"Wait, did you hear that?" Hawk turned around with caution. "Sounded like heavy footsteps."

Badger spoke, his tone soft. "Confirm. Multiple contacts, about one hundred meters out. Formation's breaking up."

"This is it. No heroes today," Shrike said.

Nomad lowered behind a wide tree trunk. "I've got visual. Three Zodarks, moving east to west. They haven't spotted us... yet."

Spark hid behind a tree, aiming her weapon around it. "Perfect. Let's introduce ourselves, shall we? On my mark..."

Lucky grimaced. "No, hold your fire. Don't want them to alert thousands more."

"Roger," Spark said.

Above, Coop and Riggs watched the scene unfold. Riggs rested his elbows on his knees. His brow creased in concentration as he studied the readouts on the control panel in front of him.

"They're doing all right," Riggs said. "They're staying alert, keeping their eyes open for any sign of danger. Spark's got a trigger finger. I thought she'd be more of a leader, but it seems Lucky's the one. Honestly, Badger's more aware than the rest of them."

"I've been working with him. He thinks he's the best at everything but keeps quiet about it. Nonetheless, he's improved as of late." Coop studied the screen. "They're all learning. Pilots aren't used to being on the ground. Yes, Lucky's a leader. Shrike can adapt to this life. Heck, I'd say he could be one hell of a soldier. Did you see his last simulation? He aced it while the rest of his team floundered. Embarrassing."

"Yeah, I saw it. Tried not to after I heard about it from you, but watched the holovid replay," Riggs replied.

The pilots moved behind cover, their eyes darting from side to side as they searched for any sign of further movement.

"They're passing us by," Lucky said, her chest on the forest floor, rifle steady as she lay on the ground. "Close call."

"Stay down," Badger said. He remained behind a tree, his body well hidden.

"Hand signals from now on," Lucky said.

"Roger," a few in the team replied.

Shrike's voice burst over the pilots' helmets. "Zodarks, fast approaching, five o'clock! Open fire!"

Two Zodarks emerged from the trees, leaping down from the branches with their weapons drawn. Their holographic forms appeared as real as anything, even to Coop, and he'd seen this type of scenario hundreds of times.

The pilots opened fire. The muzzles flashed, lighting up the plant life in brief strobe-like bursts.

The Zodarks moved with inhuman speed. Their holographic forms shimmered as they dodged the hail of holographic fire.

The Zodarks began shooting, returning fire at them. The air crackled with the sound of energy blasts. The melting foliage sizzled all around.

Lucky crawled behind a fallen log. Bark splintered inches from her head as enemy fire tore through the vegetation.

"Spark, on your six!" Lucky shouted.

Spark spun, her rifle barking. Blood erupted out the side of a Zodark's head. It fell facefirst with a thud.

"Ten-four on the warning," Spark shouted back.

Nomad killed another Zodark mere meters from him. He crouched and darted between two trees. "More coming from the east."

Shrike grunted, hefting his weapon. "I've got it covered." He went to climb up a tree, and his hand went through the hologram. "Damn, forgot."

He unleashed a torrent of suppressing fire, forcing a group of advancing Zodarks to take cover.

Shrike's voice crackled over the comm as he went to one knee next to a boulder. "Multiple hostiles, this time coming from the north quadrant. Tango is unaware of my position. Have positive ID on targets. Weapons free, engaging." He picked off several Zodarks as each shot found its mark. For every fallen enemy, two more took its place. Some dropped from the trees fifty meters away. Others popped up from the ground seventy meters from Shrike.

Hawk weaved through the underbrush. He flanked a group of Zodarks and caught them by surprise. Three enemies went down before they could react.

"Nice work, Hawk," Lucky said.

To Coop, the rigorous training he'd inflicted on his pilots was working. He noticed it with this group more so than the rest of his space crews, but they'd been improving by the day.

Right now, these pilots below him in the simulation chamber floor were spread out in a loose semicircle formation. Every one of them used the dense jungle terrain for cover. Lucky found position behind another fallen log about twenty meters ahead of them. She provided leadership, coordinating their efforts. Spark was fifteen meters to Lucky's right, using a large tree trunk for cover. Nomad took up a spot twenty-five meters to Lucky's left, concealed by thick underbrush. Hawk was the furthest forward, about thirty meters ahead of Lucky, having just completed his successful flanking maneuver. Shrike was ten meters behind Lucky, elevated slightly on a small rise, which gave him a better vantage point for sniping. Between Lucky and Spark, Badger lay on his stomach about five meters behind them. The man was providing suppressing fire and doing a good job.

The Zodarks approached from multiple directions, surrounding the team. The main force advanced from the north, with eight Zodarks spread out in a line about fifty to seventy-five meters away. Another group of twelve Zodarks moved from the east, about sixty meters from Spark's position. A smaller contingent of four just dropped from the trees to the west, about forty meters from Nomad. Two more groups, each consisting of six to seven Zodarks, were closing in from the southeast and southwest, both about eighty meters out.

"Fall back!" Lucky ducked behind a massive rock. "Spark, move!"

Spark sprinted from her position, zigzagging between trees. She dove into a shallow ditch just as energy bolts scorched the air where she'd been.

"Clear!" she called.

Lucky burst from cover and ran low and fast. She slid into position next to Spark, panting heavily.

"Nomad, you're up!" Lucky said.

Nomad vaulted over a fallen log. His boots squelched in the mud. He sprinted from tree to tree, using each as momentary cover.

A nearby explosion sent shockwaves through the ground. Dirt and leaves rained down. Through the settling debris, Nomad tumbled into a small clearing.

"I'm good," Nomad said.

"Covering fire!" Lucky popped up, laying down suppressing fire.

Badger was next. He lumbered forward. Enemy fire shot past him, leaving scorch marks on nearby trees.

Spark followed suit as Badger made it to safety, sliding in next to Nomad.

Lucky continued to fire. "Hawk, go!"

Hawk moved like a ghost, barely disturbing the underbrush. He flitted from shadow to shadow, almost invisible, until he materialized next to Badger.

"Shrike, what's your status?" Lucky asked.

"Moving to a new position." Shrike crawled between patches of heavy thicket. When he made it close to Lucky, he lined up his sights and shot at enemy targets, downing several. "Come on, guys. We gotta go. Time to evac is ticking!"

A blast rocked the jungle. This time, the explosion was close enough to send Lucky and Spark tumbling from the shockwave. They scrambled to their feet, ears ringing, as they tried to shake off its effects.

The flight suits worn in this particular simulation were specially enhanced for the holographic engagement arena. While similar to the ones they wore in the cockpit, these had been embedded with countless haptic feedback nodes that translated simulated impacts from nearby explosions or blaster fire into physical sensations against their bodies. It made the virtual explosions or the impact of a Zodark blaster feel disturbingly real. Even the chamber's advanced gravimetric floor plates could shift beneath their feet, mimicking uneven terrain and the force of nearby detonations. Added atmospheric emitters that could fill the air with the aroma of cordite or burning foliage added yet another layer of realism that, when combined with the overhead mesh of microscopic projectors, created a seamless 360-degree environment in which a person's brain struggled to differentiate reality from illusion.

"Damn, that hurt," groaned Lucky, wiping sweat and dirt from her brow. As she looked around, she saw that flames licked up a nearby tree. It spread through the canopy, smoke building up until it billowed around them, reducing their visibility.

Spark coughed a couple of times. "We need to exfil. Get out of here before the Zodarks encircle and trap us!"

"Yeah, copy that," Lucky concurred. "This path isn't going to work, guys. Our path to RP-Alpha is blocked. I'm calling an audible. I want everyone to head to RP-Bravo. I'll alert the extraction team!"

Spark and Lucky ran past Hawk, who yelped. "Ouch! Damn! Even a near miss from a blaster can hurt like hell!" he bemoaned as he took off after Spark and Lucky, nursing a singed arm.

Badger popped up from his position and laid down another barrage of covering fire. "Move it, people! I can't hold them off forever!"

Nomad hurried after Lucky and Spark. Hawk had rounded a tree and prepared to lay down his own covering fire so Badger could bound backwards to set up another firing position as the team continued to race toward the evac location.

The enemy kept coming. Badger and Hawk could cut down several Zodarks, only to see their numbers replaced and more following after them. The enemy force was beginning to overwhelm them.

"Oh, come on! I've got multiple new hostiles racing toward us. If we don't figure something out quick, we're dead," Shrike exclaimed, exasperated as the pressure of the simulation continued to build.

Lucky cut in, countering hotly, "Negative, Shrike. We're not out of luck yet, but you are right about too many of them closing in on our path. We gotta move faster. We can't allow them to encircle us."

Shrike popped out of cover, squeezing off quick bursts. Two Zodarks went down, but a third returned fire. Shrike ducked just as the volley of enemy fire tore through the space where he'd been standing as the tree behind him erupted in a shower of burning leaves.

The pilots continued their fighting retreat, but the Zodarks pressed their advantage.

"We can't keep this up," Nomad said, his breathing labored.

Hawk crawled behind a small hill. "They're herding us. We're running out of options."

"Any bright ideas?" Badger asked between firing short bursts from his rifle.

From the data streaming on the screens, Coop monitored Badger's M87, which was running dangerously low on power. "They're doing better than I expected. They're almost as good as a Ranger team."

Riggs gave him a sideways look. "Rangers...I take it you haven't seen a Ranger team in action before, have you?"

Coop glanced at Riggs, then turned his eyes to the biggest holodisplay in the viewing room. "OK, I'm exaggerating, but still, I'm impressed."

"I hate to say it, but me too," Riggs added.

Lucky's rifle kicked back against her shoulder when she fired. A Zodark hit the ground, the impact slicing through its chest. "Contact, two o'clock!"

As the pilots executed a tactical withdrawal, the Zodarks consolidated their force and shifted from an encirclement pattern to a frontal assault formation.

Spark aimed her M87 at the nearest Zodark, which was coming around a tree, its hackles raised and mouth wide. It showed its spiked teeth. "Engaging!" Her rifle chattered. The Zodark shook from the hits, its skin ripped apart before it lay lifeless on the forest floor.

"Nomad, watch your left flank!" Lucky shouted.

Nomad watched the tree line. "Roger that. Area secure."

Badger's weapon roared to life. "Suppressing fire, east quadrant!" His rounds forced a group of advancing Zodarks to scatter.

"Textbook, Badger. Well done!" Lucky said. "Hawk, how's our six?"

"All clear for now," Hawk replied. "But they're massing for another push."

The six-pilot team continued to retreat strategically. They split into pairs. One duo provided covering fire while the others quickly fell back. Then they'd switch roles, ensuring constant protection as they withdrew. Every pilot kept about five meters away from their teammates. They were close enough to help each other but far enough apart to avoid being easy targets.

Suddenly, Zodarks burst from the underbrush and charged forward toward Hawk.

"Open fire!" shouted Lucky.

The air filled with the sound of weapons discharging and guttural howls from Zodarks. Holographic rounds crisscrossed the battlefield between the two groups.

"They're flanking us again!" Nomad yelled in frustration. They were constantly falling back further and further away from the extraction point.

Lucky saw the threat and spun to face it. She fired in short, controlled bursts. "Fall back! Now!" she shouted angrily.

The pilots began leapfrogging from cover to cover.

"Shrike, what's your status?" Lucky asked.

"Relocating," he replied. "New position in ten seconds."

A Zodark jumped down from a tree near Hawk, its blade attempting to slash him.

Startled by the beast's sudden appearance and the blade arcing down toward him, Hawk fell backward as he fired his rifle into the Zodark's chest at near-point-blank range.

"Oh, that was a close one," Hawk commented as he scrambled back to his feet.

The Zodarks pressed harder, coming faster and seemingly materializing out of thin air.

"We can't keep this up," Spark said. "I'm running low on power."

The Zodarks were too many, too quick. In this simulation, they moved with perfect synchronization.

At this point, the pilots had formed a tight circle, beating back teams of two or three Zodarks as they bum-rushed the pilots, attempting to overwhelm them.

Lucky turned to check on Shrike and Nomad when she saw Nomad take several blaster shots to the chest. His suit instantly locked up, and his body collapsed to the ground in an uncontrolled fall. Then, before she could react, a Zodark jumped over his lifeless body, standing in the midst of them, his twin blasters firing away.

Lucky screamed in panicked horror, bringing her rifle to bear as she fired at this intruder within their ranks. The Zodark fell to the ground and was quickly replaced by several more who had rushed the gap in their lines when Shrike and Nomad had gone down. Before Lucky could respond, she felt her body being punched in multiple places before her suit locked up too, her body falling to the ground.

In the blink of an eye, the fight was over. They had been wiped out before they'd had a chance to even get close to either rally point for extraction.

****

"All right, Riggs, let's end the simulation and turn it off," announced Coop.

Riggs acknowledged, his fingers typing commands. In moments, the holograms creating this realistic training environment blinked off, fading away to reveal white walls covered in the tiny LED strips that made things look so real.

Coop pressed the intercom to speak, clapping slowly as the sound of it echoed throughout the chamber before commenting. "Well done, everyone. This was an outstanding effort—maybe the best of your squadron."

In truth, Coop was satisfied with the junior officers' performance. In the past few weeks, they had been tested to the limit; the process had laid bare their command of the new skills they'd been taught as well as their growth or lack thereof as leaders who could think under pressure.

The pilots stood, their faces stoic as they listened to their commander's words.

"I know you're likely feeling disappointed at not making it to either rally point. The fact is, you weren't supposed to. No one is, and that's not what we were testing. We were testing how well you could work together while facing overwhelming odds. In that regard, you passed," Coop explained, encouraging them. "Now get out of here. Get yourselves cleaned up, and instead of reporting to the briefing room for more instructions, I'm giving you the rest of the afternoon and evening off. Report to the auditorium tomorrow at 0700. It's time to return to the sim pods before we begin squadron, group, and wing tactics. Get some sleep—you earned it."

Coop smiled as he swiveled his chair to face Riggs. "Time to bring in the next group. Let's see if we can't nudge the intensity a little more."

Chapter Eighteen

Early September 2114
RNS *Vega*
Titan Training Facility
Sol System

Aboard the RNS *Vega*, crew members busied themselves at their stations. Seated near the rear of the bridge, Lee was enjoying his new, all-time favorite command chair while overseeing the flurry of coordinated tasks as his people began putting lessons learned into practice.

Admiral Ripley Lee had been settling into his position on a new ship, both figuratively and literally. He was quickly becoming familiar with this seat, breaking it in and exploring its numerous features. The armrest panels housed an array of controls, from holographic displays to tactical interfaces. A built-in seat comm device allowed for instant shipwide communications while biometric sensors monitored the occupant's vital signs in case the ship's captain was injured during a battle. The chair even boasted a climate control system along with a discreet storage compartment for personal items.

Lee eased into the new leather of his command chair, positioning himself at the heart of operations in *Vega*—one of the most advanced vessels in the fleet. Initially, when Command had contacted Lee from the battlefront, they had planned on giving Lee two months to train, but they'd needed his ship, his crew, and his space wings at the front much sooner. So he'd had to hurry up the training process at the Proving Grounds and push everyone that much harder.

To Lee's right, Commander Noriko Sato stood beside her chair, surveying the various readouts on the main viewscreen at the front of the bridge. After taking her seat, she activated a control on her chair's panel. A small holographic display materialized, rising from her armrest. Using this display, Sato made final adjustments to the parameters of the Pallas Training Protocol or PTP they were about to initiate. "Bringing up our fleet, Admiral. Looks like Pallas gave us the RNS *Virginia*, *Artemis*, *Orion*, *Nebraska*, *Trident*, and *Harbinger* to play with."

"Hmm, very well. Let's go ahead and initiate Pallas—bring the ships up on the main screen, and let's begin," Lee ordered.

"Aye-aye, sir. Alerting Titan Station. The *Vega* is activating Pallas. We'll advise them of our return to ready status once PTP is complete."

This was the part that amazed Lee the most about the new warships the Fleet had been fielding. The Pallas Training Protocol was an incredible multimodal Metaverse training program that would integrate a ship's onboard computers and systems into a training mode that would allow the crew to operate the ship as if it were in a real-world situation. With Pallas, a captain could test his crew's ability to fight fires, a decompression event, or simulated battles. Inside these simulated battles, they could construct scenarios that involved strictly the use of their fighters or the ship's weapon systems or just about any other of the myriad of training events the ship's captain might want to use to test his crew and further hone their skills.

When Pallas was activated, the crew would wear specialized full-spectrum eyewear and earbuds that would immerse the wearer into the simulation. If the ship was supposed to be under attack, the eyewear and the earbuds would simulate the damage it sustained, shaking or vibrating in response. The eyewear would show sparks, smoke, and other visual phenomena in coordination with the auditory effects, creating a truly immersive training experience unlike anything Lee had ever seen. The best part was that the ship's captain could run the training events as often as they liked, even while deployed, by simply having the ship's secondary bridge crew operate the ship and make sure nothing outside the simulation posed a threat or required the termination of the simulation. Pallas was a truly remarkable program. Lee only wished it had been around during the First Zodark War. Sometimes, the key difference between survival or defeat, victory or death, was the proficiency of a ship's crew and their ability to use the ship's capabilities to their maximum extent. Experience gained in battle was invaluable. Surviving a battle to gain and then use that experience in the next battle was a lot easier said than done.

It was important to note that when Pallas was in use, the ships with which the *Vega* would interact were part of the simulation. They weren't real but rather highly sophisticated simulations within the training protocol. The commanders of these virtual vessels were also simulated entities. They were carefully programmed to mimic the personalities, decision-making processes, and communication styles of

131

their real-life counterparts. As a result, they'd react to situations, give orders, and communicate in ways that closely mirrored how the real captains would behave in similar circumstances.

At the helm of *Vega*'s bridge, Commander Lewis Reynolds, the ship's navigator, hunched over his console. His hands hovered above the controls. Wrinkles etched deep lines around his eyes. He'd spent years charting courses through the stars and had mostly done so for Lee no matter the ship he commanded. Reynolds muttered softly to himself as he ran through preflight checks.

Data streamed across the interfaces at the communications station while Commander Lucia Rodriguez, the ship's comm officer, monitored incoming transmissions.

The tactical officer, Commander Connor Rhom, occupied his post to Lee's left, his muscular frame coiled with anticipation. He rubbed the scar that ran along his jawline, a souvenir from an engagement gone wrong a few years back.

These were the three R's—Reynolds, Rodriguez, and Rhom. Or, as many jokingly referred to them, "the R-Team." Lee had been with them for years, requesting their transfers to whatever new ship he was commanding. They were a team, and a team sticks together.

A dozen other officers filled the other stations on the bridge. A warship of this size with this much firepower required a large crew. Sitting in his chair, Lee surveyed them, a mix of seasoned veterans he had come to rely on and a sprinkling of newly trained officers and enlisted fresh from the Academy, the *Vega* their first assignment. Each of them carried a huge weight of responsibility on their shoulders.

In his early years on Navy vessels, Lee had learned much from his mentor, Captain James Oldendorf. Tragically, the man had died on the bridge before Lee's very eyes. Since that tragic day over twenty years ago, only a few of Lee's officers had fallen in combat. He silently thanked the heavens that he had been blessed with an incredible team for such a long time and was thankful he hadn't lost many ships during the past couple of decades.

Lee pushed the comm button, opening a channel to the fighter bay. "Captain Cooper, this is the admiral. We have activated Pallas and are ready to begin the simulation. Are your pilots geared up and ready to begin?"

The bridge fell silent before the speakers crackled to life. "Affirmative, Captain. All pilots are prepped and in position in the sim pods. We're ready to launch on your mark."

"Excellent," Lee said. "Stand by for my command." He swiveled in his chair, addressing the bridge crew. "All stations, prepare for combat simulation. We're gonna run this op until it's burned into our bones. I want every crewman to push their limits, breathe through the pain, and overcome the obstacles thrown our way. Mental or tactical, it doesn't matter. We break through whatever's thrown at us, no matter what."

Commander Rodriguez typed on her comms' holographic display. "Captain, all systems are linked to Pallas. We are green across the board."

"Tactical is ready, sir," Commander Rhom reported at the weapons station. "Sim rounds loaded, targeting systems calibrated."

Commander Reynolds dipped his head at the admiral. "Navigation plotting multiple evasive patterns, Admiral. Ready to execute on your command."

The main viewscreen darkened, filling the bridge with the vast emptiness of space. Stars shined against the blackness. It was a deceptive calm before the storm.

"Activate Pallas. Let's see what kind of simulated battle it has in store for us," Lee commanded.

Angry red dots blossomed across the main display—each representing an enemy vessel.

"Zoom in."

"Zooming in, Admiral."

Lee examined the enemy formation. At the center, massive Zodark battleships lumbered. Their hulls bristled with weapon emplacements. Flanking these behemoths were Zodark cruisers, their engines glowing hot as they maneuvered into attack positions. Mixed into the fray were swarms of Vultures—Zodark fighters circling the larger ships like angry hornets. In the rear, an Orbot capital ship, known as a base star, nearly six thousand meters long, flew toward the *Vega*, the immense craft heavily armed and disgorging swarms of drone fighters.

"Wow, looks like Pallas is bringing us a fight today," Lee commented as he took in the sight of it all. "You guys know what to do—

let's send 'em packing." He punched in a command, connecting him to Flight Ops. "Captain Cooper, you seeing this?"

Coop's heavy tone burst through the speakers. "Affirmative, Admiral. My pilots are chomping at the bit. Permission to launch?"

"Negative. Hold position." Lee turned to his tactical officer. "Rhom, give me a threat assessment."

Rhom was reading his display as he took in the information. "Sir, I'm counting eighteen Zodark battleships, nineteen cruisers, one capital ship, and... wow, at least three hundred Vulture fighters, and that's not counting the swarm of eight hundred drone fighters we know that Orbot ship is capable of deploying. They've got us outgunned and outmanned for sure."

"Then we'll just have to outsmart 'em, won't we?" Lee replied, then turned to Navigation. "Reynolds, plot an intercept course. Bring us in at heading zero-four-seven mark three. Plot a course between those ships, Alpha Two and Bravo Six—all ahead flank speed," Lee directed before turning to look at Commander Rhom. "Tactical, bring our missile batteries online and start charging the magrail capacitors. Tell the gunners to stand by for close-quarter battle. We're going to get in close and let our guns rip them apart."

Sato's facial expression was a cross between concern and horror as she leaned in close to Lee, whispering, "Sir, that'll put us right in the crossfire of—"

"I'm aware it will, XO. Trust me on this. It's going to work," he tried to reassure her. Turning to his navigation officer, he said, "Reynolds, have the helm guide us in and continue with my orders."

"Aye, sir. We're on it."

Lee nodded, a smile forming on his face as he connected to Flight Ops. "Coop, we're about to thread the needle between some bad hombres. I'm going to need your Gripens to clear us a path through these Vultures and your Valkyries to pummel those Zodark frigates and corvettes. We gotta keep those torpedo boats off our asses, or they'll shiv us to death once they get inside the range of our secondary batteries. You think you're pilots are up for some high-stakes, big-reward flying?"

Coop laughed at his comment before offering, "Sir, if my pilots aren't ready for action after the weeks of hell I've put them through, I'll surrender my wings and sweep floors. Just say the word, and I'll cut them loose."

"They better be, Coop. I pulled a lot of strings to get your wing access to those training sims. I better see results from it," Lee cockily replied to his ace pilot. He was counting on Coop to come through for him in a big way with this strategy he was going to try.

As Lee disconnected from Flight Ops, he turned back to his bridge crew, his stomach churning unnervingly from the stress of his decisions and the battle that was about to take place. No matter how long he'd commanded a ship, on the eve of battle or in an important training operation, his nerves liked to make themselves known in one form or another—sweat forming on his brow, his hands becoming clammy.

"All right, people, this is our chance to impress the brass and demonstrate to ourselves we have what it takes to win, what it's going to take to achieve victory and finally end this war once and for all," he exclaimed to everyone on the bridge, then turned to face Sato. "XO, start Pallas in three... two... one..."

The second Pallas went live, the swarm of angry Vultures surged forward, rapidly closing the sixty-eight thousand kilometers between them. While the Vultures raced toward them, the giant engines of the Zodark capital ships illuminated the darkness behind them as the plumes of energy propelled them forward, the speed of these giant warships steadily increasing as the distance between them shrank, the two battle lines converging until the enemy was within range of their guns.

Lee watched the scene unfold for a moment before his voice rang out. "Commander Rhom, weapons free—light 'em up and score us some trophies!"

A few officers howled excitedly in response. Those manning the offensive and defensive weapon systems were calling out targets to each other and engaging that ships that AI had delineated as most important first.

Lee couldn't help but look on in awe at the twenty-four-foot-wide floor-to-ceiling main monitor on the bridge. Despite all the warships he had seen, the images had never been this crisp or realistic, drawing him into the action.

On each side of the *Vega* were ten twenty-four-inch twin-barreled magnetic railguns. As they fired in rapid succession, Lee knew that when those giant projectiles careened into the armor of a Zodark ship, their two-thousand-pound high-explosive incendiary warheads would explode within the guts of the enemy ship, tearing it apart from the inside out.

The *Vega* also had twelve twin-barrel turbo lasers on each side. Each barrel was capable of delivering a one-gigaton shot every twenty-five seconds.

Damn, that packs one hell of a punch, thought Lee in astonishment as he watched the battle unfold.

When needed, the capacitors on the turbo lasers could release a maximum charge into the barrels, delivering a pair of two-and-a-half-gigaton shots. The only downside to this strategy was that the lasers would then require a hundred-and-eighty-second recharge cycle before they would be ready to fire again. Lee imagined it being the longest three-minute wait of his life between salvos.

"Admiral, enemy capital ships are attempting to burn through our jamming—we've got multiple heavy cruisers and corvettes accelerating rapidly," announced Commander Rhom from his tactical action officer or TAO position.

"Acknowledged, Rhom. Get your gunners on those ships while they're still outside of torpedo range," replied Lee before connecting to Flight Ops. "Coop, launch fighters—get after those Vultures and have your bombers take out those corvettes!" he shouted, disconnecting the call before Coop could respond as he pivoted to Commander Reynolds. "Comms, connect to the *Artemis* and *Orion* and tell them to form up on our flanks, tight. Order the *Virginia* and *Nebraska* to pull ahead of us and take the point position for the group. Then, I want the *Trident* and *Harbinger* to fall back slightly and take up a rearguard position."

"Aye-aye, sir. We're on it," replied Reynolds confidently, cool as a cucumber.

With orders being shouted and information being passed about, the bridge erupted into a flurry of activity and controlled chaos. Seconds turned to minutes as status reports steadily rolled in from stations throughout the *Vega* and the fleet as the ships moved into formation.

Rodriguez relayed orders and coordinated movements, calling them out as the data came in. "*Artemis* acknowledged, moving to the port flank, bearing two-seven-zero mark fifteen. *Orion* confirming, starboard flank secured, heading zero-nine-zero mark twenty-two."

Reynolds adjusted the *Vega*'s course to align with the forming battle group. "*Virginia* and *Nebraska* advancing to forward positions, eight thousand kilometers ahead."

The main viewscreen showed Coop's Gripen fighters and Valkyrie bombers streaking out from the *Vega*'s launch bays. The craft accelerated rapidly, putting distance between themselves and the *Vega*. They formed up into tight attack squadrons, vectoring toward incoming Vultures.

"Coop, status report," Lee asked, watching the fighter squadrons launch one after the other.

"Strike Wing 14 is fully deployed, Admiral. The 15th should be following us out of the launch tubes shortly. We're moving to engage Vultures in Sectors Five-Charlie and Five-Hotel—thirty-three thousand kilometers and closing."

Lee's mind was racing as he processed the information coming in fast from all directions. Then, he saw the first sign of victory; the lead battleship they had opened fire on with their magrails had suffered a catastrophic explosion that looked to have started in the forward section before cascading into the center of the ship, after which a giant explosion had practically ripped the vessel apart. With its power gone and its engines dark, the ship was adrift, quickly falling out of formation and to the rear of the enemy force.

Smiling at the quick victory, Lee called out, "Good shooting, TAO! Now get us a bead on that new battleship moving into the lead position. Hit 'em with the turbo lasers and a full spread of Hydra missiles."

Rhom's fingers moved across his console. "Aye, sir. Turbo lasers are locked on and engaging. Missile batteries one and three are acquiring missile lock... firing missiles one through ten and thirty through forty!" Rhom declared as he punched the launch command. "Missile batteries one and three, firing!"

Lee was smiling with excitement as he watched the missiles race ahead of the *Vega*. He checked the status of the guns—magrail turrets showed across the board, turbo lasers showed charged and ready. "TAO, fire at will. Lay into that battleship."

The space around the *Vega* lit up as weapons fire lanced out toward the distant Zodark formation. Countering this brilliant display of weapons fire heading in one direction were the periodic streaks of energy that zipped past the *Vega*, an occasional energy bolt slamming into the giant star carrier or one of the nearby ships in close formation.

On the tactical display, friendly signatures burned bright green while hostile targets pulsed an angry red. The distant readouts of starfighters quickly changed as the formations merged into a giant melee.

"Admiral, our sensors are updating the enemy position relative to our own—at nine hundred thirty-two thousand, four hundred kilometers and closely quickly," announced Commander Reynolds as he swiveled in his chair to face Lee. "Sir, our sensors are showing the Zodark ships to have increased their initial speed from one hundred and twenty kilometers per second to now one hundred and eighty kps. At their new speed and our present speed of three hundred and seventy-five kps, our ships will cross paths in twenty-eight minutes."

"Very well, Commander. Keep us apprised of any changes in speed by the enemy fleet," acknowledged Lee before turning to face his TAO officer. "Rhom, what's the status of those corvettes closing in on our flanks?"

"Our heavy cruisers are handling it, sir. Our Valkyries have already taken two of them down and heavily damaged three more," Rhom replied. Then the *Vega* shook violently as it felt like a hammer had smashed into the front of the vessel. A few yellow lights flicked on, but nothing red, or worse, flashing red, indicating something serious.

As the battle continued to rage, Lee and the rest of the crew watched the first volley of missiles cross the vast distance, racing toward their targets. The seconds felt like they stretched into eternity before Rhom announced, "Sir, impact on lead Zodark battleship in three... two... one..."

On the main bridge monitor, dozens of fiery blooms erupted against the armor of the Zodark battleship. It took a few moments for the cameras to relay the blast of the second wave of Hydra missiles as they impacted against the giant warship—a series of new explosions and fiery jets of flame stretching dozens of meters into the blackness, illuminating the damaged warship. As the barrage of twenty-four-inch magrail slugs pummeled the outer hull of the ship's armor, new jets of flame were ejected from dozens of newly created holes across the ship.

When the second Zodark battleship of the fight was blown apart from internal damage, it drifted out of its formation, falling further and further behind the fleet as the remaining vessels continued forward, their lasers stabbing high-energy beams into the darkness toward the Republic warships.

"Helm! Turn one-six-seven degrees to starboard now!" shouted Commander Rhom.

Oh crap! Those torpedoes are still going to hit! Lee patched himself into the ship's 1MC, shouting to everyone, "Torpedoes inbound—brace for impact!"

The *Vega* shuddered as one, then a second torpedo slammed into the forward port side of the ship. Alarm bells and new alerts sounded on the bridge—someone else shouting to brace for impact yet again as the next volley of torpedoes hit.

*Boom...*Lee felt the floor of the bridge shake from the force of the blast. Wherever that torpedo had hit, it had nailed something important. The violence of the explosion brought on a momentary flashback to his first space battle, the one where he'd found himself suddenly thrust into command of the battleship when the captain and chain of command had been killed and he was all that was left.

Lee held the sides of his chair tightly, grimacing as the damage control board was illuminated with red warnings flashing for attention. "Reynolds, activate evasive pattern Delta-One-One. We need to turn our damaged side away from the enemy until we can figure out how badly we've been hit."

"Aye, Admiral, initiating evasive pattern Delta-One-One," Reynolds acknowledged.

Shifting his gaze back to the monitor. Lee studied the enemy's disposition and remaining forces as he evaluated how his own force was holding up. Lee highlighted one of the Zodark battleships that was pummeling one of his battle cruisers. "Rhom, shift the portside guns to target that battleship I just highlighted and see if we can't punch some holes into that section here." Lee pointed to an area along the lower rear third of the ship. "If we can land a few rounds into that section, it should knock their guns off-line."

"Ah, going for the power capacitors—good call, sir. Adjusting the portside main guns now," Rhom acknowledged, sending the change of targets to the gun crews.

Lee looked on in frustration as he watched one of his battleships and a pair of heavy cruisers clumsily engage different targets based on their proximity instead of coordinating their fire. Tapping on the controls, he opened a comms channel that connected him to the command channel for each of the ships.

"This is Admiral Lee. I'm ordering the *Artemis* and *Orion* to execute a pincer maneuver along vector zero-four-four mark twenty-nine. I want you both to close within forty-seven thousand kilometers and hammer the starboard flank of that battleship with your primary turbo lasers and Hydra missiles. Decrease your speed to thirty-two percent, turn that battleship into slag!" ordered Lee, then turned his attention to the *Virginia* and *Nebraska*. He wanted the pair of heavy cruisers to keep the enemy's eyes and attention on them and what they were doing so the *Artemis* and *Orion* would have more time to hopefully take another battleship off the board. While they would attempt to force the enemy to spread their ships out, Lee directed the *Trident* and the *Harbinger* to come forward from the rearguard position along the starboard side of the *Vega*, using its size to help cover their repositioning. Once they were ready to cross in front of the *Vega*, he wanted them to accelerate to maximum speed to slash their way through at least a third of the enemy fleet, pummeling them with plasma torpedoes and Hydra missiles the entire time. If they didn't thin the enemy ships out soon, it would start to get ugly, quickly.

The simulated battle Pallas had drawn up for them continued to unfold across the viewscreen and tactical displays. Stealing a glance at the damage control board, Lee felt relieved to see that the flashing bright red sections of the ship had turned to either static red or yellow. He winced at the two sections of the ship showing black. He knew those sections contained the portside torpedo launchers and a single bank of fifty Hydra missiles. If a section of the vessel was highlighted in black, it was inoperable—damaged beyond their capability to repair it during a battle. Returning his attention to the main screen, he watched the battle still happening between Coop's fighters and the hundreds of Zodark Vultures still very much in the fight.

"Sorry to bug you, Coop. What's the status of those Vultures and where are your Valkyries at?" pressed Lee, not completely satisfied with the performance of his space wings just yet.

"Still engaging, Admiral. We've got a couple of different fights happening right now. Some are happening as far as eighteen thousand kilometers. Others are happening at knife range," replied Coop, as calm as he could.

In the background, Lee heard the sounds of simulated weapons fire and engines screaming, likely from radical maneuvers at high speeds. "I just checked the wing's log—it's showing we've downed ninety-seven Vultures and thirty-four Glaives. I've got my Valk squadrons attempting to go after those corvettes and frigates—I'm sorry we couldn't have stopped that one corvette from hitting the *Vega* with that spread of torpedoes. We were pummeling the ship. Still, it managed to get a spread of torps fired off before it blew apart. We're trying, Admiral, we're just heavily outnumbered here," Coop explained, doing his best to bring Lee up to speed while still obviously engaged in some sort of a dogfight or sniping battle of his own.

Lee sighed as he listened. He had hoped somehow that his fighter corps might be faring better by this point in the battle. "Thanks, Coop, for the update. Just keep the pressure on and keep trying to thin them out," Lee finally replied, not sure what else to say at this point. He knew they were doing the best they could given the situation they found themselves in.

The battle continued to rage. Ships maneuvered across thousands of kilometers of simulated space. Lee shouted orders, coordinating the efforts of his fleet like a master conductor.

"*Artemis*, adjust course to three-one-two mark twenty-one. Shift fire onto new hostile. Range thirty-seven thousand, five hundred klicks. Target that cruiser's starboard engine nacelle. Concentrate all batteries."

The main viewscreen showed the *Artemis* turning, its engines flaring as it changed direction. A new enemy cruiser appeared, growing bigger as the *Artemis* got closer. Then the *Artemis* fired a burst of lasers, hitting the cruiser's exposed portside engine nacelle. It exploded in a brilliant flash, sending debris flying into space. The enemy cruiser tilted to one side, leaking atmospheric fluids and gases from the now exposed rear portion of the ship.

"*Orion*," Lee ordered, "I need you at coordinates five-zero-zero by two-zero-zero by minus-three-five-zero. Enemy cruiser trying to slip through our lines."

The screen changed, showing the *Orion* speeding to the coordinates. When it got there, an enemy cruiser came into view, trying to sneak through a gap. The *Orion* fired a volley of Hydra missiles. The enemy vessel tried to maneuver away from the trajectory of the incoming missiles, to no avail. When the barrage of some fifteen out of the twenty Hydras fired at the cruiser impacted along the whole length of the Zodark ship, it caused a series of explosions to ripple along the line of the vessel. Moments later, the entire ship blew apart, breaking up into multiple large chunks of debris.

Lee began to privately feel they were doing well—that was until he saw how far the *Virginia* and *Nebraska* had moved from the *Vega*. They had gotten themselves too far ahead and had fallen out of the kind of interlocking fields of fire they called the *box*, a means of leveraging the defensive weapons of the warships around you to provide a better, more robust defense of each other when flying in a tight formation.

Connecting to the ships in question, Lee ordered, "*Virginia*, *Nebraska*, this is the *Vega*. You've pushed beyond the box. Fall back eight thousand kilometers and stay within the box. Out."

Lee had the screen split so he could observe them separately. As they fell back toward the *Vega*, the enemy must have realized the same thing as Lee had—the volume of enemy fire hitting them now increased exponentially. The ships were slammed with high-energy laser beams, ripping rents and gashes across the hulls of both vessels. Several torpedoes slammed into the *Virginia*, severely damaging its port side. The *Nebraska* fared better, though its bow took heavy damage as it retreated.

Then, Lee noticed how the lead Zodark battleship had also strayed too far ahead of its armada, exposing it to a similar fate to the one that had just befallen *Virginia* and *Nebraska*. Not one to miss an opportunity when one presented itself, Lee seized the opportunity, ordering, "All ships, target lead battleship at bearing zero-three-three mark zero-one-seven. Range twenty-nine thousand kilometers. Concentrate all primary magrails on the target!"

All ships, including the *Vega*, opened fire. When the magrail rounds burst from Lee's ship, the bridge vibrated. A few moments later, the lead enemy battleship took a direct hit from a concentrated volley. A massive explosion tore through its midsection, causing the craft to break apart. The two halves of the ship drifted in opposite directions, secondary explosions blasting along their length as power cores and ammunition stores detonated.

Rhom checked the damage sustained by all ships in the fleet. "Sir, *Artemis* has small hull breaches on decks three and four. *Orion* only sustained surface damage. *Virginia*'s starboard maneuvering thrusters are out, and several decks have hull breaches. *Nebraska*'s front missile turrets are inoperable, and front sections have lost air pressure. No one's reported dead or injured. RNS *Vega*, *Trident*, and *Harbinger* are all operating at one hundred percent capacity."

The hostile fleet flew ever closer, now a mere twenty-five thousand kilometers away. Lee's eyes moved between the main viewscreen and the tactical readouts, analyzing the information.

"Reynolds, bring us to heading zero-nine-two mark four-six. Rhom, prepare to fire another salvo of antiship missiles. Target their new lead cruiser. I want the projectiles set for proximity detonation."

"Aye, sir. Armed and ready."

"*Artemis*, *Orion*," Lee said, "focus fire on the cruiser, second from the lead, vector zero-nine-eight mark five-three. *Virginia*, *Nebraska*, provide cover for our fighters."

Lee nodded, his eyes never leaving the tactical display. "*Artemis*, *Orion*, fire on my mark. Three… two… one… mark!"

The space around the *Vega* illuminated as missiles streaked toward their targets. Lee held his breath, counting the seconds until impact.

Missiles converged on the lead cruiser, which seemed to absorb the assault without much effect. For a beat, nothing happened. Then, unexpectedly, the cruiser's hull began to burst open. Its form distorted, bulging outward in places and caving in others. The ship's surface glistened with an iridescent glow, growing brighter until it was painful to look at.

The cruiser imploded with a silent flash, collapsing in on itself. Where a massive warship had been moments before now floated a perfect shining sphere no larger than a beach ball. The sphere pulsed once, twice, then winked out of existence, leaving behind nothing but an empty void in the starfield.

The same thing occurred with the second cruiser behind the now-vanished lead enemy vessel. It too turned into a ball and blinked out, disappearing.

For a millisecond, Lee furrowed his brow. *Must be a glitch in the sim system.*

The comm blared to life, Coop's tone slicing through the thick atmosphere. "Admiral, our forces are sustaining damage. Vultures outnumber us significantly. Enemy reinforcements have launched. We're detecting an additional six hundred hostile starfighters swarming our position. I repeat, we're now significantly outnumbered."

Lee's jaw clenched, his mind racing through potential solutions. He knew Coop wouldn't call for help unless the situation was dire. The captain's voice carried a hint of strain that Lee had rarely heard before.

"Understood, Coop," Lee responded. "*Trident, Harbinger,* break formation and provide suppressing fire for our fighters."

As the orders were relayed, Lee's mind whirled with more possibilities. This was why they ran these simulations, he reminded himself. To learn, to adapt, to overcome unexpected challenges. Sometimes, the simulation intentionally created impossibilities, which was good. It kept the captain sharp and the crew on top of their game. He examined the tactical display, noting the positions of each ship, each fighter squadron.

Lee patched into all vessels and fighters. "We're shifting to Viper Formation Delta. *Artemis, Orion,* tighten your perimeter. *Virginia, Nebraska,* fall back to coordinates five-zero-zero by three-zero-zero. We're going to create a kill box for these Vultures."

As he spoke, the enemy starfighters flew past the Zodark vessels toward *Vega* and her fleet.

"Vultures nine thousand klicks and closing. Closest enemy cruiser, seventeen thousand kilometers," Rhom said.

Lee viewed the holo. Nine torpedoes headed toward their ship. "Rhom, initiate point defense! Target those torpedoes with laser fire!"

Rhom punched in the commands on the tactical console. "Engaging point-defense system, Admiral!"

The ship's laser batteries came to life, spewing rapid pulses of energy at the incoming projectiles. Bright flashes illuminated the viewscreen as six torpedoes detonated prematurely, torn apart by the precise laser fire. However, three torpedoes slipped through the defensive screen.

"Brace for impact!" Lee shouted.

The ship shuddered violently as the torpedoes slammed into the starboard side. The bridge lurched and alarms blared.

"Damage report!" Lee called out, steadying himself as the ship simulated the disaster around them.

Rhom pulled up the damage assessment. "Captain, we've sustained significant damage to the starboard hull. Decks five through eight have been breached and emergency protocols are in place. Main power is fluctuating. We've lost thirty percent of our weapon systems on the starboard side. Engineering reports the starboard nacelle has taken a direct hit and FTL capability is compromised. Life support is holding, but we're venting atmosphere in sections twelve and fourteen. Casualty reports are coming in from multiple decks."

Admiral Lee tapped his comm device. "Engineering, what's your status down there?"

Chief Engineer MacGregor spoke through the speakers, punctuated by simulated klaxons. "Admiral, if this wasn't a simulation, we'd be up to our eyeballs in power surges! Right now, we're sustaining critical damage across the board. Engines two and six are completely out, and the rest are screaming for mercy. With all due respect, sir, you need to fly this bird better than this if we're to survive in real combat."

"Noted, Chief. I'll try to dodge the torpedoes next time. Maybe you could make the ship a bit faster?"

"Aye, sir," MacGregor replied. "I'll see what I can do about boosting our maneuverability for the next round. But remember, even I can't make a silk purse out of a sow's ear."

As Lee was about to respond, his attention snapped back to the main holoscreen. The enemy starfighters were closing in fast, two thousand kilometers away. The Zodarks cruisers and battleships were a mere eight thousand klicks from the *Virginia*, twelve thousand from the *Vega*.

The simulator wanted close-quarter combat, and it wanted to overwhelm us. We're not going to make it out of this one with a success.

"Coop," Lee called, his fingers already tapping out new coordinates on his chair's interface, "I'm sending you a new attack vector. Bring your squadrons around to heading three-one-four mark two-two. We're going to funnel those Vultures right into our waiting guns."

"Copy that, Admiral," Coop said.

On the screen, Coop's fighters executed the maneuver flawlessly as they reared back and headed for *Vega*.

"I count twenty torpedoes heading our way, impact in five seconds, sir," Rhom reported. "Shooting down as many as possible. Sixteen left. Fourteen. Twelve."

The viewscreen flashed as torpedoes detonated. Their proximity fuses triggered a massive chain reaction of bursts as a handful hit *Vega* head-on.

The mighty ship gave a simulated jolt and then shook. The bridge rocked, holographic sparks erupting from consoles in a display of simulated damage. The viewscreen flickered, static cutting through the image of the attacking ships.

"Damage report!" Lee demanded.

"Rhom's console is out of commission," Sato said, bringing up her holographic screen from her chair's armrest. "Armor at thirty-one percent, Captain. Hull breaches on decks four through seven."

Lee searched for options. They needed more power, more speed, more of everything if they were going to survive this encounter.

"Reverse thrust!" Lee commanded.

"Engines not responding, Admiral," said Reynolds at Navigation.

"Engineering," Lee said into his comm. "MacGregor, we need more power!"

The chief engineer's voice came back strained. "The simulated reactor's already at one hundred and ten percent capacity. Any more and we risk a breach. If so, we're dead in the water."

"Reroute emergency power to maneuvering engines," Lee ordered. "And get me a firing solution on that cruiser bearing two-seven-zero, range six thousand kilometers!"

"Firing solution ready, sir." Rhom squinted his eyes against the glow of his monitor. "All forward weapons locked and loaded."

"Fire everything we've got!"

The viewscreen brightened as the *Vega* unleashed its full arsenal. Missiles streaked across space, leaving fiery trails in their wake. Lasers pulsed with deadly energy, cutting through the void toward their target. Tungsten rounds burst from the magrails.

The Zodark cruiser attempted to evade. Its engines flared as it tried to break off its attack run.

The first missile struck home, their detonations blasting across the cruiser's underbelly. Lasers followed, scoring deep gashes in the enemy bow. As the cruiser continued its turn, magrails punctured its port.

"Direct hit!" Rhom shouted. "Multiple hull breaches detected!"

Another devastating hit rocked the *Vega*, sending shockwaves through the hull. The bridge lights blinked off and on, plunging the crew into momentary darkness before sputtering back to life.

"Weapons off-line, sir. We're defenseless." Rhom's shoulders slumped a little.

"*Virginia, Nebraska*, I need you to—"

Before Lee could complete his sentence, on the main holodisplay, the *Vega*'s holographic representation broke apart under relentless enemy fire. Pieces of the once-proud ship scattered across the simulated void.

The words "SIMULATION TERMINATED" flashed across every screen on the bridge, bathing the crew in harsh red light. Lee grimaced, his fist clenching involuntarily. Sometimes the simulator tested them with the impossible, but for the better. Always for the better.

"Reset the simulation. We go again, and this time, we surpass our previous efforts." Lee stood, his posture straight as he spoke to his crew. "Listen up, people. We're not leaving this room until we get this right. Every move, every command, every response must be perfect. We gotta brush off whatever rust we have left within us."

Lee's mind drifted briefly to his mentor, James Oldendorf. The best captain he'd ever served under, a man whose relentless pursuit of perfection had shaped Lee into the leader he was today. He could almost hear Oldendorf's voice, urging him to push harder, to demand more from himself and his crew.

"I once served under a captain who understood the value of these simulations," Lee continued, his voice taking on a more personal tone. "Captain James Oldendorf. He'd run the same scenarios over and over, tweaking our responses, honing our skills until we could react without thinking. It was grueling, exhausting work, but it saved our lives more times than I can count. So we're going to run this simulation again. And again. And again. Until every one of us can perform our duties in our dreams and in our nightmares. Until we can anticipate each other's moves before they happen. Until we become a single, unstoppable force capable of taking on anything the enemy throws at us."

One by one, the crew nodded, straightening in their seats. They turned back to their consoles and reset their stations. Lee sat back in his chair and visualized the recent battle in his mind's eye, analyzing every move, every decision that had led to their defeat.

He saw the *Vega* flanked by its support ships, forming a tighter defensive perimeter. Fighters swarmed in patterns, drawing enemy fire away from vulnerable Republic vessels. He imagined coordinated missile strikes, timed to coincide with precisely targeted magrail barrages.

Lee's fingers tapped rhythmically on the arm of his chair as he considered different approaches. Perhaps they could use the debris field from destroyed ships as cover, or program their signal disrupters to rotate frequencies more rapidly to confuse enemy targeting systems.

He thought about the Zodark tactics they'd encountered, searching for weaknesses to exploit. Their reliance on overwhelming numbers could be turned against them with the right strategy. If he could find a way to divide their forces, to isolate and eliminate key ships...

As the simulation reset to readiness, the bridge came alive once more. Holos blinked to life as the simulated battle began anew. Lee took a deep breath, centering himself. This time would be different. This time, they would prevail.

Chapter Nineteen

Late September 2114
RNS *Vega*
Titan Training Facility

The office room, typically a sanctuary of order, now felt charged with an electric disarray. Maps flickered on the walls, each one a reminder of the mission looming before everyone on RNS *Vega*. Here, Admiral Lee stood in front of his desk.

Lee drummed his fingers against his thigh. The Pfeinstgard and Gravaxia systems had been on every officer's lips for weeks. Intelligence reports, troop movements, supply chains—all of it was building towards the final campaign—the invasion of Zodark space.

He glanced at the chronometer on his desk. Ten minutes until he needed to be on the bridge. Ten minutes to gather his thoughts, to steel himself for the challenges ahead. Lee took a deep breath, inhaling the familiar scent of recycled air that permeated every starship.

Eight weeks ago, they'd started training. Today, they were leaving and heading to the front.

He looked at a framed photo on his desk. A younger version of him stood next to Captain James Oldendorf, both grinning after a successful training exercise. Lee's throat tightened. *What would Oldendorf do in this situation?* The question, as always, brought both comfort and a renewed sense of purpose.

Lee straightened his uniform, tugging at the cuffs and smoothing down nonexistent wrinkles. Every detail mattered. The crew would look to him for strength, for leadership. He couldn't allow himself to display even the slightest trace of uncertainty or weariness, particularly in the wake of this past week—the most challenging and grueling period he or any member of his crew had ever endured.

With a final glance around his office, Lee strode toward the door. His hand had just brushed the door's control panel when a sharp, insistent beep cut through the air. Lee froze, his fingers hovering mere centimeters from the door's surface.

The beep came again, more urgent this time. Lee's brow furrowed as he turned back to his desk—the communication console pulsed with a red light, indicating a priority message on a secure channel.

Lee crossed the room in three long strides. *A secure message moments before departure?* It could mean that a change of orders or new intelligence had arrived and it had changed something—information that could dramatically alter their mission parameters.

He pressed his palm against the console's biometric scanner. The desk's holoscreen illuminated to life. Within it materialized a three-dimensional image of the official seal of the Republic.

The hologram changed, the screen going white before a message appeared:

// TOP SECRET // EYES ONLY//

"URGENT: To Rear Admiral Ripley Lee. You are to accompany Colonel Jeremy Eliason, Commander, 2nd Regiment, 3rd Special Forces Group, and Captain Tim Haas, Commander, ODA3236, Charlie Company, 2nd Regiment, 3rd Special Forces Group, to Fort Yarborough on New Eden in the Rhea system forthwith. Upon arrival to Fort Yarborough, you will report to Headquarters, Republic Army Special Forces, and later, to the Office of the Viceroy for consultation with Viceroy Miles Hunt, Head of Space Command, Fleet Admiral Chester Bailey, and Army Chief of Staff, Field Marshal John Reiker, General. END OF MESSAGE."

// TOP SECRET // EYES ONLY//

Lee blinked after reading the short message, wondering what it meant and why *he* was being directed to accompany two Army Special Forces officers to New Eden. What could have transpired recently that had attracted the attention of the Viceroy and the heads of Navy and Army? Whatever it was, he'd been summoned. In fact, he just received a message from Colonel Eliason that he and Captain Haas were catching a transport to the *Vega* and would join him in twenty minutes.

Damn, twenty minutes isn't exactly a lot of time to brief Sato, Lee realized. What really gnawed at him was the lack of context or reason behind this urgent request. *It sounds like someone within the Army got themselves in serious trouble, but why would I be dragged into this?*

As he hastily packed a go-bag, Lee ran through recent events in mind as he tried to figure out what this could be about. He had maintained a stellar record since leaving the Academy. He wasn't aware of any mistakes or accidents he had committed along the way that could be coming back to bite him now, on the eve of redeploying to the front.

He sighed to himself. Orders were orders, especially when they came from the very top. *I'll have to wait until I get there.*

Lee activated the comm link to Flight Ops, connecting to the duty officer. "This is Admiral Lee," he announced. "I need MARS028 and its flights crew made ready for departure in thirty minutes to Fort Yarborough, New Eden. Inform the pilot we should be gone no more than ninety-six hours. Oh, and there is a shuttle from the *Maddox* on their way here. Give them priority landing permission and provide them with whatever assistance that Colonel Eliason and Captain Haas need to need to join me aboard MARS028."

"Yes, sir," the duty officer replied. "We are showing MAD011 on approach to Docking Bay 2-Alpha. I'll go ahead and reroute them to Docking Bay 3-Alpha instead. That's where MARS028 is parked and being made ready, Admiral. Will there be anything else?" he asked.

"No, Lieutenant. That'll be all," Lee confirmed before he terminated the connection.

Lee swiftly called for his XO and Chief of the Boat to report to his office ASAP. He needed to bring them up to speed and ensure the ship and the rest of the fleet continued their final preparations to deploy.

Taking a breath, he took a seat at his desk and began downloading critical mission logs he might need onto a secure datapad. He typed on the console, selecting files and encrypting them. Unsure of what this meeting was about, he opted to bring the mission logs from their last deployment, in case these events were somehow related.

As he waited for his second-in-command to arrive, Lee turned his attention to the task at hand. He pulled open a drawer, revealing a small ornate box. Inside lay a collection of personal items—a worn leather-bound journal, a pocket watch that had belonged to his father, a smooth river stone from Earth, and a necklace with a cross pendant. Lee placed each item into a small travel bag, just in case he wouldn't be returning or he was reassigned.

Suddenly, the door beeped, causing Lee to jump for some reason.

"Enter," he called out.

The door slid open. Lee looked up to see his XO, Captain Sato, her tall, lean frame standing in the doorway. She scanned the room, taking in Lee's travel bag and the state of his desk. Her posture stiffened a bit, a subtle tell that she sensed something had changed.

"You wanted to see me, Admiral?" Captain Sato asked as she entered Lee's quarters.

"I do, Captain. I just received an urgent order to accompany a pair of Special Forces officers to Fort Yarborough on New Eden. I haven't a clue why, and even if I did, I wouldn't be at liberty share due to operational security. As the Captain of the *Vega* and the senior ranking officer within the Fleet, I am designating you as the temporary Fleet Commander, effective immediately, until my return," Lee explained rapidly to a bewildered Sato.

"I don't have a lot of time before I need to leave, Sato, but I trust you. I need you to proceed with the Fleet to our first waypoint, Intus—where you will take on additional supplies and personnel during the port call to include eight Primord heavy transports that will travel as part of our fleet. We are only scheduled to be in port for five-days, more than enough to accomplish what needs to be done. If I haven't linked up with you by then, I want you to proceed with the Fleet on our regular schedule to Pfeinstgard as planned. The Primord garrison is waiting on the supply ships merging with our Fleet. It's important that we deliver those supplies as the buildup for next operations continues. If, for some strange reason, my status as the Fleet Commander changes, I will send you a secure message and do my best to explain what happened. Do you understand your orders, Captain Sato?"

Sato's eyes widened in shock. Seconds later, she schooled her expression back to professional neutrality. Her spine straightened as she absorbed the gravity of Lee's words, and assumed the increased responsibility.

"Yes. Understood, sir," replied Sato. "I'll ensure all operations continue smoothly in your absence. Is something else going on?" she pressed. "Something I need to be aware of, sir?"

Lee smiled as he shook his head. "That's unclear at the moment. This situation is… fluid. Yeah, that's the word that comes to mind. For now, I'm being given the mushroom treatment...you know, kept in the dark, and fed BS," he replied, eliciting a laugh. "As soon as I know more, I'll pass it along. Hopefully, whatever this is, it'll get sorted quickly and I can return to the *Vega*."

He stood, moving around his desk. "Captain, I know this is sudden, especially given our imminent approach to the front. On my desk is a secured datapad with all the critical information you'll need: the battle plans we went over and war-gamed during our months of training, and the contingency plans for the myriad of scenarios and the latest intelligence reports pertaining to our mission area of responsibility. I've also included my personal notes should you want to read them."

Sato nodded. "I'll review everything thoroughly, sir."

"Good," Lee said. He hesitated for a moment, then continued, "Sato, you know as well as I do that the situation at Pfeinstgard and the border region is volatile. Trust your instincts, but don't hesitate to consult with the senior staff, especially the Chief of the Boat—he has a good read on the crew and how they're doing. Don't forget to leverage Commander Connor Rhom from Tactical. I think he has some valuable insights into the enemy's recent movements."

"Aye, Admiral. I'll make full use of the team's expertise."

"I have full confidence in your abilities, Captain. This ship, this crew—they're in good hands. Remember, in combat, decisive action is key. Don't second-guess yourself."

"Aye, sir. *Vega* will be ready for whatever comes our way."

"I know she will," Lee said. He extended his hand, which Sato shook firmly.

"Safe travels, Admiral," she said.

"And should I be delayed, good hunting, Captain," Lee replied. "Dismissed."

As Sato turned to leave, Lee added, "Oh, and, Sato? Keep an eye on Engineering. MacGregor has been pushing the engines hard lately during drills. We may need that extra power, but make sure he doesn't burn them out before we even engage the enemy."

"Understood, sir. I'll keep them in check."

After Sato left, Lee reached for his bag, his fingers closing around the strap. He strode out of his office and into the corridor.

The hallway outside stretched endlessly before him, the familiar walls and fixtures blurring as Lee picked up his pace. Crew members scurried out of his way as he marched along, their curious glances bouncing off his stony expression. An admiral leaving his post on the eve of a crucial mission, with his travel bag in hand? They knew something was up. It was unprecedented, the kind of thing that would set tongues wagging for weeks.

Once he approached the turbo lift, Lee caught sight of his reflection in a polished bulkhead. For a moment, he hardly recognized the man staring back at him. The lines around his eyes had grown deeper, the set of his mouth more or less turned into a frown. Stress did that to a captain—more so to him during the months of training, it seemed.

The elevator's doors opened, and Lee stepped inside. As they closed behind him, he said, "Docking Bay 3-Alpha."

Whatever the Viceroy and the Fleet Admiral have in store, I'll meet it head-on, he determined.

The turbo lift slowed. The doors slid open, revealing the bustling activity of the docking bay. Lee stepped out and headed toward the Multipurpose Advanced Response Ship or MARS. It was an executive travel FTL-capable ship the Navy had acquired for senior military officers needing dedicated interstellar transport. Lee seldom used the luxury ship despite it being a perk of his position; it made him feel weird to travel aboard such a luxury.

Approaching the ship, Lee spotted Colonel Eliason and Captain Haas standing near it, waiting patiently for him to board before they would follow suit.

"Morning, Admiral," Colonel Eliason greeted as Lee walked aboard. "Any ideas what this might be about?"

Lee dropped his go-bag next to the overstuffed leather recliner in the cabin behind the flight deck. Taking a seat in the chair, he motioned with a hand for the colonel to sit across from him. "Honestly, I haven't a clue. When I count the ships that are part of our fleet here and those still in Pfeinstgard, I have more than one and forty-six warships under my command. I am sure once we arrive, someone will eventually clue us in."

Chapter Twenty

30 Hours Later
Alliance City, New Eden

Admiral Lee watched out the viewport as the shuttle descended through New Eden's atmosphere. When the shuttle dropped below the cloud cover, it revealed the lush, densely forested landscape that stretched from the towering mountains west of the planet's capital—Emerald City. Having started as a planned city, it was built along the turquoise coast of the planet's ocean. Extending in several directions like the hub of a wheel, its spokes stretched from its core to equally planned and designed cities—connecting New Cambria, Londonian, and Alliance City with transportation nodes such as hyperloops, maglev rail networks, and multilane highways.

As the pilot continued their descent toward New Eden, he eventually banked the shuttle away from the capital and toward Alliance City. Each time Lee visited New Eden, he marveled at how much progress had been made toward finishing each of the new skyscrapers that sprouted like weeds in a garden. Sure, the towering structures were beautiful. But Lee couldn't help but wonder if such megacities were ideal for raising a family, rather than allowing for more urban sprawl and smaller cities to spring up. Not having a family of his own, Lee had decided he didn't have a dog in this fight, so for the time being, he abstained from voting in local referenda that dealt with such issues.

"Sir, we're approaching Alliance City. We should be on the ground shortly," announced the pilot as they began their final approach to the spaceport.

Lee nodded. "Thank you, Lieutenant Reaves. Let Flight Ops know I'll need a ride and escort to the building the Viceroy's Office is located in. Man…so much has changed since I was here last year."

"Aye, Admiral. It sure has," Reaves replied, then pointed in the distance. "Those three towers, they're new condos that were recently completed. The only reason I know anything about them is my brother-in-law is big into real estate. He convinced me to go in on purchasing a couple of units in one of those towers."

"Huh, not a bad idea, Lieutenant," Lee commented, making small talk and distracting himself from thinking about the reason he had been summoned—which was still a giant mystery.

As they drew closer to the capital city of the alliance, the lushness of the double- and triple-canopy jungle seemed to cocoon it in its own world. What made the autonomous city-state of Alliance City stand out in contrast to the other cities of New Eden was the diversity in style and construction of the different neighborhoods. Some areas of the city catered to Altairians, others to the Tully. The Ry'lians, Primords and humans all had their own sections too, unique to the design and culture of each group.

"Vega One Actual, Flight Control One-One. You are clear to land on pad Charlie Five," a voice from Flight Ops announced over the shuttle speaker.

Lee listened as Lieutenant Reaves acknowledged the order, landing on pad Charlie Five.

The engines powered down, and the subtle shift in gravity signaled their touchdown. Standing, Lee grabbed for his flight bag as the cabin door slid open. A Republic Army captain stepped in to greet him.

"Admiral Lee, welcome to New Eden. I'm Captain Lam from the Provost's Office," he said. "I've been instructed to collect you the moment your shuttle touched down and take you to see the Viceroy and the Fleet Admiral immediately. If you'll come with me, sir, we've got a vehicle waiting to take you there."

Whoa, this really is serious, Lee thought.

He nodded at his new host. "Thank you, Captain Lam. I've got a flight bag with a change of clothes inside. If one of your soldiers can grab it for me, we can get on our way."

"Not a problem, Admiral. If you'll come with us..." Lam gestured for Lee to exit the shuttle.

When Lee stepped on the tarmac outside, the heat and humidity of New Eden's atmosphere enveloped him like a wet embrace. The sun was still high, with a few puddles of water that were evidence of an earlier afternoon shower. The soldiers fell in behind him as they escorted him to a waiting vehicle that would drive them the short distance to their destination.

When they arrived at a building marked Alliance Headquarters, the van came to a halt. Exiting the vehicle, they approached a set of weighty doors. A pair of heavily armed guards snapped to attention, then rendered Admiral Lee a customary salute before opening the doors leading into the building.

Ah, the wonders of air conditioning, Lee mused. He had almost gotten used to the back of his uniform shirt sticking to him.

The group moved swiftly. The white walls seemed to close in around Lee; the pictures reminded him of a recruitment office more than what he'd expect of an alliance commander's office.

They passed several security checkpoints, each more stringent than the last. At each one, Captain Lam presented his credentials, and Lee was subjected to increasingly thorough scans. As they delved deeper into the complex, the corridors grew slightly wider, the lighting a touch softer. The air took on a different quality, hinting at larger spaces beyond the blank walls.

After what felt like an eternity of twists and turns, they came to a stop before an unmarked door. The lead soldier placed his hand on a scanner, and the door opened. Lam turned to Lee, his expression unreadable.

"Admiral, this is as far as I go. Please head in," Lam offered as he motioned for Lee to enter.

Lee entered what appeared to be a small conference room. In its center stood a solitary table and chair, drenched in lighting so focused, it created a spotlight effect. Lee raised his hand to shade his eyes and squinted against the brightness. When he took in the rest of the room, he noticed the Republic insignias that decorated the walls.

What the heck is this, and why am I here? Lee wondered.

Lee's footsteps echoed as he approached the table and chair. As he drew nearer to the focal point of the room, oddly, the hair on the back of his neck stood on end. His every instinct screamed that he was on display, a specimen now under intense scrutiny. He'd been through battles, the worst of the worst, and his friends' and companions' deaths, but for some reason, this felt direr, and he didn't know why.

"Take your seat, Admiral Lee," said someone in the darkness, someone who the intense lighting made almost impossible to see except for the man's shadow.

The metal legs scraped against the floor as Lee pulled the seat out. As his eyes adjusted to the glare, he became conscious of movement from the shadows. A few more figures emerged from the darkness, walking toward him until they had arranged themselves in a semicircle looming in front of him. Then, as if a switch had been flicked, a soft light powered on, and the faces of those before him came into view.

At the center of this imposing array, two people commanded Lee's attention. Viceroy Miles Hunt, and beside him, Fleet Admiral Chester Bailey. Also present were Admiral Fran McKee, General John Reiker the head of the Army, and another general he hadn't heard of but saw he headed up Republic Special Forces.

They brought in all the heavy hitters, thought Lee.

Viceroy Hunt spoke first. His voice boomed through the chamber. "Admiral Lee, we're sorry to summon you like this, so I'll get to the point. Were you aware of Captain Tim Haas and his actions during the reconnaissance mission to Lunakor?"

"Lunakor, sir?" Lee thought for a moment. "Negative, sir. I wasn't aware of Captain Haas's assignment to Lunakor or of the specifics of his actions during that operation. In fact, I don't know who the man is, Viceroy. I wasn't briefed on Delta mission parameters and objectives."

Viceroy Hunt's face was as serious and sullen as Lee had ever seen. "Admiral Lee, under your watch, Captain Tim Haas smuggled a biological weapon, a virus engineered to attack the Zodarks, and released it on Lunakor."

"What?!" Lee asked, practically shouting.

"Yes," said Hunt. "We haven't brought him in for his own disciplinary hearing yet, but we have him dead to rights. His actions almost cost us our place in the Alliance."

"My God…" The implications of what the Viceroy had just told him made Lee's skin crawl.

"Frankly, if we weren't in the middle of a war right now, you'd be relieved of your command," Hunt explained. "However, we are short experienced officers at your level."

Admiral Lee shifted uncomfortably in his seat. *How hard is the hammer about to hit?* he wondered.

"The rank you've currently attained is the highest you are going to go," Hunt proclaimed. "Some time after the war has ended, you will be retired, honorably of course."

This effectively ends my career, Lee realized, feeling like he'd been punched in the gut. He had been on a trajectory to become a four-star admiral, and now he was going to go away into obscurity, drifting away into the dark of night.

He straightened his spine. "I disagree with your decision, but I accept it. I would like to make one request," said Admiral Lee.

"Understandable. What's your request?" asked Hunt.

"I'd like to be here when you mete out Captain Tim Haas's punishment," Lee replied.

"Done."

****

Captain Tim Haas strode into the meeting room with a bit of swagger. All of the heavy hitters were there, including the Viceroy himself. His Special Forces group commander and his Fleet commander were also present, but there was no sense in being downtrodden.

I know what this is, he realized. *It's time to pay the piper.*

"Captain Haas, we have convened this tribunal to investigate something that happened in the Gravaxia system," announced Viceroy Miles Hunt, cutting to the chase. "We suspect that you know what happened and why you've been summoned here. Would you like to *tell* us what happened?"

Captain Haas swallowed, pulled back his shoulders, and replied, "You're right, I do know why this tribunal has been convened. In fact, I was wondering when this was going to happen."

Admiral McKee gasped quietly at his audacity.

Haas turned to his commander. "I take full responsibility for what I did, but I'm not sorry that I did it," he said. "My cousins, aunts, and uncles were all killed—murdered in cold blood—and someone needed to make the Zodarks pay for that."

"That's not your decision to make, Captain," said Bailey, speaking with a booming voice that almost caused Haas to shrink back. "Your decision could impact *all* of humanity and our standing in this alliance. Your selfishness and your pursuit of vengeance have endangered everything we've worked for."

"There's no reason to hold a trial," said Viceroy Hunt. "You're guilty. You've admitted that you're guilty. We have all the evidence, and your co-conspirator has admitted he provided it to you."

Captain Tim Haas nodded ever so slightly, acknowledging that what the Viceroy had just said was all true.

"The Emperor recalled *me* to interrogate me about this incident," Hunt explained. "He has extended some grace to the Republic, but that grace was not extended to you. Emperor Tiberius SuVee has demanded your life as punishment. To keep this matter quiet, you will be transferred immediately to the Gallentines and your sentence will be carried out with them.

"As far as your family is concerned, you will have died in a training accident, not combat. You lost that honor. Your benefits will be paid out to your family, which is more than you deserve. May God have mercy on your soul."

Captain Haas didn't cry as he was led away. The only regret that he had was knowing that his children would grow up without him. His vengeance may have put their alliance in danger, but he also knew it could have been the very thing that saved them.

Chapter Twenty-One

Early December 2114
RNS *Vega*
Task Force 28
Pfeinstgard System

Admiral Lee had resumed command of TF 28 upon his arrival in the system. A holographic display floated above Lee's desk. He scrolled through the data from the recent simulated orbital bombardment and ground invasion against a Zodark system.

Even though his visit to speak with the Viceroy and Admiral Bailey bit at him, he did his best to put the odd meeting out of his mind. After several days of travel, he'd finally landed back on the *Vega*. In preparation to enter the Gravaxia system through the massive stargate looming nearby, he and the fleet had spent the last few days engaged in training exercises with the Primord fleet.

The aroma of freshly brewed coffee freshened up the air, a luxury Lee indulged in daily. Beside the coffeemaker, a small table held an assortment of mugs, each bearing the insignia of a ship he'd served on throughout his career. Above the coffee, a wooden cross hung on the wall. A well-worn Bible rested on a small shelf across from it, its pages dog-eared and filled with handwritten notes.

While he reviewed the simulation data, Lee's mind drifted back to the intense practice session. The simulation results were promising, but real combat was unpredictable. The Zodarks were a formidable enemy, and he couldn't shake the feeling that this conflict would test them in ways they couldn't anticipate. Unlike the last time they'd pushed into Sol, this time, the Zodarks would be more prepared.

Lee closed his eyes, replaying key moments from the simulation in his mind. The initial bombardment had been perfect, striking the Zodarks with devastating effect. The swift adjustments made to firing patterns, covering weak spots that emerged into different sectors, and the deployment of ground forces had gone smoothly.

A soft chime interrupted him. His office screen flickered, revealing the sharp features of Primord Admiral Bjork Stavanger. The man's stern expression filled the screen, his eyes looking right through Lee.

161

What imposing features, he thought. Stavanger's elongated, pointed ears framed a face dominated by an extremely prominent needlelike nose.

"Admiral Lee." Stavanger's deep voice resonated through the room. "I trust you've reviewed the simulation data?"

Lee straightened in his chair. "Yes, Admiral. We've made significant improvements in our response times and coordination."

"Good. Admiral, our combined fleet is nearly assembled at the rally point. The final contingent of our heavy cruisers will arrive soon. I've received new intelligence suggesting the Zodarks have fortified their defenses, but they're not expecting a strike of this magnitude. We have the element of surprise, but we can't afford to be complacent. I've ordered all our ships to run final systems checks. We should review the assault strategy one last time before we make the jump."

"New intelligence? What exactly have you learned?" Lee asked.

"The reports indicate they're reinforcing their orbital platforms," Stavanger explained. "But new intelligence confirms that even though Zodarks are indeed bolstering their orbital defenses, their stargate perimeter patrols have noticeably decreased. It's an unusual tactical shift. This change in their patrol patterns is... concerning. Perhaps they're reallocating resources due to internal pressures we're unaware of."

"Then we need to revise our initial approach," Lee countered.

"Aye, Admiral," Stavanger said. "I want our recon units on high alert as we approach. We'll need to proceed with extreme caution and be prepared for any eventuality."

"Agreed."

"From your shift in posture, I can see you have a little disagreement with something I've suggested." Stavanger leaned forward. "What would you suggest, Admiral?"

Lee unfolded his arms, which he now realized he had crossed reflexively. "Our stealth tech worked well last time, but they've had time to adapt," he explained. "We can't rely solely on that advantage."

"With all due respect, our stealth capabilities are still our best bet for infiltration," Stavanger insisted. "We've made improvements since your last incursion."

"I appreciate the upgrades, but we need more than just technological superiority. We need tactical unpredictability—a multipronged approach," Lee said, pulling up a holographic display of the Gravaxia system. "I've been looking this over recently. I say we use stealth tech, yes, but we also create a diversion—something to keep their sensors occupied while we slip the bulk of our forces through."

Stavanger studied the display, his expression thoughtful. "A feint attack on their outer defense perimeter?"

"Precisely. We send in a small, highly maneuverable task force to engage their outer defenses. Make it look like we're probing for weaknesses."

"While our main fleet slips through under stealth," Stavanger finished. "It could work, but the timing would be critical. We'd need perfect synchronization."

"That's where you come in, Stavanger," Lee said. "Will some of your fleet be willing to lead the diversionary force? Your military's expertise in hit-and-run tactics will be crucial."

"My task force would be extremely vulnerable," Stavanger insisted.

"I'm aware of the risks," Lee said. "But we need people we can trust to pull this off. Those who can improvise if things go sideways. You have experts among your fleet who've been at war for over a hundred years and have the ability to do what I'm thinking."

"Interesting," Stavanger said. "We can make it work. So, let's talk specifics."

"I want to utilize our new ECM suites to create false sensor readings. Make it look like we have a larger force than we actually do."

"Our force is very large."

"We'll make it appear even bigger."

"I see."

"And," Lee continued, "we'll need to time it perfectly with our main thrust through the stargate."

"How long do you calculate we can maintain the element of surprise once we're through?"

Lee's face darkened with concern. "Realistically? No more than thirty minutes. Maybe less if they've improved their detection capabilities."

"That's not much time," Stavanger said.

"No, it's not. Which is why we need to prioritize our objectives," Lee said. "So, here's what we do. Your diversionary force engages their outer defenses here and here." He indicated points on the display. "Meanwhile, a few ships in what I'll label your stealth fleet push through the stargate and make a beeline for that control node where our intelligence suggests the primary command is located. If we can take it out, we'll cripple their ability to coordinate a system-wide defense. It's the best way to crack these Zodarks wide open, and they'll lose the fight before they know what's happening."

"We'll need to punch through their defensive screen quickly," Stavanger said.

"Agreed," Lee replied.

"Remember, our window of opportunity is small," explained Stavanger.

"Just one thing," Lee said. "If things go south, don't hesitate to pull out. We need your teams alive for the long game."

Stavanger remained expressionless. "For this, I'm calling a comm meeting of all commanders in the fleet in two hours. We need to adjust our plans accordingly."

"I'll be there, Admiral."

Stavanger held up a finger. "I have some concerns about your initial bombardment strategy from what I observed in the simulations."

Oh, I guess we're going to talk some more, thought Lee. "I'm eager to hear your assessment, sir," he said aloud.

"In your most recent sims, your attack patterns were far too predictable," Stavanger said. "The concentrated fire on the simulated moon at sector one-two-seven-point-five by four-five-point-three left your flanks exposed. Any competent Zodark commander would have exploited that weakness."

"Thank you for pointing that out, sir," Lee said. "I'll adjust our approach to incorporate more randomized targeting sequences. We'll get back into the training simulations soon and see where we calculated the approach incorrectly."

"See that you do," Stavanger replied. "And what about your coverage of Sectors Two and Five? The lag time in your fire support was unacceptable."

"Acknowledged, and that didn't slip by me. We've already implemented new protocols to reduce response times. I estimate we can cut the lag by forty percent in our next drill."

"Better. Now, explain your rationale for the ground force deployment along vector two-two-five."

"Yes, Admiral," Lee said, calling up the relevant data on his screen. "We chose a thirty-degree approach angle to maximize cover from the terrain features in quadrant Beta-9. Our simulations showed a sixty-two percent reduction in projected casualties compared to a direct assault."

"Interesting. But did you consider the impact on your air support capabilities? That approach severely limits your options for close-air support."

"A valid point. We'll reassess our air support coordination to ensure we maintain optimal coverage throughout the engagement."

"See that you do, Lee."

"Understood, Admiral. We'll revise our strategies and run additional simulations to address these issues. I assure you, we'll be ready before we invade."

Stavanger held Lee's gaze for a long moment before nodding. "Very well. I expect a full report on your revised battle plans within forty-eight hours."

"I'll have that report to you in thirty-six."

As Lee absorbed the critique, Stavanger's tone shifted. "Now, I must commend you on your quick adaptation to the Zodarks' simulated frequency jamming. Your decision to switch to light signaling communications was brilliant. I've never seen a captain act so effectively in the face of unexpected electronic warfare. Your fleet maintained cohesion. They continued to execute difficult maneuvers despite the communications blackout."

The edges of Lee's mouth curled up ever so slightly. It was the best he could do at accepting the compliment.

During the training exercise, the simulation had included the loss of all electronic and quantum communication across all ships in Lee's fleet. All communication officers were trained in Morse code, and they had worked flawlessly with one another, using directional light beams to transmit messages from ship to ship.

Stavanger replayed a segment of the battle, highlighting Lee's star carrier. "At timestamp 05:12:09, you recognized the jamming field's signature and immediately ordered the switch to light signaling comms. Within forty-seven seconds, your entire fleet had adapted, and you were able to coordinate a devastating counterattack on the Zodarks."

Lee allowed himself a small nod of acknowledgment. "Thank you, Admiral."

"Keep honing that adaptability. It may well be the key to our victory in Gravaxia. From this point forward, I'll continue to observe our combined sim operations. We'll become one, Admiral."

"Agreed, sir," said Lee.

"Good."

As Admiral Stavanger's image faded from the holodisplay, Admiral Lee felt the Primord's after-action report had been fair. He pivoted to his battle management system and accessed recent combat simulations. He'd review all scenarios, from the initial sim engagement to yesterday's, and he'd do so prior to the joint operations briefing with his task force commanders. In the simulations, he'd identify both vulnerabilities and force multipliers in the combined Earther and Primord fleet maneuvers, committing all of it to memory while logging pertinent data for further analysis.

Post-briefing, he'd resume his intensive study of simulated offensive and defensive strategies until the end of the day. Tomorrow, his crew and fleet would return to war games, ironing out inefficiencies until they achieved peak combat effectiveness. The next day promised another grueling cycle of preparation.

"Here we go," he told himself, rolling up his sleeves and hunkering down. "Time to dig in."

Chapter Twenty-Two

High Council Chamber
Drokanis, Zinconia
Zodark Home World

Zon Otro entered the High Council Chamber with the weight of the Empire pressing heavily on his shoulders. The air was thick with tension as the Council members stood to acknowledge his presence before taking their seats. The chamber, usually filled with the murmur of discussion, was now eerily silent, the gravity of the situation hanging over them all like a dark cloud.

Otro took his seat at the head of the long table, his eyes narrowing as he looked at the assembled Council members. Mavkah Griglag, the head of the Malvari, and his deputy, NOS Tarvox Nilkar, sat at the opposite end of the room, their expressions hard and resolute as they waited to be called forward to walk through the blue flames of the Circle of Truth. Notably absent, of course, was the Groff. This was a deliberate move on Otro's part. He wanted to focus solely on the military situation at hand, not petty issues or the perceived personal slights in which Vak'Atioth found comfort in wallowing these days.

"We all know why we're here," Otro began, his voice low and steady. "The Gravaxia system is on the verge of being invaded again, this time by a combined force from the Republic, the Primords, the Altairians, and even the Tully. If the Groff is to be believed, even the Tully—as weak as they are—have committed half a million of their soldiers to this fight. This is not the first time the Republic and their allies have attempted to seize control of Gravaxia. We were fortunate that during their last attempt to seize the system, the Malvari had devised a clever ambush that caught the Republic by surprise, ultimately forcing a hasty retreat from the system after sustaining heavy losses. That plan worked last time. Now, we need a new plan, a stratagem that will once again turn the tide of battle in our favor," explained Otro as he made eye contact with each of the Council members before turning his gaze to settle on the Mavkah and his deputy. "We cannot afford to lose Gravaxia, but we also cannot ignore the threat that loss will pose to Tueblets. I need to know what the Malvari is doing to ensure this system doesn't fall and what you are doing to fortify Tueblets. Now step forward into the Circle of Truth and answer our questions."

Griglag stood and looked to the center of the Council Chamber, where the Circle of Truth sat, casting long shadows under the harsh lights and glaring eyes of those who sat in judgment on the Council and guided the Empire. He stepped forward and walked through the blue flame, its ominous light enhancing the scars of countless battles that lined his face.

Once through the cleansing flame of Lindow, Griglag returned his gaze, unwavering as he stood ready to speak. "Great Zon, Council members, I bring with me good news from the shipyards of Tueblets. Three of our new *Plarix*-class heavy battleships, the *Drexol*, the *Fendal*, and the *Grax*, have completed their training to join the fleet. In the days following my appointment as Mavkah, the Malvari commissioned the construction of thirty of these hulls to be built at an accelerated pace. As we speak, every seven days, a new hull is laid down and another is completed. To address your question about reinforcing Gravaxia and Tueblets, out of every two ships we complete, we are sending one to join the defenses in Gravaxia while the other stays to reinforce Tueblets—"

"Three battleships!" interrupted Councillor Gorax as he shouted in shocked disbelief at what he was hearing. "Zon Otro, surely within the Malvari we have more competent NOSs we can make Mavkah than this berinx."[3] Gorax spat the words out of his mouth like warm water, glaring with contempt at Griglag as he continued his rant. "We ask what the Malvari are doing to prepare the Gravaxia system to repel an invasion and all the Mavkah can tell us is the Malvari is sending three battleships!" screeched Gorax.

Bang, bang.

"Enough, Gorax!" Zon Otro shouted as he slammed the Rock of Order against the surface of the dais they sat upon. "You go too far, Gorax, insulting the Mavkah! I have called this meeting to learn what steps the Malvari are taking to prepare for this invasion, not to have the Mavkah insulted by you over whatever hurt feelings you still harbor over the loss of a few ship-building contracts. Mavkah, why don't you explain to the Council how these new warships are going to make a difference in the coming battles to assuage their concerns?"

---

[3] Berinx is the Zodark word for children up to the age of six, similar to toddler.

Griglag nodded. "Yes, of course, Great Zon. These new Plarix-class battleships are unlike any warships we have previously built, and it is the Plarix that the Malvari believe will save the Empire and restore what has been lost. The size of the ship has been greatly increased, allowing us to double the complement of starfighters and bombers they can carry. Another major change with this class of battleship is our introduction of a magnetic railgun system into the main armaments. The Republic has shown us just how powerful a kinetic-based weapon can be. The Plarix battleships will now boast this offensive capability as well. Defense-wise, we have redesigned the armor belt and added a meter of specially engineered metallurgical and composite materials designed to protect against the Republic's kinetic weapons. This is in addition to the improved laser batteries and antiship missile magazines. The Plarix ships will be more than a match to counter the Republic's new class of star carriers and battleships. These ships are the most powerful we've ever built, and they'll be at the forefront of our defense in the Gravaxia and Tueblets systems."

Otro nodded along as he listened, though his expression remained grim. "Mavkah, three Plarix battleships are a start, but we both know it won't be enough to stem the tide of warships marshaling against us in Pfeinstgard. The allied fleet, led by the Republic, has grown into a vast armada. This isn't a skirmish or probing attack. This is an invasion fleet, a force assembled for one purpose—to conquer. Tell us, Mavkah, how do you and the Malvari plan on defending Gravaxia? What is your stratagem to hold it, to beat back this invasion force gathering along our border?"

Griglag breathed slowly, allowing his mind to form the thoughts, then put words to them. He exchanged a glance with NOS Tarvox, who had joined him in the Circle of Truth, before responding. "Great Zon, I have given the situation much thought, examining previous battles we have waged against the Altairians, the Primords, and the Tully prior to the appearance of the human-led Republic. I recalled battles of the past in search of a stratagem that might yet work. One day, while I was thinking, I fell into a deep slumber. It was during this period of sleep when I believe the great god Lindow replayed a series of battles you and I fought together. Do you remember the Siege of Intus?" asked Griglag.

Zon Otro nodded. "I do, Mavkah—that was many dracmas ago. What of this long-ago battle, and how does it pertain to our current situation?"

Griglag nodded at the question. "During the siege of the planet Intus, the Primords would not give up control of the system no matter how hard we fought. And then we discovered they had built a series of forts and other defensive structures within the Spritzers ice belt, not far from the stargate, that connected the rest of the Primord territory. Each time we would engage one of their forts or defensive structures, two or three more would be in range to help protect it. This defensive strategy caused us to lose many ships until we eventually overwhelmed them with our mass.

"What I propose doing with the Gravaxia system is to expand upon this strategy and make it ours. It worked back then for the Primords. I believe we can make it work in Gravaxia," explained Griglag. "What we have begun to do is reinforce our positions on the key planets and moons in the system. Additional ground forces have been deployed, and fighter and bomber squadrons have been increased and dispersed to operate from many smaller makeshift bases we have established in the different asteroids and ice belts. The Malvari is doing everything within our power to strengthen our defenses and prepare to repel this invasion."

Tarvox, who had remained silent to this point, leaned in, his voice more measured but no less determined. "My Zon, we also have another option—a more... unconventional approach. We've begun modifying our groupings of interplanetary fast-patrol boats, transforming them into what we're calling 'Victory ships.' These vessels will be rigged with specially configured Arkanorian reactors. For the purpose we have in mind, we have changed how the magnetic shielding around the reactor operates. In this situation, we have deliberately configured the containment field to fail upon the ship's destruction or impact with an enemy vessel or something of similar mass."

He paused, letting the words and meaning of this sink in before continuing. "When the containment field fails, the reactor will go critical, unleashing an explosion comparable to fifty megatons of explosive power and radiation damage. The power of this detonation against or near the hull of a Republic warship could destroy or severely cripple it. To be clear, we aren't talking about a handful or even a few dozen patrol ships being rigged like this. We are looking at rigging hundreds, perhaps

170

even a thousand of these ships, lying dormant in wait to hurl themselves en masse to overwhelm the enemy's ability to defend against them."

The room suddenly became deathly silent as Otro and the Council members processed this information. The idea was bold, brutal, and utterly ruthless—exactly what the situation demanded.

"The Republic has pushed us to the brink," Zon Otro said, his voice growing colder with each word. "They've turned the Guristas against us; they're threatening the very heart of the Empire—Tueblets. If we lose Gravaxia, Tueblets will be next, and with it, everything we have ever fought for—the Empire."

Zon Otro fixed his gaze on Griglag. "Mavkah, how many of these Victory ships does the Malvari have, and how fast can we build more?"

Tarvox whispered to Griglag before he answered, "We have one hundred and thirty-seven ready for immediate use. Another seventy-three are being converted to Victory ships, with shipyard capacity now reaching ninety-two new vessels a month."

Otro bunched his eyebrows. "Mavkah, if my math is correct, this means we have two hundred and ten ready or nearly ready for immediate use, with no more than ninety-two additional ships each month. Is that correct?"

Griglag nodded. "Ninety-two vessels is the most we can rig for this kind of use—the bottleneck isn't the shipyards, it's the reactors. Since we can only build so many a month, that is why I don't recommend we deploy them to Gravaxia. The moment these vessels are used, their element of surprise will be gone. We will have one chance for these Victory ships to surprise our enemies—it needs to count."

Zon Otro stared down Tarvox. "I want as many of these Victory ships built and deployed to protect Tueblets as possible. We will give the enemy no quarter. The Republic thinks they can defeat us with their numbers and technology, but they underestimate our resolve."

Griglag nodded firmly. "The ships will be ready, my Zon. We'll make sure the Republic understands what the true cost of trying to defeat our Empire."

A sadistic smile spread across Otro's lips. His eyes swept over the Council, his resolve hardening. "We fight for our survival, for the future of the Zodark Empire. We must prepare for battle, and may Lindow guide us to victory."

The Council members stood as Zon Otro rose from his seat, the weight of his decision clear in his eyes. The Zodark Empire was on the brink of invasion, but under his leadership, they would fight until their last breath. The Republic would learn the hard way that the Zodarks were not to be underestimated.

Chapter Twenty-Three

RNS *Vega*
Task Force 28
Pfeinstgard System

Coop's brow furrowed as he swiped through the data on his pad. "Looks like Nomad pulled off some impressive maneuvers in the asteroid field simulation," he said.

"Barely scraped by, if you ask me," Riggs grunted. "His vector control was sloppy at best."

"Come on, Riggs. He navigated that debris field like a pro," Coop insisted.

"A 'pro' wouldn't have clipped that chunk of space rock at the 2:13 mark. In real combat, that's the difference between coming home and being space dust."

"It was either that or finding himself splattered across the asteroid," said Coop. "He made a split-second decision, and it was correct."

Riggs only nodded. "Maybe I need to see the vid again."

Thing was, Coop knew that Riggs had a point, as usual. Normally, Nomad would have slipped through that narrow a margin without a scrape to the expensive starfighter he piloted. He'd need to keep an eye on Nomad these next few training sessions. Sometimes, Coop needed was a good night's sleep, and his reflexes returned to normal—he hoped the same would be true for Nomad.

Coop moved on to the next report. "Badger's kill ratio in the dogfight sim is off the charts."

"Nothing new there," Riggs insisted. "His fuel management could use work. He's burning too hot on his attack runs."

"Still grounding him when we go into combat. I don't think he understands the concept of, let alone the word, 'wingman.'"

"You should keep him on the ground," Riggs said. "Kill counts won't mean much if he flames out midbattle."

They continued through the sim reports, Coop finding positives where he could, while Riggs's ability to uncover every flaw kept a good balance between the two.

As they neared the end, Coop exhaled. "Lance and Boomer have really stepped up their game. They'll be ready for Gravaxia."

Riggs raised an eyebrow. "You sure about that, Coop? Their formation flying still needs work. Saw some dangerous gaps in their last patrol sim."

"True, but their reaction times have improved drastically. They're anticipating each other better now. Still, we'll run them through more tight-quarters drills. Get that muscle memory locked in."

"Roger that," Riggs said. "And make sure they're prepped for long-range engagement scenarios."

"This invasion... we're going to lose good people, Riggs. Just like Alfheim."

Riggs's eyes darkened at the mention of that bloody engagement. "Hell of a fight, that one. Lost what, half our squadron? We had a good commander, though."

"Seventeen pilots dead," Coop said, the number etched into his memory. "We gave as good as we got, though. Took out two of those damned *Tikiona*-class supercarriers."

"Damn straight we did." Riggs nodded. "Watched Kiwi and her wingman fly straight into that carrier's bow, missiles blazing. Never seen anything like it."

Coop's throat tightened at the memory. "They knew what they were signing up for. Took out that wormhole tech and cut off the Orbots' reinforcements."

"Between you and me, I think that move saved the whole system," Riggs agreed, a rare note of admiration in his voice. "But the cost..."

A heavy silence fell between them. Coop stared at the data pad in his hand, but his mind was light-years away, replaying the fiery destruction of those supercarriers, the desperate maneuvers of his fellow pilots as they fought against overwhelming odds.

"Losing good souls is never easy," Coop said.

Riggs grunted in agreement, his eyes staring at the far wall. He rubbed his hands together slowly as if remembering an unpleasant time in his life.

"We lead our space wing from the front," Coop said. "Like usual. They need to see us out there taking the same risks."

Riggs rested back in his chair, a ghost of a smile on his face. "You know, Cooper, sometimes I think you're too soft on officers, on everyone. But then you say something like that, and I remember why you're in charge of this motley crew."

"High praise, coming from you, old man."

"Don't let it go to your head. We've got a long road ahead of us." Riggs's expression lifted when he grinned. "At break, to clear my head, I watched the latest episode of *Galactic Hedge*. Did you take a gander?"

Coop's eyes lit up. "Oh man, that twist with the Centauri hedge fund manager? I didn't see that coming!"

"Right?" Riggs chuckled. "Thought for sure he was working with the cartel."

"Same here. But then, bam—he's actually a deep-cover agent for the securities commission. And that scene where he's transferring the encrypted ledgers while dodging weapons fire?"

Riggs snorted. "Pure fantasy. No way you're pulling off those moves in a three-piece suit."

"Hey, maybe Centauri tailoring is just that good," Coop laughed. "But seriously, when Zara hacked into the vault using that modified tachyon emitter? No way that would work in real life, though. You'd need, what, a small star's worth of energy to generate those kinds of tachyon fluxes?"

"At least. But it made for some good TV. And that chase sequence through the zero-g trading floor?"

"Oh yeah, when the gravity cut out and all those holoscreens started floating?" Coop's eyes glimmered with excitement. "I was on the edge of my seat."

"You should've seen your face just now. Looked just like Dimes after his first successful barrel roll."

"Hey, can you blame me? It's not every day you see a firefight break out in the middle of a futures trade."

"True enough. Though I've got to say, if I was writing it, I'd have had Zara use that quantum entanglement device she picked up in episode three."

Coop nodded. "Yep, that would've been perfect. Instant secure comms, no chance of interception."

"Exactly. And maybe throw in a double-cross from that info broker. What was his name again?"

"Connor," Coop said. "Or something like that. And, yeah, that guy's definitely playing both sides. No way he's just a 'concerned citizen.'"

Riggs snorted. "My money's on him being the real mastermind behind the whole scheme."

"Well, theoretically—" Coop began but was interrupted by a burst of static from the room's holodisplay.

The air shimmered, coalescing into the stern visage of Admiral Lee. His voice filled the room as it reverberated through the ship's intercom system.

"Attention, all personnel. This is Admiral Lee. The fleet is preparing for imminent departure through the stargate. All hands to battle stations. I repeat, all hands to battle stations. We jump in twenty minutes."

The hologram flickered out, leaving Coop and Riggs staring at each other. They, along with all personnel aboard the carrier, had just received orders for an imminent jump through the stargate into the Gravaxia system. A prior mission briefing had emphasized minimal prep time, as their window of opportunity was narrow.

Covert Primord special operation teams had been tasked with sabotaging the enemy's early-warning systems and defensive grid. The entire fleet would be given the go-ahead when intel came through showing that Zodark forces were at reduced readiness with their perimeter defenses compromised.

This opening would allow the entire Republic and Primord armada to make a coordinated jump into the Gravaxia system, catching the Zodarks off guard, initiating the invasion when the enemy's response time would be at its slowest.

"Well," Riggs said, pushing himself to his feet. "Guess *Galactic Hedge* will have to wait."

"Looks like we're about to star in our own high-stakes drama," Coop responded.

Riggs headed for the door. "Let's hope it has a better ending than last season's finale."

Coop followed close behind. The weight of responsibility settled heavily onto his shoulders as they stepped into the corridor, the ship already abuzz with increased activity.

As they made their way to the flight deck, crewmen rushed past, each focused on their assigned tasks.

Coop ran through preflight checklists in his mind, the easy camaraderie of their TV discussion a distant memory, replaced by the cold reality of impending combat.

Once they reached the flight deck, the space was alive with the whine of engines, along with the shouts of deck crews. Pilots scrambled to their fighters, and tech teams performed last-minute checks, the air thick with the smell of fuel.

"See you on the other side, Captain," Riggs said.

With a final nod, they parted ways. Each headed to his respective fighter. After Coop climbed into his cockpit, the canopy lowered, sealing him in. Around him, the other pilots of his large space wing ran through their preflight sequences. Through the comms, he could hear the steady stream of status reports and system checks for nearly ten minutes.

As the launch countdown began, Coop took a deep breath, centering himself. The familiar cockpit surrounded him, every switch and display exactly where it should be. This was real, and every time he went into combat, he always felt numb until his first engagement.

The deck officer's voice blared over the comms. "All fighters, prepare for launch when Admiral Lee gives the go."

Coop's fingers moved over the controls: engines primed, weapons systems online, armor at full capacity. He pressed the comm. "This is Captain Cooper. Stay sharp out there. Watch each other's backs, stick to your training, and we'll all come home. Good hunting."

"Alpha Squadron, we're the initial fliers in our wing. We'll be launching immediately after the jump to establish space superiority. Bravo and Charlie Squadrons will follow on my mark. Delta and Echo Squadrons, you're our reserve. Be ready to launch at a moment's notice. Remember, our primary objectives are to neutralize any remaining orbital defenses and screen for *Vega* and other ally vessels. Omega Squadron, you're on standby for close space support. Keep those engines hot." Omega was where he'd placed Badger, right where the man belonged.

"Any questions?" Coop asked.

A chorus of "No, sir!" came through the comms.

"All right, people. Let's make it count. Cooper out."

Affirmative responses echoed back. Everyone was ready. The plan was set. Moments after *Vega* and the rest of the fleet entered and exited the stargate, Coop's space wing would launch. Their mission: to shoot down as many Zodark fighters as possible.

Chapter Twenty-Four

RNS *Vega*
Task Force 28
Pfeinstgard System

Admiral Lee stood on the RNS *Vega*'s bridge, his hands clasped behind his back as he gazed out at space beyond the viewscreen. His crew busied themselves at their stations, waiting for the imminent call.

Without warning, the main screen came to life. The official seal of the Primord fleet materialized on the display until it faded, replaced by the visage of Admiral Bjork Stavanger.

"Admiral Lee." Stavanger's voice blared through the speakers. "Given that our previous strategy has already been implemented with exceptional outcomes, I'm pleased to inform you that everything has progressed according to plan thus far."

"It's good to see you, Admiral," Lee replied. "As you can tell, I have returned, and brought along some new toys for us to play with. Our new flagship, the *Vega*, packs a hell of a punch, and we are now carrying nearly four hundred starfighters and bombers."

"Those two space wings will sure come in handy," Stavanger commented. "I have more good news. The deployment of our compact task forces to challenge the Zodarks' external defenses went better than planned. We are now prepared to advance to the next stage of our attack."

"Excellent, sir," said Lee.

"Your fleet will spearhead the diversionary force, and you will take lead," Stavanger said, reminding him of the battle plan they'd discussed weeks prior. "We've positioned specialized satellites in strategic locations across the system. When we activate them, they will begin spoofing the Zodark sensors, making them believe there is a larger force than there is, and that we are headed in different directions from our actual intended destination.

"Despite our force already being substantial, we are determined to make it appear even more formidable as you suggested. The timing of our move through the stargate must also align flawlessly with the diversion to maximize surprise.

"So, Admiral, the time is now. Not too long ago, we located the node housing the primary command center and have neutralized it. This single act will greatly disrupt their capacity to coordinate a system-wide defense. Get your men and women ready—it's time to move through the star system and start our incursion."

Lee's spine stiffened. They were going to war. "Understood, sir. Follow my lead."

Stavanger's image nodded once, then vanished, leaving the bridge in a moment of silence.

Lee eyed the faces of his bridge crew as they all waited for his word. His eyes settled on the communications officer, Rodriguez, her dark hair pulled back, her fingers hovering over her console. "Lieutenant Rodriguez, broadcast to all ships in the fleet. Prepare for immediate stargate entry. I'll be on the comms soon."

"Aye, sir. Broadcasting now." Rodriguez pressed a holographic button, her voice clear as she relayed the order across all fleet command channels.

"Navigator," Lee called out. "Status report."

Lieutenant Reynolds kept his focus on the monitors at his station. "Sir, coordinates for the Gravaxia system stargate locked in. Awaiting your command."

The main viewscreen shifted, displaying the massive structure that would catapult them across light-years in the blink of an eye. The stargate's outer ring shined silver, crafted from an alloy harder than diamond. Within the ring swirled the heart of the gate—a field of energy pulsing with mystical hues. Streaks of electric blue and vibrant purple twisted around each other, occasionally shot through with flashes of crimson and gold.

Lee allowed himself a moment to marvel at the sight. No matter how many times he'd seen it, the raw power contained within the breathtaking vortex never failed to instill amazement.

Lee sat in his captain's chair, his XO sitting to his right. They gave a respectful nod to one another before Lee tapped the comm panel on his command seat's armrest. "Engineering, status. I'm talking to you, MacGregor."

"Aye, Admiral. Engines purring like a kitten that's had too much catnip, sir," said MacGregor. "We're ready to dance with the devil."

"Colorful as always, MacGregor. How's our core stability?"

"Steady as a rock, sir," MacGregor said. "I've got her at one hundred and three percent efficiency. Any more and she might start singing opera."

"Emergency power reserves?" Lee asked.

"Topped off and eager to join the party. I've rigged up a little surprise too. If we need it, I can divert power from nonessential systems faster than you can say 'haggis.'"

"Good work." Lee nodded. "I need every ounce of power you can give us, as always."

"Don't you worry, Admiral," MacGregor replied. "My crew down here are ready."

"Keep them in line, Mac. We're counting on you."

"Aye, sir. Won't let you down."

As the comm channel closed, Commander Connor Rhom spoke up. "Weapon systems primed and ready, sir. All ships reporting battle-ready status. The *Vega*'s at full combat readiness as well. Twenty-four twin-barreled antiship turbo lasers all charged, targeting systems calibrated. Twenty twin-barreled twenty-four-inch magrail turrets, locked and loaded. Two hundred fifty antiship missiles ready, sir. Fighter complement at full strength."

"Outstanding." Lee pressed the button to activate the fleet-wide communication channel. "Attention, all personnel. In moments, we will cross into Zodark territory. The next few hours will test us in ways we've never been tested before. Each of you represents the best of humanity—your training, your dedication, your unwavering commitment to protecting our way of life. Our actions today will echo through the ages. We fight not just for ourselves, but for every man, woman, and child across the galaxy who looks to the stars and dreams of peace.

"I have faith: faith in each of you, faith in our cause, faith in the unbreakable spirit of humanity. To your stations, all of you. Whatever comes, we face it together. For Earth, for humanity, for the future!"

He switched off the comms. "Helm, take us in."

Several screens popped up on the main display, showing a panoramic view of their fleet. The sight took Lee's breath away. The RNS *Vega* was second in the formation. Flanking her on either side, the battle cruisers RNS *Artemis* and RNS *Orion* sliced through the darkness like twin blades of steel.

Ahead of them all, the form of the heavy cruiser RNS *Detroit* glided gracefully toward the stargate. This was Lee's old ship, one he had come to feel a deep connection to. And as the *Detroit* approached the event horizon of the gate, the ship's silhouette stretched and distorted for a moment before it was swallowed by the twisting energy field.

The viewscreen panned, revealing more of their armada, including the battleship RNS *Virginia*, its massive gun turrets glinting across its hull. Near the rear of the formation was the bulky shape of the *Jupiter*-class troop transport RNS *Vanguard*, flanked by several of its sister ships. Beside them, a massive orbital assault ship, the RNS *Maddox*, stood at the ready. Their presence was a reminder of the ground forces they carried—men and women ready to fight on alien soil.

The fleet's support vessels came into view next. Lee noted the distinctive profile of several *Saturn*-class fleet replenishment ships, their holds packed with supplies vital for a prolonged campaign. Darting between the larger vessels, corvettes maintained a vigilant patrol, their thinner forms distinctly different compared to the lumbering capital ships.

As the cams moved back to the front of the formation, more ships came into view—the RNS *Nebraska*, its hull scarred from previous engagements, and the pristine forms of the RNS *Liberty* and RNS *Pioneer*, both flak frigates bristling with point-defense weaponry. All in all, fifty human ships and thirty Primord vessels made up Lee's Task Force 28.

Lee nodded to his navigator. "Reynolds, take us through."

On the viewscreen, the stargate loomed larger. As they approached, the gate's energy pulsed with increased intensity—an ethereal light show.

The RNS *Vega* reached the threshold of the gate. For a heartbeat, everything stopped, like time had been paused. With a flash of light momentarily blinding everyone on the bridge, they plunged into the vortex.

Lee's stomach lurched as the familiar sensation of stargate transit came over him. It lasted only a second, but in that instant, he felt his body expanding across light-years of space, only to snap into place like a rubber band.

As quickly as it had begun, it was over. The viewscreen cleared, and straight ahead, a menacing number of Zodark warships hung in space, their predatory bodies in wait to attack.

Before Lee could issue a command, the space between the two fleets erupted in weapons fire. Beams of searing energy lanced out from the Zodark ships, stabbing the human fleet still emerging from the gate.

The *Vega*'s bridge erupted into a flurry of activity. Alarms blared, status reports flooded in from all decks, and crew members shouted updates.

"Execute immediate evasive action," Lee said. "Come to heading zero-nine-five. Redline the engines. I want a thirty-degree starboard turn, now!"

"Aye, Captain. Coming to heading zero-nine-five, executing thirty-degree starboard turn at all ahead flank."

Blast it, Lee thought. So much for his strategy of using their Primord allies to hit the Zodarks' key defensive positions to delay them. All it had done was make the Zodarks angrier.

Lee gripped the arms of his command chair as the RNS *Vega* banked hard, enemy fire clipping her bow. "Once we complete the turn, be ready to adjust course to one-two-zero if needed," he ordered. "We need to close some distance between us and those contacts."

Zodarks disliked close-quarter fighting when it came to fleet battles. Apparently, the pounding of magrails had drilled too many holes in their heads.

"Understood, sir. Standing by for further course adjustments."

Admiral Lee opened a channel to the entire armada. "All ships, return fire! The battle starts now!"

The *Vega* shuddered as its magrails opened up, sending rounds of destructive death hurtling toward the Zodark fleet. Across the formation, other human ships joined in, filling space with a maelstrom of weapons fire.

****

Several Hours Later

The battle assessments kept pouring in for Admiral Lee. So far, he felt cautiously optimistic. Ground forces had established a strong foothold on the moon they'd targeted for capture.

The RA and Primord ground commanders had sent him requests, asking for the remaining ground troops to be committed to finishing the capture of the rest of the Gravaxia system and the other Zodark ground installations there.

Admiral Lee had been impressed by how thoroughly the Primords had defeated the Zodark Navy in the Pfeinstgard system during their absence. The tales of their glorious exploits in battle had already become somewhat legendary among his troops. This newfound confidence in their ally made the decision easy.

Approved, Lee thought as he filled out the appropriate memo via neurolink.

With the stroke of a virtual pen, he had just assigned the rest of his Republic Navy and Primord reserve forces still waiting in Pfeinstgard to be committed to the final capture of the Gravaxia system, which would set the stage for what he believed would become the defining battle to defeat the Zodarks once and for all—the battle for Tueblets. With control of this vital transit system, they would effectively cut the Zodark forces into multiple small sections where none of them would be able to provide the other with help or support.

Chapter Twenty-Five

RNS *Vega*
Task Force 28
Gravaxia System

The RNS *Vega*'s bridge lit up with the flashes of incoming energy beams. Emergency alerts blinked on the main screen, showing damage reports from combat.

Gotta get closer, Lee thought. Close range was where the Republic always did the most damage.

"Reynolds, hard to starboard! Bring us about to heading three-one-five, pitch negative twenty degrees!"

"Aye, sir. Bringing about to heading three-one-five, pitch negative twenty degrees."

Lee felt the deck shift beneath his feet as the giant star carrier responded. The stars on the main viewscreen blurred into streaks as the *Vega* heeled over, narrowly avoiding a barrage of enemy fire.

"New heading zero-four-five, full impulse!" Lee ordered.

Reynolds nodded. "Aye, Admiral. Course zero-four-five, full impulse."

Lee watched the tactical display. A cluster of Zodark ships were attempting to move farther from Lee's task force, but Lee's fleet closed in fast. The entire Zodark fleet filled the main display. Wicked-looking protrusions jutted from their hulls at odd angles, each one bristling with weaponry.

"Multiple heavy cruisers and battleships launching torpedoes," Commander Rhom reported.

Dozens of glowing projectiles streaked toward the Republic and Primord fleet. Moments later, lances of light shot out from the Zodark vessels.

"Incoming laser fire!" Rhom shouted.

The bridge rocked as a salvo found its mark.

"Status report," Lee said.

"Armor at ninety-seven, sir," replied XO Sato. "Minor damage to port side. No hull breaches detected."

"Casualties?" Lee asked.

"None reported so far, Admiral," Sato replied. "But Engineering reports power fluctuations in the aft generators. They're working to stabilize them now."

"Good. Keep me updated." Lee's attention moved back to the tactical display. The Zodark battleships formed up into a wedge formation, clearly preparing to punch through Task Force 28's lines. There were sixty-five hostile vessels in all.

Lee keyed the comm. "Coop, launch all squadrons immediately. I want our entire space wing out there. Primary objective: defend the fleet, with emphasis on capital ship protection. Execute! Take out as many Vultures as you can in the process."

Coop's voice answered through the intercom. "Aye-aye, Admiral. Initiating launch sequence for all fighters and bombers. Delta and Echo Squadrons will take point for fleet defense. Alpha, Bravo, and Charlie will form a protective screen around our capital ships. Omega Squadron on standby for rapid response. Launching in T minus thirty seconds."

"Very good, Coop. Keep me updated on squadron status and enemy movements," Lee directed. "We can't afford to lose any of our big guns out there."

"Understood, sir," Coop said. "All pilots are green across the board. First wave launching now. Will maintain open comms and provide real-time tactical updates. Cooper out."

Lee turned his attention back to the main viewscreen, studying the enemy formation. One Zodark battleship stood out, larger than the others—a command ship.

"Concentrate fire on that nearest Zodark battleship," Lee ordered. "Vector zero-four-five mark two."

"Aye, sir," Rhom responded. "Targeting solution locked. Twin-barreled twenty-four-inch magrail turrets aligned. Ready to fire."

Sensor data streamed across a secondary display. Range, velocity, and targeting information scrolled past, updating in real-time. The computer's predictive algorithms outlined the optimal firing solution, factoring in the enemy ship's speed and trajectory.

"Fire!" Lee commanded.

The deck trembled as the *Vega*'s main batteries unleashed their fury. On the viewscreen, brilliant streaks of light darted out toward the targeted Zodark battleship. The magnetically accelerated rounds crossed the space between the vessels in the blink of an eye.

The rounds punched through, slamming into the Zodark ship's hull. Explosions blossomed along its surface, and debris spun away into the void.

"Direct hit," Rhom called out. "Enemy battleship showing significant damage to its port side."

"Good. Maintain fire on that target," Lee said. "Let's take it out of the fight."

As the *Vega*'s guns spoke again, the rest of the human armada and the emerging Primord fleet began engaging the Zodark forces. Eruptions riddled both enemy and ally vessels alike.

The bridge shook as a torpedo found its mark. The armor continued to hold. On the screen, the RNS *Artemis* and RNS *Orion*, two of the fleet's most formidable battle cruisers, moved into position, flanking the damaged Zodark battleship.

"*Artemis* and *Orion* in position, sir," Rhom confirmed. "They're preparing to fire."

"Tell them to let loose everything they've got."

Missiles streaked from the Republic ships. The projectiles impacted against the alien vessel's weakened armor, creating a series of bright flashes that momentarily overloaded the viewscreen's filters.

As the missile barrage subsided, both RNS vessels opened up with their magrail turrets. Streams of hypervelocity rounds tore into the Zodark ship's hull, piercing through armor plating.

The alien vessel shuddered, then, with a silent flash lighting up the battlefield, it exploded. The blast wave rippled outward, scattering metallic fragments in all directions. Remnants of the once-mighty warship spun away into the void, some still glowing from the heat of the explosion.

Lee scanned information streaming across the personal holo projecting off his chair's armrest, taking in the overall picture of the engagement. His fleet held its own, but the Zodarks pressed hard. Several of his own ships had taken damage, and the RNS *Intrepid* was reporting critical system failures.

As Lee studied the hologram, new data flashed across the display. Five new enemy contacts appeared at the edge of the battle zone.

"Sir, five more Zodark ships approaching from coordinates one-seven-eight by six-seven," Reynolds announced.

"On screen," Lee ordered.

The main viewscreen shifted, zooming out to show the new threat. The five new Zodark vessels were advancing on their flank. The lead ship, larger than the others, was clearly another flagship.

Numbers scrolled across the bottom of Lee's screen, updating with each passing second:

Range to lead Zodark vessel: 48,457 kilometers

Closing speed: 0.15C

Time to optimal weapons range: 0:32

Lee pressed his comms button. "RNS *Detroit*, RNS *Virginia*, RNS *Nebraska*, form a wedge," he directed. "Push through their line."

On the main holoscreen, the three heavy cruisers responded to his order. The ships moved into a tight arrowhead formation, with the *Detroit* at the point and the *Virginia* and *Nebraska* flanking it.

The wedge of human warships accelerated, driving straight toward the heart of the five-ship Zodark formation. Energy beams and missiles from the alien vessels lashed out at the advancing cruisers, but their armor held firm.

As they closed with the enemy, the three cruisers opened fire. Magrail rounds, lasers, and swarms of missiles erupted from their hulls in a devastating fusillade.

The lead Zodark ship, caught off guard by the sudden, aggressive maneuver, took the brunt of the assault. Its engines failed under the onslaught and the enemy vessel's hull buckled. Secondary explosions moved along its length before it broke apart in a spectacular burst of light.

The *Virginia* and *Nebraska* peeled off to either side, bracketing the remaining Zodark ships with withering fire. The *Detroit*, meanwhile, plowed straight ahead. Its reinforced prow smashed through the wreckage of the destroyed Zodark vessel, scattering fragments. The cruiser's point-defense systems worked overtime, swatting away missiles and smaller craft trying to impede its progress. Two more Zodark battleships succumbed to allied fire, going out of commission and out of the fight.

All around, the combined Primord and Republic forces fought off enemy ships. Chaos reigned.

Lee bent slightly forward in his chair, his eyes never leaving the tactical display. He watched as the three Republic flak frigates, two heavy cruisers, and a handful of Primord vessels tore through the Zodark line, leaving a trail of destruction. Two more hostile ships fell to the onslaught, their hulls shattering.

"Sir," Rhom said. "The Zodark line is breaking. They're attempting to disengage."

"Excellent," Lee said, his voice carrying across the bridge. "Tell *Detroit*, *Virginia*, and *Nebraska* to hold position and continue engaging any targets of opportunity. We need to press our advantage."

As the battle continued to rage around them, new data streaming across the display showed the shifting balance of power. The human and Primord fleet had seized the initiative.

"Another enemy ship neutralized, sir," Rhom announced, his brow furrowing as more information materialized across his console. "Massive energy signature detected at bearing two-seven-zero, range five hundred and twelve thousand kilometers."

The main holographic display changed, zooming out to encompass a wider view of the battlefield. A pulsing red icon appeared at the edge of the sensor range, accompanied by data scrolling rapidly across the bottom of the projection:

Unknown Contact

Bearing: 270

Range: 512,000 kilometers

Mass: 1.8E7 tons

Energy Output: 9.7E12 MW

Classification: Anomalous

Lee squinted as he studied the readout. "Magnify."

The main viewscreen quivered, resolving into a high-resolution image, making Lee's breath catch in his throat. A colossal Zodark flagship dominated the display. The alien ship dwarfed its escort fleet, which consisted of over ninety smaller vessels arranged in a protective formation around their mammoth leader.

Lee's mind raced as he calculated the odds. His own task force was just over eighty ships. With the ships in the current engagement, the Zodarks would outnumber them almost two to one.

"Admiral, we've got incoming!" Rhom's eyes widened as he stared at his sensor display. "Minimeteoroid storm dead ahead!"

"What?" Lee asked. "How close?"

"It'll be on us in less than a minute, sir," Rhom said. "Density readings are off the charts."

How did we miss this? Lee wondered. *Where was intel on this?* This was one of the reasons why their ships had such robust armor, but Lee questioned if it would be enough.

"All hands," Lee commanded, "brace for impact! Helm, adjust our heading. Try to minimize our profile."

The bridge crew scrambled to secure themselves as the first particles struck the *Vega*. A cacophony of pings and thuds reverberated through the hull, growing in intensity with each passing second.

On the main viewscreen, the space ahead of them shimmered and distorted. Tiny flecks of light appeared, streaking past at incredible speeds. As they watched, a Zodark Vulture was caught in the storm. The ship itself disintegrated, torn apart by the relentless barrage.

"Damage reports coming in from all decks," Rhom said, his voice tight with tension. "Hull breaches on decks four and seven. Bulkheads automatically sealing now."

"Sir, we've lost contact with the RNS *Sovereign* and RNS *Dauntless*," Rodriguez reported, her face pale. "Last transmission indicated multiple hull breaches."

Lee's jaw clenched. Those were good ships with good crews. "Keep trying to raise them. What's the status of the rest of the fleet?"

Before anyone could answer, a brilliant flash lit up the viewscreen. One of the Zodark cruisers had strayed too close to a particularly dense patch of micrometeoroids. The vessel came apart at the seams, explosions tearing it to pieces.

"Sir, Cooper's space wing is in trouble," Rodriguez reported, her pitch barely audible over the constant impacts. "They're getting torn apart out there."

The storm was playing havoc with their sensors. Coop's fighters and bombers were scattered, trying desperately to evade both the Zodark attackers and the lethal debris field.

"Coop, get your people out of there," Lee said into the comm. "Fall back to the *Vega*'s defensive perimeter."

"Trying, sir," Coop's voice crackled back, filled with static. "We've lost... can't... make it—"

The transmission cut out. A cold knot formed in Lee's stomach. More blips vanished from his display—each one representing a pilot, a person he'd sworn to protect.

"Sir, we've lost over thirty fighters," Rhom said, his tone hollow. "Requesting immediate shuttle launch for search and rescue for ejected pilots."

Lee nodded. "Do it. Get as many of our people back as we can."

As the rescue shuttles launched, Lee focused on the battle at large. Despite the devastation wrought by the micrometeoroid storm, he saw an opportunity. The Zodark fleet was in disarray, their formation shattered by the unexpected onslaught.

"That's our primary target," Lee said, gesturing to the large Zodark flagship. "All ships, maintain distance at four hundred thousand kilometers. Prepare for long-range engagement."

The crew relayed orders, coordinating with the rest of the fleet. Lee's task force, accompanied by the Primord armada, maneuvered into position, their formation tightening despite the ongoing storm.

"Sir," Rhom said, "hostiles entering maximum effective range in T minus two-seventeen."

"Tactical, begin plotting firing solutions," Lee replied. "I want our first salvo to hit them the moment they cross the four-hundred-and-twenty-five-thousand-kilometer threshold."

"Aye, sir. Targeting computers are calculating enemy vectors now. We're factoring in their current speed and projected evasive maneuvers."

Ghostly projections appeared on the tactical hologram, showing the anticipated paths of the Zodark ships. The computer's predictive algorithms were impressive, but Lee knew the aliens were crafty.

"Adjust fire control for a twenty percent random deviation from predicted paths," Lee ordered. "Let's make it difficult for them to guess our targeting priorities."

As the seconds ticked down, Lee's chest tightened. More reports about meteoroid impacts came in from his fleet. Another dozen Gripens and Valkyries had met their end.

"Rhom," Lee asked, "what's the status of this meteoroid field? When can we expect it to clear?"

"Admiral, I've been analyzing the sensor data continuously. I'm afraid the readings show no sign that the shower is abating. At its current intensity and spread... it'll take days before we see any significant reduction in particle density."

"Days? That's not acceptable. We need to clear this area ASAP."

Just then, Reynolds's voice chimed in. "Sir, I've been mapping the particle density and velocity patterns. There's a path of least resistance we could exploit. It takes us on a trajectory near Lunakor."

"The moon? That's a short detour, Reynolds. Are you certain?" It was where they were heading, along with many of his *Jupiter*-class troop transports. This was good news, and it lightened the load off Lee's chest a little.

"Yes, sir. It's our best option. Coordinates are as follows: bearing zero-four-seven mark two-eight-three, range two-point-seven million kilometers. We'll need to maintain that heading at this speed to reach coordinates in eighteen minutes."

"Very well, Reynolds. Plot the course." Lee activated the fleet-wide communication channel. "Attention, all ships. We're adjusting course to navigate through this meteoroid storm. All vessels are to form up on the RNS *Vega* and match our course and speed precisely. Set new heading to zero-four-seven mark two-eight-three. I say again, zero-four-seven mark two-eight-three. Maintain this course for the next eighteen minutes. We'll be skirting the moon Lunakor. Obviously, we're facing the largest Zodark force we've ever encountered, not to mention this meteoroid storm. I will need everyone's all, and more. Lee out."

The *Vega* and the entirety of Task Force 28 altered their course. The new trajectory, while safer from the meteoroid storm, still kept them on an intercept path with the larger Zodark fleet. The imposing Zodark flagship loomed at the center of this huge force. Meanwhile, the smaller Zodark armada they had initially engaged right after emerging from the stargate was regrouping, struggling to maintain formation in the turbulent space weather.

Lee now found himself in a precarious position, facing two separate Zodark armadas. Even with the allied Primord ships fighting alongside them, Task Force 28's forces were significantly outnumbered.

"Range to enemy fleet: four hundred and sixty thousand kilometers," Rhom said. "Designate distant enemy formation as Fleet Beta. Closer Zodark formation, designate Fleet Alpha. Acknowledge."

"Acknowledged," Lee said. "Tactical, confirm designations and update the fleet-wide tactical network with these new designations. Ensure all ships are aware."

"Aye, sir." Rhom typed in the information, his eyes shifting over to a second screen on his console. "Fleet Beta at a range of four hundred and thirty-one thousand kilometers and closing. Our optimal long-range firing distance is four hundred and twenty-five thousand kilometers. We'll reach optimal range in approximately eight seconds at current speeds."

When eight seconds had passed, Lee spoke over the comms. "All ships, open fire."

Missiles launched from the Republic and Primord ships. Moments later, beams of energy shot out from the fleet's laser batteries.

The first salvo crossed the vast distance between the fleets. The Zodark vessels took evasive action, their movements even more erratic than the tactical computer had predicted. Despite their best efforts, though, not all of them could avoid the incoming fire.

Several smaller Zodark ships erupted as missiles found their mark. Others suffered glancing blows from the laser fire, but the massive Zodark flagship remained untouched, protected by layers of escort ships and its own formidable defenses.

More minimeteoroids struck the *Vega*. As miniature rocks punctured the ship's armored hull, klaxons blared.

The tactical display burst with warnings. A swarm of new contacts presented. Hundreds of small craft poured from Zodark Fleet Beta.

"Zodark Vultures incoming, closing in quickly," Rhom said. "At least three hundred fighters."

An approaching cloud of enemy starfighters came into view on the screen. A hail of energy bolts streaked across the void, peppering the human-led ships. With the *Vega* being the largest ship in the system, it was a magnet for enemy fire—even the most inexperienced Zodark pilot couldn't possibly miss hitting the thirty-two-hundred-meter-long pride of the Republic Navy.

"Coop?" Lee keyed into Coop's channel. "Are you with us?"

"Communication… lit… choppy, sir, but sti… here."

Lee breathed a sigh of relief. *Damn Zodarks have so much jamming going on.*

He turned to his comms officer. "Rodriguez, anything we can do to clear up that signal?"

"I'll do my best, sir," she replied.

Lee tried to get through to Coop again. "Those Vultures need a lesson in dogfighting, and many are approaching. Knock them out before they get here," he directed.

"Negative, sir...fighter... damaged. I'm RTB. My XO, Riggs, is taking over."

The radio went silent.

"Coop? Do you read?" Lee asked. "Coop?"

There was no response.

Lee grimaced. "RNS *Ortega* and *Intrepid*," he said, keying his comms, "accompany the fighters and try to keep up. Run interference. End as many of those Vultures as possible. Keep their fighters off our capital ships."

As the Gripen fighters streamed in formation toward the incoming Vultures from enemy fleet Beta, Lee looked at the distance of the Zodark fleet Alpha: thirty-eight thousand kilometers, and they were beginning to fire again. Meteoroids seemed to grow bigger, hitting all ships at a faster clip.

The bridge of the RNS *Vega* quaked under the impact of another wave of minimeteoroids.

"Admiral," Rhom said, "the meteoroids are getting more intense. Our sensors are having trouble distinguishing between debris and enemy fire."

On the screen, a particularly large chunk of space rock hurtled toward them. The ship's point-defense lasers fired rapidly, vaporizing the incoming threat into a cloud of smaller fragments.

"Turn off all laser weapons for long-range battle engagement," Lee ordered. "Continue to use them as point defense against the meteoroids. We'll rely on missiles and magrails for offensive operations."

As his crew scrambled to comply, Lee studied the main viewscreen. The Zodark fleet Alpha was shifting, their formations breaking apart as they struggled to maintain cohesion in the face of the intensifying storm.

"Sir," Rodriguez reported, "the enemy is reversing course. They appear to be retreating from the meteoroid field."

"And our missiles?"

"Still tracking, sir," Rhom confirmed. "The storm is interfering with the Zodarks' laser defenses. Their accuracy is significantly reduced."

The storm threatening to tear Lee's fleet apart was also providing an unexpected advantage.

"XO Sato," Lee said, turning to his second-in-command, "I'd like your input on our current situation. Do you have any suggestions for our strategy moving forward?"

Sato considered for a moment before responding. "Sir, I recommend we use the storm to our advantage. We can use it as cover to maneuver closer to the enemy while they're struggling with their defenses. It's risky, but it could give us the opening we need."

"We'll need to coordinate closely with the rest of the fleet and our Primord allies." He pressed the wide-channel comm. "Attention, all ships, the situation has changed, and so must our strategy. We're initiating a divide-and-conquer operation, effective immediately."

Lee outlined the new plan, dividing the fleet into three task forces—the main battle group, the Lunakor invasion force, and the reserve/support group. As he spoke, the tactical display on the main screen updated, showing the new formations taking shape.

"The main battle group will engage the primary Zodark forces, serving as both our main offensive thrust and a diversion," Lee continued. "While we draw their attention, the Lunakor invasion force will use the cover of the meteoroid storm to break away and approach the moon via the circuitous route I'm sending you now. The reserve group will provide support where needed and act as a screen for the invasion force. This is a complex operation, people. We'll be using every trick in the book—ECM to mask the invasion force's departure, specialized ships with enhanced meteoroid deflection capabilities as escorts, and a series of deceptive maneuvers to keep the enemy guessing."

As Lee finished speaking, the fleet continued to reshape itself on the tactical display. The Lunakor invasion force, led by the RNS *Maddox*, peeled away from the main group, using the intensifying meteoroid storm as cover.

"Sir," Rodriguez said, "Zodark fleet Beta is approaching from three hundred and thirty-nine thousand kilometers out, but they're slowing. It looks like they're attempting to reverse course to avoid the meteoroid storm as well."

Lee nodded. "Good. That gives us more time to execute our plan. Keep an eye on them, but focus on the immediate threat."

The bridge shook again as another wave of meteoroids peppered the *Vega*'s hull. Lee gritted his teeth, knowing that every impact incrementally weakened their defenses.

"Damage report," he said.

"Minor hull breaches on decks seven and twelve," Rodriguez reported. "Repair teams are responding. Armor holding at seventy-seven percent."

The main battle group was now fully engaged with the Zodark fleet Alpha forces, unleashing a barrage of missiles and magrail fire. The space between the fleets was a frenzy of explosions, vaporized rock, and lethal projectiles.

"Sir," Sato said, "multiple hostile torpedo launches detected. We're looking at a full spread, sir."

The storm made it nearly impossible to accurately use laser technology in long-range targeting, as the meteoroid disturbances scattered and refracted the beams, reducing their effectiveness at extended distances. So, without their lasers, the Zodarks were relying on their torpedo arsenals. It was a dangerous gambit—torpedoes were slower and easier to intercept than energy weapons, but they packed a much bigger punch.

"All ships, prepare for incoming torpedoes," Lee ordered over the fleet-wide channel. "Point-defense systems on full auto. Evasive maneuvers at your discretion. Knock these torpedoes out!"

Chapter Twenty-Six

RNS *Vega*
Task Force 28
Gravaxia System

The minimeteoroid storm turned Coop's battlefield into a treacherous obstacle course. Debris bounced off his hull as he wove through meteoroid hell. Around him, RNS ships battled two Zodark fleets coming from different directions, which were mere lights off his cockpit window. Some hostiles were over three hundred thousand kilometers away, while some enemy vessels were only twenty-five thousand kilometers from him and opened up with rapid fire on allied forces.

Coop spotted a Vulture closing in on his wingman's tail. "Watch your six, Riggs."

Coop snap-rolled his fighter, bringing his weapons to bear. The magrail guns roared to life, spitting superheated slugs at the enemy craft. The Vulture erupted in a brilliant fireball, and Coop plunged through the fiery cloud, his sensors momentarily overwhelmed.

"Thanks for the save, boss," Riggs's voice crackled over the comm. "These rocks are playing hell with my targeting systems."

"Tell me about it," Coop said, juking hard to avoid a particularly nasty cluster of space rocks. "All units, report in."

The comm channels boomed with chatter as his pilots checked in. Amidst the confusion, Coop caught snippets of the larger battle unfolding around them.

"Nomad here, engaging three bandits at Sector Seven."

"Shrike to Coop, we've lost Bullseye and Tex to meteoroid impacts. Requesting reinforcements."

"This is Rogue," a cool female voice cut through the noise. "Valkyrie Beta Squadron just took out an enemy battleship. You're welcome, boys."

Coop grinned. At least something was going their way. "Good work, Rogue. Keep the pressure on their capital ships."

"Coop, this is Phoenix! We've lost half our squadron to these damn rocks and Vulture crossfire. We need backup!"

"Bee here. Echo Squadron is down to a quarter strength. These meteoroids are tearing us apart!"

"Phantom calling in. Lost my wingman and three others. The Vultures are picking us off while we dodge this meteoroid minefield!"

Coop absorbed the grim updates, and it was even more grim reading what was coming in on his screen. The display showed ninety-eight fighters lost in his space wing, leaving only 202 remaining. The odds were overwhelming, even with allied Gripens from other RNS ships defending as many Republic vessels as possible.

He had to act fast. "Omega Squadron, this is Coop. Launch immediately from the RNS *Vega*. We need you out here now."

"Roger that, Coop," Badger's voice burst over the comms. "Omega Squadron launching. We're on our way."

While Coop watched Omega Squadron's markers appeared on his tactical screen, he thought more about Badger. The pilot was a wild card, a true maverick. You never knew which version of him you'd get in any engagement—the one who was just out to rack up Vulture kills, or the team player who'd risk everything to save a fellow pilot.

"All squadrons, this is Coop. Omega is joining the fight."

"Aye, sir," came the replies over the intercom in near unison.

A proximity alert blared. Coop's attention swept back to his immediate surroundings. Three Vultures had broken through the melee, zeroing in on his position. At the moment, he flew close to the *Vega*, protecting her as best he could.

"Riggs, full thrusters port!" Coop hauled his stick hard to starboard. "We've got company!"

Coop's Gripen shuddered as a torpedo detonated nearby, the shockwave buffeting his craft. Coop grimaced hard, fighting to maintain control as he evaded more incoming fire.

"I can't shake 'em, Coop!" Riggs's tone was tight with tension. "These Vultures are persistent!"

The minimeteoroid storm was wreaking havoc on their systems, making accurate shots nearly impossible.

"Riggs, we're gonna split up," Coop announced. "Try to draw them away from each other. Use the debris field for cover."

"Copy that," Riggs responded. "Good luck, boss."

Coop dove into a dense cluster of meteoroids, his Gripen's hull groaning under the impacts. Warning lights flashed across his console as his armor strained to deflect the barrage. Behind him, the Vultures struggled to keep pace, their larger frames less maneuverable.

A large piece of rock loomed ahead. Coop waited until the last possible second before rolling hard, skimming the surface of the meteoroid. One of the pursuing Vultures wasn't so lucky, smashing headlong into the obstacle and disappearing in a wild explosion.

"One down," Coop said.

His elation was short-lived as his fighter rocked violently, klaxons blaring. A lucky shot from one of the remaining Vultures found its mark, and Coop's systems were going haywire.

"Riggs, I'm hit!" Coop said, fighting to keep his craft under control. He diverted coolant to an overheating engine, preventing a catastrophic meltdown. "How're you doing over there?"

"Not great. I've got two on my tail, and my weapons are barely functioning in this mess!"

Coop's heart raced as he searched for a way out of their predicament. Streaks of weapons fire lanced past his canopy, striking the Vulture behind him. The enemy fighter disintegrated, and Coop's sensors picked up two new contacts closing fast.

"Yeehaw!" a familiar voice whooped over the comm. "Looked like you could use a hand there, Captain."

"Badger." Relief washed over Coop. "Nice of you to join us."

"Anytime, sir," Badger replied. "Nova and I will mop up the rest of these jokers."

"Much obliged," Coop said. "Riggs, you still with us?"

"Still here. Thanks for the assist, Badger."

"Our pleasure, gentlemen," a new female voice chimed in. "Two Vultures in our sights. Planning to take them down in a few seconds. Stand by."

As Badger and Nova veered off to engage the remaining Vultures, Coop took a moment to assess the larger battle. His tactical display was a frenzy of friendly and enemy contacts, all swirling in the maelstrom of the meteoroid storm. With a sinking feeling, it hit him how many of his squadrons had indeed been decimated by the combined threats of enemy fire and space debris.

"All units, this is Coop," he broadcast. "Regroup and form up on my position. We need to consolidate our forces and push back against the enemy offensive."

Coop scanned his tactical display. Something caught his attention—a group of Republic ships breaking away from the main task force. He zoomed in, recognizing the IFF signatures of the Lunakor invasion force. They were making a covert move toward the moon, hoping to slip away unnoticed.

A few Vultures spotted the maneuver as Coop's display lit up with a new threat. Ten Vulture fighters peeling off from the enemy formation, giving chase to the invasion force.

"Damn it," Coop muttered, assessing the situation. The Lunakor force was too far to reach quickly, but someone had to intercept those Vultures. He keyed his comm, searching for the nearest friendly units.

"Coop to Hawk, Shrike, Lucky, Spark, Badger, Nova, Nomad, and Riggs. Form up on me. We've got a situation. Phantom, you have the lead of our space wing. I'm breaking off to provide immediate air support for the Lunakor invasion force. They'll be taking heavy fire and need CAS ASAP. Maintain standard combat spread and keep comms open on Tac Channel Three. I'll relay updates as they come in. Phantom, you're cleared hot. The rest of you, maintain formation integrity and follow Phantom's orders. Coop out."

Acknowledgments crackled over the comm as Coop vectored toward the invasion force. His fighter screamed through the meteoroid field, the other pilots falling into formation behind him.

"Lunakor invasion force is making their move," Coop said, his eyes fixed on the distant invasion force. "But they've picked up some unwanted attention. We need to clear their six."

As they raced across space, the verdant moon Lunakor came into view. Its green aura shimmered against the starry backdrop.

"I see 'em," Nova called out. "Vultures, dead ahead. They're engaging the invasion force."

Flashes of weapons fire tore into the darkness in the distance.

"All right, people. Let's crash this party. Weapons free, but watch your targets," Coop commanded. "We can't risk hitting our own."

"We're leaving the meteoroid field," Riggs said.

"That means we can use our blasters." Coop's newly formed small squadron dove into the fray. Free from the interference of the meteoroid field, their laser targeting systems sang with renewed vigor.

"Got one!" Badger whooped as his shots connected, turning a Vulture into an expanding ball of metal shards. "These boys picked the wrong day to play hero."

Coop veered his fighter, lining up a shot on a Vulture harassing one of the invasion force's troop transports. His lasers spread out, catching the enemy fighter squarely in its engines. It spiraled away, trailing fire and smoke.

"Excellent shot, boss," Riggs called out, his own fighter flying past in pursuit of another target.

The battle intensified as the Republic fighters tore into the Vulture formation. Coop's cockpit was filled with a cacophony of comm chatter, status reports, and the constant thrumming of his ship's systems.

"Shrike here, I've got two on my tail!"

"I see 'em, Shrike. Spark, change vectors and give 'em hell!"

"Roger that, engaging now."

Coop banked hard, avoiding a volley of enemy fire. He rolled, bringing his guns to bear on another Vulture. The enemy fighter exploded in a satisfying blast of fire.

"Nomad to Coop," the comm crackled. "The invasion force is almost in range. They're starting their approach to Lunakor."

"Copy that, Nomad. Let's finish this up and provide escort."

The remaining Vultures, outmatched and outnumbered, scattered. Coop and his squadron gave chase, determined to eliminate any stragglers.

As they pursued, Coop found himself drawing closer to Lunakor's upper atmosphere. The green haze of the moon filled his canopy, growing larger.

"Coop, watch yourself," Riggs said. "You're getting awful close to atmo."

"I see it," Coop replied, lining up a shot on one of the last Vultures. "Just need to finish this guy off."

He fired, sending a stream of laser fire that quickly found its mark. The enemy fighter disappeared in a flash of light. Coop pulled back on his stick, ready to rejoin the squadron, when a proximity alarm blared.

"Coop, behind you!" Riggs shouted.

Before Coop could react, his fighter quivered violently. Warning lights flashed across his console as a grinding sound filled the cockpit.

"I'm hit!" Coop yelled, fighting with the controls. "One of my engines is down!"

Riggs came to his rescue, destroying the Zodark fighter before it could hit him again.

"Thanks, Riggs," Coop said sullenly, wishing he hadn't needed assistance.

"I've got your six," Riggs replied.

Coop was feeling a bit conflicted; he wanted to get back into the fight, but his mental risk-benefit analysis told him he should sit this one out.

Just then, Coop spotted one of the newer pilots trying to nurse his damaged fighter back to the *Vega*. When Coop contacted him, the newbie's voice was audibly shaking. "I, I don't think I can make it," Turbo managed to stutter.

Coop knew at that moment exactly what he had to do. "Riggs, you have control of the flight," he declared. "I'm going to escort the new guy and get him back home in one piece."

"Roger that," Riggs acknowledged.

Coop maneuvered his fighter closer to the rookie's. "Hey, one of my engines is down, so let's head back to the *Vega* together," he explained.

The new pilot was practically hyperventilating but acknowledged he'd heard him.

"Breathe," Coop directed. "Remember your training. Work the problems one at a time. You've got this."

There was a brief pause, but Turbo must have taken the advice to finally slow down and get some air, because the next time he spoke, he sounded like he was in a much better headspace.

"Thank you, sir," he replied. "I really thought I was a goner back there."

"Aw, don't get all sappy on me—I think we're going to have to change your call sign from Turbo to Waterworks with those tears of fear running down your cheeks," Coop teased him good-naturedly. "But seriously, Turbo, we all have close calls. One day, you'll get to return the favor and help someone else out."

202

Chapter Twenty-Seven

RNS *Vega*
Task Force 28
Gravaxia System

The next few minutes were tense. Each ship in Task Force 28 evaded in calculated patterns, their point-defense systems working overtime to intercept the incoming swarm of Zodark missiles and torpedoes. Explosions bloomed in space as many were destroyed, but some found their marks.

A Primord cruiser succumbed to direct hits, its outer layers fracturing like brittle glass. Even as Lee mourned their loss, he saw the Lunakor invasion force slipping further away, now almost invisible amidst the intensifying storm.

Rhom spoke up. "Captain, we've lost contact with RNS *Cutlass* and RNS *Longbow*. Last known positions indicate they were at the forefront of the meteoroid storm. No distress signals detected. Presumed destroyed, sir."

"Understood," said Lee. "Relay their last known coordinates to search and rescue. Adjust fleet formation to close the gap. Tactical, recalibrate our firing solutions to compensate for their absence."

Damn it. Three ships, three crews… gone in an instant, thought Lee. This storm was turning into a meat grinder. They needed to adapt fast, or they'd lose this battle in no time.

"Sir!" Rhom displayed the flagship of the Zodarks' Fleet Alpha on the main viewscreen. The massive warship loomed against the starfield, its port side vulnerable and unprotected. Beside it, the twisted, smoldering wreckage of what had once been a Zodark cruiser drifted lifelessly. Debris and bodies floated in the vacuum. "The flagship. It's exposed!"

"All vessels, target primary weapons on enemy command ship, designation Zodark-One. Converge fire for maximum impact," Lee commanded. "This is our window for a critical strike."

The fleet responded immediately, a constellation of missiles and magrail projectiles converging on the exposed Zodark vessel. Bright flashes cascaded across the alien ship's exterior, armor-piercing projectiles and antiship missiles tearing great rents along hundreds of meters of its armor.

As the Zodark flagship reeled under the assault, the rest of their fleet was regrouping, forming a protective screen around their wounded command ship.

"Sir," Sato said, leaning closer to Lee, "the meteoroid storm is intensifying again. We're taking heavy damage across the fleet."

Lee's chest tightened at the news. They'd pressed their advantage, but now the very phenomenon giving them an edge was threatening to overwhelm them too.

"All ships, initiate tactical withdrawal," Lee ordered bitterly. The screen showed a safer zone in the system, coordinates farther from Lunakor, but he had to pull his fleet out of this mess. "Fall back to rally point Zeta. Maintain fire on the Zodark flagship. Lunakor invasion force, continue your approach to the moon. You have a clear path. We will continue to engage the enemy fleet."

As the main task force began its coordinated retreat, Lee watched the Lunakor invasion force on the small holo hovering above his armrest. The force was well on its way to Lunakor. ETA, two minutes.

"Helm, set course for rally point Zeta," Lee said. "Let's regroup and prepare for the next phase of the battle."

"On it, Admiral," Reynolds said.

"Good man," Lee replied.

While the RNS *Vega* turned, a beam of energy so bright that it made Lee's eyes water even through the viewscreen's filters was expelled from the Zodark flagship. It swept across space with terrifying speed, slicing through several of the aircraft in Coop's space wing, disintegrating Valkyries and Gripens until it slammed into the RNS *Liberty*. The battlecruiser ruptured into several segments as the ship broke apart.

Before Lee could process the loss, the beam found another target—the RNS *Pioneer* was caught in the ray's path. It suffered the same fate as its sister ship. In the span of seconds, two more of the fleet's second-most-powerful vessels had been reduced to expanding clouds of dust.

A violent tremor ran through the *Vega* as a glancing blow struck its hull. Lee gripped his command chair, fighting to stay upright as the ship rocked beneath him.

"Hull breach on deck two, Section R. Auto containment initiated!" Rhom interjected. "Another direct hit to that area may gut the lower decks."

"Acknowledged, Commander Rhom," said Lee hastily.

He switched to shipwide communications. "All hands, brace for evasive action," Lee warned, then disconnected.

"Helm, veer to port, bearing zero-four-five mark two-seven-zero. Engineering—redistribute power to the engines and primary weapons. Rhom, target enemy's forward battery and fire at will."

Again, Lee keyed the fleet-wide communication channel. "All vessels converge on rally point Zeta, coordinates one-seven-three zero-five-eight nine-two-one. Frigate Group Charlie, form a defensive screen around our damaged quadrant. Heavy Cruiser Group Epsilon, provide covering fire. We'll regroup and repair at Zeta before pressing our advantage." He eyed Reynolds at Navigation. "Plot the quickest course to those coordinates that minimizes our exposure. Engineering, I need options for emergency repairs once we reach the rally point. Let's move, people."

"I'll get on that, Admiral," came MacGregor's raspy voice from the engineering section. "Right now, we have a critical situation that has to be addressed," he continued. "Our portside propulsion is off-line, starboard is beginning to fail. That hit we took to deck two caused all sorts of problems across the ship's main power distribution line. In order to repair it, we need to conduct an emergency power reroute to bypass the damaged distribution line until it can be repaired," McGregor explained. I need five minutes to disconnect the reactor from the damaged distribution line while we reattach a new line and connect it to the reactor. If we don't do this now—we'll lose propulsion entirely and the weapons with it."

"What the heck, Mac? Five minutes in the middle of a battle— I'll give you two," Lee shot back, blindsided by the severity of the damage they had sustained. "I don't care what you have to do, Mac, but you gotta make it happen in two minutes or less."

"Two minutes?" growled MacGregor. "We're on it as we speak, skipper, but I can't change the fundamental laws of the universe. These engines aren't bloody magic wands."

"I get it. Just do what you can. We're counting on you. Out."

"Sir, Zodark cruiser at bearing zero-four-seven just went up," Rhom said. "RNS *Kraken* reports a direct hit on its reactor core." He brought it up on the display, the fiery entrails from the debris field dwindling.

"Keep pressing," he ordered. "Target any ship that looks vulnerable."

The tactical display flickered with constant updates as the battle raged on. Zodark vessels collapsed to the task force's desperate attack during their retreat, the enemy's exteriors shattering under concentrated fire.

"RNS *Helios* reports two kills," Rodriguez announced. "Zodark battleships from Fleet Beta at coordinates two-two-five by one-one-eight, and closing at two hundred and eighty-four thousand kilometers. They're attempting to go through the meteoroid storm."

"Let them," grunted Lee. "Rhom, given our momentum while we wait for a miracle from engineering, what's our estimated time to clear the debris field?"

"Based on our current trajectory and the density of the debris field, I estimate we'll clear it in approximately three minutes, forty-six seconds. However, I must caution that the field's composition is highly volatile. We're detecting sporadic surges in particle density that could extend our transit time by up to two additional minutes."

Reynolds's voice piped up next. "Sir, once propulsion has been restored, shall I plot any potential alternate routes as a contingency?"

"Negative. Stay the course."

"Aye, sir."

Lee's eyes locked on the form of the Zodark flagship, its massive silhouette dominating the viewscreen. Despite the losses they'd inflicted, the enemy vessel seemed virtually untouched, its defenses shrugging off the task force's most powerful attacks. "Current standing overview on the Zodark fleets," he ordered.

Rhom tapped on one of his console's interfaces. "Sir, SITREP as follows: Fleet Beta is deployed one hundred and ninety-four thousand klicks forward of our vanguard. Fleet Alpha is inbound at twenty-two thousand klicks and closing rapidly. The meteoroid field intensity is increasing."

"Tactical, coordinate with the rest of the fleet," Lee directed. "I want a constant barrage on those incoming hostiles."

As Task Force 28 pushed through the intensifying meteoroid field, the smaller rocks pinged harmlessly off their armor, but the larger ones were beginning to cause significant damage.

"Sir, multiple impacts reported across Fleet Beta," Rodriguez announced. "They're losing formation cohesion."

A series of explosions lit up the main holo as several Zodark Vultures fell to the meteoroid assault.

"Bridge, Engineering—emergency bypass is complete. Reactor reconnected. Propulsion back to one hundred percent. Weapons back to one hundred percent," MacGregor reported.

"You're a miracle worker, Mac!" Lee congratulated. "Use all the duct tape and superglue you have to, but keep us in the fight," he directed.

"Sir, Fleet Alpha is entering the densest part of the field now," Rhom reported. "They're taking heavy damage. Multiple cruisers and battleships showing noticeable critical systems failures."

Lee leaned forward, his eyes narrowing as he surveyed the enemy movements. "They're pushing too hard. They want to catch us before we reach Zeta point, but they're leaving themselves exposed."

As if to punctuate his words, a massive eruption flared on the screen. A Zodark heavy cruiser, overwhelmed by the constant barrage of meteoroids, broke apart in a fireball.

"Sir, we're approaching Zeta rally point," the helmsman announced.

"Admiral," Rhom said, "meteoroid field has cleared from our vector. All ships report navigable space."

"Excellent. Signal the fleet as soon as we reach position," Lee said, "I want us in a battle line formation."

The ships of the fleet maneuvered into position, readying for the next attack. What was left of Coop's space wing, along with the remnants of several other space wings from other ships, made a defensive shield around the fleet. Altogether, they formed the classic naval formation known as "line ahead." It was an old tactic, dating back to the days of wooden ships and cannon fire, but it remained effective even in the age of space warfare.

With their broadsides facing the incoming enemy, Task Force 28 unleashed a devastating volley. Magrails and missiles streaked across space, punching into the battered Zodark fleets.

"Concentrate fire on Alpha's flagship while it's being pummeled by those meteors," Lee ordered. "Let's see if we can't decapitate their command structure."

Volley after volley of magrail slugs were hurled into the Zodark vessel. Turbolasers and antiship missiles joined the relentless pounding the enemy ship was taking, in addition to the meteors still hammering it. Then to Lee's shock and amazement, he watched as a giant meteoroid plowed into the rear midsection of the Zodark flagship.

At first, the meteoroid appeared to have bounced off the outer hull of the vessel, turning it sideways from the impact. This sudden, radical movement caused most of the *Vega*'s magrail slugs to miss, but it simultaneously widened the amount of surface area the meteors could hit.

A bright flash blinded the bridge monitors. It took a moment for the *Vega*'s cameras to readjust as the flash dissipated, revealing the Zodark ship as it broke apart. In what amounted to a stroke of luck more than tactical brilliance, the meteors and pummeling from the Republic fleet had finally proven too much for it to bear. As the *Vega*'s weapons fire finally hit, the massive enemy ship began to break apart. Secondary explosions burst along its side as internal systems overloaded and ruptured. In a final, catastrophic detonation, the Zodark flagship broke into charred alloys.

"Flagship destroyed," Rodriguez reported, a note of triumph in her tone.

The loss of their command ship seemed to be the final straw for the Zodark fleets. Their formations, already ragged from pushing through the meteoroid field, began to disintegrate entirely.

"They're retreating," Rhom said. "Fleets Alpha and Beta are both breaking off engagement."

Lee nodded. "Press the advantage. I want maximum fire on those retreating ships. Don't let up until they're out of weapons range."

Task Force 28 surged, their weapons blazing. The retreating Zodarks, caught between the Earther and Primord assault and the intensifying meteoroid field, took heavy losses. Vulture fighters exploded by the dozen, while larger ships struggled to maneuver through the debris field.

As the battle raged on, Lee turned to his communications officer. "What's the status of our Lunakor fleet?"

After a moment of rapid communication with the Lunakor invasion force, the officer looked up. "Sir, all systems green. They've avoided the worst of the fighting so far and arrive in two-zero seconds."

"Admiral," Rhom said, "a large contingent of Zodark vessels is breaking formation. They're on an intercept course... heading straight for us, sixteen thousand klicks out."

Lee scrutinized the tactical holodisplay. Sure enough, a small portion of the remaining Zodark fleet was charging toward the *Vega* on a suicide run, their weapons already glowing with building energy.

"They've identified us as the command ship," Lee realized aloud. "Tactical, weapon status, how are we looking?"

"We're down two magrail turrets and three turbolasers on the primaries. Secondary batteries are in similar shape, but we still have some teeth to us," Rhom responded, his pitch tense before adding. "Enemy at twelve thousand klicks our fore."

"Target the lead Zodark vessel and open fire with magrails!" Lee ordered.

Rhom responded at once. "Aye, Captain. Targeting lead vessel and firing magrails."

The bridge vibrated as the magrails discharged their powerful projectiles. On the main viewscreen, the lead ship took multiple hits. Despite the barrage, it continued its advance, accompanied by eleven other enemy battleships and cruisers.

A few seconds later, several streaks of light emerged from the enemy fleet.

"Incoming torpedoes, Captain!" Rhom called out. "I count twelve."

Without hesitation, Lee ordered, "Concentrate laser fire on those torpedoes. Bring them up on screen!"

"Aye, sir. Engaging laser defense systems," Rhom acknowledged.

The main screen changed to a tactical view, showing the incoming torpedoes as bright points of light. The ship's laser batteries opened fire, lancing out with perfect accuracy.

Rhom provided a running commentary as the defense systems engaged. "First torpedo down... second and third eliminated... fourth destroyed. Energy building in the laser banks... fifth and sixth torpedoes neutralized... seventh gone... eighth and ninth destroyed simultaneously."

As the remaining torpedoes flew closer, the lasers continued their work with mounting effectiveness.

"Tenth and eleventh torpedoes eliminated... twelfth and final torpedo destroyed," Rhom announced. "All enemy torpedoes neutralized, Captain, but hostiles continue their vector run toward us, sir."

"All ships, this is Admiral Lee. The contingent of enemy vessels, approximately one dozen strong, are on an intercept course toward our flagship, *Vega*. Intel suggests they're initiating a suicide run. They're aiming to broadside us with maximum impact. All defensive systems to full power. Point defense, prepare for heavy engagement. Brace for imminent hostile contact. We need covering fire, now!"

The expanse of space around the *Vega* erupted with magrails and missile fire as Task Force 28 responded to Lee's call. The approaching Zodark ships found themselves caught in a quagmire, their tight formation working against them as they struggled to evade the volley.

"Six thousand klicks to our fore, Admiral."

Lee gripped his command chair as Republic and Primord ships continued to unleash weapons fire. A pair of enemy vessels ignited in quick succession, rupturing in brilliant flashes of orange and white. Debris from the destroyed vessels hurtled through space.

"Evasive action!" Lee commanded.

The helmsman responded instantly, maneuvering the *Vega* to miss the expanding cloud of destruction.

"Nearest hostile, three thousand klicks!" Rhom shouted.

Just then, three more enemy cruisers fell to the combined firepower of the allied fleet. Their broken forms tumbled end over end. One of them, its engines still firing sporadically, veered directly into the *Vega*'s path.

"Brace for impact!" Lee shouted as *Vega* collided with the damaged Zodark cruiser. The two ships ground against each other, armor plating shrieking as it tore away.

The bridge shook as chunks of the enemy vessel smashed against *Vega*'s exterior. Warning klaxons blared, and damage reports hurried in from all decks. A massive section of another Zodark cruiser's superstructure broke free, spinning wildly toward the *Vega*'s starboard nacelle.

"Auxiliary power to starboard engines, full ahead!" Lee said.

As the *Vega* broke free from the wreckage and the debris flew past them, data scrolled across Lee's armchair's holographic screen. *Vega*'s armor had been severely compromised in a few sections, requiring the emergency doors to close to isolate the breaches until engineering repair Synths were able to patch a few of the gaping holes in the ship.

Lee took in the battlefield at a glance on the main viewscreen. A smile spread across his face as the last of the incoming enemy ships winked out of existence while the rest of enemy Fleet Alpha and Beta were in full retreat.

"Situation update," Lee said.

"We've neutralized their offensive capability," Sato responded. "If I can suggest, sir, this lull as the enemy retreats presents us with a short window to consolidate our forces and initiate critical repairs to restore some weapon stations and plug some holes we still have in a few sections of the ship."

Lee agreed, ordering her to make it so. It was time to lick their wounds and assess the situation before the enemy returned.

Chapter Twenty-Eight

Republic Chancellor's Office
New Cambria
New Eden, Rhea System

Chancellor Aimes Morgan sat down at the table with Viceroy Miles Hunt and the Humtar governor of what had become the Northeastern State of Africa, a woman named Nisaba. Also present were the Chancellor's head of overall reconstruction efforts, Chul Kim, and the Humtar head of recovery efforts, a man named Akkil. He was eager to get an update on how things were going with the rebuilding and with the Humtars settling on Earth.

Chul Kim began. "As you know, tens of millions of people were displaced by the attack, but the Humtars have established temporary housing for many in the region, and they are restoring major services, such as electricity and running water, to all the remaining regions and pockets across the planet that are still struggling with recovery efforts. However, these are only interim solutions. The Humtars have presented us with many proposed improvements to these regions and to the State of Northeast Africa, which I invite my colleague Akkil to share with you and answer any potential questions you may have."

"Thank you, Chul," said Akkil. "As you know, our methods of construction are vastly different from yours here on Earth. Our people have developed methods of sustainable construction that work in harmony with the surrounding environment. We have been conducting research into how to most effectively manage the arid conditions of northeast Africa, and we are now beginning work on the more permanent dwellings. The buildings will foster the growth of local flora and fauna and will harness solar energy to reduce the amount of external power production needed."

"That sounds great," said Chancellor Morgan. "I do hope you will be willing to share some of your advancements in construction with us."

"Most certainly," said Akkil. "We recognize that tearing down and replacing all existing buildings may cause more damage to Earth. However, there is certainly a lot of new construction that is needed on

Earth, and it is self-serving for us to ensure that as much of the planet can be housed sustainably as possible."

Morgan laughed. "Self-serving? How so?" he asked.

Akkil smiled. "You see, our people are greatly concerned with health. We have put a great deal of study into epigenetics, and we have learned many of the secrets to keeping good genes turned on and problematic genes turned off. It is how we manage to look as though we never age, even after many years of life. So, we would like the environment surrounding us to promote well-being as much as possible. It's also why we have begun construction on our air filtration systems."

"Air filtration systems?" asked Viceroy Hunt, his left eyebrow raised.

"Yes," Akkil confirmed. "They utilize some of the same principles as we employ on our capital planet, with our air lock system that encases the planet. If it pleases you, we'd like to bring air filtration towers to New Eden, Alpha Centauri, and the former Sumerian planets and colonies now under Republic control. They have extended the life expectancy of our people and reduced the incidence of disease since widespread integration of this system went into effect."

"That is certainly an amazing offer," said Viceroy Hunt. "I would love to learn more about this technology," he said.

"Well, I suppose we should spend a little more time going over the finer points," said Chancellor Morgan, "but I'm very pleased with this update."
******

Two Days Later
Office of the Viceroy
Alliance City, New Eden

Another meeting, thought Viceroy Miles Hunt. It was an inevitable part of the job title he held, but sometimes, he did wish he could get back to being the captain of a ship, diving directly into the action.

At this table were Humtar governors of the settlements at Alpha Centauri, at Earth, and at the New Eden moon of Pishon. There was a Humtar Navy advisor and a Humtar Army advisor, and a head of overall recovery efforts. On the Republic side were Miles's old friend Chester

Bailey, Admiral Fran McKee, Admiral William "Willie" Rosentreter, Lieutenant General Jayden Hopper, and General Bates, the new head of the Republic Army. It was set to be a real barn burner.

After the obligatory niceties and introductions, Chester Bailey cleared his throat. "Well, ladies and gentlemen," he said, "I guess I'll be the one to open this discussion up. During our last meeting, you had mentioned sending advisors to assess the current state of our technology, education, manufacturing capabilities, our shipyards, and current warships in production. Have your advisors completed their assessments, and if so, what are their conclusions?"

The Humtar Navy advisor, Admiral Urnam, didn't seem the least bit bothered by Bailey's bluntness. "I would like to assure you, as far as the Humtar people are concerned, the Republic territory will be protected as if it were Humtar territory," he replied. "As such, four squadrons of three battleships, five cruisers, and twelve frigates will deploy to protect the systems at Sol, Rhea, Alpha Centauri, and the Qatana system."

Urnam held a hand up to forestall some of the questions he anticipated at that moment. "I do want to clarify that we will still not be fighting the Zodarks directly on behalf of the Republic. However, providing a defense force to protect Republic systems from attack *does* free up additional warships and soldiers for the war against them."

Admiral Fran McKee interjected, "Are the Humtars willing to help the Republic turn our existing warships into more powerful ships? Or perhaps we are able to take the ships that are still under construction at the Republic shipyards and improve on those vessels that are still under construction?"

Admiral Urnam nodded. "We will provide the Republic with our quantum fusion technology, enabling you to utilize the same Humtar quantum fusion reactors we use in our warships. The QFRs will produce even greater power levels than the known Gallentine, Collective, and Legion warships."

"Well, that's a huge deal," said Viceroy Hunt, unable to contain his own awe.

Urnam smiled. "We will, of course, provide technical and engineering assistance in creating these QFRs on the planets that the Republic controls as well. Those ships that are still under construction and future warships should be able to be upgraded using the quantum

214

fusion technology, but we will have to evaluate existing warships to determine if they can be brought back into a shipyard and retrofitted to integrate with the new QFRs."

Admiral Urnam had a mischievous twinkle in his eye. "Who wants to talk about weapons?" he asked.

Bailey took the bait. "All right, me. Tell us what you've got," he said jovially.

"These QFRs will do more than just make your ships more powerful and efficient," Urnam explained. "They will increase the power of your current turbo lasers by a factor of three."

"Wow," said Bailey. "OK, I'm impressed."

That will make our weapons more powerful than the Gallentine ships, Hunt realized immediately, *and the Collective ships as well...*

Admiral Urnam pulled up some information using his tablet, and several Republic ship designs populated as 3-D holographic images above the table. "Admiral McKee, we could look at retrofitting the Republic's newest star carrier, the RNS *Draco*, which is still in the shipyard. Not only can we add the QFR as we just discussed, but we can include our wormhole bridging technology. I think you will agree that this will increase the capability of this warship and the Republic Navy. I can also look into doing the same with the battleships, the RNS *Gladiator*, *Centurion*, and *Majestic*, although this is about as close to direct military intervention as our Humtar people are willing to go at this point."

Viceroy Hunt and the Republic admirals and generals were generally pleased and in good spirits after learning about these newfound advantages that would soon be coming their way. Now that they'd found out what gifts had been waiting under the Christmas tree for them, however, the conversation turned to how they planned to finish off the last of the Pharaonis and the Zodarks.

Chapter Twenty-Nine

RNS *Maddox*
Task Force 28
Gravaxia System

The ghosts of a thousand battles whispered in her ears as Captain Naomi Love surveyed the hangar bay on the orbital assault ship. It stretched before her like a metal canyon, alive with pre-mission preparations. Pilots and ground crews swarmed around the Osprey and Scarab troop transports.

Naomi's mind drifted to her late husband, Jack. She'd lost him aboard a civilian ship, of all places. The man had conducted hundreds of missions as a troop transport pilot in hostile enemy territory, and yet he'd died aboard a Blue Horizon Meridian vessel when a random laser had sliced through the cabin. It had happened years ago, and although the pain of it all still clung to her, it had numbed significantly.

Technicians in grease-stained jumpsuits crawled over her Osprey's hull, making last-minute adjustments. Pilots in their flight suits clustered in small groups, going over mission parameters one last time on their datapads.

Love stood in the elevated command-and-control center, a glass-walled room jutting out from the hangar's upper deck. This vantage point gave her a commanding view of the entire operation below. The transparent floor beneath her feet added to the sensation of floating above the bustle.

Beside her, Master Chief Brian Ford was reading data reports from his console.

"Chief, how're we looking on fuel cells?" she asked.

"All ships topped off, Captain. We've got enough juice to make it moonside and back with room to spare."

"And the new stealth coating?" asked Love. "Any issues with application?"

"Negative," Ford said. "Every bird's got a fresh coat."

Just then, the Rangers they were going to transport started to enter the hangar. She tapped her comm unit, opening a channel to all aviators.

"Attention, all pilots," Love's voice rang out in the helmets of every flier under her command. "Our passengers are arriving—that means it's time to put our war faces on and kick some Zodark ass. While the Rangers load their gear, I want to remind everyone of our objective: to land the Ranger regiment near Tumikhala Spaceport and support the seizure of this critical Zodark facility. You've been briefed on the approach vectors and landing zones. Stay low, stay fast, and stick to your assigned corridors."

"Captain," Ford said, grabbing her attention, "take a look at this."

She eyed his station's monitor and pressed the comms a second time. "Listen up, everyone. We just received a last-minute intel update I need to pass along to you. One of our recon drones spotted the Zodarks deploying mobile SAM units around the perimeter. These weren't in the original briefing, so keep your heads on a swivel and stay alert for this new threat. Remember your training, stay calm and use the tools you have to get you through this. ECM suites should be on the moment you leave the ship. Once the Rangers are deployed, Scarabs, Valkyries and Gripens will provide close-air support. Flight Charlie, Wolfpack, is on standby for medevac and evac duty should things go sideways and we need to pull our people. Any questions, direct them to your flight division leaders. That is all."

As the pilots absorbed the new information, Love turned her attention to a datapad Ford held out. They reviewed the technical readouts of the squadrons, the ships' schematics and weapons, checking and double-checking every detail.

The two of them did a quick check of the Scarabs assigned to Overwatch One, Two, and Three, providing overwatch and close-air support over the battlespace once the assault against the spaceport was underway. Each of the Scarabs was fitted with sixteen multipurpose smart missiles, twenty-two antipersonnel fragmentation missiles and twelve of the nastiest weapons the Republic had—a fuel-air explosive multifunction glide bomb. After the munitions had been checked, mechanics had gone over every inch of those ships. Magrails and blaster turrets were online and calibrated. Full diagnostic runs, checked. No issues detected. The Scarabs were ready to rain hell on the Zodarks.

Switching to another schematic, Love did a final check on the Ospreys. Like the Scarabs, they carried the same multipurpose smart

217

missiles and tiny antipersonnel Kamikaze drones in addition to the pair of .50-caliber rotary magrail cannons and the chin-mounted blaster turret. Oh, how she loved to use that chin gun as it swiveled wherever her helmet faced.

Who wouldn't love strafing runs with a pair of miniguns? she wondered. *The Ospreys are good to go*, she confirmed before closing the file she'd been reviewing.

On the flight line, the Rangers strode toward the waiting troop transports, their armor gleaming under the lights. Each soldier carried an assortment of weapons and gear, ready to kill.

"Anything else I should know before we launch, Chief?" Love asked.

Ford shook his head. "Negative, Captain. We're as ready as we'll ever be."

"Good," Love replied. "Then let's begin."

Love and Ford exited the flight operations center and made their way down to the flight line, where they approached their Osprey. The Rangers fiddled with some gear before loading it into the troop bay. Love and Ford briefly conferred with the crew chief and the maintainers before climbing aboard themselves. Ascending the ramp into the cabin, Love paused as she approached a plaque mounted on the wall. Reaching her fingers out to touch it, she traced the Latin words inscribed there: "Vivere Pugnare Alium Diem." The cool metal under her fingertips helped ground her, as did the meaning of the phrase, which translated to "Live to Fight Another Day."

Ford followed suit, his calloused hand brushing the plaque. Love nodded and walked deeper into the troop bay, rows of seats lining the walls. The space felt hollow, awaiting the Rangers who would soon fill it with their presence.

Love made her way to the cockpit. She slid into the pilot's seat, studying the array of controls and displays. Taped to the dashboard, a photo of Jack looked back at her, his lips upturned into a smile. After kissing her index finger, she touched Jack's lips. "Watch over me again. Keep all our men and women safe, got it?" she said to Jack.

As Ford settled into the copilot's seat, the first of the Rangers appeared at the top of the ramp. Love turned, watching as each soldier filed in. One by one, they reached out to touch the plaque, a solemn ritual that had become deeply ingrained in everyone who entered Love's

Osprey. Over the years she'd been flying, this simple act had spread throughout the ranks. It rippled across the Republic military like a wave of tradition. Even new passengers, Rangers, and troops who boarded her transport had been told by others to touch the plaque, transforming it into a cherished good luck charm. The ritual had taken on a life of its own, passed down from veteran to rookie, creating an unspoken bond among those who served.

Love strapped herself in. "All systems check, Ford. Let's make sure this bird's ready to fly."

"Roger that, Captain. Initiating preflight sequence."

As the Rangers continued to board, Love and Ford ran through their checklist one more time, their voices a steady back-and-forth of technical jargon.

"Fuel cells?" she asked.

"Optimal charge, Captain," Ford replied.

"Hydraulics?"

"Pressure nominal across all systems."

"Weapon systems?"

"Online and calibrated."

As the last Ranger filed in, Love pushed the intercom icon on the dashboard's holodisplay. "Strap in tight, folks. We're launching in sixty seconds."

A holographic countdown appeared on the windshield. Love's hand hovered over the ignition sequence, her attention fixed on the timer.

When the countdown hit zero, Love spoke through her squadron's comms. "All units, this is Wolfpack Lead. Launch sequence initiated. Form up on me."

She initiated engines and her craft hummed beneath her. She eased the transport off the hangar floor.

The hangar bay doors yawned open, revealing the vast expanse of space beyond. Love guided her troop transport through the opening, the transition from artificial gravity to zero-g barely noticeable thanks to the ship's compensators.

As they cleared the orbital assault ship, the moon Lunakor dominated Love's view. Behind her, the rest of the squadron poured out of the assault ship. Scarabs and Ospreys alike emerged, their forms glinting in the system's bright sunlight. Love kept an eye on her display as the squadron fell into formation, each ship taking its assigned place.

While they approached Lunakor's atmosphere, Love's voice boomed over the comms once more. "Wolfpack, initiating atmospheric entry. Vector two-two-five, approach angle seven degrees. Prepare for turbulence."

She adjusted their trajectory, angling the Osprey's nose downward. The ship shuddered as it hit the outer layers of Lunakor's atmosphere. The resulting friction caused the temperature in the cockpit to rise noticeably.

Love remained steady on the controls, making minute adjustments to keep them on course. Beside her, Ford called out readings amidst the growing turbulence.

"Hull temperature rising, within acceptable limits."

"Structural integrity holding at ninety-eight percent."

"Velocity decreasing as expected, currently at Mach 2 as we enter the lower atmosphere."

The shaking intensified, rattling Love's teeth. The muffled grunts and shifting of the Rangers sounded in the cabin behind her. They penetrated deeper into the atmosphere, the sky outside glowing an eerie reddish-orange as the sun set.

Love updated her pilots. "Wolfpack, we're experiencing expected turbulence. Maintain formation and current vector. Prepare for course correction in T minus thirty seconds."

The Osprey bucked, fighting against Love's controls. Ford's voice became a constant stream of data, calling out their rapidly changing status.

"Hull temperature stabilizing."

"Velocity now Mach 1 and decelerating."

"Atmospheric density increasing, adjusting life support accordingly."

As they pierced through a shimmering veil of mist, the landscape bloomed into view beneath them. Sprawling across the horizon was a lush forest of towering trees. Their canopies erupted in a variety of emerald and jade foliage. Several crystal-clear lakes dotted the panorama.

Love began the preprogrammed course correction, guiding the Osprey onto its final approach vector. The rest of the squadrons emulated the action, their formations tightening as they neared the LZ.

"Wolfpack, we are on final approach," Love announced. "Overwatch One, prepare to break formation and stand by for CAS. Wolfpack, stand by for landing instructions. ETA to drop zone: four minutes."

Love's grip tightened on the controls as the Osprey plunged deeper into Lunakor's atmosphere. The ship quivered, buffeted by turbulence as it pushed through layers of gases and particulates. Suddenly, the sky lit up with fire. Bursts of searing energy streaked past the transports, so close that Love could feel the heat through the hull. The cockpit illuminated with each passing volley.

"Incoming fire!" Ford said, his eyes glued to the tactical display. "Crap! Sensors are detecting multiple search and target radars going active!"

Love's jaw clenched as the lethal fireworks show unfolded around them. The energy blasts painted burning bloom patterns across the sky, each one a potential harbinger of destruction.

"Evasive maneuvers!" Love shouted. Her Osprey lurched to the side, narrowly avoiding an explosion that would have torn through them. "Overwatch—weapons free! Engage ground radars and commence suppression of enemy air defense *now!*" ordered Love. She jinked her Osprey to the right before angling her nose down—shedding altitude while accelerating rapidly toward the surface.

She activated the comms. "All Wolfpack squadrons—execute evasive pattern Delta and haul ass to the surface, *now!* You are weapons free—clear your assigned LZ and eliminate any active radars or surface-to-air weapons you find!"

Love was breathing hard now, her muscles strained as she gripped the flight controls, beads of sweat running down the sides of her face. *Stay calm—just breathe*, she told herself before briefly glancing to Ford.

"Ford, damage report!" she exclaimed through gritted teeth.

"We took a hit near the rear of the troop bay! A piece of shrapnel punched a hole there. Mayfield's on it and should have the hull breach sealed momentarily. He's using that new autosealant stuff they gave us to try out," replied Ford.

"Damn, a piece of shrapnel actually managed to rip open the troop bay?" Love replied. She cursed loudly as she hit the air brake, dodging multiple laser beams that nearly cut them apart. She shoved the throttle forward, rapidly accelerating them forward as more lasers cut through the air they'd occupied just moments earlier.

"Oommff—structural integrity at ninety-two percent after that stunt," commented Ford. "Don't forget we've got a hole in the troop compartment that's temporarily sealed with putty and prayers."

Love juked them hard to starboard, then port, weaving a path through a barrage of enemy fire so thick she was surprised they hadn't been sliced apart yet.

"Wolfpacks, this is Lead," she called out over the wing frequency. "Tighten your formations up—LZ in sixty seconds. Overwatch Two and Three: you are weapons free! Prioritize enemy search and targeting radars. Destroy those SAM sites at bearing zero-six-zero degrees, range—four kilometers."

Acknowledgments came over the comm as her pilots responded. A large cloud of flames to her port drew Love's attention. Her heart sank as she realized two of the Ospreys on her flank were falling to the ground as fiery wrecks.

Comms chatter flooded in. "Wolfpack Actual, this is Wolfpack One-Seven, we've lost engines!"

"Wolfpack One-One. Taking heavy fire! Hull integrity critical!"

Another explosion rocked the formation. This time it was a Scarab to her right-front quadrant as it blew up.

"Wolfpack One-Nine is down!" someone said over the comm. "I repeat, Wolfpack One-Nine is down!"

Love grew increasingly frustrated until she shouted, "Enough! Clear the comms and cut the chatter! We're approaching the LZ, thirty seconds—we're almost there!"

Through the viewport, the expanse of Tumikhala Spaceport came into view. The facility bristled with Zodark defenses, gun emplacements and missile batteries littering its perimeter. Surrounding the spaceport, a dense jungle spanned into the distance. Love's tactical display lit up, pinpointing designated landing zones near the base's outskirts.

"Wolfpacks, this is Lead," Love called out. "LZ in sight. Prepare for final approach. Overwatch elements, maintain covering fire."

She guided her craft toward the nearest landing zone, a small clearing just beyond the jungle's edge. Enemy fire continued to streak past, but it was less intense now as they neared the ground.

"Ford, give me a status update on our Rangers," Love said.

"Rangers are prepped and ready, Captain," Ford reported. "No injuries from the turbulence. They're good to go.

"Thirty seconds to touchdown," she announced over the Osprey's intercom system. "Rangers, prepare for deployment. Watch each other's backs down there. I want you all coming back in one piece! All of you."

The Osprey's landing gear extended as they neared the clearing. Other surviving transports touched down, forming a loose perimeter around the landing zone.

"Touching down in three... two... one..."

The Osprey trembled as its landing gear made contact with the lunar soil. Love powered down the engines and activated the deployment ramp.

"Go, go, go!" came the shouts of the Rangers.

The thunderous sound of the Rangers charging down the ramp reverberated through the troop bay, their boots pounding against the metal floor.

As the last Ranger disembarked, her Osprey's sensors beeped incessantly.

"Ford, give me a SITREP," Love directed.

"Huh, that's not good," he mumbled. "One of our scout drones is reporting multiple large groups of Zodark soldiers approaching from all vectors. Closest group is at our two o'clock, five hundred meters and closing fast. I count at least three battalions' worth converging on our position."

"Geez...who invited those guys to our kegger?" Love joked, breaking some of the tension of the moment. "Ford, we've got to buy time for our ground forces to secure the area."

She activated the comms. "All Wolfpacks, we've got enemy ground force inbound to the LZ. We need to maintain defensive positions around the LZ and give our Rangers a chance to fortify it while additional Ranger units are brought in. Find your targets and engage at will."

With the orders given, she brought the Osprey into a low hover, just meters above the ground. As she activated the gun system, targets suddenly began to appear—two hundred meters, one hundred and fifty meters, one hundred meters...she pulled the trigger, her eyes going wide at what she saw next.

Chapter Thirty

RNS *Jack*
Task Force 28
Lunakor Moon

"Tangos incoming!" Ford's voice cut through the din. "Multiple hostiles, eleven o'clock!"

Zodark soldiers materialized from the dense foliage, some leaping from towering trees with inhuman agility. The jungle erupted in a hail of weapons fire. Several Rangers crumpled to the ground, dead from a hail of blaster fire.

"Deploying APM drones," Love said, her fingers tapping the tactical display.

A swarm of drones shot from the Osprey's launch tubes. They streaked toward the enemy. Love activated the chin-mounted blaster turret.

"Ford, engage with the magrails."

"Aye, Captain."

The air ignited with tracer fire as the twin .50-caliber five-barrel magrail cannons roared to life. Trees splintered and exploded as they were cut to pieces. In the distance, Zodark soldiers were torn apart by the hypersonic projectiles ripping through the air.

"Good effect on target!" Ford said.

As the Kamikaze drones reached their targets, diving into clusters of enemy troops, explosions rocked the jungle floor, sending plumes of dirt and dismembered Zodarks skyward.

"Multiple KIAs confirmed," Ford reported. "They're still coming, Captain!"

Love swung the turret, laying down suppressing fire as more Rangers sprinted for cover. "Come on," she muttered, picking off Zodarks as quickly as her guns could fire.

A rocket shot through the woods, heading right for them.

BAM!

The massive explosion rocked the Osprey, sending dirt, rocks, and pieces of trees raining down on them. Warning klaxons blared as the craft shuddered.

"Status!" Love shouted over the roar of the guns.

"We're good—it missed us. Just taking splash damage to the paint job."

The jungle in front of them had turned into a hellscape of smoke, severed tree trunks, and the bodies of dead Zodarks. To the right and left of them, Rangers and Zodarks were locked in brutal close-quarter combat, exchanging intense fire.

"Captain, our power cells are overheating." Ford's voice was edged with stress. "The magrails are drawing too much juice."

Love cursed under her breath. "Divert power from nonessential systems. We can't lose those guns!"

With the turret synced to her helmet, wherever she looked, that was where the gun aimed. Catching a flash of movement to her left, she turned to see what it was just in time to catch a Zodark squad attempting to flank a group of pinned-down Rangers. She pulled the trigger, holding it down as the blaster spewed the hate and anger she felt toward this insidious race of monsters. The blaster bolts shredded their bodies apart, eliminating them before they could attack the Rangers.

BOOM!

Another explosion erupted near them—the concussive blastwave shook their Osprey as shrapnel pelted its armored hull.

"Look out! Multiple hostiles, six o'clock high!" Ford shouted, pointing at the new threat. "They're in the damn trees."

Love spun the turret, unleashing a withering barrage into the canopy. Zodark snipers and machine gunners fell from their perches, their bodies riddled with holes.

"How're we looking on ammo?" Love asked, a hint of concern in her voice.

"Not good," Ford replied. "Magrails down to thirty percent, and we're out of APM drones!"

"Roger that. Maintain fire. Call out priority targets. We need to make every round count."

The dim lighting in the cockpit flickered briefly.

"Captain, power cells are critical. We're gonna lose the guns!"

Almost on cue, the chin-mounted blaster turret went dead—followed by the magrails moments later.

"Whoa! What the hell just happened?" Love yelled.

Ford's tone lowered, his eyes on the dashboard's interface. "Wow, we actually melted the power cells to the weapons systems. The cooling systems couldn't handle the strain. Captain, we need to get off the ground and back to the *Maddox* for repairs before we lose any more systems."

"OK, on it." Love lifted the craft off the jungle floor. All around her, other Scarabs and Ospreys rose into the sky. While they were ascending, Love spotted a missile leap into the air. It took off with blinding speed toward one of her Valkyrie bombers. The bomber was in the middle of releasing a stick of a dozen five-hundred-pound bombs over top the length of a defensive trench work protecting the outer perimeter of the spaceport.

She watched the event unfold like it was in slow motion. There was nothing Love could do to stop that missile or warn the pilot of the danger heading toward him. The Valk's automated defense suite spotted the threat and released flares and chaff canisters to try and spoof the missile's guidance system. However, it flew past the flares and through the chaff, detonating once it had closed the distance to get within range of its proximity sensor.

Love watched as the left wing of the Valkyrie was torn off the fuselage, causing the bomber to spin out of control as flames enveloped it. Within seconds, a small figure ejected from the doomed craft—the parachute blossoming above the individual.

At that moment, Love ignored her bleeding heart instincts and followed her training with automaticity. "Ford, I want you to geotag the downed pilot's location. Pass it along to any nearby Ranger units on the ground. Also send it to the *Maddox* search and recovery squadron."

"On it," Ford replied.

When that had been completed, Love led the rest of her force back to the *Maddox* for round two, delivering more troops to the surface.

Chapter Thirty-One

11th Spartacus Armor Regiment
DreamScape MWR
RNS *Callisto*

Kennedy paddled hard, feeling the resistance of the water beneath him; he caught the wave just as it began to crest. He popped up on his surfboard, the rush of adrenaline and excitement surging through his veins. As he dropped into the barrel, the wave curved around him, forming a perfect tube. He crouched low, his hand skimming the wall of the wave, the sensation of the cold, misty spray hitting his face as he shot through the tunnel.

This is incredible. Back on Earth, Kennedy had been one of his state's best surfers, spending countless hours in the ocean to perfect his skills. It was rare for him to find another surfer who was even close to as good as he was.

Kennedy extended his hand toward the churning water. The speed of the wave continued to propel him and his board through the water. He had to remind himself this was all part of the Metaverse—as real as he wanted it to be. It was just an illusion, a digital mind trip to spoof his body into believing it was real.

He brushed away the droplets of water from his face. For the briefest of moments, he forgot that he was in a virtual reality sim pod, his body encased in a Metaverse suit from head to toe aboard the RNS *Callisto*.

As the wave began to die out, Kennedy launched himself off his board. He hit the water with a splash, the sensation so authentic that his mind momentarily struggled to reconcile the fact that he wasn't in the ocean at all. He surfaced, the familiar salty taste of seawater on his lips, only to blink and remember that this was all a simulation. The Metaverse suit had replicated everything perfectly—the cold water, the weightlessness, even the sound of waves crashing around him.

Kennedy paddled back out to where Wilson and Captain Martin waited, a grin stretching from ear to ear. The transition from the hyperrealistic surf to the sterile awareness of his true surroundings was jarring, but in that moment, he didn't care. The DreamScape MWR Metaverse had done its job—given him a taste of home, an escape from the harsh realities of life aboard a starship. For now, he was content to ride the virtual waves, even if it was all just a dream.

"Nice run, Kennedy," Wilson called out, giving him a high-five as he approached.

"Thanks, man. These suits are something else, huh? Feels like we're really here."

All three sat straddling their boards. The warm water lapped at their legs as they watched their fellow soldiers catching waves in the distance. The simulation was so realistic. They were light-years from any real ocean, but while inside their suits and wearing virtual reality goggles, there was almost no difference between fake and real.

An hour ago, just before Kennedy had walked through the VR room's entrance, he'd noticed that the words emblazoned above the door read "Where Reality and Illusion Converge." No truer words were ever written.

"So, what do you guys think about this upcoming operation on Eurysa?" Kennedy asked. He squinted against the virtual sun's glare.

Martin huffed. "We've got three days until our R&R's dead and gone. Let's talk about something else, like—"

Wilson shrugged Martin off. "It's on our minds, so why not? You know, I heard it's supposed to be a real paradise there. There's more to what we saw in briefing with the general. I've looked more into it in private. Lots of green, plenty of water. Fruits everywhere, most of which we can eat, they say…"

"If we can secure those archipelagos, we'll get the upper hand on the Pharaonis," Kennedy said. "And it's important, because—"

"Seriously?" Martin slowly grinned. "You can't keep your mind in one place, can you?"

"Not when it comes to surf…" Kennedy gave a thumbs-up. "After we kick those Pharaonis' heads off, I say we find some trees, carve out some boards, and hit those alien waves."

Martin laughed. "You really think they'll let us go surfing in the middle of a war?"

"After the operation's over, why not? We'll have earned a little pat on the back and some fun. Besides, can you imagine the kind of waves a planet like that might have? We could be talking twenty meters, easy."

Wilson let out a low whistle. "Twenty meters? That's insane. I don't know if I could handle that. Where did you get that info?"

"Ah, just guessing. OK, OK, maybe not twenty. But even ten would be incredible."

"We can dream," Martin said. "But, hey, none of us have been to the surface of Eurysa, and those intel weenies are protecting whatever information they have about the planet like it's your daughter's virginity—"

Wilson slugged Martin in the arm, causing him to wince.

"Ouch, what the hell, sir?"

Wilson stared daggers at the young man until he wilted and apologized.

"Well, the point was, for all we know, it could be a surfer's nightmare," Martin explained.

Wilson's face softened. "Don't ruin Kennedy's wet dream, and I mean that literally," he said with a laugh. "Who knows, we could be talking ten-, fifteen-, twenty-meter waves."

"All right." Martin shook his head, another small grin creeping across his face. "If we do manage to catch some waves on Eurysa, I call dibs on the first ride."

"Deal," Kennedy said, extending his hand.

As Martin went to shake, he jerked away when a shark swam past him, jumping on his board so fast it slipped out from under him and he fell into the water. "Whoa! What the hell?" He swam like his life depended on it back onto his board, his eyes wild. "Did you see that?"

Wilson cackled so hard he fell off his own board. After he climbed back on top, he wiped the salt out of his eyes. "Relax, Martin. It's not real. It can't actually bite you. You should have seen your face."

"OK, tough guy." Martin shifted on his board. "I still remember when a spider crawled onto your cot while you were sleeping. You woke up with a shriek. Never heard a man scream so high."

Kennedy chuckled. "Woke up everyone." He blew air through his lips. "Come on. Let's head in. I could use a break from all this excitement."

The three of them lay facedown on their boards and padded toward the shore.

"You think it'll ever end?" Kennedy asked, his voice matching what he felt deep down—somber.

Martin exhaled loudly. "Sometimes it feels like we're just spinning our wheels out here. No matter how many Zodarks or Pharaonis or whoever we take out, there always seem to be more waiting somewhere else."

"It's a big galaxy," Wilson commented.

Kennedy paddled harder. "As long as even one Zodark is still alive, they're going to keep fighting. It's in their blood. They won't stop until they've wiped us out completely, or we wipe them out."

Martin frowned, looking like he didn't agree with Kennedy's assessment. "I don't know. I mean, sure, the Zodarks are a violent species, but maybe they're not all the same? I might be dreaming here, but there could be some out there who want peace just as much as we do."

"Dreaming? No, you're living in la-la land." Wilson scoffed. "The only good Zodark is a dead Zodark."

When they reached the shore, lounge chairs conjured by some unseen digital force materialized on the pristine white sand. They set their boards down and sank into the chairs.

All around them, the Metaverse thrived with life. In the distance, other soldiers caught waves. Their shouts of exhilaration carried across the water. Palm trees swayed in a gentle breeze, their palm leafs rustling. The ocean stretched out before them—a sparkling blue expanse going on forever. There were even pods of dolphins that would periodically leapt and spun through the waves bringing even more realism to what people saw.

"Hey, Wilson, maybe you can answer this question that's been bugging me for a while," Kennedy started. "Crewing the colonel's tank, you probably hear a lot, especially conversations between him and the general from time to time, right?"

Wilson's demeanor turned serious. "Maybe," he replied. "That depends what you are asking. The colonel's a good man, a good commander. How about you ask your question, and I'll tell you if I can answer it."

"That's fair," said Kennedy. "Here's my question—why are we doing this? Invading another planet, I mean. Why not reduce the planet to rubble unless they surrender? It just seems like we are wasting lives doing what we are doing."

Martin looked like he was about to say something, but he paused to hear Wilson's response.

Wilson leaned forward. "I asked the colonel the same thing," he admitted. "He said bombarding an enemy's cities to dust from space leaves the enemy with no outs, no reason to surrender, no reason to end their resistance. He said unless the Republic or the alliance wants to eradicate an entire species, we have to convince the enemy to surrender—"

"And how do you do that?" interrupted Kennedy. "Convince the Pharaonis, or the Zodarks for that matter, to surrender?"

Wilson smiled, undeterred by the interruption. "Easy," he replied. "You remind them of what they have, what they stand to lose should they continue to fight. You were too young to have served during the first and second battles of Alfheim that ended the First Zodark War. The reason the war ended was because the Viceroy offered the Orbots a shared occupation of that frozen wasteland. At the time, no one realized the importance of the planet, but it was one of the few places you could mine that rare material, Bronkis5—the stuff that makes our ship armor so tough.

"When the Orbots were presented with an offer allowing them to still have access to the material they wanted if they agreed to end the war, they took it." Wilson held a hand up to forestall any questions Kennedy was about to ask. "The reason for putting boots on the ground is to remind the enemy we aren't restricted to flatten their cities from space. We can just as easily eradicate them from the surface. But more than that, the ground campaign gives the enemy time to think, time to accept the situation as it is: yield and be allowed to live, resist and watch as your species is slowly eradicated one city, one village at a time. If the people want to live, eventually they overthrow their government to seek terms or force their government into accepting them."

As Wilson finished explaining, Kennedy started to see the logic in the plan, even if he didn't like it. "Man, war is messed up, isn't it?" he managed to reply.

"Yeah, it is. I just hope after we defeat the Pharaonis and turn our attention to finishing this war with the Zodarks, it all ends," Martin offered. "I sometimes imagine how things might have turned out if our first contact team hadn't been attacked when we first met the Zodarks."

Wilson laughed. "Yeah, I could see it now—us palling around with those blue beasts like we're best friends."

They joked around about how things would have been different if that fateful day had turned out differently. The conversation soon drifted to family, Wilson and Martin doing most of the talking.

"Hey, Kennedy, did you ever talk to your kiddos?" Martin asked.

Kennedy hesitated. "Uh, a little."

Martin raised his eyebrows. "And?"

"It was good," Kennedy said. He'd taken his therapist's advice on letting her coach him through a comm call with his soon-to-be ex-wife. They had focused on effective communication techniques like active listening and empathetic "I" statements. Appealing to his ex-wife's desire for their children's well-being, he had asked her to let him speak with the twins more often. To his surprise, she'd agreed, and he'd been able to have a long conversation with his children just a few days ago.

Wilson rolled his head toward Martin. "You know, you can be a little too nosy sometimes."

"It's my most loved asset," Martin replied.

"Nope, not even close."

As his friends bantered back and forth, Kennedy's thoughts drifted to his conversation with his kids. It had been harder than he had expected, trying to explain why he was so far away and when he would be coming home. He had wanted to tell them everything, to pour out his heart and let them know how much he loved and missed them. With kids that young, though, it wasn't easy.

What Kennedy also hadn't told his friends was that he had spoken to the twins twice in the past week. He'd stayed up late into the night cycle just to hear their voices. With each passing day, the reality of their upcoming mission on Eurysa loomed larger. Kennedy grew more and more anxious.

He knew that the fighting would be brutal. That there was a very real chance he might not make it back alive. Any combat presented that possibility. The thought of leaving his children fatherless… he didn't want to think about it. He did his best to divert his thoughts elsewhere.

Kennedy held up a hand. "Server!"

An older gentleman wearing a butler outfit popped onto the virtual reality space next to Kennedy. "How may I be of service, sir?"

"Hey, could you bring us the best wine you've got?" Kennedy asked, a glint in his eye. "Something really special, like a 2012 Château Lafite, a 2005 Petrus, and maybe a 2015 Screaming Eagle. Three bottles, if you don't mind."

The butler inclined his head. "Of course, sir. I shall fetch them right away."

With a faint pop, the butler vanished. He reappeared seconds later with a silver tray bearing three elegant bottles of wine. Kennedy reached out to take one, then paused. "Too bad we can't actually drink these." He ran a finger along one of the labels. "Wouldn't that be something, getting buzzed in the Metaverse?"

Wilson snorted. "Yeah, and then waking up with a hangover in the real world. No, thanks."

Kennedy waved the butler away. "Never mind. Come back when you have the real stuff, OK?"

The butler raised an eyebrow. "I'm afraid that would be quite impossible, sir. As you know, this is only a simulation."

"Yeah, yeah, I know." Kennedy leaned back in his chair. "It's OK, Wilson will get me the real stuff when we beat the Pharaonis. Right, buddy?"

Wilson yawned. "Not in a million years."

"Aw, come on." Kennedy clapped his hands together. "You can't blame a guy for trying."

The butler cleared his throat. "Will there be anything else, sir?"

"No, that's all for now. Thanks."

With another faint pop, the butler disappeared, leaving the three friends alone on the beach once more.

Chapter Thirty-Two

Early April 2115
RNS *Valiant*
Zanthea Star System
En Route to Eurysa, Pharaonis Home World

Captain Joe Wright stood at the center of the *Valiant*'s bridge, his eyes locked on the holographic display of the planet Eurysa, now dominating the viewscreen. It was beautiful, very much like Earth, New Eden, or even Sumer and Alpha Centauri. He studied the distant planet as it glowed like a precious stone with blue and green hues. It was an incredible contrast to the black void of space surrounding it. Wright's hands rested on the cool metal of the railing as he observed the incoming data feeds, each one confirming what he already suspected—the Pharaonis weren't going to surrender. They were going to fight. "XO, what's our current distance to the Pharaonis fleet?" asked Wright, his voice calm yet carrying the weight of command—honed through years of space combat.

Commander Shane Weber, standing just off to the right, kept his eyes on his tactical screen. "Two million kilometers, Captain. We're beginning to receive some good data on their fleet from those drones the *Sirius* launched a while back. We've got eyes on what's left of their fleet. They look to be clustered near the northern pole of the planet. But these readings…they seem off somehow."

Wright raised an eyebrow, a pang of concern rising within him. He still had flashbacks from the last time a clever trap had ambushed his ship the Pharaonis had set up. His crew, his ship, the *Teddy*, had barely escaped destruction. The *Teddy*, his first command of a major warship, would likely spend the better part of one or even two years in the shipyard before she'd be ready to rejoin the Fleet. After that fateful encounter, his entire crew had been transferred to the newly built *Victory*-class battleship, the RNS *Valiant*.

"Here, look at this." Wright pointed to the Pharaonis ships on the tactical action map. "See what I mean? Now that they know we're here, look at what they're doing. They're positioning themselves in low orbit over both of the polar caps. This will let them leverage the planet's gravity and likely planetary defense weapons on the surface. It's actually a brilliant idea, considering the situation. But look over here, at this moon." He pointed toward the moon Zephyra, in orbit of the planet Skiron. "If I were in charge of their fleet, I'd position our weakest ships there. Then, I would have the remainder of my fleet positioned on the dark side of Zephyra and wait—wait until our forces are in high orbit over Eurysa, then spring the trap and come at us from the rear."

Weber's face now looked concerned. "Huh, that makes a lot of sense," he replied, apparently trying to play it cool. "Oh, check this out, sir. Speak of the Devil—it seems the admiral must have had the same thought. It looks like he's sending a squadron to investigate it—two battleships, eight cruisers, and fourteen frigates. Damn, that's a lot of firepower."

"Yeah, it is," Wright acknowledged with a nod. "I'm glad we didn't get pulled off our mission. You've seen how those Pharaonis fight. They're savages. If our orbital bombardments can soften them up before the ground force is dirtside, we might be able to save some lives. Have I told you about my youngest brother?" he asked, changing topics. "The one who had to buck the family tradition and joined the Army instead of the Fleet?"

"No, I didn't realize you had a younger brother in the Army," said Weber. "What does he do, if you don't mind me asking?"

"He's a regimental commander in the 11th Infantry Division, the 22nd Dubliners," Wright proudly extolled.

"Ah, isn't that General Varinius's division?" asked Weber.

"It sure is—good ole Spartacus Varinius. He grew up on the mean streets of Rome before his family immigrated to the Republic. But, like I was saying earlier, I'm glad we're still on a mission. The more we can beat the Pharaonis into submission from orbit, the fewer casualties we'll likely take once the orbital assault begins," explained Wright.

"Just remember something, Shane," he continued. "Desperate people fight with everything they've got. This is why we mustn't allow ourselves to underestimate the enemy. The Pharaonis know this is the final battle. They'll be defending their home and their families, just like we did during the Battle of Sol. That's the kind of motivation you can't ignore and dismiss at your own peril."

"Aye, Captain. The crew is sharp. They won't let you down," replied Weber, his tone more serious. "It looks like we'll have a little bit of time before we're within weapons range. I'll have the gunnery crews ready the batteries for long-range engagements. Unless you tell me otherwise, I'm going to talk to Flight Ops and have them ready the bomber strike packages for antiship missions and the fighters for space dominance. Just give the word, and they'll launch."

Wright smiled widely at his XO, who had practically read his mind. "Good call, XO. In the meantime, I'm going to my quarters to try and catch a bit of shut-eye. We should have a few hours before things start happening. Wake me if you need to. Otherwise, you have the bridge."

"Aye, Captain! The XO has the bridge," Commander Weber declared firmly as he sat in the captain's chair.
****

Five Hours Later
Bridge of the RNS *Defiant*
En Route to Eurysa, Pharaonis Home World
Zanthea System

"Admiral, we're receiving an urgent communiqué from the *Rass*," announced Lieutenant Willard. "Sir, you were right. The *Rass* has detected thirty-eight warships in low lunar orbit of the moon Zephyra. Captain DeWolf of the *Rass* and Captain Lionel of the *Triumph* are deploying their squadrons and moving to attack the enemy force."

Vice Admiral Rosentreter stood from his seat as he looked at Lieutenant Willard. "You said thirty-eight warships—what's the composition? What kinds of ships are they facing?"

Willard contorted his face as he continued to read the report. "Whoa, sorry about that, sir. Captain DeWolf is reporting fourteen of those Blacktips—frigates, basically—nine Makos cruisers, six Thresher battleships, and nine of those Hammerheads—those heavy destroyers that pummeled the Fleet pretty hard during the Serenea campaign."

Admiral Rosentreter nodded as he took it all in. His mind was racing with possible scenarios of whether Captain DeWolf's squadron would be enough to handle this larger Pharaonis warship or if he should dispatch additional ships now before the heaviest of the fight started.

As he was about to speak, his XO, Captain Luke Bucee, walked up to him, "Sir, I'm pretty sure DeWolf and Lionel can handle this. But maybe it wouldn't hurt our position if we directed a squadron of Altairian warships to back them up."

He turned to face his XO. "That's a good idea, Bucee—Lieutenant Willard, send a FRAGO to the Altairian battleship, *Berkimon A2*, and have them proceed with maximum speed to assist the *Rass* and *Triumph* squadrons in neutralizing that Pharaonis fleet in orbit of Zephyra."

"Aye, Admiral, generating the fragmentary order now," Willard replied quickly, his fingers typing away.

"Lieutenant Lando, I think it's time we open the throttle on the engine, throw ourselves into the battle to seize the high ground over Eurysa and begin the work of finishing this war," exclaimed Admiral Rosentreter, a devilish grin spreading from ear to ear.

It's time we end this, he thought, relishing the opportunity to get some payback for the invasion of Sol.
****

Five Hours Later
Bridge of the RNS *Valiant*
Approaching High Orbit Over the Planet Eurysa

Captain Joe Wright gripped the armrest of his command chair. His eyes narrowed as the bridge monitor flickered from the intense flash of a nearby explosion. The Pharaonis Makos cruiser had erupted into a brilliant ball of fire, its shattered hull spiraling into the black void. For a moment, the bridge was bathed in white light, the sheer brilliance of the explosion washing out the display. Then, as quickly as it had flared, the light faded, leaving behind the grim reality of battle.

The external cameras adjusted, and the chaos of the fight happening around them resumed its relentless assault. Bright streaks of red and yellow laser fire crisscrossed in and around allied warships, with the occasional burst connecting against the outer hull of allied vessels. It was almost like watching an artist splashing strands of bright colors in haphazard patterns that made it nearly impossible to avoid being hit.

Captain Wright watched the battle intensify as the rate of fire from what remained of the Pharaonis fleet and the antiorbital guns on the surface picked up. It felt like each shot, each burst of energy was a signal of the weight of desperation—the weight of knowing their defeat was imminent, their near-certain extermination unavoidable. Wright knew if the Pharaonis refused to surrender and refused to submit to the alliance, this battle would be the beginning of the end of the Pharaonis as a spacefaring people.

"Ack, damn! That was bright," exclaimed Lieutenant Commander Becerra from her comms station. "Ensign House, I just modified the auto dimmers for the OmniView. I know you're focusing on driving the ship, but don't forget to check it when the ship goes to Condition One."

"Aye-aye, ma'am. My apologies. I won't let it happen again," House acknowledged.

BOOM!

The *Valiant* shook violently from whatever had just hit them. Captain Wright released his white-knuckled grip on his chair as sparks rained overtop the tactical section of the bridge.

"What the hell just hit us?" shouted the XO as he walked briskly toward the tactical section.

Tapping his communicator, Wright demanded, "Engineering, Bridge—what hit us, and how bad was it?"

It took a moment for someone to respond. "We took a hit along the belly of the ship. Damage reports are still coming in, but it looks like the bulk of the impact occurred in the vicinity of the starboard recovery bay. Give me five minutes to figure out how bad it is, and I'll get back to you," Commander Peter Mertes explained.

"Did I hear that right?" asked Commander Weber, a look of concern on his face.

"Yeah, starboard recovery bay—get in touch with Flight Ops and see how they're doing. Ask if or how badly this might impact our flight operations. We can scale back our use of the bomber squadrons, but I want to make sure we have plenty of fighters deployed. We've got too many transports relying on us for protection," ordered Captain Wright.

"Aye, sir. Maybe we got lucky, and it won't have been that bad of a hit," his XO offered optimistically before returning to check on some other crewmen.

Captain Wright shook his head. *If we can't use that recovery bay, that is a serious problem*, he realized.

When he looked up, he caught the eye of his Chief of the Boat, Master Chief Petty Officer Bill Walters. "COB, I need a couple of things from you," Wright called out. "First, discreetly run a diagnostic on the OmniView to see if any of the lenses were damaged during the last couple of flashes. We're going to need it once we start bombarding the planet, and if it's damaged, we need to know now so we can get the auto shop crafting repair parts for it. I also want you to check on the wounded—head down to sickbay, and get a sense of how things are going with the crew as you pass their stations."

"That's a good idea, sir. I'll see how everyone is holding up. I may pay a visit to Engineering and Flight Ops on my way to sickbay," the COB replied. He promptly turned to head for the exit and check on the crew.

Wright marveled at times at how much new tech had been integrated into this third generation of the *Victory*-class battleships. He wished they had been given more time to familiarize themselves with the new Gallentine and Humtar technologies—they had essentially turned this battleship into a new warship altogether. The addition of the superior Gallentine sensors, the Omni-Spectral Array (OSA), and the Pulsar Echo Location System or PELS greatly enhanced their ability to find, fix, and destroy enemy ships almost instantly after exiting a stargate or a wormhole bridge. The comms system had also been upgraded with the quantum beam link or QB system, enabling real-time in-system comms and near-real-time comms to nearly anywhere in the Milky Way.

"Captain, Engineering," his comms device chirped.

Wright bristled. *Finally, it's about time he called with an update.* Tapping the comms unit, he replied, "Pete, give me a status update."

"We took a torpedo hit adjacent to the starboard recovery bay— the right side of the bay," he explained, then paused. "That's the fuel storage side, Captain."

Oh, crap—that could have been a lot worse.

"We think we have the fires under control right now, but the bay...she'll be nonoperational for a while. I've got two magrail turrets on the port side down and a single turbo laser on the starboard side—"

"How badly damaged are the guns, Pete?" Wright interrupted.

"The turbo laser should be operational in a few hours. Once the fighting subsides, I'll be sending a repair team outside to finish some repairs we can't finish inside the ship. On the port side, turret seven is toast—it's slag at this point. We'll need to put her in the shipyard for that kind of repair. Turret nine should be back in action within the hour. How's the fight looking? Are we almost through it?" the chief engineer asked.

"Thanks for the update, Pete. As to the fight—they're down to a few ships. It won't be long now," Wright answered.

"I gotta go, Captain. The kids need supervising," Commander Mertes joked before the connection terminated.

Wright returned to his captain's chair as he studied the tactical situation. This was one of the features he really enjoyed about the new warship. The captain's chair was designed in such a way that it allowed him to pull up multiple holographic displays, showing a three-dimensional overview of the battle happening around them. It could even show him the trajectory lines his gun turrets were aimed at and track the projectiles or missiles fired at enemy targets. He was still familiarizing himself with all the different features available to him. "I really wish we had been given more to acquaint ourselves with the *Valiant*'s upgrades before we left the Titan Proving Grounds," he mumbled to himself.

What really excited him about the new capabilities being added to the newest generation of *Victory*-class battleships was the addition of the Humtar version of the quantum conduit bridge. This was the same bridging technology the Gallentine and Humtar ships possessed that allowed them to create wormholes between two points in space and time. It was a technological wonder he would probably never fully understand, and he was OK with that.

Hell, even Pete, as brilliant an engineer as he is, doesn't fully understand how either of those quantum fusion reactors works—and for now, he doesn't need to, he thought.

When the *Valiant* had received orders to rejoin Admiral Rosentreter's Third Fleet, they had been in the midst of an extensive and intensive training program with several Humtar engineering experts. With their deployment imminent, the Humtar instructors had worked feverishly to program six of the thirty E200 engineering Synths that worked alongside their human engineering counterparts to be able to maintain and or conduct maintenance and repairs of the QF reactors should a problem arise while the ship was deployed. Once it became clear they needed at least one person beyond the engineering Synths who knew what they were doing, the Humtar ambassador to the Republic consented to allow one of the Humtars, named Kursag, to accompany them into battle, just in case a repair or situation was beyond the Synths' ability to identify or fix. It also meant their Humtar instructor, Kursag, would be able to continue training Commander Mertes's engineers.

"Good shooting!" Lieutenant Commander Becerra congratulated.

Captain Wright pushed aside the holographic displays he'd been studying to see what was happening. When he turned to face the main monitor on the bridge, he was just in time to see a volley of thirty-six-inch magrail slugs hammer the exterior hull of the Pharaonis warship. Traveling at a velocity of twenty-five thousand meters per second, the kinetic energy alone was powerful enough to cause significant damage to the outer hull of a warship. Watching the volley of projectiles hammering away at the Pharaonis battleship, Wright spied a couple of flashes, a telltale sign of a ricochet. Some of the shells impacted at the wrong angle, causing them to bounce off the armored shell and tumble harmlessly into space. While this occasionally happened to some of the projectiles, more often than not, several would score direct hits, causing immense damage once the multistage warheads exploded deep within the ship.

One of the more closely guarded military secrets within the Republic was how their projectiles worked and what made them deadly. Buried deep within the core of this multistage thirty-six-inch projectile was a five-thousand-pound unique mixture of a chemically engineered high-explosive material designed at first to detonate, creating a cavernous pocket before the second stage exploded, scattering a sticky gelatin-like material against anything and everything it touched. Within three to five seconds of exposure to oxygen, the gelatin-like material would chemically ignite, burning rapidly until it reached temperatures in excess of two thousand degrees Fahrenheit. The newly created firestorm rapidly consumed all available oxygen and atmosphere within the ship. As the heat of the fire begins to melt through the inner decks of the ship, the structural integrity of the targeted vessel would begin to buckle and fail. In the vacuum of space, the insides of the ship would be constantly sucked outward until it exploded.

"It's finally going down, sir," Wright's XO said confidently as he stood next to him. "If I'm not mistaken, that's the final Thresher from what's left of their fleet."

Captain Wright nodded to himself, smiling. "That's correct. It's the last of their Threshers. Seeing them explode like this, it never gets old, XO. Watching these once majestic, enormous warships being torn apart from within—it's a beautiful thing to watch," he shared, just as multiple jets of flame ejected from at least four of the entry wounds in the armor of the ship. It didn't take long before a series of explosions rippled across the giant vessel and the ship broke apart.

Wright was satisfied with what he saw and knew his escort ships were more than a match to finish off the remaining Pharaonis warships. He turned to his XO. "Shane, that was a good fight," he commented. "I'm going to my quarters to consult privately with Admiral Rosentreter on our next steps. In the meantime, you have the bridge. Stay on top of any repairs that might slow us up or need to be performed before we enter the planet's upper atmosphere."

"Aye-aye, Captain. I'll stay on it and make sure Commander Mertes and his engineers have us ready to begin our next mission," Commander Weber assured him. He then loudly said, "Lieutenant Baker, have your gunners focus their fire on the best available targets. Commander Little, I need your CIC section to begin identifying targets. See if *Draco*'s CIC has generated a priority target list they want our battleships to begin going after."

In a lowered, almost hushed tone, Commander Mertes whispered, "We got this, sir. If something happens—we'll get you."

"Very well, XO. You have the bridge," Wright replied as he walked toward the exit, heading toward his office and quarters just beyond the bridge.
****

Five Hours Later
Bridge of the RNS *Valiant*
In Orbit of Planet Eurysa

With a warrior's admiration, Captain Wright observed how the different Pharaonis antiship batteries had gone from firing random beams of ionized particles to well-coordinated ion beams that bracketed an allied ship. Several of the ionized particle beams cut deep gashes and lines across their victims.

This was the first time Wright had seen the discharge of an ion cannon. It was different from what he had expected. When the cannon fired, it hit its target with a bright blue glowing beam as the expelled energy plowed into its target.

One thing was certain as the allied fleet descended into low orbit—something seemed to have changed with whoever was commanding the planetary defensive batteries. Where moments earlier, the firing patterns had been a disjointed randomized firing pattern, now the batteries were coordinating their fire and had gone from a nuisance to a dangerous threat the fleet had to prioritize destroying.

The ion batteries were soon joined by giant magnetic railguns, hurling giant projectiles in similar coordinated firing patterns, focusing their fire against one allied ship at a time until it was disabled or destroyed. The fleet suddenly found itself in a fight it had to win and win quickly before the Pharaonis guns picked them apart.

These Pharaonis continue to surprise me, Wright conceded.

"Captain, we're receiving a message from Admiral Rosentreter," announced Lieutenant Commander Becerra.

Wright turned to face his comms officer. "Go ahead and put him through. Put it on the main viewer," he directed, watching his bridge crew quickly fix their uniform blouses on the off chance the admiral might see them.

Admiral Rosentreter's image filled the floor-to-ceiling bridge monitor. Rosentreter was the first to speak. "Captain, I believe you are aware of the recent change in how the Pharaonis are using their ion cannons, correct?"

Wright nodded. "We noticed the change immediately after descending into low orbit. In fact, Commander Little from our CIC believes this might actually be part of a greater stratagem by the Pharaonis."

"That may be true, Captain, and perhaps your Commander Little and your CIC can study this theory further after the battle is over. Right now, the *Valiant* is the only vessel in the Fleet with a Humtar reactor, and those upgraded turbo laser turrets that are immediately available—*Majestic* and *Centurion* should arrive shortly," explained Rosentreter.

"Joe, I'm going to ask you to do something that's going to place your ship and crew in more danger than I have a right to ask of you," he continued. "These ion batteries need to be taken out expediently. I need you to bring the *Valiant* down, down into the planet's atmosphere—to an altitude of between forty thousand and eighty thousand feet. At that altitude, not only will your primary turbo laser batteries be able to independently engage those ion batteries, your secondary guns should be able to engage those smaller quad-barrel turrets. If we don't find a way to take those smaller turbo lasers out—we'll lose a lot of OATs in the first couple of assaults. It's imperative the *Valiant* take them out—I'd order someone else to do it if they could. Your ship is all I've got."

Commander Weber tried to conceal a grimace as he approached the captain, standing next to him.

"Admiral, we understand the risk, and we know what's at stake if we fail to eliminate those guns. You can count on us to get it done," Wright responded confidently. He then added, "Sir, if I could make a couple of requests that I believe will aid in our cause?"

The admiral motioned with his wrist. "Yes, of course," he said. "What can we do to help?"

"Sir, as the *Valiant* descends to the appropriate altitude, I would like to request six of the Fleet's fourteen *Cyclone*-class flak frigates to operate alongside us. Their additional point-defense weapons, magrail turrets, and extensive missile interceptors will greatly aid in our mission to neutralize the gun emplacements."

Wright watched as the admiral appeared to mull over his request. Lowering their ships into the planet's atmosphere was extremely dangerous and not often done. Should their engines or antigravity systems become damaged, they could very likely find themselves crash-landing on the planet with little hope of returning to space.

"OK, Joe, the mission's too important not to use every advantage we have. This is a risky move that I'm ordering you and these corvette commanders to take—we must clear a path for the OATs so they can at least make it to the surface. My CIC section is going to send you a set of coordinates I want you to clear. The data packet will also contain as many real-time satellite and video overviews of the ion and magrail cannon emplacements and the locations for those smaller, more deadly quad-barrel turbo lasers. Those guns, in particular, may be hard to see and engage, but they are the very type of guns that'll wreak havoc on our

Ospreys, Scarabs, and Starlifters. Do what you can to remove them and clear a path for the Army. Get it done, Joe," the admiral concluded. With his orders given, the line disconnected.

"OK, everyone! You heard the admiral—we have a mission, and it's a tough one, but I believe in you and your abilities to the *Valiant* with everything you've got," boomed the voice of the XO. He then turned to face Wright.

Captain Wright stood a little straighter and pulled his blouse tight. In his most serious tone of voice, he spoke with conviction and energy. "The XO's right," he began. "Each of you was chosen to serve aboard the *Valiant* for a purpose. There is a reason why you're here and not assigned to some other ship. You're here aboard the best battleship in the Republic because *you* are the best at what you do.

"The admiral, the Fleet commander himself, has given us a mission—a job only the *Valiant* could do. I need everyone to dig deep within you, to put your war faces on and find that inner warrior inside yourselves and unleash it against the Pharaonis. This looks to be the final fight, the battle to end this war. Let's show the enemy why we're the toughest bastards in the Milky Way," he concluded.

Then Wright turned to face his helmsman. "Ensign House, bring the *Valiant* down to an altitude of fifty thousand feet above the ground. CIC, Commander Little—identify the best path and altitude the *Valiant* should maintain during this mission. Coordinate your efforts with Ensign House at the helm.

"XO, order the ship to be rigged for atmospheric flight—ensure antinausea medication is properly distributed to the crew along with the first dosage of stims. Establish a twenty-four-hour crew, especially for the guns and fabricators. Get in touch with the Commander, Flight Operations, and tell him to report to the CO immediately," Wright said, rattling off a series of orders as the ship prepared itself to leave low orbit and enter the atmosphere of its first planet.

He then turned to face his tactical action officer, Lieutenant Levi Baker. "TAO, in the coming hour, a lot of responsibility is going to fall onto your shoulders. The CIC is going to be inundating you with target packages like you've never seen. I need you to remain calm, maintain your composure, and continue assigning appropriate targets to the specific gun turrets that can neutralize said targets. Communicate with your gun crews, encourage them, and rally them to continue hitting targets. Our first pass over these positions will likely be done at speed—approximately twenty-five hundred miles per hour or Mach 3.26. This should keep the *Valiant* at a speed that will make it harder for ground weapons to track and score hits."

Lieutenant Baker slowly nodded as he took in the information. He typed feverishly before looking back to the captain, a question forming on his lips as he spoke. "Sir, if I may. There's a question I have regarding the kind of munitions our gunners can use—"

"You mean, will we be allowed to use atomic weapons, right?" the captain interrupted.

The lieutenant's cheeks flushed at the question. He then nodded slowly, not saying anything right away.

Wright saw everyone on the bridge was now staring at him, waiting with bated breath for his answer to a question they felt uneasy asking, let alone considering its use. He got their attention and addressed them all at once. "Listen, so everyone understands, this question about the use of atomic weapons was asked and deliberated on extensively during a preinvasion meeting and tabletop exercise a few weeks back. The use of atomic weapons was not ruled out, but it was also not considered acceptable for wide use against any and all Pharaonis targets. If, after analysis of a fortified position, it couldn't be disabled or destroyed via conventional munitions, the limited use of atomic munitions has been authorized during the preparatory bombardment prior to the landing of OATs and SOF Forces on the planet. This will be at the discretion of the captain. TAO, if you believe you have a target that qualifies to receive a little extra atomic love—bring it to the XO. If he agrees, he'll bring it to me. If I concur, I'll sign off on it and authorize the use of the weapon. Now, unless there's something urgent we haven't discussed yet—this discussion is over. We have work to do, and the clock is ticking."

A flurry of activity broke out across the ship as spacers from every shop and department began tying down equipment and locking drawers and cabinets as they prepared the ship to enter the planet's atmosphere. While the bridge crew moved with purpose and determination, the commander of the *Valiant*'s pair of strike wings strolled onto the bridge, making his way to the captain.

Wright was talking to his XO when he heard, "Excuse me, Skipper, you said you needed to speak with me in person?" It was Captain Kenny Hamlin, call sign Ken.

He turned around to see the *Valiant*'s wing commander, a smile forming as he spoke. "Thanks for coming up here, Kenny. I don't think I could peel away from the bridge right now. So here's what's happening," Wright said. He explained what they were about to do, then asked for Kenny's ideas on how best to utilize his pair of strike wings to support the *Valiant*'s overall mission.

The Fleet's newest addition to the squadrons, the E-12B Phantoms, were electronic warfare wizards that were adept at blinding enemy fighters and bombers, and occasionally jacking up an enemy warship if they were lucky. With twenty-four of the Phantoms assigned to the *Valiant*, they had their work cut out for them if they wanted to prove they belonged with frontline units and not in some sort of specialty squadron used for one-off missions.

"Hmm, OK, given the mission parameters, here's what I think will work," Ken began to explain.

The more he spoke, the more confident Wright felt. Flight operations weren't exactly his forte. He'd come up through the ranks aboard a *Rook*-class battle cruiser in the lead-up to the First Zodark War. Later, he'd transferred to the *Ryan*-class battleships, then back to a battle cruiser under Admiral Amy Dobbs. From then on, he'd followed Dobbs's career; as she'd progressed, so had he until he was eventually assigned the *Valiant*.

"OK, Skipper. I think we've got our plan. I'll head back to the flight deck and brief my pilots. We'll get airborne within the hour—we'll be in position then for the *Valiant* to begin its descent to firing altitude. If there's anything else, you know how to reach me," explained Captain Hamlin before turning to leave the bridge.

Chapter Thirty-Three

Bridge of the RNS *Valiant*
High Orbit Over Eurysa

"Target those ion cannons now!" shouted Captain Wright, watching helplessly as the ion cannons continued to target the corvettes and frigates escorting the *Valiant*, slicing a second corvette in half. "Hit 'em with a full salvo—railguns and turbo lasers. I want that place turned to dust."

"Aye, Captain. Targeting solutions locked," responded Commander Weber, his XO, who stood at the tactical station. The man's fingers moved with precision, entering commands that would soon translate into death from above as he helped Lieutenant Baker with targeting.

The *Valiant* shuddered slightly as its massive railguns and turbo lasers roared to life. The twin-barreled thirty-six-inch magnetic railguns discharged their projectiles at blistering speed, the shells piercing the void between ship and planet, leaving trails of ionized gas in their wake. Almost simultaneously, the twin-barrel turbo lasers fired, each bolt a lance of concentrated energy capable of vaporizing steel and stone alike.

From the bridge, Wright could see the impacts below. The first volley slammed into a Pharaonis ion cannon installation, turning it into a geyser of fire and debris. The ground buckled and split, flames erupting as secondary explosions rippled through the site. The second volley targeted a magnetic railgun battery perched atop a mountain range. The mountain itself seemed to shudder as the explosive power of the *Valiant*'s weapons tore through rock and metal, sending fragments of the gun battery and boulders tumbling into the valleys below.

"Enemy defensive positions neutralized," Weber reported, his voice steady but with a hint of satisfaction.

"Good. Let's not give them a chance to recover," Wright replied. "Prepare for the next salvo. Target their secondary defenses. I want everything they have at that base destroyed before we commence phase two."

As the *Valiant* shifted to bring more of its weapons to bear, the ship shuddered slightly from incoming fire. A Pharaonis railgun struck a nearby battleship, the kinetic impact slamming into its thick Bronkis5-

reinforced armor. The armor, made from carbon and steel composite materials enhanced with the rare mineral, absorbed the brunt of the force, deflecting some of the energy away from the point of impact. Sparks flew as the metal groaned under the stress, but it held.

Wright's gaze hardened, watching the scene unfold on the tactical display. The Pharaonis defensive weapons were formidable, firing enormous projectiles from their magnetic railguns at incredible speeds. Their ion cannons flashed with a deadly blue hue as they unleashed bolts of supercharged particles. The projectiles hurtled through space, each one capable of puncturing through meters of armor, sending devastating ripples through even the most reinforced ships.

"Evasive maneuvers, Helm!" Wright ordered. "We're not here to be target practice. Bring us around—find their blind spots."

The ship's engines roared as the *Valiant* began its maneuver, its armor shimmering slightly from the heat and force of near misses. Wright could see the bright trails of ion cannon fire streaking past the ship, narrowly missing them by mere meters. When those weapons hit, it wasn't just a kinetic impact—it was a cascading storm of electromagnetic energy that could fry internal systems and cripple a ship.

"I hope one of those hits doesn't punch right through us," Wright muttered, watching as a nearby cruiser was struck by a direct hit from an ion cannon. The energy slammed into its armor, burning through sections of its hull plating, exposing internal systems. Secondary explosions erupted as the ship lost power in key sectors.

"All PDGs active!" Wright ordered, and almost immediately, the point-defense turrets on the *Valiant* lit up, spraying streams of tracer fire into the air around them. Swarms of incoming missiles fired from hidden launchers on the surface were headed right for them. The Pharaonis were attempting to overwhelm their ships' defenses, but the *Valiant*'s PDGs were cutting them down. The missiles exploded in rapid succession as they were intercepted, sending shockwaves harmlessly through the air but causing no damage.

"Captain, we're beginning to take concentrated fire from several ground batteries!" Weber shouted over the din of the bridge, the tension mounting.

Wright's eyes narrowed as the ship shook under the pressure of enemy fire. He watched as another railgun slug slammed into one of their sister ships, the RNS *Centurion*. The kinetic force of the impact sent a ripple across the hull, causing a series of metal plates to peel away as the round punched through the outer layer of armor.

"They'll have to pull back and make repairs, but we stay in the fight," Wright declared. "We need to take out those railguns and ion cannons before we can even think about softening their cities."

Wright watched the devastation on the planet's surface as their railgun shells and turbo lasers returned fire. A brilliant flash of light illuminated the surface as one of the planetary defense installations exploded, sending debris flying into the atmosphere. The sheer impact of the *Valiant*'s turbo lasers was mind-boggling, vaporizing everything in their path while the magnetic railguns tore deep gouges in the ground. Each round was designed not just to hit but to leave a path of destruction in its wake—collapsing fortifications and creating zones of chaos in Pharaonis defenses.

The first targets were eliminated, but more lay ahead. Wright glanced at the tactical map, knowing they still had work to do.

"Reload the railguns. Ready the next salvo, and keep those turbo lasers firing. We're not done yet."

Wright felt the rumble of the ship beneath him, the vibrations from the firing of the massive guns resonating through the decks. As they pressed the assault, the enemy's defenses began to falter, but Wright knew the fight was far from over. With each salvo, the Republic inched closer to dominating the skies over Eurysa, but the cost of victory was still unknown.

****

Eight Hours Later
Bridge of the RNS *Valiant*
Planet Eurysa, 50,000 Feet Above the Surface

"Stay sharp, XO," Wright warned, his nerves still on edge. "We're not out of the woods yet. Keep the weapons primed and ready. Let's make sure any stragglers or hidden batteries are dealt with before they can become a problem."

The ship's engines hummed softly as the *Valiant* glided through the thin upper atmosphere. Below them, the surface of Eurysa was a patchwork of greens and blues, scarred by the violence of their bombardment. Smoke plumed from craters where cities had once stood, and fires raged unchecked across vast swaths of land. Yet, despite the devastation, Wright knew their work was far from over.

"Bring us around to the northern hemisphere," Wright ordered. "Target the military installations and troop concentrations near the capital. Let's clear the way for our boys on the ground."

"Aye, Captain," Weber acknowledged, inputting the commands into his console. The *Valiant*'s massive railguns and turbo lasers pivoted into position, ready to unleash their fury.

Through the viewport, Wright watched as the first salvo was unleashed. Twin barrels of the thirty-six-inch magnetic railguns discharged with a flash of light, sending their deadly payload hurtling toward the surface. The impact was catastrophic, the ground erupting in a shower of debris as the rounds tore through hardened fortifications and troop bunkers.

"Direct hit on the primary target, Captain," one of the weapons officers reported, his voice filled with a mix of satisfaction and urgency. "Secondary explosions detected—looks like we hit a munitions depot."

Wright allowed himself a small smile, but it quickly faded. There was no time for celebration, not yet.

"Good work. Keep up the pressure. We need to soften them up before the assault ships move in. And watch for any new heat signatures—anything that looks like it might be a weapon we missed."

The tension on the bridge was palpable. Every crew member was on edge, their eyes flicking between their screens and the view outside. The planet's surface, now marred by craters and burning wreckage, seemed to pulse with an unnatural light as their weapons continued to pound the remaining military targets.

"Captain, the orbital assault ships are moving into position," Weber reported, his tone growing more serious. "They'll be deploying the first wave of Ospreys and Scarabs in fifteen minutes."

Wright nodded, his jaw set. This was the moment of truth. The Pharaonis had already proven themselves a dangerous foe, and there was no telling what traps they might have laid for the incoming assault troops.

"Increase our scans," Wright ordered. "I want every square meter of that surface under scrutiny. If there's anything down there that looks even remotely like a weapon, I want it taken out before our boys hit the ground."

"Aye, Captain. Scanning now," Weber confirmed.

Wright's eyes narrowed as he stared at the planet below, willing his ship and crew to find any remaining threats. The Republic forces had come too far, sacrificed too much, to lose now. The *Valiant* was their shield, and Wright was determined to make sure it held firm.

The minutes ticked by as the *Valiant* continued its bombardment, each shot fired with precision and purpose. The surface of Eurysa lit up with the fires of destruction, yet Wright knew it was necessary to ensure the safety of the soldiers about to make their descent.

"Sir, sensors are picking up something!" Weber called out, his voice tinged with alarm. "New energy signatures—looks like hidden batteries coming online!"

"Target and fire! We're not letting them get a shot off!" Wright barked.

The *Valiant*'s weapons roared to life, turbo lasers and railguns unleashing a barrage of firepower. The ground below shuddered as the hidden batteries were obliterated before they could pose a threat.

"That was close," Wright muttered, his heart pounding in his chest. "Good work, everyone. Let's finish this."

The *Valiant* pressed on, its guns blazing as it cleared the way for the ground forces. The planet Eurysa, once the jewel of the Pharaonis, was now a battlefield—a testament to the Republic's resolve and the power of its fleet.

As the final targets were destroyed, Wright allowed himself a brief moment of satisfaction. But the battle was far from over. The ground assault was about to begin, and the fate of Eurysa—and perhaps the entire war—hung in the balance.

****

48 Hours into the Battle
Bridge of the RNS *Valiant*
Planet Eurysa, 30,000 Feet Above the Surface

Captain Joe Wright leaned over the tactical console, his face etched with exhaustion and resolve. Two days of relentless combat had transformed the *Valiant* from a battleship into a floating firebase, a lifeline for the ground forces slugging it out on the surface. The ship's crew had been running on adrenaline and sheer willpower, executing precision strikes in support of the Orbital Assault Troops (OATs), Rangers, and Delta Special Forces units.

"Captain, another fire support request coming in from Delta Company, 2nd Rangers," Commander Weber reported, his voice carrying the strain of long hours at his station. "They're pinned down near the southern ridge of Sector Seventeen. Requesting immediate air support and a railgun strike on enemy armor moving up from the valley."

"Understood," Wright replied, his voice firm despite the fatigue. "Load batteries one through four with high-explosive rounds. Prepare to fire on my command. Alert Flight Ops to scramble a squadron of Gripens and a flight of Valkyrie bombers."

"Aye, Captain," Weber acknowledged, already relaying the orders to the weapons and flight control officers.

The *Valiant*'s secondary weapons, the quad-barrel sixteen-inch magnetic railguns, rotated into position, their barrels adjusting to the precise coordinates provided by the Rangers. Through the viewports, Wright could see the distant flashes of explosions on the surface—a grim reminder of the ongoing battle that raged below.

"Fire!" Wright commanded.

The railguns discharged with a deafening thud, sending their deadly payload hurtling toward the columns of Pharaonis armor below. The rounds impacted with devastating force, bracketing their positions as a series of bright, blinding flashes lighting up the surface as enemy vehicles were tossed through the air like a child's toy or simply torn apart by the explosions.

"Direct hits on enemy armor, Captain," Weber confirmed. "Rangers report the threat has been neutralized."

Wright allowed himself a brief nod of satisfaction, but the battle was far from over. The demands for fire support kept coming in, one after another, a signal of the intensity of the ground combat.

"Captain, Flight Ops reports that the Gripens and Valkyrie are en route to support Delta Company," Weber continued. "We've also launched a swarm of Reaper drones to provide additional close-air support. Should we deploy more anti-air batteries to cover their advance?"

"Yes, do it," Wright replied. "The last thing we need is to lose any of our birds to ground fire. Make sure the Reapers have their targeting systems locked on anything that moves near our guys."

As the *Valiant* continued to hover over the battlefield, the bridge crew worked tirelessly to keep the ship's systems running at peak efficiency. The battle was a relentless grind, the crew's movements precise and practiced despite their fatigue. Wright could feel the tension in the air, the unspoken fear that one missed target or delayed reaction could spell disaster for the troops below.

"Incoming transmission from Alpha Company, 23rd Regiment," Weber called out. "They're advancing on a heavily fortified enemy position in Sector Twelve, but they're taking heavy fire from an entrenched Pharaonis artillery battery. They need a railgun strike to clear the way."

"Target that battery and fire at will," Wright ordered. "Make sure they have a clear path to their objective."

The railguns thundered once more, their destructive power unleashed on the enemy's fortifications. The *Valiant*'s sensors registered the destruction of the artillery battery.

"Target destroyed, Captain," Weber reported, his voice carrying a note of grim satisfaction. "Alpha Company reports good effects on target. They are advancing."

Wright's gaze remained fixed on the tactical display, his mind racing as he juggled the demands of the battle. The *Valiant* was holding the line, providing the firepower needed to turn the tide, but he knew they couldn't afford to let up, not even for a moment.

"Prepare to shift targets to Sector Nine," Wright instructed. "We've got reports of enemy reinforcements moving in from the east. Let's make sure they never get the chance to engage our troops."

The battle continued to rage, the *Valiant*'s guns firing in a steady, relentless rhythm. The bridge was a hive of activity, the crew working in perfect unison to carry out Wright's orders. Despite the exhaustion, the tension, and the unrelenting pressure, the *Valiant*'s crew remained focused, determined to see the battle through to its end.

For Captain Wright, the fate of the Republic's ground forces—and perhaps the entire campaign—rested on their ability to deliver the firepower needed to break the enemy's resistance. And he was determined to do just that, no matter the cost.

Chapter Thirty-Four

Early May 2115
23rd Texas Mechanized Infantry Regiment
Tharnix Flats, Eurysa

Major Paul Vaughn smiled as he heard Colonel Thomas mention how his Texans were pairing up with his tanks to form the iron fist of the division. His tanks would punch holes in the enemy positions while Vaughn's Mech units would sweep aside any Pharaonis infantry.

The moment Colonel Thomas wrapped up his speech, Major Paul Vaughn, call sign Lone Star-6, made a beeline to catch the attention of Lieutenant Kinkaid, his soon-to-be Beaumont Company commander. He moved with purpose, his eyes locking on Lieutenant Kinkaid and Master Sergeant Dausch. "Lieutenant, Master Sergeant, a word before we head out," he called, his tone leaving no room for debate.

Both men turned, surprised. Dausch's expression hardened almost immediately, like he knew what was coming.

"Everything all right, sir?" Dausch asked, his voice calm but wary.

Vaughn cut straight to it. "Not exactly. We took a beating during the last campaign—especially in the officer ranks. We were supposed to get replacements, but things went sideways in transit. General Varinius gave the green light for battlefield promotions to fill the gaps, and I'm under orders to act."

Kinkaid looked like he'd been caught in a crossfire, while Dausch clenched his jaw, already bracing for the inevitable. Vaughn didn't give him the chance to argue. "Stand down, Chris. I've kept you in that Master Sergeant role as long as I could, but this is over. I'm not promoting someone with less experience over you, and I'm sure as hell not catching flak from the general for it. You're getting the bars."

Before Dausch could protest, Vaughn pulled a set of Lieutenant's insignia from his pocket and tossed them his way. "Congratulations, Lieutenant. You're the new Platoon Leader for Second Platoon—call sign Mustang One. Pick your replacement for Master Sergeant and fill the other two sergeant slots. You've got thirty minutes before we marshal the vehicles and head out. Dismissed, Lieutenant."

Vaughn didn't wait for a response. He turned to Kinkaid, pulling out the captain's bars with the same no-nonsense approach. "Congratulations, Captain. You're now the Beaumont Company CO—call sign Longhorn Six."

Kinkaid looked like he might be sick. "Sir, I'm—I'm not sure I'm the best person for the job."

Vaughn met his eyes. "You're right; you're not," he said flatly. "But that's war. We have to Semper Gumbi—stay flexible. We have to be like water and move around the obstacles in front of us. You've been taught that no plan survives contact with the enemy, and you'll see that soon enough. For now, lean on your platoon leaders, give your NCOs the room they need, and keep your focus on leading the company. This is one of those moments, Kinkaid, where you'll either rise to the occasion, or you won't."

He paused, letting his words sink in. "I know you have doubts. But here's what I know—you've got a good team around you with a lot of combat experience. They will help and you will learn from them. Now get your company ready to roll. The 9th OAR is waiting on us."
****

2nd Platoon
Beaumont Company

"Ah, shucks. Would you look at that?" called out Corporal Jackie Walkup as soon as he spotted Dausch wearing his new lieutenant bars.

Dausch shot him a look but didn't break stride. "Knock it off, Walkup. I don't want to hear another word about it. That goes for everyone," he said firmly, turning his attention to the platoon as they began readying the vehicles. His tone left no room for argument. The platoon had learned long ago that when Dausch wasn't in the mood for jokes, it was best not to poke the bear.

Staff Sergeant Olaf Breuer stepped forward, giving Dausch a curt nod, but didn't comment on the promotion. Breuer wasn't the type for small talk, and Dausch appreciated that. He motioned for Breuer to follow toward one of the Bobcats. He then caught the attention of Sergeant Moshen Mica and Corporal Walkup, telling them to join him.

Breuer bunched his eyebrows, questioning, "Everything all right, Chris?"

"Yeah, what's up, Hoss?" pressed Mica.

"Things are fine, Olaf, and I appreciate you're asking," said Dausch, irritated. "Look, I didn't *want* this promotion to lieutenant, and you know damn well if I could have wiggled my way out of it, I would have," Dausch explained, his right hand digging inside his pocket for the rank insignia he was about to spring on them. "Here's the deal, guys. My promotion to lieutenant means we've got a vacancy to fill, and no new replacements are on the horizon. The Major told me to promote who I see fit, but he also made it clear the platoons and company were to fill these vacancies from the existing squads and platoons.

"Olaf, I hate that I must do this to you, but I can't think of a more competent person to fill the vacancy my promotion created. With that said, congratulations, Master Sergeant," Dausch explained as he pulled the rank insignia from his pocket, handing it to him.

He turned to face Corporal Walkup and Sergeant Mica, handing both a set of rank insignias a grade higher than the ones they wore. "As you can guess, Breuer's promotion means the two of you are moving up a grade yourselves—and no, you don't get to turn it down any more than I could. Now let's get ready to roll; it won't be long until the Major gives the go-ahead."

"Sounds good, Lieutenant," commented Mica as he replaced his rank with the new staff sergeant chevrons and rocker. "Perhaps this is for the best. Besides, we're totally digging these new call signs. I mean, we're the 23rd Texas and up until now, none of our units were named after anything Texas."

"Ha," Dausch chuckled. "Yeah, I guess that's one of the privileges of being a regiment commander for a general with the name 'Spartacus Varinius.' I heard Major Rick Ahlstrom from the 24th Spartan Infantry Regiment changed the names of his companies to resemble Greek names and mythology."

Breuer shook his head dismissively. When General Varinius allowed the regiment commanders to change the names of their companies and call-signs to improve morale, many of the soldiers loved it. Breuer wasn't one of them. "While you were at the commander's call, I put the platoon to work getting our vehicles and gear ready," he said. "I figured you might return with orders. If you look over there—" he pointed to where a cluster of vehicles and soldiers were gaggled, "—I had the vehicles readied and lined up in the assembly area near where they are setting up a new motor pool."

Dausch smiled. "And *this* is why you are the new Master Sergeant, Breuer. You know exactly what needs to happen to get the platoon ready to leave the FOB, and you make it happen."

"Eh, I've seen how you handle things, and it seems to work. I'm just doing what I believed you would do if you were here," replied Breuer as he tried to downplay the compliment.

"Well, I appreciate it," Dausch commented, giving a sigh before turning serious. "Here's how I want the vehicles laid out—squad leaders for First, Second, and Third Squad ride in the IFVs. Fourth Squad leader in a Puma, and Fifth Squad leader in a Bobcat. I'll ride Bravo Eleven—that command module upgrade looks sick in those Bobcats. Talk about situational awareness of your platoon or company—those recce drones are going to make it easy to know what's happening around us."

"Hell yeah, they will," agreed Staff Sergeant Mica with a grin. "Hey, so did they tell you how our regiment is going to be working with those tankers?" he asked. "Are we acting as recon ahead of them, a screening force, or fully integrating our platoons with their platoons?"

Dausch grinned. He liked having NCOs who weren't afraid to ask questions. "It's kind of a mix, I suppose. Our Company, Beaumont, was tagged with providing recon for the combined force. Christi, Dallas, and Eagle are integrating themselves with the tankers. Amarillo and Flower Company are integrating with one of the tank companies to form a quick reaction force or ready reserve that'll stay here on the FOB, unless needed. With that said, our platoon is going to take lead and be the recce force to link us up with the 9th Orbital Assault Regiment."

Dausch pulled his Qpad from his pocket before adding, "I've just sent a copy of the operations order and our specific instructions to your Qpads. Our vehicle waypoints and routes should already have been pushed to the vehicle nav systems. Unless you guys have further questions, I think I've gone over everything you need to know before we push off." He paused just long enough to glance as his watch. "In twenty-eight minutes, Major Vaughn said the colonel wants us on the road."

"Wow, they're really throwing us into the fight right out the gate, aren't they?" Breuer commented. "I guess I best be off to check on the guys and make sure we're ready then."

Dausch and the platoon finished their vehicle loadouts and gathered the gear they planned to bring. Meanwhile, the sound of Army Mongoose transport ships continued to grow. Scores of these transports delivered everything from specialized containers configured to function as medical units to mobile Arkanorian power generators. If there was a domain of war the Republic excelled at—it was logistics.

"Second Squad!" shouted the squad leader. "Check your rifles, then buddy check. It's time to load up in the vehicles and prepare to roll."

A chorus of "yes, sergeant," echoed in return as soldiers from the different squads loaded into their vehicles.

After a quick check of his squads, Lieutenant Dausch made his way to Bravo Eleven, the Bobcat recently converted to be more of a command vehicle than an assaulter like the others. Sliding into the passenger side back seat, Dausch locked his rifle in place and went to log in to his computer to ready the system. Once they got on the road, the drones would get airborne and begin streaming video surveillance of a three-kilometer roving bubble around the convoy. If the drones spotted a threat or something that needed further attention, the AI-assisted targeting software would take over, highlighting the threat for further analysis or termination.

System ready—drones ready to deploy, the computer prompt told him. Dausch nodded to himself in satisfaction, then looked to Mica, who was seated in front of him. "Turret systems all good?" Dausch asked out of routine.

"Good to go, LT," Mica replied with a thumbs up.

Just then, a targeting reticle appeared to hover in front of the passenger-side windshield. He watched a second more as the reticle moved side-to-side as Mica used the joystick to direct the remotely controlled twin-barrel blaster turret mounted to the top of the vehicle. That turret allowed the vehicle to provide suppressive fire when dismounted infantry needed it most.

With the platoon in position, Dausch gave one final sweep of the formation. Four Pumas, four Bobcats, and three Linebackers—all humming, their engines ready for what lay ahead.

"Second Platoon, listen up," Dausch called over comms. "We're leading this convoy. We are the recce platoon for the company, who in turn is the screening force for the rest of the regiment and the 11th Spartacus tank Regiment. It's our job to spot anything out of place along the T1 North-South Highway leading us to Objective Gold—a combat outpost the 9th OAR set up controlling a major highway interchange leading to their capital. Now maybe we'll get lucky, and the enemy won't try to reassert their control over this major piece of infrastructure. Perhaps luck has been good to you in life; it hasn't for me. So, we're not taking any chances the enemy is just gonna let us take this highway without a fight. Everyone needs to keep your heads on a swivel and be ready for anything. I want the platoon ready to roll in five minutes. Out."

Dausch switched the comms channel to the one his squad leaders were on. "Mustang Twelve, Sergeant Walkup—you're in Bravo Twenty-One. I want your Puma to lead us off the FOB onto the highway once we're ready to roll. Mustang Two, Master Sergeant Breuer, will be riding in Bravo One. If we run into Pharaonis infantry, we'll figure out if we're going to dismount the vehicles and engage them or stay mobile. If we dismount—direct the APCs where you think it's best. Is everyone ready?" he asked.

"Hooah, let's roll," replied the squad leaders in unison.
****

ECP-6
FOB Sparta

Dausch took a breath, eyes fixed ahead. "All right. Let's get this done."

Although Dausch could feel the weight of the new bars on his collar, he didn't dwell on it. His focus was where it always was—on the soldiers under his command.

Lieutenant Dausch sat in the back seat of the Bobcat, eyes scanning the data pad providing an overview of the vehicles ready to exit the FOB when Captain Kinkaid's voice crackled over the comms. "Mustang, you're cleared to proceed. Maintain spacing and move with caution. Let's clear the route and make sure the Pharaonis didn't leave any surprises for us."

Dausch keyed his mic, his voice calm but firm. "Longhorn Six, copy that. Mustang moving out."

He glanced up, his view from the Bobcat limited but clear enough to see the Pumas up ahead starting to pull forward. The convoy began to roll, slow and steady, the hum of engines filling the air as they left the perimeter of FOB Sparta behind. Dausch flicked his eyes back to the data pad, keeping an eye on the terrain markers, the route ahead, and the positioning of his vehicles.

They merged onto the highway without problems or fanfare, the vehicles steadily building up space between each other as the pace of the convoy continued to pick up. In front of him, Staff Sergeant Moshen Mica was looking intently at the screen where he monitored control of the twin-barrel laser blaster turret atop the Bobcat.

With his head forward, his eyes sharp as they scanned the horizon, Dausch asked, "Anything?"

"Nothing yet, LT. Clear so far," Mica replied, though clearly, neither of them felt entirely at ease.

As they moved along the highway, the landscape began to shift. What had once been a relatively barren stretch of road opened into something more alive. Strange, alien trees lined the sides of the road, their twisted trunks and translucent leaves catching the light in a way that made them shimmer. Patches of prairies and dense clusters of forest dotted the landscape, interspersed with wide, open spaces that looked untouched by the war raging on this planet.
****

Bravo One

Private Doug Donnie, sitting in the rear Linebacker, was the first to break the silence on the open comms. "Damn, look at this place. Looks like a mix between a jungle and some kind of alien savanna. Anyone else half-expect something to jump out at us?" he asked.

Sergeant Walkup's voice from the lead Puma cut in. "Whoa, Donnie, shut up. We're only thirty minutes into this convoy and here you are—about to jinx us."

Seated next to Donnie was Private Jesus Martinez who was clearly unable to resist. "Hey, it could be a friendly creature that jumps out at us," he teased. "Like one of those flying things over there. You see those birds?" he asked, pointing a finger at the monitor as a small flock of winged creatures soared into view of the turret camera.

These birds were unlike anything they had ever seen up to this point in their lives. Their wings were somewhat translucent while also iridescent and shining their soft colors for all to see. Their strange cries echoed through the sky.

Breuer, seated near the vehicle commander, glanced at the birds, his grip on the command pad tightening slightly. He wasn't one for distractions and wanted their attention focused on what was happening on the road and its immediate vicinity.

"Cut the chatter, guys. Stay focused on the mission," Breuer said evenly. "We're not here to birdwatch and you're not doing a Big Year," he said, referring to an annual competition among birders to see who could spot and identify the most species of birds in a year.

"Ah, come on. We would clean up at the annual Big Year event," Martinez joked. "No one is seeing the kinds and types of birds and flying creatures back home like we are."

The chatter subsided as the convoy pressed forward, engines humming steadily. They advanced down the cracked, weathered highway. The soldiers, once relaxed in their banter, now sat in tense silence, eyes constantly scanning the tree lines, alert for any sign of danger. The alien landscape around them was as captivating as it was unsettling—a world that seemed both alive and unfamiliar, full of mystery and menace.

Massive trees loomed in the distance, their bark a deep, almost obsidian-black, with branches twisting upwards like gnarled hands clawing at the pale sky. Between the trees, faint movements flickered—alien fauna, too far to identify. The animals' shapes and movements were strange, unsettling in their fluidity. Some seemed to dart between the shadows, others watched with an eerie stillness from the undergrowth. The leaves of the trees shimmered in odd hues, their radiant edges catching the light in a way that made them seem to pulse, like veins of an alien heart, beating in rhythm with the planet.

The open prairies between the clusters of trees were dotted with strange, pale grasses swaying in the wind, their long tendrils reaching toward the passing convoy as if drawn by some unseen force. Occasionally, bizarre, bird-like creatures swooped overhead, their wings stretched wide, casting dark silhouettes across the ground. Their high-pitched calls added to the growing sense of unease.

Inside the vehicles, the tension was palpable. Every soldier felt it—a gnawing sensation that something was watching from the shadows.

The calm before the storm, broken only by the rhythmic clank of the vehicles and the occasional ping of sensor sweeps.

"Master Sergeant Breuer, you've been on a few planets," said Private Donnie. "Ever seen anything like this before?" he asked, his eyes never leaving the window of the APC.

Breuer, sitting beside him, took in the strange sights outside. "Not like this, Donnie," he finally replied, his tone flat. "This place... it's got a pulse. Feels like it's alive in a way the other planets weren't. You'd do well to keep your eyes sharp. Just because it's quiet, doesn't mean it's safe."

As the convoy pushed further into the alien landscape, the horizon shifted, revealing more towering forests and deeper valleys. They had entered a world that felt less like a battlefield and more like a predatory beast, lying in wait for the right moment to strike.
****

Bravo Eleven

Dausch kept his eyes on the map, tracking their approach to the forest section up ahead. The trees ahead were denser, the kind of cover that could hide anything—or anyone. He toggled the comms. "Mustangs, tighten your spacing to three vehicle lengths. Keep an eye on those tree lines," he directed. The spacing between their vehicles had stretched to more than six lengths, creating wider and greater gaps between them. "Watch those trees Mica—the left flank."

"Aye, LT," Mica responded, swiveling the turret to cover the tree line as they neared the forest's edge.

Suddenly, the sensors in Dausch's Bobcat pinged on something. The vehicle's radar and IR sensors detected something moving in the distance. His command pad lit up with a faint marker, outlines of something moving in the trees. "Bravo Twenty-One, hold up," Dausch ordered, urgency in his voice. "Possible movement, left flank."

"Copy that, Mustang One. Slowing down to ten kilometers an hour," Sergeant Walkup confirmed, his Puma slowing, the turret swiveling to face the possible threat.

The convoy slowed, the hum of the engines quieting as the vehicles adjusted their positions. Dausch deployed a couple of drones, sending them to investigate. He felt his heart rate tick up as the drones approached the edges of the forest. His mind raced through the possibilities. It could be nothing—just wildlife—or it could be something else.

"Mustangs, stay sharp. Mica, give me a visual check with IR, thermals, and spectral analysis. I can't shake the feeling something is out there," Dausch said, his voice dropping lower.

Mica nodded; the turret locked onto the tree line as he scanned it using the three different modalities to see if they could detect something. "Hey, I think I got something... can't totally make it out. It might be animals, given how low it is to the ground..."

Dausch narrowed his eyes, looking at the faint blips on his data pad. "Let's not take chances. We'll approach that bend ahead nice and slow until we know it's clear."

The tension thickened as they inched closer to the forest, every soldier now waiting for what might come next.

The eerie stillness of the forest shattered in an instant. Blaster fire erupted from the tree line, bright streaks of energy cutting through the air as the Pharaonis launched their ambush.

"Contact, left flank!" Dausch barked, his hand instinctively gripping the command data pad as the Bobcat jerked to a halt. He heard Mica shout something about return fire when an explosion rocketed their Bobcat, showering them with shrapnel and debris.

Dausch shook off the effects of the blast. Mica shouted orders to his squads, firing the blasters atop the vehicle with precision accuracy. He looked out the windshield in time to see the Puma's 50mm cannons firing explosive rounds into the tree line, the roar of explosions around drowning everything out.

Two of the Pumas near the front of the convoy had turned off the highway in the direction of the tree line with a Bobcat trailing behind them. The trio were unleashing hell on the attackers—streams of blaster bolts and bursting shells ripping tree limbs and trunks apart.

Vehicles from the rear of the convoy raced forward as Dausch directed the drivers where he wanted them in the rapidly forming battle line of armored vehicles. As trucks came to a halt and their gunners joined the fray, soldiers spilled out of the vehicles to take up positions near them. They brought their rifles to bear, joining in.

"Seoul Two-One, Longhorn Tango. Fire mission, fire mission, grid attached. Requesting one round, high-explosive, ten-meter airburst—how copy?" Sergeant Sciallo called over the radio. Sciallo was the forward observer attached to Beaumont Company from the 11th Korean AR—the division's artillery regiment.

"Longhorn Tango, good copy—grid confirmed. One round HE, ten-meter airburst," Dausch heard over the comms.

"Missile incoming!" shouted Mica as the vehicle's dazzler and countermeasures activated. The missile zeroed in on the lead Puma that was currently pummeling the Pharaonis infantry in the tree line. It zipped across the two-kilometer distance, exploding fractions of a second later as it flew into a hail of steel pellets from the vehicle's self-defense system.

"Found 'em! Nine o'clock! Missile team!" shouted the driver to Mica as he brought their vehicle's twin blasters to bear.

Crack, crack, crack.

The blaster cut loose, firing a barrage of energy bolts into the enemy missile team, preventing them from launching another attack.

"Longhorn Tango—shot out. Splash in five seconds," announced Seoul Two-One.

"Confirmed, shot out. Splash imminent," Sciallo barely replied when the 240mm high-explosive shell exploded over top of the forest and the Pharaonis still firing at them.

BOOM!

The ten-meter-high explosion flattened all the trees in a fifty meter circle from its epicenter.

"Ceasefire! Ceasefire!" Dausch ordered as bits and pieces of trees, dirt, and other debris fell from the sky.

As Dausch watched the drone feeds on his tablet, he saw that the enemy fire stopped completely. He wasn't sure at first if they had killed the ambushers or if they were stunned and would resume firing. Ten seconds went gone by with no resumption in enemy fire—then thirty seconds, and still nothing.

"Mustang One, Longhorn Six. Status report on that contact! Do you need assistance?" asked Captain Kinkaid over the comms, his voice nervous.

"Longhorn Six, negative. It appears the Pharaonis were lying in ambush for whatever vehicles or convoy passed by. No casualties on our end, two vehicles with minor damage but operational. Drones confirm two missile teams and three heavy blaster teams—total enemy KIA is fourteen," Dausch calmly relayed.

"Good copy, Mustang," Kinkaid replied. "Go ahead and get back on the move. I suspect this won't be the last ambush we'll encounter before reaching Objective Gold." Then he added, "I'm going to see if we can get some aerial support from the Iron Eagles or the Fleet. Stay safe, out."

Dausch had barely finished speaking to Kinkaid when Breuer's voice came through, steady but with a hint of pride. "We did it, LT. Wiped the floor with 'em and not a single casualty."

Dausch grunted to himself as the realization of surviving their first ambush on this new planet set in. "Yeah, I guess we did," he acknowledged. "Let's get the platoon back on the move. The old man wants to press on."

"OK, Mustangs. The LT says the breaks over," Breuer directed. "Let's get the party buses back on the hardball and get moving. We've got another sixty-two kilometers to go."

They'd drawn first blood, but Dausch doubted today would be the last.

Chapter Thirty-Five

Mid-May 2115
2nd Platoon Mustangs, Beaumont Company, 23rd Texas MIR
Bravo Three, T4 Highway

"Hurry up, Hollis. We need to get back to the fight," Lieutenant Dausch snapped, his voice sharp with impatience. He grabbed another 50mm shell from Sergeant Barton, tension rising with his every move.

"We're going as fast as we can, LT," Corporal Hollis replied, his breath coming in ragged gasps as he loaded the shell. Hollis was the driver of Bravo Three, one of their Puma light tanks, and exhaustion clung to him like a second skin.

Sergeant Barton wiped the sweat from his brow, his tone grim. "We're almost done, Lieutenant. If it weren't for Colonel Horn and his brass balls, those supply POGs would never have risked coming this close after what happened to Cully Company." His words carried weight, a grim reminder of the ambush on an ammo carrier from the 11th Lugano Logistical Support Regiment. The Pharaonis had left no mercy, and the brutal end of those soldiers was still fresh in everyone's mind.

Barton patted the Puma's side like a trusted companion. "We were down to four rounds, LT. That's all the ammo we had for this Pig."

"I know," Dausch muttered. "But every second we're out here, we've got guys fighting without the firepower they need. We've got to get back."

The distant rumble of artillery reverberated through the air, a constant reminder of the chaos just over the horizon. It had been nearly two weeks since they'd left FOB Sparta, pushing toward Objective Gold—two hundred and sixty-two kilometers west of Vrahk'tol. The highway and railway intersection they were fighting for ran through three cities, a spaceport, and an industrial center. The allied forces had spared these areas from bombardment, hoping to preserve them for the aftermath.

If Dausch had had it his way, he would have leveled the cities, encircled the capital with the entire Fifth Corps, and ended this hellish push. But it wasn't his call. Instead, they were stuck grinding through kilometers of enemy resistance, every inch of ground paid for in blood and sweat.

"Hey, LT. Still bummed over losing the Bobcat?" Hollis asked as he shut the ammo locker on the Puma's turret with a loud clank.

Dausch shot him a stern look. "You mean, do I miss the one vehicle designed to let me run this platoon without roasting in this metal coffin?" he shot back. "Or are you asking if I'm enjoying the scent you've unleashed on us all?"

Barton nearly lost his grip on the 50mm shell, laughing. "Man, Hollis—I told you that 'perfume' of yours wasn't gonna win any awards."

Hollis looked genuinely wounded. "It's not that bad!" he insisted. "I'm just trying to bring a little refinement to the battlefield. My dad's been running a perfumery for years back home. Figured I'd carry on the tradition."

Dausch shook his head, the hint of a grin creeping in. "Refinement? Hollis, whatever you concocted back on Serenea didn't attract customers—it attracted chortillas. You know, the hairy, skunk-scented nightmares?"

Barton snorted. "Yeah, remember when those things wouldn't leave you alone?" he reminisced. "You were like the Pied Piper of chortillas. We could barely keep them off your gear."

Dausch's left eyebrow rose. "Wait, are you telling me that *you're* the reason those eight-legged furballs were stuck to us the whole time?" he asked. "That smell—that was *your* doing?"

Hollis shuffled awkwardly. "It wasn't exactly intentional..."

Barton clapped Hollis on the shoulder, still grinning. "Well, whatever you were aiming for, all it did was piss off the chortillas and everyone else aboard the *Callisto*. That little 'mishap' caused a serious stink—literally."

Dausch snickered. "And you wonder why Major General Spartacus was livid when that thing got loose? Three weeks, Hollis. That creature stunk up half the ship, and no one could catch it."

Barton shook his head, still chuckling. "Yeah, and remember when we hit Combat Outpost Gold? Major Vaughn practically turned purple when he smelled that funk. You could see the realization hit him that it came from our unit, not somebody else's."

Dausch wiped away a tear of laughter. "Vaughn was beyond embarrassed. First, he had to explain to Spartacus why one of those walking glue traps made it aboard. Then he had to deal with the fact that his regiment was the one spreading that stench all over the *Callisto*."

Hollis sighed, resigned. "You guys really don't appreciate innovation."

"Don't worry, Hollis," Dausch said with a smirk. "We'll find a way to use your talents... just not when it comes to 'fragrance.' Now, let's get back into the fight."

After thanking the supply team for the much-needed resupply, the three climbed back into the Puma. Since Dausch's Bobcat had taken a rocket to the axle, disabling it, he'd been forced to find another ride until Bravo Eleven could be repaired or replaced. Bravo Three, the Puma, wasn't ideal for leading the platoon, but it gave him better control over its 50mm magnetic railgun, allowing him to provide direct fire support to his infantry.

The Puma was no lightweight—its multipurpose warheads packed a punch. The targeting computer could calculate the power needed for each shot, adapting the warhead to suit the target. Sometimes, it sent a solid slug to punch through armor; other times, it unleashed maximum explosive force. With sixty-four shells in the magazine, it could keep firing long after other vehicles ran dry. The twin laser blasters mounted beside the main gun offered even more versatility, helping to support infantry or defend the Puma from direct assaults.

"Stand by, vehicle ignition," Hollis announced, his voice steady.

Dausch and Barton prepped their systems, their helmets connecting wirelessly to the Puma's network as soon as the ignition sequence started. The electric drive train hummed quietly, waiting for Hollis to shift it into gear.

"Weapons system online—ECM and countermeasures active— main gun and blasters good to go," Barton reported, checking off each system.

Dausch glanced at his monitor, watching as the platoon's status updated. The picture painted on his screen was grim. The company was still locked in the fight they'd left earlier, struggling to break through.

"Damn," Dausch muttered, mostly to himself. "The whole time we've been rearming, and they still haven't broken through that tree line."

"They will once we're back in the fight," replied Barton as he centered the turret toward one of the Bobcats still burning from a missile hit. "Come on, let's go, Hollis. Get us on the move."

The Puma lurched forward as Hollis gave the electric motors some juice, accelerating the six-wheeled tank up to 30 kph in seconds. Craters, charred ground, and the wreckage of vehicles stretched out around them.

The air vibrated with magrail fire and the distant booms of explosions, even muffled through the Puma's reinforced hull. Dausch scanned the carnage through the night vision cameras, watching as a Pharaonis body came into view—twisted and broken. Another soon followed, lifeless, and then a third, torn apart mid-stride by incoming fire. The battlefield was littered with insectoid corpses, their once-fearsome forms now just twisted remnants of a relentless enemy.

This was the part of combat that wasn't talked about in the news, in movies, books, or by recruiters and politicians—the insatiable appetite of fresh souls fed through the meat grinder of war. Battle didn't discriminate and it didn't care who you were—man, machine, or alien. It chewed through everything with brutal efficiency, leaving nothing in its wake aside from the blood-soaked soil and shattered lives. This was something Dausch knew well, having led his platoon through many battles. It was never easy, losing soldiers, friends and even mentors. However, it was war, and Dausch knew that the sooner a soldier accepted they were already dead—only then could they live.

If it's your time, then there's nothing that's going to change or stop it.

Dausch continue to watch the Puma's camera feed as it displayed a high-resolution view of the battlefield that stretched on before them. Shattered trees, craters, and the twisted bodies of Pharaonis warriors dotted the landscape in clusters near shattered bunkers and fighting positions. The enemy had fought hard, resolute in their defense and will to make sure the Republic and Primord Forces paid dearly for every inch of Pharaonis territory they took.

When they began to approach what loosely stood for the front lines, the bark of a Yeti tank rang out. The roaring sound of artillery shells pierced the air. Radio traffic of a Talon strike fighter confirming targets with a forward air controller spoke of the intensity of the battle they were quickly approaching.

BOOM...BOOM.

"Holy hell—would you look at that?" commented Hollis as they watched a pair of billowing smoke towers rising into the air.

"Whoa, those had to be two-thousand-pounders or more," exclaimed Barton as the shockwave reached them. It wasn't a danger-close mission, but it wasn't far off.

Dausch pointed to something in the distance, highlighting it on the nav map. "Take us there, Hollis," he directed. "That's where the platoon is."

"Hey, that vehicle over there—the one on fire. Isn't that Walkup's vehicle?" Barton asked, concern in his voice. "I'm going to see if I can call him—Mustang Twelve, Mustang One. Come in, over."

When he couldn't readily reach Sergeant Walkup, Dausch felt his heart begin to pound. He keyed his own mic. "Sergeant Walkup, come in. What's your SITREP?"

Nothing but static crackled through the comms. Dausch clenched his jaw. "Hollis, get me thermals on Walkup's vehicle and see if they bailed out nearby!"

If the Pharaonis had killed his friend, Dausch would make sure they paid for it in blood.

"On it, Lieutenant," Hollis replied, fingers flying across his control panel. A thermal image flickered to life on the screen, casting the battlefield in eerie ghostly hues. Heat signatures flared in bright red amidst cool blues and greens—live weapons fire, spread across the tree line.

"There, twenty or so meters to the right of their vehicle," Dausch said, jabbing a finger at the display. "Oh, damn. Looks like multiple hostiles converging on their position! Barton, see if you can't hit 'em with a couple of rounds and take 'em out."

"On it, LT," Barton replied as he worked the gun, zeroing in on the charging Pharaonis.

Bang, bang.

The cannon barked twice—the magnetic railgun hurling the projectile into a cluster of Pharaonis before exploding in the midst of them. It tossed many of them aside, injured from the blast. When the second round exploded in the same spot—the concussive blast tore into the enemy soldiers.

"Good shooting, Barton!" Dausch congratulated him before ordering, "Hollis, get us on the move and head right for our guys before those Pharaonis have a chance to recover."

The Puma roared forward, crashing through dense underbrush as Hollis punched it. The vehicle plowed through branches and hanging vines. Inside the Puma, the scraping of twigs against its armored hull sounded like nails against a chalkboard as they barreled through the underbrush.

"LT, can you work the blaster while I stay on the cannon?" Barton asked, the cannon firing quick shots at something Dausch couldn't see.

"Yeah, I can do that. Hollis. Share the windshield so I can see what I'm shooting at," Dausch ordered, placing his command tablet next to him. He reached for the joystick that would control the independent blasters on the turret and activated it. A second later, the monitor in front of him displayed the view he'd have if the Puma had a front windshield.

The targeting reticle appeared on the screen; the gun was live and ready to fire. What Dausch saw was a hurried firefight. Pharaonis soldiers fought fiercely; Republic soldiers held ground in some areas and advanced in others. As they exited a thick patch of underbrush, Dausch caught sight of a Republic trooper leaning beside a shattered tree, her rifle steady as she aimed. He swiveled the blasters in her direction when he saw a Pharaonis skitter into her sights. She fired a single shot, connecting with its head, the force of the projectile exploding it.

"Damn, that was a good shot," Dausch muttered to himself. He watched her bound forward, her rifle tucked into her shoulder as she fired to cover her move.

Dausch cut loose a barrage of rapid-fire blaster shots over her head to help shield her until she ducked behind the trunk of a fallen tree. A few meters to her right, he saw another soldier crouching nearby, his hands trembling as he fumbled to reload his rifle. The soldier slammed the mag into the rifle on his second try, then repositioned his body and fired into the advancing enemy.

"Missile team, three o'clock—he's going to fire!" Hollis shouted frantically.

Barton was already swiveling the main gun in their direction when Dausch spotted the Pharaonis aiming a missile right at them. Just as he thought the enemy was about to fire, Dausch felt the recoil of the

Puma's main gun. The Pharaonis soldier disappeared from the explosion that enveloped it.

"Whoa…oh my God, that was close," Dausch heard Hollis exclaim in shock. "I owe you a beer, Barton. We were dead if he got that missile off."

Dausch grunted at the grim assessment. Hollis was likely right. The distance between them and that missile was so close that it would have hit them before the vehicle's self-defense system could react. "Good shooting, Barton. Now, after I change my underwear, I'll put you in for an award—you've earned it," Dausch jokingly complimented, and they laughed at the near-death experience.

Hollis slowed the Puma as they neared where Sergeant Walkup and his squad had taken cover after their vehicle was hit. The ground approaching Walkup and his squad was littered with the bodies of torn and shredded Pharaonis soldiers. Whatever had happened before Dausch and their Puma had arrived left no doubt about the intensity of the battle they had just fought. With a pair of M91 heavy blasters and the squad's M12 338LMG, they had probably slayed a platoon or two worth of enemy soldiers on their own.

Dear Lord, could they have possibly managed to survive this? Dausch wondered as the Puma halted. The vehicle's radio came to life, and the sound of Walkup's voice crackled over the comm, breathless.

"Lieutenant Dausch, you there?"

"Loud and clear, Sergeant," Dausch replied, relief washing over him. "Well done."

"Yeah, well, it was them or us. Sorry, I didn't respond earlier. The bugs were trying to overrun us again. Was that you guys who took out a cluster of them with the fifty-mike-mike? If it was—thanks. I don't think we would have made it otherwise," explained Walkup as he approached a wounded soldier kneeling next to him. "Sir, I've got three wounded—one's urgent surgical, the other two need an evac but aren't staring at death for now. Can you see what the holdup is?"

Dausch's jaw tightened. "Yeah, copy that. What happened to Doc? Why isn't he helping?" Doc was the platoon's C200 combat medical synthetic. The C200s had proven so wildly successful during the last war that they were now being distributed down to the platoon level.

"Doc's gone," Walkup answered. "Got blown up when they nailed our APC. He went back in to recover Harris, our driver, but then the Linebacker exploded."

Dausch cursed angrily inside the vehicle and pounded his fist on the armrest of his chair. "We should have been here! They needed us, and we weren't there," he shouted in frustration.

"It's Murphy's Law, LT—don't beat yourself up over it," Barton said. "Half the platoon's ammo status had gone from red to black. When those ammo trucks caught up to us you made the right call to resupply. If this is anyone's fault, it's those tankers in Eagle and Falcon Companies for not waiting around to let our units rearm before pressing on again."

"Yeah, I get it. You're right, Barton," Dausch acknowledged. "It doesn't make it any easier to accept more losses, even if it wasn't my orders that led to them."

"Losses? Did we lose more vehicles than Walkup's Linebacker?" asked Hollis.

Before Dausch could respond, the sound of an approaching Chickenhawk drew their attention. "Mustang Twelve, Angel Two. We have a visual on your position—heading to you now," announced the pilot flying the medevac.

"Angel Two, Mustang Twelve—we have one urgent surgical, two critical, and three KIA," Walkup replied. "Our platoon doc was taken out. We're doing what we can without him, but if you can spare one, we'll gladly take it."

When Dausch heard Walkup mention three KIAs in addition to his wounded, he realized he hadn't checked on the status of his other troops in the platoon. He felt panicked, and he cycled through apps until he found the one he was looking for. He discovered that a Bobcat had been destroyed; however, the soldiers riding in the vehicle reported no injuries. He breathed a sigh of relief.

"Hollis, we lost a Bobcat in addition to Walkup's Linebacker. Aside from being down another vehicle, we're doing all right," Dausch explained, responding to Hollis's earlier question.

The sounds of more explosions in the distance seemed muffled inside the Puma, despite the shaking of the ground with each boom. Yeti's main gun cracked sharply as it repeatedly fired at targets unknown. Either Eagle or Falcon Company, or both, had resumed their push to relieve the 9th Orbital Assault Regiment after capturing the strategically positioned Aetherport. This fortress-like structure controlled the high ground approaching the Pharaonis industrial city of Verdanthia. Its position also enabled it to project fire control over a twelve-kilometer stretch of the T4 highway—the same highway leading to the Pharaonis capital.

Dausch paused for a moment, lost in thought as he considered their next move and what to do with the five soldiers that couldn't fit into his remaining vehicles. He was just about to contact Major Vaughn when the radio crackled to life. "Mustang One, Lone Star Six. Status report," said Vaughn.

Speak of the devil. Dausch shook his head before responding. "Lone Star Six, Mustang One. I have three wounded being evacuated right now and three KIA—one Linebacker and one Bobcat destroyed. I'm short vehicle space for five soldiers. Any chance a spare Linebacker is sitting around waiting for a new home?"

There was a moment of silence as he waited for the major to respond. "Mustang One, that's a good copy. Stand by, I'll check with Fribourg Company for a loner."

"Huh," said Hollis. "That's interesting, LT. Do you think the LSR has spare vehicles for instances like this?" he asked.

Dausch shrugged. If they did, it was news to him.

"Mustang One, Fribourg is sending a loner—a Linebacker was just assigned to your platoon. Transfer control of the vehicle to one of your hitchhikers and prepare your platoon to move out and catch up to Eagle and Falcon Companies. It seems Spartacus Six forgot to wait for his infantry support until they ran into more of those missile teams. Now they're screaming for it, and your platoon is the closest unit I've got," Vaughn explained.

Great. Where the hell is the rest of the company? Dausch wondered.

"Lone Star Six, that's a good copy. Is the rest of the company or the regiment going to join us?" asked Dausch.

"Good hunting, Mustang One. Save a seat if you beat us to Aetherport. Out."

"Damn, that's cold, LT. Sending us off on our own like this," Hollis commented after Vaughn ended the transmission.

"Water off the back, Hollis," said Dausch. "Don't let it bug you. Get us in gear and back on the move. We've got some distance to make up for," he ordered. He sent the new coordinates to the other vehicles in the platoon.

"Listen up, Mustangs," Dausch said over the comms. "The day is not over, and we've got new orders. Everyone should have received the new coordinates I sent. It seems that in Eagle and Falcon Companies' haste, they forgot to wait for their infantry support. They've run into a bit of a hornet's nest with missile teams spread out in those tree lines in sector five and need our help clearing them out. They've temporarily stopped while they wait for us to catch up and deal with it.

"Mustang Eleven, I want First Squad to lead the platoon in a wedge formation with Mustang Twenty-One and Mustang Thirty-One following, in that order. Mustang Two will trail the platoon with the Linebackers until we need to dismount our infantry," Dausch explained as his platoon of vehicles moved out.
****

Forty Minutes Later
Bravo Three, T4 Highway

Dausch watched the monitor intently as his platoon moved past the tanks of Falcon Company. The Bobcats in First Squad weaved their way through the dense foliage. Dausch's monitor showed their infrared lasers probing through the shadows between the trees. Suddenly, a flurry of movement caught his attention. Without warning, the tree line erupted in laser fire. Missiles streaked toward his platoon. The fight was on.

"Barton, missile team, bearing two-six-eight," Dausch urgently called out. "Light 'em up!"

Barton was already in motion. The Puma's turret swiveled into position with whirring servos and fired. The 50mm magrail hurled the multipurpose projectile into the tree line where an enemy missile team was preparing to fire. The round airburst near the Pharaonis, spraying them with shrapnel and tossing them to the ground with the concussive blast.

"Got 'em!" declared Barton. "LT, I'm going to work this side over with a few more rounds. Can you hammer it with the blaster at the same time?"

"Yeah. We gotta thin this missile teams out, or we'll run out of countermeasures," Dausch replied, switching his monitor to take control of the blaster. "Hollis, don't forget to change positions periodically, so we don't become a sitting duck. Stay on top of those countermeasures. When we're down to our last charge, stop the vehicle, pop the smoke screen, and go reload them."

"Hell yeah, LT. Let's do this thing!" Hollis hollered excitedly.

Bam, bam, bam!

The cracking sound of sonic booms reverberated inside the Puma with each shot Barton fired. Using the thermals, it was incredible to see just how many Pharaonis soldiers were being hidden by this unusual kind of underbrush that seemed to be everywhere on this strange planet. The foliage of small- to medium-sized bushes and this arid moss functioned like an organic camouflage. It was difficult to spot the enemy with standard lenses.

"Missiles inbound! Hornets engaging!" Hollis warned as alarms alerted them to the incoming threat.

Pop...Pop.

The loud bursting noises momentarily distracted Dausch, but he fired the blasters relentlessly into clusters of moving heat signatures shooting at them. Suddenly, a pair of flashes bloomed in front the vehicle, momentarily blinding his thermals.

Dausch was annoyed that his view of the enemy was temporarily interrupted but also felt relieved knowing their Hornet antimissile system scored a pair of hits against the missiles heading for them. It was moments like this he was glad the Republic made use of what other races considered "legacy" or "ancient" tech. The Hornet's antimissile system was a more high-tech multipurpose version of the early 21st Century Trophy active protection system that was used extensively on armored vehicles during the battles leading up to the AI war of the 2040s. As far as Dausch was concerned, it was the Republic's ingenuity of fusing of human and alien technology that continued to give the Republic its military edge.

"Mustang Two, Mustang One. I'm sending a map marker where I want your Linebackers to dismount the rest of the platoon," Dausch directed. "Sciallo is ordering a strike to hammer them while your vehicles move into position."

He opened a shared digital map to outline how he wanted the attack to happen. While Breuer and Dausch were finalizing the plans for the attack and repositioning their Linebackers and Pumas, the first volley of artillery shells began to arrive. The 240mm shells were a mixture of air- and ground-bursting high-explosive shells and white phosphorus, also known as "Willie Pete."

The Republic Army used Willie Pete shells in the same way they had been used nearly two hundred years ago, when they were first introduced in 1916, during the First World War. When a white phosphorus shell exploded in the air, it released two hundred and ten canisters of air bursting submunitions that disbursed in a circular arc, two hundred and fifty to three hundred and fifty meters in diameter. What made this kind of smoke generator deadly was that once the white phosphorus was exposed to oxygen, it ignited. The white smoke that was released occurred due to combustion temperatures of 800 to 2,5000 degrees Celsius, melting and consuming everything it touched.

As the third volley pummeled the forested area that it had turned into a fiery cauldron, the alien trees and underbrush burst into flames. Isolated fires from the descending canisters soon merged. Dausch was staring into the flames when something strange happened. He heard a strange shrieking sound. After a moment, it dawned on him that he was hearing cries of agony, shouts of Pharaonis soldiers being burned alive in their hidden positions within the forest now fully ablaze. Dausch reached over to the audio controls and turned it all off—silencing the cries of his enemy. He realized in that moment they wouldn't need to attack this position. The fire and air bursting high explosive shells were doing the job better than they could.

He contacted the commanders of Eagle and Falcon Companies, letting them know the missile teams had been dealt with. The path to the Aetherport, the giant Starport outside the city Verdanthia was now clear. This was the last major structure standing between the allied force and the Pharaonis capital city of Vrahk'tol. The 9th and 13th Orbital Assault Regiments had seized the spaceport a few days prior. Now it was the job of the 11th Division to relieve them and prepare to support the final assault against the capital.

With these missile teams dealt with, Dausch wanted to focus on keeping his platoon alive and making it to the Aetherport in one piece. It wasn't long before the tanks of Eagle and Falcon Companies reached their positions. He steadily merged his platoon of vehicles with the tanks, like the original plan had called for.

****

Two hours had passed since the skirmish in the forest, and there was still no sign of the enemy. They eventually left the more forested areas near the T4 highway, turning off the main road to drive across the more flat, expansive plains. It wasn't long before the convoy of wheeled vehicles and tank treads churned up clouds of dust following behind them.

When they approached an elevated rise in the terrain, Dausch lost sight of what lay beyond until their vehicles reached the crest. When they did, what he saw as the terrain descended into a wide plain caught Dausch's breath in amazement. The map showed the structure sprawled out before them was in fact the Aetherport they had been fighting to reach. The Starport was massive, sprawling across the landscape like some colossal hive-like structure.

How big is that thing? he wondered as they continued to drive closer to it.

It appeared to be constructed entirely of earthen materials—a jumble of dirt mounds and twisting spires—and it rose high toward the sky. The Aetherport's pockmarked walls had been carved out of the very soil itself. There was no way to tell how old the structure was or what it might have been originally built for. It had jagged ridges, and deep crevasses ran along its surface, creating a rough, organic texture. In places, the walls bulged outward in a way that made it look like they were about to pop.

As they approached, Dausch noticed a series of interconnected mounds and tunnels that wove in and out of each other like a vast maze. Openings dotted the Starport's surface like gaping mouths leading into the depths of the earth.

When they drew closer, the carnage from the battle to seize the Aetherport came into view. Like battles before it, the ground approaching the structure was littered with the dead and disfigured bodies of the enemy—bloated as the sun baked their lifeless forms.

A couple of times, the column of tanks had to snake its approach to the entrance to avoid falling into craters deep enough to swallow a Yeti tank or Puma. The closer they got to the walled structure, the more shattered pieces of earthen material they found strewn about. It was obvious to anyone this was the site of a major recent battle and a testament to the ferocity and firepower the orbital assault divisions attacked with. The shock troops of the Republic had a well-earned reputation, and no doubt, this battle would add to it.

Up ahead, as they neared the walled structure, they saw more signs of battle damage—a deep gash created a hole through the earthen outer wall. It had likely been hit with a bunker busting missile or bomb, or maybe even a turbolaser from a Navy corvette or frigate that descended to low altitude to provide this very kind of direct fire support. What Dausch found most interesting was the tangled web of chambers built within these incredibly thick walls.

"Wow, this must have been one hell of a fight—these scorch marks around this hole must've come from a Republic warship," Dausch observed. "They're too symmetrical to have been caused by anything else."

"Yeah, it's incredible, LT," said Barton. "It makes me happy as hell to be part of the regular army and not an OAT, Ranger, or Delta. The kinds of battles they're thrown into are astounding."

Barton cleared his throat, then added, "I had an uncle in the 82nd OAD during the last war—the battles he regaled us with as young boys made him sound like a supersoldier. When I told him I wanted to become an OAT like him, he took me to a bar he hung out at with his friends and shared the unvarnished, uncensored reality of what the OATs had been like for him. He said that if I wanted to live, to one day have a family, I should join the regular Army, not the OATs or Deltas. After twelve years in the RA, I can't thank him enough for being honest with me."

"Ha ha. Wow, that's practically the same thing my dad told me when they announced a draft as the Zodarks invaded Sol," Hollis chimed in. "He told me to go to the recruiting station the next day and join the RA before I could get drafted into the OATs or SOF."

"Listen to you two, bunch of pussies," Dausch joked with them. "Hollis, keep following the tanks inside. We'll tail them to the marshalling point and wait for the rest of the regiment to catch up."

Once they rolled into the makeshift staging area, a welcoming party of units who arrived ahead of them waved and welcomed them to the Starport. They were guided to some parking ramps and told to park the vehicles and get some rest. Dausch made sure to let everyone know he wanted the vehicles topped off on ammo and all repairs that needed to be made completed before they sacked out for the night. If they needed to roll quickly for whatever reason, Dausch wanted to make sure his platoon was green on ammo and the vehicles ready to fight.

Dausch heard the radio just as he was about to step out of the vehicle. "Mustang One, Longhorn Six. How copy?"

He reached for his comms. "Longhorn Six, Mustang One. We just arrived at the Spaceport."

There was a pause. "That's good to hear, Dausch. I wanted to say that was a hell of job your platoon did today. The rest of the company should join you shortly, along with the rest of the regiment. Major Vaughn wanted me to pass along a set of orders for your platoon."

Dausch sighed. All he wanted to do was stretch his legs and back, maybe sleep ten or fifteen hours if he was allowed to.

"Mustang Platoon is ordered to stand down for the next twenty-four hours. You are to use that time as you see fit, but you are not to work. You and your platoon have earned a day of rest. I'll see you in twenty-four hours. Out."

Huh, well I'll be, thought Dausch. *I guess I can get 15 hours of sleep...*

Chapter Thirty-Six

ZN *Kryzal*
Planet Shwani, Varkorion System

The *Kryzal* entered the Varkorion system after a long journey to the edge of Zodark-controlled space, to a place called the Skadi Fields on the edge of Primord territory. Back in the time before the Zodark and Primord people were in a perpetual state of war, this zone, a dark region of space with almost no stars, making it eerily quiet and isolated, had boasted some of the most valuable ice and mineral fields one could mine. In time, the Zodarks began calling it the Skadi, allowing and occasionally even supporting the mining stations or the formation of some trade outpost.

The miners, Zodark and Primord alike, generally got along, trading amongst each other from time to time, at least until the war between them had ended the friendly working relationship the miners had forged on their own. Now, this region of space was largely empty, devoid of the mining outfits that used to operate the various outposts and mining stations. All that remained in the area was Vargr Outpost. In this quiet, desolate place, rogue traders and those working the illicit black markets between each other's territory still thrived, even growing in the absence of any official government presence.

Heltet fancied himself a spymaster, an intelligence operative who spent much of his time lurking among the shadows of the Groff. In his mind, the Vargr Outpost was an ideal place for an in-person meeting with his Karaffs, a rare occasion given the extreme risk of discovery it posed to his spy chiefs, the few he still had. Yet the urgency of the information he sought necessitated a meeting regardless of the risk it posed. Now, having met with them, he felt foolish for having forced them to make this journey only to provide him with the news he feared most—the Republic was coming, and there was nothing they could do to stop that eventuality from coming to fruition.

Feeling glum at the news his Karaffs had provided, Heltet began asking questions and familiarizing himself with the *Kryzal*—an upgraded destroyer class they called the Thoraxian heavy destroyer. Unlike the Malvari's version, the Plarix Drexol class, the Thoraxian had been designed and commissioned by the Groff, not the Malvari, and built in secrecy at the Tarkun Shipyards of Nightra, a moon orbiting the planet Skorvald, not far from the planet Shwani, the Groff headquarters. Heltet suspected that if the Groff or Malvari were headquartered in Zinconia, this kind of secret project would likely never happen. Too many prying eyes and too many ways a Council member could stumble upon the truth. Regardless, he enjoyed the separation between the Groff and the Malvari.

*If the Mavkah knew we had built a more powerful, more potent version of their beloved Plarix Drexol...*Heltet smiled as he imagined Mavkah Griglag losing his mind in a fury at the Groff for having taken their destroyer and made it better. If there was one thing Heltet loathed about the Malvari, it had to be their inflexibility about old traditions and their inability to adapt to change. Brute force could only work for so long. Eventually, you had to rely on that spongy substance between your ears called brains.

I wonder how many of these Thoraxians Vak'Atioth has ordered to be built, Heltet thought to himself. In a way, he was surprised by the kinds of upgrades the Malvari had failed to make since their first encounters with the Republic or the other races. It seemed silly to him that the Malvari wouldn't modify new warship designs to adjust to the enemy they were currently fighting. Then again, he recalled the inflexibility in ship designs for which the Malvari were notorious.

As Heltet continued to sit at his desk, reviewing the reports his Karaffs had given him, he knew this wasn't going to please the Director. The news was not good. There was just no way to sugarcoat it. He knew the Director had hoped they might deliver new information they could act on to prevent the inevitable, but sadly, there was nothing. They would have to get creative in figuring out how best to fight the Republic and its allies into a stalemate—freezing territory to bring about peace. It wouldn't last, of course, but it would give them time to rebuild their fleets, and to finish their preparations to fully integrate the Gorgonian tribes into the Zodark Army. They would make fine shock troops, disposable, replaceable—just as the Guristas had been cultivated to be.

Heltet heard someone approaching the door. *Bang, bang...*

"Enter!" he shouted, waiting to see who was interrupting him.

"Laktish, sorry for the intrusion. You asked to be notified when we began the final approach to Shwani," announced NOS Jakrim, the captain of the *Kryzal*. "Would you still like us to approach the orbital platforms so you may inspect their progress yourself?" he asked, a bit of skepticism in the tone of his question.

Heltet gave a curt nod, ignoring his curiosity as to why the Laktish would want to inspect a defensive platform like this, but he wasn't about to question him either. With his answer, Jakrim turned to leave to head up to the bridge. Heltet stood, then walked after him, allowing nothing but silence and curiosity to fill the void as they approached the bridge.

When they reached the bridge, the Zodarks manning the different stations snapped to attention, mindful of who had just entered with their captain. While Heltet held no military rank, he was the Laktish—the Groff enforcer and by far the most feared Zodark outside of the Director himself or the Zon, for it was the Laktish that administered the punishments that kept the Empire under control.

NOS Jakrim told his crewmen to return to their stations and to put the asteroid on the main monitor. When it appeared, the feed showed hundreds of construction robots crawling across the outside of the asteroid, some busily affixing laser turrets or pods of antiship missiles and intercept missiles.

Jakrim looked at Heltet. "It's hard to believe it has come to this, isn't it?"

Heltet nodded, then explained, "There is a proverb I learned from the humans—the ones from the Republic. It said something to the effect of *it is better to have something and not need it than to need it and not have it.* I agree with you, Jakrim, it is sad the day has come when the Empire faces invasion. It is, however, better to have these platforms at our disposal than to need them and not have them."

Heltet could see his comment had unnerved Jakrim. The idea of an invasion of Zodark territory was so foreign, so abstract, that most had a hard time fathoming such an event happening, yet it had happened several times and would happen again shortly.

Brushing his own concerns aside, he added, "Regardless of why these platforms are having to be built, NOS Jakrim, the reality is they should have been built dracmas ago and improved upon as new technologies revealed themselves. Yet here we are, hastily cobbling together whatever sort of defenses we can to counter this scourge, to prevent these quants from invading *our* Empire." Heltet placed extra emphasis on the word *our*.

Jakrim furrowed his brow, sneering at the suggestion that these defensive platforms should have already been built. "A strong Mavkah paired with a Zon guided by Lindow never would have allowed the Empire to be placed in such a position." He shook his head dismissively. "We are lions led by a lamb who seeks counsel from donkeys. Alas, what can we expect from the Zon who gave us the greatest military defeat the Empire has suffered?" whispered Jakrim in disgust.

Heltet snorted in amusement at this NOS's perceptiveness— even he felt little confidence in this Zon. It did not seem right, elevating the former Mavkah to the High Council following his utter defeat in Sol, crippling the Malvari in the process. When barely a moona had passed and he was voted to replace Utulf as Zon, questions of nepotism and corruption had spread. Utulf and Otro were both from the Ishukat tribe, one of several tribes within the Blood Raider Clan—the most powerful clan in the Empire.

Leaning closer to Jakrim so only he could hear him, Heltet whispered, "You are not wrong, Jakrim—but you should keep those comments to yourself, lest you speak them in the company of the wrong person and find your loyalty and honor questioned."

Jakrim's face flushed as he realized he had just disparaged the Zon in front of the Laktish of all people. "My apologies, Laktish. I want only the best for the Empire."

"As we all do. I have seen what I need to see. Take us to the Ministry's spaceport. I have much work I must attend to," Heltet ordered. It was time to report his findings to Vak'Atioth.

As the *Kryzal* moved past the rock being transformed into a defensive platform, Heltet studied the specifications of the asteroid he assumed had been plucked from one of the several ore belts within the system. The rock they had chosen was good—five kilometers in length, one kilometer in height, and two and a half kilometers in width. To his surprise, it wasn't the only one being turned into a weapons platform— six others were undergoing a similar process of transformation. If nothing else, they would make any attempt to seize the planet or bombard it from space terribly costly in terms of ships and personnel.

Jakrim stepped next to him, commenting, "Laktish, the spec sheet you are looking at is not the most up-to-date version. That is the one being shown just in case the Republic or its allies might acquire it. The real one says these Eyes of Shwani will have more than two hundred primary laser batteries—the same batteries with which we recently upgraded our battleships and heavy battleships."

Heltet chuckled when he heard the name of these platforms, which seemed to annoy Jakrim. "Haha, my laughter is not at you, NOS Jakrim—I am just surprised Vak'Atioth retained the name for these giant rocks—the Eyes of Shwani." He laughed some more before regaining control of himself. "When I heard Zon Otro refer to these massive floating bases as the 'Eyes' of whatever planet it was going to protect, I had to laugh—as if it's looking down on the planet and not outward into the abyss."

Heltet then pounded his chest twice with both his right hands. "We, the Groff, we are the Eyes of the Empire—not some floating rock with lasers and missiles. Frankly, I'm surprised the Director went along with the name, but then again, I have been gone away for many months, so I am sure much has happened in my absence."

The *Kryzal* began its entry into the planet's atmosphere. Heltet walked to an empty chair, strapped himself in, and watched like everyone else as the ship reentered the atmosphere, a brief flame swirling about the front chin of the warship as its heat shield protected the armor beneath it. It wasn't long until they touched down, the Groff headquarters a few hundred meters from where the pilot parked the *Kryzal* until its next mission.

****

Drokanis, Ministry of Groff
Planet Shwani, Varkorion System

Director Vak'Atioth's office at the Groff headquarters was just the way he liked it—austere and imposing. He felt it was a good reflection of himself and the institution he had commanded for going on twenty-three years at this point. He could have his office on any floor, any view he wanted from the towering structure built to intimidate the residents and any who had business within the planet's capital city, Drokanis. Instead, the office of the most feared Zodark in the Empire wasn't located in some fancy office with a view. It was in the bowels of the building—sublevel three. Arguably the most secure and fortified location in the building. In an age where orbital strikes could easily occur, Vak'Atioth left nothing to chance, especially his privacy and safety.

When asked how he would like his office to be constructed, he'd told the designer he wanted an office that exuded an air of authority and dread. They had accomplished this with a large dark wooden desk made from native trees, its polished surface unmarred save for a single comms console and holographic interface for conducting video calls. Located behind the desk was a wall of screens silently streaming newscasts from across the Empire, images of shipyards busily rebuilding the Malvari's fleet of battleships. It was a visual reminder to all who entered—nothing happened within the Empire that he didn't already know about.

Of course, there were his trophies, mementos of past victories or wins, and the occasional symbol of his ruthless efficiency. His pride and joy was the preserved skull of a fearsome Gjallar beast, a creature all Zodark youth of note would hunt when coming of age. He had placed a series of ceremonial weapons mounted to either side in perfect alignment. They ranged from a Zodark plasma lance to the blade of an ancient Zodark warrior king to and a personal artifact from his days as the Laktish, the enforcer.

Focus, Vak, think your way out of this problem, he told himself for probably the tenth time. Spread across the desk before him were half a dozen tablets with intelligence reports informing him of all sorts of troubles and problems needing to be solved. All the while, the three tablets he'd placed in his top drawer warned him of the allied buildup taking place in the Primord system of Pfeinstgard.

Damn that fool Otro…he just had to gamble the Empire on his desire to defeat the Republic, cursed Vak, contemplating the situation the Zodarks now found themselves in. He was just about to go for a walk when a message said the *Kryzal* had landed—Laktish Heltet was on his way to see him.

"I pray to Lindow, Heltet, that you bring us good news—Lindow knows we need some about now," Vak muttered to himself.
****

"Enter, my Laktish. How was your journey?" Vak asked, stepping toward Heltet to greet him.

"It was a much longer journey than I remembered," answered Heltet as the two of them embraced.

"Come, Heltet, let us drink to your safe return and Lindow's protection. I suspect we have much to talk about," commented Vak. He guided them toward a set of chairs arranged in front of a fireplace and rang one of his aides to have a bottle of Budarian wine brought in. Then he retrieved a pair of pipes and some Brill from his secret stash in the bottom drawer of his desk.

When they had finished their glass of wine and smoked the Brill, Vak decided it was time to find out what Heltet had learned during his covert meeting. "Heltet, the suspense is killing me. What did you uncover?"

Heltet was a little slow in responding. Vak wasn't sure if that was because of the wine and Brill or because he didn't know how to deliver bad news. "Just rip the bandage off, Laktish. Good, bad, or indifferent, we need to know what your Karaffs shared," Vak prodded softly.

Sighing, Heltet began, "My Karaff of the Republic, the one who replaced the traitor—he has confirmed the Gurista resistance against the Republic has ended. In fact, he says there wasn't much of a resistance to begin with. But that's not all he provided—"

Vak hissed, irritated at the pace at which Heltet was explaining things. "This news from the Orinda system—this isn't new or of value to us now. If this Karaff provided valuable intelligence—share it now. Do not test my patience, Heltet. The situation around here has shifted in your absence, and I fear not for the better."

"Yes, of course. My Karaff has informed me of something incredible happening within the Republic. The ancient race—the Humtars—they have returned. In fact, it would appear the humans are direct descendants of the Humtars. The ancient race that built the stargates were humans," Heltet revealed.

A look of shock washed over the face of Vak'Atioth, who stammered, "I, um, your Karaff is certain of this?"

Heltet nodded. He reached for his satchel, retrieving an ornate box. He pressed an index finger down across the face of some dragon-looking creature. When he lifted his finger, Vak saw a tiny drop of blood seep through the skin before Heltet placed the finger in his mouth. "It's a DNA lock," shared Heltet as the ornate box unlocked and he retrieved a P2 device.

When Heltet placed the priority pad or P2 on the table beside them, he turned it on, and an image of his Karaff appeared. In Sumerian, the man explained what he knew of these Humtars. He shared information about what sounded like incredible and impossible feats of technological capabilities these Humtars seemed to possess. He then began to share multiple video clips of the Humtars speaking in large and small groups to various people on Earth.

As Vak listened to the words of this Karaff and to the words of these Humtars themselves, he found himself awestruck by not just what he was hearing but what his eyes were seeing. There was no doubt the humans of the Republic, the Sumerians, and the Guristas were direct descendants of the Humtars. But as he studied the faces and bodies of these Humtars, he couldn't help but notice how flawless, how perfect they appeared. They were a few inches taller than the average Republic human, but their skin looked flawless, and their physiques appeared trim, athletic, and fit.

When the Karaff showed videos of the unimaginable means these Humtars were using to build new cities and repair damaged ones from the attack on Earth, Vak knew the Empire was in trouble. *If these Humtars can rebuild cities like this...what could their shipyards be like?* he thought to himself. With a sense of fear and foreboding, he contemplated what the future might hold for the Zodark people if they did not either defeat the Republic quickly or find a way to stalemate the war and secure an armistice or peace before these Humtars could transfer the kind of military technology that would likely brush aside the Zodark Navy and end the Empire.

"This next video is of my Karaff in the Primord Kingdom. He has done well for us—acquiring a substantial amount of information, plans, and details of alliance activities taking place in the Pfeinstgard system," Heltet confirmed. He resumed his briefing, further explaining the Groff's beliefs and the Malvari's fears. "Our suspicions about the alliance using the system as a springboard to invade the Empire are well founded. One of his sources was able to acquire a substantial amount of details of troop and ship movements, training regimens, and buildups of supplies for what can only be a full-scale invasion of the Gravaxia system. Unlike the Republic's previous incursion into the system, it would seem they intend to capture and occupy at least one or more of the system's planets and/or moons," explained Heltet in a very matter-of-fact way.

When Heltet finished his briefing and provided his own overview and analysis of what it meant in the grand scheme of things, he asked, "Vak, I have served the Groff and the Empire for more than fifty dracmas. I have witnessed some incredible military victories—some attributable directly to the intelligence you and the Groff have provided. Given what we now know of these Humtars and their obvious intent to help their fellow humans—their direct descendants, no less—what can we possibly do to save ourselves and prevent the alliance from dismantling and occupying the empire our people have spent the past centuries building?"

Vak stared at Heltet for a moment before speaking. "You have done well, Heltet. You have brought great honor to the D'Shawni Clan through your service. Your present position—Laktish—it has certain duties that, at times, can conflict with some of the activities of the Groff. Activities from which I have been forced to shield you in order to give you plausible deniability."

"Is this in reference to the civil unrest and the blasphemy being spoken against the Zon and the High Council?" Heltet prodded, his appearance becoming more guarded.

Nodding slowly, Vak explained, "It pains me to admit this, Heltet, but I have failed the Empire—I have failed as the director of this agency—"

"Failed? You are too harsh on yourself," Heltet interrupted.

Vak raised a hand to forestall Heltet from speaking further. "I appreciate your support and confidence in my leadership, Heltet. For too long, I have watched the rot grow within the Malvari and done nothing to stop it. I selfishly saw it as a means for personal gain. If I stood by and allowed the rot to grow, it would weaken the standing of the Malvari in the eyes of the Council. It would position me to be selected to serve on the Council. At least, that was Councilman Tanhilff's intention when he conspired with me. I was to be his benefactor, his vote toward his own ascension to become Zon.

"That was the plan until the Battle of Myrkarian," Vak explained, his demeanor becoming angry. "Otro is from the same tribe as Utulf. I was not aware of that until after he had been appointed

Mavkah. By that point, it was too late for me to intercede and try to prevent his appointment. With Otro as the new Mavkah, Zon Utulf had a protégé in Otro and essentially had the military in his back pocket. The man is utterly incompetent and should never have been appointed Mavkah, but he was, and it was for a singular purpose—to allow Utulf to remain the Zon long after he officially stepped down. Otro owed his position to Mavkah, then to the Council, and then to Zon Utulf.

"Try as I might to reveal the depths of his incompetence and unfitness to be Mavkah, there was nothing more I could do after his shocking victory against the Primords, his second dracma in office. When he unbelievably smashed the Primord fleet at the Battle of Myrkarian, not only did he end the Primord threat to our conquest of their planet Intus and Rass. He made himself a national hero—something Utulf promoted heavily across the Empire. At that point, the rot within the Malvari could not be removed. It just grew and festered under the ineptitude of Otro. I mean, look at his own deputy, Damavik—that traitorous bastard," ranted Vak, muttering obscenities as he listed off the failures of Otro until he mentioned the Battle for Alfheim.

"When the Orbots forced us into accepting a peace treaty with the Republic and their allies during the Second Battle for Alfheim, Otro became incensed. He believed we could have finished the Republic and conquered their territories if the Orbots had not stymied his plans," Vak explained. "He pressured Zon Utulf to push the Groff into finding the location of Earth and preparing the way for the war to resume once the *Nefantar* was ready. Well, you know how that ended." Vak sighed audibly, shaking his head. "Otro should have been frocked for what he did—bypassing the Groff and speaking directly to your Karaff. For all we know, his contact with your Karaff could have been what triggered this Dakkuri person to change sides. In a single failed battle, he lost more than half of the Malvari's entire fleet, much of it our newer class of warships. It crippled us while accomplishing nothing—"

Heltet cut in to ask, "Vak, I understand your frustration with the Malvari and Otro—and, yes, I share your opinion that he should have been frocked for what he did. But are you saying this civil unrest, this blasphemy being spoken against the Zon and the Council, is being directed and fueled by the Groff, by you?"

Vak could see Heltet looked conflicted. Technically, it was his job to find the culprits of this whisper campaign and shut it down. He probably would have if Vak had not included Heltet's deputy—Zelron Velix. Zelron had done a superb job of cherry-picking the information Heltet was given while intercepting reports that would have revealed the Groff's growing role in subverting the Council's control over the Empire and the groundwork that was being laid to remove Zon Otro from power.

"Let me ask you something, Heltet. Are you willing to do whatever is necessary to preserve the Empire—to prevent it from being defeated?"

Heltet bunched his eyebrows together, his facial expression forming a question he looked unsure of asking. "You know the answer to that question. Of course I am, and I will do whatever is necessary to protect the Empire from a loss that would see us cede territory to weaken us even in defeat. Does this mean the Groff is actually plotting something against the Zon, against the Council?"

"Heltet, sometimes you have to get dirty before you can become clean. The situation such as it is has reached a point where if someone doesn't intercede now, there won't be an Empire to protect much longer," replied Vak, his eyes searching Heltet's for signs he might turn on the Groff.

For a moment, no one spoke. Vak observed Heltet like a hawk. For his part, Heltet seemed to be playing out different scenarios in his mind before he spoke. "I believe I understand what is happening, but that doesn't change the underlying issue that we are an intelligence agency—not a military organization. How would any of this work?"

Vak breathed a sigh of relief. His Laktish appeared to be on board. Standing, Vak began to explain as he brought up a live feed of the Tarkun Shipyards of Nightra. "Heltet, I think it's time to include you in Operation Vhextar..."

New images appeared on the giant center monitor against the back wall of Vak's office. The moment Heltet saw them, his mouth fell open in shock. "How...how is this possible?" he finally managed to stammer.

"It's simple, Heltet. Remember when I spoke of the rot and decay that has taken root within the Malvari? We stand on the verge of being invaded from at least one and possibly two directions instead of incorporating lessons learned from battles with the Republic, the Primords, and even the Altairians. Yet the Malvari has made few if any changes to the designs of our warships. Under Otro's leadership, it took the Malvari more than fifteen dracmas to finalize the designs of the *Plarix Drexol*—our first destroyer class of warships. When this warship first went into battle, the deficiencies and problems became apparent despite the success of the ship. Did the Malvari look to fix these deficiencies? No—instead, they focused the majority of their shipyard production capacity on building their toy, the *Plarix*-class heavy battleships.

"Did you know the resources and materials that go into building just one Plarix battleship could be used to build four of these new Thoraxian heavy destroyers?" Vak asked. "Think about that, Heltet—four Thoraxians. Those four warships could tear a Plarix battleship apart. Imagine how much stronger our fleet would be if, instead of building twenty Plarix battleships, those resources and shipyard capacity had been thrown into mass-producing Thoraxian destroyers. Instead of having twenty battleships, we would have eighty Thoraxian destroyers. Can you imagine how powerful our fleets could be if we fielded hundreds of these? We would overwhelm the enemy and reclaim lost territories."

Heltet continued to look surprised by what Vak was saying. He then dared to ask, "So you have had the Tarkun Shipyards of Nightra building these Thoraxian destroyers for the Groff?"

Vak nodded, not saying a word.

"By Lindow's grace—I am amazed, Vak. How many of them has the Groff built?"

"While the Malvari have built fourteen of their Plarix battleships, the Tarkun Shipyards have built one hundred and sixty heavy destroyers. Once we have two hundred of them…that's when we will move against Zon Otro and the High Council. With the people behind us, we will levy charges of corruption and treason against the Council members. That is where you fit in to all of this, Heltet. As the Groff Laktish, it falls upon you to read the charges against the members of the Council. You will strip them of their authority, of their position on the Council, and take them into custody, where you shall implement the punishment of frocking, placing their fate firmly in the hands of Lindow," explained Vak with a smile of satisfaction.

Leaning forward in his chair, he stared into Heltet's eyes. "I know that you have just returned from a long journey and I have given you much to think about. I would like an answer to the question I am about to ask, but should you require some time to deliberate on your response, the most I can give you is till sunset. So, Laktish of the Groff, can we count on you to fulfill your duties as Laktish...or will you force me to ask for your resignation and detain you until your replacement has acted?"

With his ultimatum delivered, Vak sat back in his chair, his eyes focused on Heltet as he awaited his response.

Chapter Thirty-Seven

Mid-June 2115
11th Spartacus Armor Regiment
Oretheon Industrial Complex
Lindenzia, Planet Eurysa

Colonel Steve Thomas sat in the command seat of his Yeti main battle tank, leading the 11th Spartacus Regiment toward the Pharaonis city of Lindenzia. The landscape ahead shifted from open plains to dense city structures, and while Thomas's tank was a beast in open terrain, the thought of urban combat gnawed at him. Back home, he was a country boy, preferring wide-open spaces over the claustrophobia of megacities. In combat, those urban areas were death traps—missile and laser magnets for tanks like his Yeti. He knew the infantry appreciated the tanks soaking up the enemy's attention, but they weren't designed for city fighting. That was a job for Pumas, Linebackers, and Bobcats—faster, more agile vehicles built to handle the tight spaces and ambushes that cities bred.

When the Pharaonis had first rolled out their heavily armored vehicles, the Yetis had found their match. As soon as Republic forces started pushing beyond the initial beachheads, those Pharaonis tanks became a threat in urban areas. It wasn't ideal, but it was the new reality. And so, the Yetis were thrust into the fray, forced to slug it out in the streets where they had little room to maneuver.

As the Republic pressed deeper toward Vrahk'tol, the Pharaonis shifted tactics. Instead of throwing wave after wave of soldiers to overwhelm the Republic's advance, they began digging in, holding ground until the last possible moment, and then retreating to the next fortified position. Cities, industrial complexes, defensive outposts—it didn't matter. The Republic gained ground, but the Pharaonis were always one step ahead, slipping away before they could be pinned down. Thomas couldn't shake the feeling that their enemy had grown smarter over the course of the war. But by now, it was too late. The outcome had already been decided—the Pharaonis were delaying the inevitable.

Thomas's regiment neared the last natural barrier between them and the Pharaonis capital: the Lindenzia River. Earlier attempts by Orbital Assault Regiments to seize the bridges had failed—except for one. The 9th OAR had managed to save the sole crossing still standing, a critical victory. But for Colonel Thomas, it meant his regiment would have to pass through Lindenzia, one of the few cities spared from orbital bombardment. The reason was obvious—it lay less than fifty kilometers from the capital.

As they drew closer, the bridge came into view. It was an imposing structure—a four-lane road with two rail lines crossing over a massive archway, its design a mix of steel and some composite material, woven together in intricate patterns. Wood, or something that resembled it, adorned the arch, blending seamlessly with the industrial design. Fifty meters of engineering brilliance stretched across the river.

Thomas had to hand it to the Pharaonis—their architecture was as strange as it was beautiful. *All we've got to do is make it across and through the city to Oretheon,* he told himself, already thinking ahead to the next battle.

The sun hung high overhead, baking the landscape in relentless heat. Despite the sweltering conditions, life thrived on this strange planet. Purple flora with flat, spiny leaves clustered in the shade of bent trees, their massive roots sprawling across the soil like tangled webs. Pods filled with spores clung to the branches, occasionally bursting and releasing clouds of particles that made Thomas sneeze whenever they drifted too close.

At its narrowest point, River Lindenzia stretched fifty meters—the exact length of the bridge the regiment was crossing. Elsewhere, the river widened significantly, creating vast marshlands and bogs that made crossing a nightmare. Its fast-moving current clocked in at over ten kilometers an hour, and at an average depth of fourteen meters—fording it definitely wasn't on the table.

"The scouts made it across—still no contact. That's a good sign, sir," Sergeant Wilson said, eyes glued to the gun camera feed.

"Knock on wood, it stays that way, Sergeant," Thomas replied, though he knew better than to trust calm in a war zone.

Ahead, the scout-recon element of Bobcat light tactical vehicles and Puma tanks from the 23rd Texas Mechanized Infantry Regiment pushed forward. They were acting as the eyes and ears for his tanks, screening for enemy missile teams that might try to ambush them. Though lightly armored, those vehicles packed enough firepower to deal with any Pharaonis squads that popped up.

As the rest of the reconnaissance element secured both sides of the bridge, Thomas continued scanning the horizon, instincts on edge. "What's loaded in the tube, Wilson?" he asked.

"AP, Sir. Power capacitors show full charge. Railguns ready to fire," Staff Sergeant Joe Wilson replied. "I can swap it for AMP if you want more versatility."

Thomas mulled it over. The armor-piercing round in the chamber was solid for heavy targets, but an advanced multipurpose round would give them more options—programming it to airburst or detonate on contact, even adding a delay. The AMP's flexibility made it deadly against infantry or fortifications, and he had a gut feeling they'd need that edge soon.

"Swap it out for AMP. We'll be needing them," Thomas said.

Wilson gave a nod and quickly made the switch, his confidence evident. "Good call, sir."

Staff Sergeant Colton Mayfield, their driver, eased the tank forward. "Looks like we're still in the clear. No bottlenecks and no sign of enemy contact."

Thomas smirked at the rare moment of calm. "No contact, huh? Guess using a Yeti for recon would've been like waving a big, shiny target for missile teams."

Wilson chuckled. "I'll take the quiet before the storm any day, sir. Twice on Sundays."

Laughter rippled through the crew, easing some of the tension. The air inside the tank was thick, heavy with the weight of uncertainty, but moments like these broke through the pressure. Riding with the colonel meant you knew everything—every good and bad detail—and sometimes ignorance really was bliss.

As the tank rumbled forward, Thomas glanced at the others. "So, rumor has it that once we clear this objective, the 13th Division's supposed to rotate in and give us some downtime at Camp Haussler. What would you guys do with five or seven days off?"

Wilson flicked a switch and adjusted the optics. "If that's true, sir, I'll take it. Seven months fighting on Serenea and a short trip aboard the *Callisto* barely scratched the surface of recovery. Now we're on another planet... who knows how long this time."

Mayfield chimed in, his eyes still on the road ahead. "First thing I'll do is sleep. Maybe send a few vids back home, let my wife and kids know I'm still breathing. Life at Fort Abrams feels like a lifetime ago."

"Sleep sounds about right," Thomas said, stretching his shoulders against the seat. "Though I doubt the general will give me more than twelve hours before he's got me running missions again. That man doesn't stop—like an Energizer bunny."

He glanced over at Wilson. "If your neck's bothering you that much, I can send you to the *Callisto* or the *Mercy* for a quick checkup. Perk of riding with the colonel."

Wilson smiled, his hand on the railgun controls. "Might take you up on that, sir," he replied. "But we're moving again, so I'd better focus on the sights."

The humor dissipated as the crew resumed their duties, their attention sharpening as the mission drew them back into the fight.

Once the reconnaissance units finished their crossing, it was time for Beaumont Company from the 23rd Texas Mechanized Infantry to follow. Beaumont was the screening force for Thomas's tanks, and if Pharaonis missile teams made an appearance, it would be their IFVs and APCs that dealt with the threat.

Thomas had a deep appreciation for the Army's Linebacker vehicles. Their versatility was unmatched. The Mech units used the infantry fighting vehicle variant, which carried ten soldiers and sported a center-mounted, remotely operated turret equipped with twin-barrel laser blasters. The rear turret held eight short-range multipurpose missiles, ideal for quick reaction against threats like the Pharaonis teams. The APC version traded firepower for capacity, carrying fourteen passengers in place of the missile turret.

But it was the command post variant that Thomas relied on most. The CP Linebacker was a mobile command hub, bristling with electronic warfare antennas, ground radars, comm systems, active defense modules, and a small army of reconnaissance drones. Inside, six workstations and a commander's station turned it into the brain of the regiment, allowing precise coordination of all six companies under his command. The CP vehicles gave the regiment an edge, working seamlessly with the division CP vehicles to provide unmatched coordination across the battlefield. Thomas made it a priority to keep these critical vehicles at the heart of the formation, well-protected from any threats.

As Berserker Company's command vehicle rolled into the city, Thomas noticed their formation was starting to break down. The vehicles were bunching up, losing the discipline that kept them safe.

"Berserker Six, you're bunching up. Get your formation back in order," Thomas barked into the comms. "We don't know what's waiting for us in that city." He hoped nothing was waiting, but with the Pharaonis, nothing was ever straightforward. They were masters of deception and ambush tactics, making it impossible to gauge how they'd respond next.

Captain Martin's voice came through the crackling comms. "Spartacus One, good copy." The convoy adjusted as they passed a building that had caused them to slow, the spacing between the vehicles gradually evening out as they pushed further into the city.

"Spartacus One, we're moving deeper into the city. Streets look clear... maybe too clear," Martin's tone carried a hint of suspicion.

"Agreed. If you need to dismount your infantry before proceeding, do it," Thomas replied. He wasn't taking any chances. If they had to slow their advance to avoid an ambush, it was worth it. The Pharaonis missile teams had proven deadly effective during the battles on Serena, and they seemed even more committed to their use here on Eurysa.

The last five weeks had been brutal, with relentless fighting as the Republic steadily deployed twenty-five of its thirty divisions in a tightening ring around the Pharaonis capital, Vrahk'tol. Lindenzia and the Oretheon Industrial Complex were the last major obstacles between them and the sprawling outskirts of the capital city. With each battle, they crept closer—now less than 50 kilometers from the Queen's Palace itself.

Thomas felt the weight of it. Every decision, every move they made brought them one step closer to the end game. But the Pharaonis were digging in deeper with every kilometer they lost.

Staff Sergeant Joe Wilson adjusted the gun sights with a precision that never wavered. Colonel Thomas valued that about him— the man had an eye for the smallest details, both inside the tank and out. It was a skill that had kept them alive.

Thomas glanced at the tactical map, tracking the regiment's movements through Lindenzia. His fingers brushed the comms switch. "All units, this is Spartacus One. We're entering Lindenzia en route to clear out any Pharaonis forces holed up in the Oretheon Industrial Complex. Stay alert for close-quarter attacks. Watch for missile teams—support our infantry, and keep your spacing. No bunching up."

Switching frequencies, Thomas reached out to Major Rick Ahlstrom, commander of the 24th Spartan Infantry Regiment, who was advancing from the east. "Spartan One, this is Spartacus One. How copy?"

The comms crackled, and Ahlstrom's voice came through, edged with strain. "Spartacus One, Spartan One here. Good copy, send traffic."

"Spartan One, our lead elements are entering Lindenzia, heading for Oretheon. No enemy contact so far. What's your status? How's it going on your end?" Thomas asked.

A moment of static followed before Ahlstrom responded, his tone revealing the weight of the fight. "Spartacus One, we've made light contact near Sector Charlie One, but we're heavily engaged on the outskirts of Sector Alpha One. We've got artillery and air support inbound for Alpha One and to assist with Charlie One. Enemy's definitely focused on us. What's your ETA to Oretheon?"

Thomas couldn't help but grin. The plan was working. By forcing the Pharaonis to split their attention between multiple attack axes, the 24th was drawing the brunt of the enemy's focus. "If we don't hit any resistance—twenty minutes, tops," Thomas replied. "Sounds like you've got their attention. Keep me posted if the situation changes, good or bad. Spartacus One, out."

Varinius had been right all along... the Pharaonis were too focused on the 24th. Meanwhile, his regiment was about to slip through and punch them hard.

Thomas switched back to the regiment frequency. "Spartacus units, listen up! The 24th Spartans have engaged the enemy on the eastern flank. It's our turn to hit them while they're distracted. Yetis, stay ready to switch between armor-piercing and AMP rounds. We'll likely need AMP for most of this fight. Be ready to counter any infantry waves.

"Pumas, you've got flank security—two pairs on each side of the column. Maintain thirty meters from the main column and stay sharp.

Cover our sides. Linebackers, hold the center. IFVs and APCs, get your infantry ready for rapid dismount. CP One, stay central and keep artillery and CAS requests rolling. If we hit trouble, Puma's flank, Linebackers dismount, and Yetis hit them head-on."

Thomas paused for effect, his voice hardening. "Let's move, Spartacus! Hooah!"

The regiment surged into motion, the rumble of tanks and armored vehicles filling the air as they prepared to punch through Lindenzia and strike at Oretheon while the Pharaonis were fixated on the 24th's assault.

It took time for the regiment to fully cross the bridge and filter into Lindenzia. In the distance, the deep rumble of artillery was constant, like a relentless drumbeat pounding Pharaonis positions. Overhead, the roar of jet engines surged and faded, followed by thunderous explosions. Each blast sent black clouds of smoke billowing into the sky, marking the destruction below.

Thomas couldn't help but be impressed by the sheer ferocity of the bombardment. It sounded like Sparta was hammering the Pharaonis hard. Artillery had become the backbone of this war in a way it never had against the Orbots. The Pharaonis, despite their insect-like appearance, were an advanced species—they'd colonized multiple planets and waged interstellar war. But compared to the Orbots, their weaponry was just... lacking. Still dangerous, still deadly, but nowhere near the precision and power of the Orbots' technology.

As his tank rolled deeper into the city, Thomas kept a close watch on the buildings they passed. Lindenzia had an almost organic quality to it. The structures seemed to grow out of the soil, rising up like some twisted version of a wasp's nest. Some towers stretched as high as a hundred meters, their gray exteriors smooth and rounded at the top. Bridges connected the taller buildings to smaller ones, and wide platforms jutted out at sharp angles, giving the whole city a disjointed, chaotic feel.

The more he observed, the more Thomas saw that the alien construction had been deliberately armored. The Pharaonis had covered many of the buildings with interlocking, turtle-like scales, each about a meter wide. They could've been metal, painted over to look organic— Thomas couldn't be sure. But the design wasn't lost on him.

Are they armoring their cities from the inside out? he wondered.

The streets were wide—twenty-five meters across—and overgrown with thick, vine-like plants that wrapped themselves around every other building. The vines, as thick as tree trunks, choked the life out of the structures, adding a splash of green to the otherwise drab, gray landscape. Thomas wondered if the vines would eventually damage the buildings, maybe even tear the city apart if given enough time.

The radio crackled. "Spartacus Six, this is Mustang Eleven. It's quiet as a ghost town, no movement detected, nothing on thermals or IR. Streets are clear. Looks like there's been recent activity—some of the stores, if you can call them that, look used. But if there were people here, they're long gone."

Thomas keyed the mic. "Mustang Eleven, good copy. Continue leading us to the rally point. Out."

He glanced at the map, already thinking ahead. The element of surprise was still on their side, but only for so long. The Pharaonis were cunning—they could be lying in wait, ready to spring a trap. He needed to get his force into position before that happened.

"They had to have seen us by now," the driver muttered. "Why haven't they shot at us yet?"

"If you saw a tank regiment rolling up to your front door, would you stick around?" Wilson replied, half-smirking.

"I'm human, not a Pharaonis."

"You make me wonder sometimes." Wilson chuckled, then glanced at the colonel. "Sir, if they're setting up an ambush—"

"Stick to the plan," Thomas interjected, his eyes scanning the skyline ahead. "If the Pharaonis engage, we hit them with everything we've got. If we're lucky, they saw us coming and bugged out."

The radio crackled to life. "Mustang Eleven to Spartacus One," came the nervous voice of the lead scout. "We've reached Marker Seven. I've got a problem you need to hear."

Thomas exchanged a glance with Wilson, who shrugged. "Mustang Eleven, Spartacus One. What's the problem?"

"Well, sir, the route Division gave us narrows from twenty-five meters down to ten for about two klicks before it opens up again at the rally point for the assault on Oretheon. It's too tight for your tanks to pass through safely. Feels like a perfect setup for an ambush. We scouted an alternate route—takes us two klicks out of the way, but it keeps us on a wide street with buildings no higher than forty meters. Your call, Colonel, but I'd recommend we deviate from the plan."

Thomas cursed under his breath. *Who in Division missed this?* He could already picture the kill box his regiment would have walked into. "Mustang Eleven, good catch. We'll take your alternate route. Lead the way. We'll follow. Out."

The column resumed its slow march, winding through the last stretches of the city. Thomas felt the weight lift slightly from his shoulders when his recon elements reached the rally point without incident. No ambush. No sign of the enemy. Aegis Company followed closely behind Mustang, and Thomas shifted to the drone feed that provided overwatch of the area. He stared at the image—something about the scene not sitting right with him.

The rally point was perfect for marshalling his forces—a space wide enough to concentrate his tanks into a lethal punch. A single Yeti was a beast of a machine, but 240 Yetis, coordinated with mechanized infantry, was an unstoppable force. Still, the gnawing feeling in his gut persisted.

Flanked on both sides by dense forest, the road stretched for six kilometers north, straight to the Oretheon Industrial Complex. The trees were thick, the vegetation dense enough to hide entire platoons of Pharaonis if they were out there.

"CP One, I want recon drones scanning the forests flanking us," Thomas ordered, his tone sharp. "Look for any signs of enemy movement. Also, coordinate with Forward Observer to get prepositioned artillery targets lined up. Be ready to call in air support if needed."

As the drones veered off into the forest, Thomas kept his eyes on the screen, watching Captain Jørgen Stenberg expertly maneuver Aegis Company into position for their assault. Berserker Company, led by his most experienced CO, Captain Michael Martin, followed close behind. Thomas had made Martin his deputy regiment commander, not out of spite, but to prepare him for what was inevitable—casualties among senior officers were high, and he knew it was only a matter of time before someone needed to step up. Martin needed to be ready.

A ping on the drone feed caught Thomas's attention. One of the recon drones, Raven Three, Aegithe forest.

"Spartacus One, this is Aegis-CP. Raven Three picked up a heat anomaly in Sector Tango Seven. It's moving in for a closer scan."

Thomas's pulse quickened. He had hoped that gnawing feeling in his gut was just nerves, but this confirmed otherwise. If the Pharaonis had set an ambush here, they knew more about his force's movement than they should.

"Copy that, Aegis-CP," Thomas responded. "Alert Aegis Six and have all elements orient to face the right flank. Potential enemy units within twenty meters of the treeline."

"Good copy, Spartacus. Aegis elements reorienting to face the right flank," came the response.

Thomas braced himself. Whatever was out there, it wouldn't stay hidden for long.

"Whoa, isn't that the rally point where we're supposed to meet up?" asked Wilson, a concerned look on his face.

"Yeah, it's supposed to be. Call it intuition, but something seems off in those trees," explained Thomas as he pointed to a spot on the monitor. "That drone may have spotted something. It's going to descend below the canopy to see what's beneath it."

While Mayfield drove the tank, Thomas and Wilson watched the drone feed intently, sharing what they saw as the Raven lowered itself beneath canopy. At first, it showed nothing but trees and shadows—until suddenly, the thermal imaging flared. The Raven reacted instantly, implementing a frenetic maneuver as beams of red and yellow lasers cut through air as the Pharaonis tried to zap the Raven from the sky.

"Holy mother! That's a lot of bugs!" exclaimed Wilson in horror at what they saw materializing before their very eyes.

"Spartacus One, Aegis-CP. We've got hundreds—no, *thousands* of heat signatures appearing within the trees. It's looks like they've amassed under the treetops with some sort of heat blanket this whole time."

As Thomas saw the confirmation he'd been right, it sent a chill through his spine. His instincts had warned him—this was indeed an ambush.

Thomas barked into the comms, "Pull the Raven out, now!"

Almost instantly, its connection was lost—Raven Three was gone.

"Damn it. I was hoping it would stay alive a little longer to keep feeding us data," lamented Thomas, his jaw clenched. The Pharaonis had made their move—now it was their turn.

"What do you want us to do, sir?" Wilson asked out from his station, his voice tense. They weren't in any position to help provide support. They were traveling with Centaur Company, and they hadn't yet reached the rally point.

Before Thomas could respond, the forest adjacent to Aegis Company erupted in enemy fire. Without warning, the treeline that had so cleverly hidden the Pharaonis soldiers exploded forth in movement. Dozens of hulking, beetle-like tanks surged forward, their massive forms breaking through the dense underbrush like monsters out of a nightmare. The beetle tanks' heavily armored shells gleamed in the sunlight, their weapons charging as arcs of blue-white energy crackled across their turrets.

"Energy weapons," Thomas muttered, his eyes narrowing. "That's a new one."

The first bolt of energy struck before anyone could react. A lightning-like blast tore across the field, hitting one of the Bobcats square in the side. The vehicle exploded in a fiery burst, debris raining down in all directions. Another bolt slammed into a Puma, its hull disintegrating in a plume of flames.

"Aegis Six, return fire! Engage those beetles with everything you've got!" Thomas ordered, his voice cutting through the chaos.

Captain Stenberg's voice shouted over the comms. "All units, open fire—engage at will!"

The battlefield exploded into a frenzy of action. The Yetis unleashed their railguns, sending rounds tearing into the advancing Pharaonis armor. The 50mm railguns on the Pumas opened up, targeting the beetle tanks with precise bursts of AP rounds. But the beetle tanks were fast, far faster than anything that size had a right to be. They rumbled forward, firing more energy blasts that sliced through the air like electric whips. Another Puma took a direct hit and was reduced to nothing but a smoking crater.

"Sir, they're pushing hard!" Wilson shouted as he adjusted the gun sights, tracking the beetle tanks' advance.

Before Thomas could respond, the ground shook. Thousands of Pharaonis soldiers followed behind the beetle tanks, pouring out of the forest in waves. They moved with terrifying speed, their insectoid limbs propelling them forward in a relentless surge. They were crossing the open ground between the forest and road, closing the gap rapidly.

"All infantry, dismount! Engage the Pharaonis soldiers head-on!" Aegis Six ordered their platoon of infantry. The 23rd Texas brought their Linebackers forward, forming with their vehicles as they dismounted their infantry.

Thomas felt the tank lurch forward. Mayfield was racing to keep pace with Centaur Company, who was rushing forward to the rally point to bring their firepower to bear. All Thomas could do was watch that the battle unfold and help bring assets to bear that could aid his forces. He watched in amazement as he saw more Linebackers screeched to a halt, the rear hatches dropping as more infantry joined the fray. As more Republic troops took up defensive positions, the Pharaonis swarm continued to close in.

The battlefield was chaos. Railguns and blasters fired in every direction. Republic soldiers threw themselves into the fight, laying down suppressive fire as the Pharaonis soldiers charged, their screeches filling the air. Close-quarter combat erupted as the enemy collided with the Republic lines, and the once-organized column dissolved into a chaotic melee.

Thomas's heart pounded as he saw dozens of missiles streaking down from the treeline, targeting his forces. "Missile teams! We've got incoming missiles!" he shouted, but the missiles were already closing in. Several impacted along Aegis Company's line, ripping through vehicles and scattering debris.

Berserker Company, led by Captain Martin, had just entered the battle, their tanks repositioning before thundering forward to engage the beetle tanks. Railguns fired relentlessly, tearing into the enemy armor, but for every beetle tank they destroyed, more Pharaonis soldiers swarmed in behind.

The comms were a cacophony of shouts and explosions. "We're being overrun!" someone screamed. "Too many of them!"

Thomas cursed under his breath, his eyes darting to the horizon. Centaur Company, the unit his command Yeti was embedded with, was still racing to join the fight. They were close, but not close enough.

"Come on... come on..." Thomas muttered, watching the swarm press harder into his forces. The Pharaonis were trying to envelop Aegis and Berserker, pinning them against the open road with little cover.

"Sir, if we don't stop those beetles, we're done for!" Wilson shouted as he swung the turret, lining up for their first shot once they rounded the bend.

"Keep firing! Focus on the beetles!" Thomas ordered any tank that could get bead on them. "Seoul Twenty-One, Spartacus One. Execute pre-planned fire missions, now! Target Sector Tango Seven and Sector Sierra Nine. Repeat, three rounds, fifty meter airburst, fire for effect!"

Seconds later, the earth shook as Republic artillery rained down on the battlefield. Explosions tore through the second and third waves of Pharaonis soldiers, turning them into charred husks before they could reinforce their front line. The artillery fire bought them precious moments, but the battle was far from over.

"Spartacus One, this is Spartan One," came the voice of Major Ahlstrom over the comms. "We've broken through! We're pushing up on your right flank. Hang in there!"

Thomas allowed himself a brief moment of relief. The 24th was moving up, just as planned. But there was no time to celebrate. The air was thick with smoke and the smell of burning metal, and the Pharaonis still swarmed in overwhelming numbers.

As if answering his unspoken prayers, the sky roared as Republic jets screamed overhead. Talon fighter-bombers and Reaper ground-attack drones swooped in, unleashing their payloads on the Pharaonis forces below. Bombs and missiles streaked toward the beetle tanks, tearing through their formations and sending plumes of fire and debris skyward.

Thomas's comms crackled again. "Spartacus One, this is Spartan One. We're moving in to reinforce Aegis and Berserker. Stand by for flanking assault."

The sound of heavy engines filled the air as Centaur Company finally arrived, their tanks tearing into the battlefield with the fury of a charging bull. The ground shook with the force of their arrival, and within seconds, they had joined the fight.

"Centaur Six, this is Spartacus One. Target the beetle tanks and break their line! All units, push forward and crush their advance!" Thomas roared into the comms.

The Republic forces rallied, their tanks surging forward with renewed momentum. Railguns fired in unison, ripping through the remaining Pharaonis armor. The Pharaonis soldiers fought with a desperate frenzied energy, but they couldn't withstand the combined might of the Republic's armored fist.

As the last of the beetle tanks exploded into a fireball, the Pharaonis swarm was cut down by the relentless artillery and airstrikes as the battlefield began to clear. The once-overwhelming swarm was now reduced to broken bodies and smoking wreckage. The Pharaonis had been defeated, but at a steep cost.

Thomas sat back in his seat, his breath heavy. The battle was over, but the war was far from won.

Chapter Thirty-Eight

Operation Orion's Hammer
RNS *Draco*
Republic Naval Shipyard, Sol

In the private study of the admiral's quarters on the star carrier *Draco*, Vice Admiral William "Willie" Rosentreter reviewed the latest battle reports from Eurysa, the Pharaonis' home planet in the Zanthea system. He closed the Zanthea report and opened the intelligence summary, or INTSUM, labeled "Pyrallis System." This neighboring system was the primary responsibility of the Altairian and Primord forces.

While reviewing the accounts of battles and skirmishes happening on the moons and planets of the Pyrallis system, Willie felt relieved to see that the Altairians and Primords were steadily defeating the remaining Pharaonis strongholds. Each victory brought the alliance a step closer to fully capturing the system and eventually defeating the Pharaonis.

Satisfied with how things were progressing in the Altairian-Primord sector, he looked for the accompanying casualty report or, as he called it, the "butcher's bill." He felt his stomach churn each time he saw the overall figure of dead, wounded, and those listed as missing or presumed captured. When they'd launched this campaign, they had expected losses to be high—they were battling for control of the Pharaonis home systems. Still, it was gut-wrenching each time he saw the number of Altairians, Primords, Tully, and Republic lives lost. Unless an offensive or big battle was underway, the numbers usually didn't change much—at least until the start of the Zanthea Campaign.

When the orbital bombardments of the planet Eurysa had begun, Willie had figured the Pharaonis's revered queen would accept the hopelessness of the situation and pursue terms of surrender. Instead, she had chosen to hunker down with her people and fight to the bitter end. As a leader, he respected her choice—even acknowledging it as a noble act despite the futility of it. In the end, it wasn't going to change the outcome. Eurysa would fall. The only question was how many Pharaonis would be left after the capture of the planet.

Willie closed the casualty report and thought about the Pharaonis. He wished they could have learned more about them—understanding their language, their culture, or how their family structures worked. As it stood, the Republic had only a rudimentary understanding of their communication. The overall lack of knowledge of the Pharaonis had made it hard to identify weaknesses they could exploit against them in battle. For better or worse, they were fighting in the dark—blinded by ignorance, despite their many attempts to understand this enemy.

Regardless of how Willie felt, he had his orders, and he intended to carry them out. Defeating the Pharaonis as swiftly as possible to bring about an end to this campaign was his highest priority.

Casualties be damned.

Lifting his cup of coffee to his lips, Willie sighed. Leaning back in his chair, he stared off into the distance, his mind drifting back to his meeting with Fleet Admiral Bailey. He had been recalled to Space Command, where, upon his arrival, he had been told his flagship, the battleship *Defiant*, was going to undergo a series of refits and overhauls to incorporate some new Humtar technologies they had recently acquired. He remembered being angry at having the *Defiant* pulled from under him. But then Admiral Bailey had told him about the *Draco*, the Republic's newest star carrier to join the fleet, and how it would now act as his flagship.

"Willie, I'm giving you the *Draco* for a specific reason—it has a special ability our other ships don't, once you'll need to leverage once you've defeated the Pharaonis. Namely, it can open a bridge between the system you're in and the destination you want to bridge to—call it a gift from our Humtar cousins. In fact, we're pairing it with their starmap of our galaxy. You can bridge between any two points you want. It's far more advanced than what even the Gallentines had aboard the *Freedom*," Admiral Bailey had explained as he brought up a holographic spec sheet of the *Draco* now floating between them.

"To that end, Willie, once you've defeated the Pharaonis, the entire focus of the alliance will shift to defeating the Zodarks. This is why the *Draco* is being assigned to your battlegroup. You will need to gather your force and bridge them to the Orinda system—Gurista space."

Willie had bunched his eyebrows in confusion. "Gurista space?" he'd pressed.

Bailey smiled. "Let me ask you, how much do you know about Admiral Dobbs's mission—Gurista Freedom 14?" he'd asked.

Willie had snorted. "You mean aside from you poaching my best task force commander and her entire complement of warships and ground force?" he'd joked. "Not much. It's all been pretty hush-hush."

Bailey had chuckled at his reply. "That's true. We intentionally tried to keep the activities of her operation as secretive as possible. Those Mukhabarat spies still linger around, and this was one operation we needed to keep them from finding out about," Bailey had explained. "But here's the deal—for more than a year, we have had Special Forces and intelligence assets on the Gurista home world. They've been steadily working to foment a coup and liberate the Gurista people from the clutches of the Zodark Empire. When the time came, Admiral Dobbs and her task force were dispatched to assist our people on the ground in executing the coup and eliminating the Zodark presence on Gurista Prime and the other planets under their control.

"As of now, the Gurista people are free from the Zodarks. The last I heard, they were looking to form their own nation, though it's also possible they'll ask to join the Republic—time will tell. For now, Admiral Dobbs is working to integrate their nascent security force into our own until the Zodarks have been defeated," Bailey had concluded.

Few people outside the senior echelon had a clue what was going on in the Orinda system; Willie was glad to finally have a better picture of what was going on. "Thank you for trusting me with this information and sharing what Amy has been up to," Willie had said. "She's a good friend and a hell of a tactician. Since you seem to be in a sharing mood"—he winked at Bailey, causing him to snicker—"what the hell is Ripley up to in the Gravaxia system? The snippets of news and dribs and drabs of intel reports suggest the Zodarks aren't ready to accept that they lost the system. Is he going to be able to hold it and finish clearing out the remaining pockets of resistance? Is the plan to use it as a base to launch further incursions into Zodark space—Tueblets, maybe?"

Bailey had studied him for a moment before speaking. "Willie, you asked a good question, and under normal circumstances, I would gladly share the answer with you. I'm not saying you or your officers can't be trusted with the truth—but we have compartmentalized operations and only share them with those outside direct involvement when necessary. This minimizes the chances of the plans being discovered by the Mukhabarat and fed back to the Zodarks."

Willie had been a little disappointed in Bailey's answer. He couldn't fault the man for giving it, though. The Mukhabarat had run roughshod over Republic Intelligence for a while in the early years of the Interstellar Marshals Service.

"Fair enough, Chester. Probably for the best that I don't know for now," Willie had replied. "This warship, the *Draco*, should aid our cause and effort on Eurysa. That battle…it was unlike anything I've seen. It's a godforsaken nightmare that none of our soldiers should ever have had to experience, Chester. If we could nuke the planet into oblivion, I wouldn't hesitate. It pains me greatly to continue authorizing one division after another to deploy to the surface. We're losing soldiers at a prodigious rate. There has got to be a way to transfer more combat Synths and allow them to do the bulk of the heavy fighting," Willie had pleaded.

Bailey just shook his head in disgust. "War brings out the worst in people. It causes a person to lose a bit of their soul and their humanity with the loss of each life. This war with the Pharaonis…we can't allow ourselves to become more bogged down than we already are. Before our meeting, I spoke with Admiral McKee about assigning additional warships to accompany the *Draco* back to Eurysa. We originally planned to reinforce your fleet once the Pharaonis surrendered—I'm going to call an audible on this and send them now.

"For more than a year, since the Zodark attack, the RA has been feverishly training new soldiers. The Army recently finished the formation of the Republic Sixth Army. At the same time, the shipyards have completed four battleships with the newest Humtar reactor technology, giving them nearly the same hitting power as a Humtar or Gallentine battleship. I'm going to go ahead and assign them to your command. After you defeat the Pharaonis, your entire force will pivot to the Orinda system, where you'll link up with Admiral Dobbs's force. Should your ground or naval forces require new replacements to backfill combat losses, the Gurista force Dobbs's command has been training will provide them.

"At that point, Willie, you will receive a detailed battle order outlining the invasion of the Zodark Empire. For now, defeat the Pharaonis, then we shall focus our attention on defeating the Zodarks and end their reign of terror across the stars," Bailey had concluded.

Returning to the present, Willie blew some air past his lips, then sat forward behind his desk. He reached for the cup of coffee, lifting it to his lips and finishing the last of it. Standing, he walked to the warming plate, where a fresh pot of Deathwish Coffee sat waiting for him. Refilling his mug, he turned his gaze to the floor-to-ceiling window that ran the length of his office. He knew the window was fake, a giant monitor connected to a series of exterior cameras providing him with a real-time view of what he might see if this were a real window. He was coming to enjoy this new feature, a digital window that could even function as a star map.

He stared at what he felt was an armada of ships, gracefully arrayed in tight formations to either side of the *Draco*. Closest to the star carrier were the lumbering hulks of the twenty-two *Jupiter*-class troop transports carrying with them the Republic Sixth Army—five hundred and fifty thousand soldiers. Intermixed within the columns of troop transports sat the fourteen equally large *Saturn*-class fleet support vessels. These were the vessels that carried much of the supplies and machinery necessary to support and sustain a fleet of warships and the army traveling with them.

Willie touched the digital window, then swiped to the left, bringing into view the forward section of the convoy. Leading this massive armada of humanity sat the four newly christened battleships—*Centurion*, *Invincible*, *Majestic*, and *Gladiator*, the ones with the newly integrated Humtar technology that massively scaled up their firepower and capabilities. While not entirely on par with a Gallentine or Humtar main battleship, they weren't far off. The remainder of his convoy consisted of two *Victory*-class battleships, two battle cruisers, twelve heavy cruisers, and a mix of three dozen frigates and corvettes. It was a large convoy—ninety-three ships in total. He just hoped it would be enough to end this war with the Pharaonis and to defeat the Zodark Empire, so it might never threaten the Republic or its allies again.

He turned away from the window in search of the communicator buzzing for his attention. "There you are," he mused, grabbing the device as he answered.

"This is the admiral," he said, hoping it was the bridge. They had a schedule to keep and a lot of ships to bridge to rejoin his fleet near the Pharaonis home world, Eurysa.

"Admiral, it's time. We're preparing to activate the bridge into the Zanthea system. Would you like to join us?" announced Captain Dan Leahy, the captain of the *Draco*.

"Ah, good to hear, Dan. I was beginning to think our departure might get delayed. This fleet is like herding cats and dogs, with how large it's gotten. But, yeah, I'm on my way. Go ahead with the jump if you need to. We've got a lot of ships to move, so don't wait on account of me," Willie calmly replied, grabbing the data pad he'd been reading as he headed for the exit.

"Affirmative, sir. We will proceed in opening the bridge—soon you shortly."

When Willie had been told the *Draco* would become his new flagship, he'd had no idea what kind of crew to expect or how trained or proficient they might be. It had been more than a year since the Zodarks and Orbots had invaded Sol. Ships, cities, military bases…these weren't the only thing the invaders had destroyed. The attacks had gutted the Navy and the Army of experienced officers, noncommissioned officers, and lower enlisted. Ships and cities could be rebuilt. People and the experiences they had were not easily or quickly replaced. It took time, and that was something the Republic was consistently short of.

When Willie met Captain Dan Leahy, he knew within moments of speaking with him that *Draco* was in good hands. Leahy had an extensive career in commanding battleships and had fought in most of the major campaigns of the last war. Whether it was fortune or fate, Leahy and the majority of his crew, raw recruits sprinkled with veteran spacers, were at a joint training base with the Altairians during the Battle of Sol. They had been spared the carnage of that day and now that the *Draco* was ready for battle, it was their time, their ship, that would bring the vengeance of a nation down upon the Zodark Empire.

"Make a hole!" a petty officer shouted as Willie made his way down the corridor. Spacers were rushing to and fro as the ship prepared to generate the temporary wormhole—connecting Sol to Zanthea.

"Hey, watch yourself—oh, um, sorry about that, Admiral," stammered a petty officer he bumped into. "I guess we're all in a rush to our stations. Sorry I lashed out at you."

Willie smiled at the brief exchange. He glanced to the man's breast pocket—Patterson. "There's nothing to be sorry about, Patterson.

You're doing your job. I'm the one who's in the way. Please, carry on, and don't let me delay you."

"Aye-aye, Admiral, and thank you for that," Patterson returned, his cheeks still flush with embarrassment. "Make a hole! The admiral is passing through!" he shouted, causing everyone to stop and step aside, standing against the wall as they waited for him to pass.

As he exited the corridor leading him to *Draco*'s internal tram system, he still marveled at how quickly and effortlessly the crew of this giant star carrier was able to rapidly move about the ship. Positioned along the spine of the ship was a series of internal trams positioned on every other deck. At thirty-two hundred meters in length and thirty-six decks in height, the ship was cleverly built with elevator banks and trams that made the ship feel less big and quick to traverse.

He walked past station E-14, heading for the elevators. The bridge was positioned four decks below, on 18—in the forward center of the ship. Waiting for the elevator, he could feel the awesome power of the ship's reactors as they charged the giant energy capacitors needed to activate the bridging technology the Humtars had given them. This new, singular capability meant the Republic would no longer be dependent on the Altairians or even the Gallentines to assist them in moving their battle groups from one location to another in a single jump. No longer needing to rely on just the stargate network was going to make the Republic more than just an up-and-coming spacefaring nation. It was going to turn them into a real regional power. The immense amount of time saved by not having to transit from stargate to stargate would transform their interstellar economy, and the importance of being able to move warships to where they were needed, when they were needed, could not be overstated.

When the doors to the elevator opened, Willie walked into the bridge and smiled. He saw a well-oiled machine with officers at different stations calling out status updates and reports. Centered on the bridge in command of it all stood the ship's captain—Dan Leahy.

"Attention! The admiral is now on the bridge!" shouted the COB or Chief of the Boat as Willie made his way toward Captain Leahy.

"Carry on," echoed Willie, approaching the skipper.

"Admiral, I'm glad you made it. We're opening the bridge as we speak," Leahy announced, the two of them turning to the main monitor.

They watched with childlike wonder as whatever physics and magic it was that created this wormhole—this bridge between Sol and Zanthea—began to appear. Moments later, when the bridge was confirmed stable, the columns of warships along *Draco* moved towards the bridge, crossing to the other side like it was nothing.

When the final ship had crossed, they closed the bridge, severing the temporary link between systems. Turning to Captain Leahy, Willie said, "Congratulations, Dan, you just completed the Republic's first bridge."

A few celebratory remarks were made, then it was back to work.

"Dan, once the ships of our convoy have been accounted for, establish contact with General Hopper and Admiral Montague, letting them know we arrived and are awaiting their status updates. Go ahead and transmit the Fleet Files—I'm sure everyone is eager for messages from home," directed Willie as he readied to leave the bridge.

"Aye, Admiral. Would you like us to coordinate our fleet with Admiral Montague, or do you want us to stay in a separate formation for now?" Leahy clarified.

Willie shrugged. "They should still be in high orbit. Let's position the fleet near the planet but not in direct orbit. We can reposition later if necessary. I'll see you in the wardroom for dinner. Make sure to invite the junior officers and NCOs to tonight's dinner. This is a big day for the Republic—we're one step closer to not having to rely on the Altairians or the Gallentines for big fleet moves like this."

"Amen to that, sir. We'll see you tonight."

Chapter Thirty-Nine

Mid-July 2115
Fifth Corps HQ
FOB Sparta

Varinius hated this kind of meeting. It was a waste of time, as far as he was concerned—endless briefs, endless talk. But they'd dragged him here, and he would sit through it because that was the job. Still, it grated on him. The Command and Control Operations Center buzzed with the frenetic energy of staff officers and techs monitoring the battle space, their fingers flying across holographic consoles, faces lit by the constant flow of tactical data. The place was a high-tech nerve center for the Corps, all shimmering holoprojections and layers of intel. He appreciated that, but the inefficiency of sitting here, discussing plans that should've been locked down days ago, gnawed at him.

The room was massive, dominated by a central holographic map that floated above the polished table, showing every critical detail of the Pharaonis capital, Vrahk'tol—the heart of the enemy. The city looked like a fortress even in miniature, with layers of defenses marked in red, and Republic forces spread in a tightening noose around it. This was the final push. Varinius knew it. They all knew it. But they were wasting time talking.

Varinius's eyes narrowed as Major General Kim Chaek stormed into the room, barking orders before his short legs even cleared the doorway. Chaek wasn't the type to waste time with pleasantries. Small in stature but with a presence that filled the space, Chaek's sharp, precise movements matched his tone—direct, no nonsense, and harsh as hell.

"Good morning. Sit down. Let's get this over with," Chaek snapped, moving toward the front of the room with the intensity of a man who couldn't be bothered with subtlety. His reputation as the "Ragin' Asian" was well-earned. He didn't mince words, and his fuse was short. Varinius respected that. At least the man didn't pretend to be something he wasn't.

Chaek wasted no time. "Yesterday's briefing was delayed for reasons beyond my control," he growled, waving off any excuse that might've been lingering in the air. "We received critical intelligence from General Hopper—intel that changes the game plan."

Varinius grunted. Chaek was laying it on thick. The 11th Spartacus Division commander crossed his arms, his eyes locked on the 3D topographical map now floating above the table. Vrahk'tol glowed in the center. Varinius's division, the 11th, was on the front line of this coming assault, tasked with punching a hole straight into the capital. That was his job—to break the enemy, fast and clean.

Chaek flicked a finger, and the map zoomed in, showing key points along the Pharaonis defenses. "Republic intelligence cracked a significant portion of the Pharaonis' comms. They've been working with some Orbot defectors, and the picture we've got now gives us a clearer view of their defensive posture. They're stretched, gentlemen, but they're dug in. This isn't going to be easy."

Varinius stayed silent, absorbing every word. He wasn't the type to talk unless he had something meaningful to add. Chaek, on the other hand, was always talking.

Chaek's eyes burned into each of the division commanders standing around the table. "Here's how it's going down. Fourth Corps will launch a feint attack three days before our main offensive. The goal is to get the Pharaonis to shift forces away from our real target—Vrahk'tol." His tone was sharp, clipped. "Twenty hours before we launch, Sixth Corps will hit them from the opposite side. They'll think that's the main assault. While their attention is split, Fifth Corps—our Corps—will strike the heart. That's us, gentlemen. We're the hammer."

Varinius shifted his stance, his eyes narrowing as the map flickered with the movements Chaek described. The plan was ambitious, maybe too ambitious. But it was bold, and bold was what they needed.

Chaek pointed at the map, his voice cutting through the room like a blade. "It'll be the 9th and 11th Divisions spearheading this. You, Varinius—your division will lead the assault. You'll punch through their defenses here." He jabbed at the line on the map. "Straub's 9th will follow. Break through, clear the way, and the rest of us will push in. The city falls, and the war's over."

There it was. The weight had dropped right onto Varinius's shoulders, but he didn't flinch. This was why he was here, why he'd fought every step of the way on this damn planet. The 11th would lead the charge. The risk was massive, but he was used to risk. The odds didn't matter when you knew your men and knew the fight.

Chaek kept going, his voice growing sharper. "You don't need me to tell you this, but I will anyway. This is on you. If you don't break their lines, this entire assault falls apart. No pressure."

Varinius shot a quick glance at the other division commanders, noting the tension in their expressions. Chaek's words had hit home. But this wasn't news to Varinius. He'd known what was riding on this from the start. His division had taken the brunt of the fighting in the lead-up to this final push, and now they'd be the ones to make the decisive blow.

Chaek, clearly pleased with himself, turned to the room. "Straub, Hentze, Toon—you'll support the advance. Once the 9th and 11th break the line, you push in hard. No hesitation. We can't let them recover. We're going to hit them fast and hard, and keep pushing until there's nothing left of their defenses."

Varinius's mind was already racing through the logistics. His regiments were ready, but the Pharaonis had been preparing for this too. They knew this was coming, and the element of surprise wouldn't last long. He needed to hit them with overwhelming force before they could dig in deeper.

Chaek's voice pierced through his thoughts, harsher than ever. "We end this in Vrahk'tol. We take the city, we crush the Queen, and we finish the Pharaonis. Get your men ready. There's no second chances here."

Varinius nodded, his expression unreadable. He didn't need second chances. He needed the opportunity, and now he had it.
****

11th Spartacus Regiment
Tactical Operation Center

The officers around the holographic map table nodded in agreement, though the air was thick with tension. This wasn't their first mission, and it certainly wouldn't be the last. Everyone knew the stakes were higher now. The Pharaonis were dug in around Vrahk'tol, and the orders they'd just received meant they'd be the ones at the tip of the spear.

Thomas tapped the map, and the holographic terrain shifted to show the paths their regiments would take. The city of Vrahk'tol loomed ahead, flanked by dense forests, with defensive fortifications glowing in red. The terrain had been heavily scouted by drones, but nothing about the upcoming assault would be easy.

"All right, let's break it down," Thomas began, his voice calm but authoritative. "We've got three days before Fifth Corps' main assault. During that time, we need to get into position. General Varinius has assigned us to spearhead the attack—23rd Mech and my 11th Spartacus tanks will lead the push. 24th Infantry will be in support, ready to flank and sweep through any breach we make. K-pop, you're on fire support, as always, but I want extra eyes on your resupply chains. This is going to be a drawn-out fight."

Major Yoon Ja-Seong, ever the sharp artilleryman, straightened and gave a quick nod. "Roger that, Colonel. I'll have the ammo dumps positioned along our route of advance. We'll maintain flexibility on fire missions in case the enemy tries to counterattack while we're advancing."

"Good," Thomas replied. His eyes scanned the other officers, then settled on Vaughn. The newly promoted CO of the 23rd Texas Mech Regiment still had a lot to prove, but Thomas trusted him. "Vaughn, your regiment's been holding its own these past few months, and you've kept pace with the tanks. I'm expecting the same on this push."

Vaughn smirked, more confident than before. "We'll keep up, Colonel. My Bobcats and Pumas are prepped, and my infantry are ready to roll. They know the drill."

Thomas gave a slight nod of approval before continuing. "Now, here's where it gets tricky. The Pharaonis have had weeks to fortify their lines. Our drones show dense defensive networks and heavy artillery emplacements. We're going to punch through here." He pointed to a section of the map where the Pharaonis defenses narrowed. "Also here," he continued, shifting his hand. "Both are heavily fortified, but we've identified gaps in their artillery coverage. That's where 23rd Mech and my tanks will hit."

Ahlstrom, ever the pragmatist, leaned in, his brow furrowed. "You're saying we're going right for the throat, then. No feints, no distractions. Full-on assault."

"Exactly," Thomas confirmed. "Fourth Corps is handling the feint three days before our push. By the time we hit them, they'll be recovering from the first attack. We need to move fast, strike hard, and break through before they can reinforce."

"Sounds simple enough," Ahlstrom grunted, though his eyes showed he knew better. Simple plans rarely stayed simple.

Thomas adjusted the map again, zooming in on the city of Vrahk'tol itself. The capital sprawled out before them like a fortress. "Once we breach the outer defenses, 24th Infantry moves in. You'll secure a perimeter, sweep for enemy forces, and reinforce our tanks. We need to keep momentum and avoid getting bogged down in the streets. We cannot afford a slow, drawn-out siege."

Ahlstrom nodded. "Understood. My infantry will be ready. Urban combat's always messy, but we'll keep things tight."

Thomas continued, his voice steady. "K-pop, you're going to need to keep our artillery fire consistent. We'll be calling in a lot of fire missions to soften up their positions. You're also on counter-battery duty. The Pharaonis have mobile artillery, and they're likely going to use it to hammer us as soon as we breach. I need your guys to find their guns and take them out fast."

Yoon's eyes gleamed with the promise of a challenge. "Consider it done. I'll have my fire control teams ready to target anything that moves."

"Good," Thomas said, his tone shifting slightly. "Now, I'm not going to sugarcoat this. This is going to be brutal. The Pharaonis know they're cornered, and they're going to fight like hell to protect their queen and their capital. We're going to be the ones they throw everything at. But I trust you. I trust your men. We've been through hell already on this campaign, and we'll get through this."

The officers around the table fell silent for a moment, the weight of what lay ahead settling on them. It was always like this before a major assault—the quiet before the storm. They knew what was coming. The chaos, the bloodshed, the uncertainty of whether they'd all make it through.

Thomas broke the silence. "One last thing. I need each of you to stay adaptable. Plans are great until the first shots are fired. After that, we're going to need to improvise. Communications will be key. Keep your units informed, keep your eyes open, and be ready to react."

Ahlstrom smirked. "Adapt or die, right?"

Thomas allowed himself a brief smile. "That's the spirit. Now, get your regiments prepped. We move at first light."

As the other officers moved away from the map table, preparing to head out to their respective units, Thomas lingered for a moment, his eyes still on the holographic map of Vrahk'tol. His mind was already racing through every possible scenario, every move the Pharaonis might make. This was it—the final battle. He could feel it. If they broke through here, it was over. The Pharaonis would fall.

****

11th Spartacus Regiment

The inside of Colonel Thomas's Yeti rattled as Sergeant Wilson fired the railgun again, sending a hypersonic round straight into one of the towering Pharaonis structures. The shot hit with precision, blowing out the base of the tower. Immediately, it crumbled, collapsing like a dying tree onto a nearby housing nest. The impact shook the ground, flattening the surrounding buildings like a bomb had gone off.

"Pumas, cover the flanks!" Thomas barked into his comm. "Laser blasters and 50mms, keep those Pharaonis heads down. Berserker, get your infantry dismounted and moving. We need boots on the ground!"

"Roger that, Spartacus One. Berserker Six copies," came Captain Martin's voice, calm and controlled, despite the chaos. "Berserker Eleven, move your platoon forward and provide cover fire. We're deploying now."

Lieutenant Loflin responded, "Berserker Eleven copies. We're on it." His platoon's Pumas wheeled out to the left, laser blasters and railguns ripping into the Pharaonis infantry as they swarmed from the wreckage.

Colonel Thomas's focus shifted as another explosion rocked the field ahead. A Yeti, point vehicle in the advance, was hit hard—its left tracks blown off, the drive sprocket torn to shreds. The Beetle tanks were hitting back, firing what looked like bolts of lightning from their energy weapons.

"Spartacus One, this is Berserker Eleven," Loflin's voice crackled over the radio. "Lead Yeti's down—sprocket's out. Repair teams are en route, but they're sitting ducks."

"Copy, Berserker Eleven," Thomas growled. "Pull it back to the reserve line once mobile. Berserker Six, you're on point now. Take out those Beetles and press the attack."

"Understood, Spartacus One," Captain Martin's voice was steady as he directed his men. "Berserker Company, let's move! Engage those tanks, and infantry, push forward!"

The Pharaonis hit back hard. From the rubble of the city streets, swarms of enemy soldiers launched themselves at the advancing Republic armor. Dozens of Pharaonis, armed with magnetic-clamp explosives, charged the Yetis, screaming as they hurled themselves into the oncoming fire.

"Linebackers, suppress that infantry!" Thomas ordered. His voice cut through the crackling comms like a whip. "Don't let them close in!"

A squad of Pharaonis broke through the suppressive fire, sprinting with antitank mines strapped to their chests. They moved too fast, too erratic for the gunners to cut them all down. One managed to get within striking range of a Yeti just as two fire teams from Lone Star Six's 23rd Mech Regiment cut it to pieces with their M-91 blasters. The mine detonated anyway.

The explosion hit the side of the Yeti like a sledgehammer. The shaped charge ripped through the tank's armor in a molten jet, turning the crew compartment into a furnace of fire and shrapnel. The Yeti went up in flames, burning bright against the darkening sky, the turret blown clean off and flipping through the air.

"Spartacus One, this is Longhorn Tango. Air and artillery ready on your mark," announced Sergeant Sciallo over the comms.

"Hold fire, Longhorn Tango," Thomas replied, his eyes locked on the battle in front of him. "Let's not waste artillery until we know what we're dealing with."

The enemy wasn't slowing down. Insectoid Pharaonis soldiers climbed over the wreckage, using the burning Yeti as cover. The Beetle tanks rumbled forward from the rear, their segmented armor glinting under the haze of battle. Lightning-like energy blasts shot from their weapons, hitting anything they could target—Bobcats, Pumas,

Linebackers. Anything they touched exploded in a cascade of fire and metal.

"Spartacus One, Berserker Eleven! Beetles closing in from the left flank, they're bringing in their Dips as well!" Lieutenant Loflin's voice was sharp, cutting through the chaos.

On his tactical display, Thomas indeed saw a mass of the Pharaonis "Dips," their APCs, spilling infantry into the fight. The Dips dipped as they offloaded soldiers, creating a wave of fresh enemy troops that surged toward the Republic lines.

"Berserker Six, hold the line! Aegis Six, Centaur Six, Dreadnought Six, form up and push those Dips back! We can't let them close on the tanks!" Thomas barked over the command channel. "All Yetis, switch to AMP rounds and focus fire on those Beetles."

"Spartacus One, this is Aegis Six. We're engaging now," Captain Stenberg confirmed as his Aegis Company shifted into formation, their Pumas flanking the advancing Beetles.

The railguns from Thomas's Yetis thundered, each shot a hypersonic punch that ripped into the Pharaonis armor. One Beetle took a direct hit, its segmented armor shattering as the tank imploded, scattering debris across the street. Another one dodged, sending a lightning bolt slamming into a Bobcat, which exploded on impact, throwing men and machines alike into the air.

"Centaur Six, this is Spartacus One. I need your company to flank right," Thomas ordered. "We've got too many Dips on that side. Take them out before they hit our infantry!"

"Roger that, Spartacus One," Captain Fordham replied. "We're moving. Centaur Company, follow my lead!"

The battle was chaos—Republic infantry dismounted from Linebackers, forming tight-knit squads that lay down suppressive fire as the Pharaonis swarmed. The enemy just kept coming, wave after wave, their morale seemingly unshaken.

"Mustang One, this is Longhorn Six. You're needed on the left flank! We've got Dips coming in hot, and Berserker's stretched thin," Lieutenant Kincaide's voice called over the battlenet.

"Copy that, Longhorn Six. Mustang One's on the move," Dausch replied, his platoon shifting toward the left, laser blasters cutting down Pharaonis as they surged forward.

Thomas's attention flicked back to the horizon, where more blips appeared on his infrared feed. Something bigger was coming. "Wilson, check those heat signatures. What the hell is that?" Thomas asked, his grip tightening on the armrest.

The screen lit up—larger, more concentrated signatures. "Sir... Beetle reinforcements," Wilson stammered. "A lot of them."

"Damn it," Thomas muttered, his heart racing. "All units, prepare for heavy armor engagement. They're bringing the fight to us."

The Beetles broke through the smoke, charging head-on at the Republic's armor. Lightning bolts shot from their cannons, crashing into Yetis and Linebackers alike. The earth shook with each impact, but the Republic forces held their ground, firing back with everything they had.

"Berserker Eleven, engage those Beetles with everything! Centaur Six, reinforce the right flank! We've got to stop them before they overrun our lines!" Thomas shouted.

The Yetis fired in unison, railguns thundering as AMP rounds tore into the oncoming Beetles. The battle had become a brutal melee, armor against armor, infantry against infantry. The streets of Vrahk'tol were awash in fire and blood, but the Republic soldiers fought with everything they had, refusing to give an inch.

"Spartacus One to all units, hold the line! We push through or we die here!" Thomas's voice echoed through the comms, rallying his men as the fight reached its brutal peak

Colonel Thomas gritted his teeth as another explosion rattled his Yeti. The Pharaonis Beetles were advancing, their lightning-like energy blasts streaking across the battlefield. His tanks were holding the line, but just barely. His gut told him they couldn't sustain this level of combat much longer without heavier support.

The tactical display inside the Yeti flickered with red blips—enemy contacts. Too many. The Pharaonis were throwing everything they had at them. Infantry swarmed the wreckage of the battlefield, Beetle tanks pushed forward, and the Dips continued offloading more soldiers. The situation was deteriorating fast.

"Wilson, keep those AMP rounds coming," Thomas barked, his eyes locked on the tactical map. "We need to slow them down. I'm calling in the big guns."

He flipped the comms to Sergeant Sciallo's frequency. "Longhorn Tango, this is Spartacus One. I need a full artillery barrage on the following coordinates: grid seven-five-three, break, seven-seven-two. We've got Pharaonis armor massing in that sector. Send everything you've got—fire for effect. Over."

Sciallo immediately replied, "Copy that, Spartacus One. Artillery inbound. Stand by for fire mission."

Thomas didn't have time to wait for the shells to land. He switched channels to coordinate air support. "Mustang, Longhorn, Aegis—this is Spartacus One. I'm calling in CAS. We need air to hammer their rear positions. Hold tight."

He keyed in the air support frequency, his voice hard and commanding. "This is Spartacus One to Reaper Control. I need immediate CAS at grid seven-five-three, break, seven-seven-two. Request Talons and Reapers for a sustained bombing run on enemy armor and infantry concentrations. Hit them hard. We've got Beetles and Dips on the ground, and we're taking heavy fire. Over."

"Spartacus One, this is Reaper Control. Good copy on CAS request. Talons and Reapers are en route. ETA three mikes. Stand by."

Thomas exhaled, his eyes scanning the battlefield through the Yeti's external cameras. The ground ahead was a warzone—a wasteland of burning tanks, crumpled buildings, and scorched earth. The Beetles were rumbling closer, their segmented legs propelling them forward like mechanical nightmares. The energy blasts from their cannons streaked through the air, striking Republic vehicles and sending plumes of smoke and debris into the sky.

His Yetis continued to fire, their railguns hammering the enemy tanks, but the Pharaonis were relentless. The air was thick with the smell of burning metal and charred flesh, and the deafening sound of battle rang in his ears, even through the thick armor of his tank. Every few seconds, the ground shook from another explosion.

In the chaos, Thomas's mind raced. He could see his men dismounting from the Linebackers, forming fire teams to engage the Pharaonis infantry. Laser blasts flashed across the battlefield, cutting down the insectoid soldiers as they surged forward. But for every Pharaonis that fell, two more seemed to take its place. The enemy was endless.

"Spartacus One, Longhorn Tango. Artillery is firing now. Splash in ten seconds," Sciallo's voice crackled over the comms.

Thomas braced himself, his eyes scanning the horizon where the Pharaonis armor was massing. In the distance, the Beetles continued their advance, their massive energy weapons glowing with power as they prepared to fire another volley.

The first artillery shells hit. The ground erupted in a series of deafening explosions. The Pharaonis position was engulfed in a wall of fire and shrapnel as shells rained down on them, obliterating everything in their path. Buildings crumbled, Beetle tanks exploded, and the alien infantry were torn apart by the relentless barrage.

Thomas watched in grim satisfaction as the Pharaonis advance faltered. The artillery was doing its job—pounding the enemy into submission. The Beetles that weren't destroyed by the initial strikes scrambled to retreat, their legs buckling under the shockwaves. But there was no escape from the firestorm.

"Keep it coming, Longhorn Tango," Thomas growled. "Don't let up."

"Roger that, Spartacus One. More rounds incoming," Sciallo confirmed.

The sky darkened as the second wave of artillery hit. The Pharaonis were caught in a relentless barrage of high-explosive rounds, each blast shaking the earth beneath Thomas's Yeti. The Beetle tanks tried to regroup, but they were being hammered too hard. Even their formidable armor couldn't withstand this level of punishment.

"Spartacus One, Reaper Control," the comms buzzed. "Talons and Reapers are entering the AO. Targeting enemy armor and infantry. Bombing run in progress."

Thomas turned his gaze skyward. In the distance, the distinctive shapes of the Talon fighter-bombers and Reaper ground-attack drones came into view, their engines roaring as they closed in on the enemy positions. Within seconds, the sky was filled with the sound of jet engines and the thunderous crack of bombs being dropped.

The Talons struck first, releasing a barrage of high-explosive bombs over the Pharaonis positions. The explosions were massive—entire sections of the enemy line were obliterated in the blink of an eye. Beetles and Dips were thrown into the air like toys, their armor shredded by the force of the blasts.

The Reapers followed up, swooping low over the battlefield and unloading their payload of precision-guided missiles. The missiles screamed through the air, homing in on the surviving Beetles and Dips. One by one, the Pharaonis vehicles erupted in fireballs, their remains scattered across the battlefield.

Thomas grinned, his heart pounding in his chest. "That's it," he muttered to himself. "Hammer them into the dirt."

The battlefield ahead of him was a scene of utter devastation. The Pharaonis advance had been shattered. Their armor lay in ruins, and their infantry were either dead or retreating. The combined firepower of the artillery and air support had turned the tide.

"Spartacus One, this is Aegis Six," Captain Stenberg's voice came over the comms. "The enemy's breaking. We're pushing forward to secure the objective."

"Good work, Aegis Six," Thomas replied. "All units, advance! Press the attack!"

The Republic forces surged forward, their tanks rolling over the wreckage of the battlefield. Infantry moved in tight formation, clearing out the remaining pockets of resistance with brutal efficiency. The Pharaonis were broken, their forces scattered and in disarray.

Thomas watched as his tanks rolled forward, their railguns firing at anything that moved. The sound of battle began to fade as the last of the enemy was mopped up. The Pharaonis had thrown everything they had at them, but it hadn't been enough.

"Spartacus One to all units," Thomas said over the comms. "The enemy's broken. Regroup and prepare for further orders. Well done."

As the smoke began to clear and the battlefield fell silent, Thomas allowed himself a moment of relief. They had held the line and survived.
****

Mustang One

The battlefield behind them still smoldered, the acrid smell of burning metal and the sharp sting of charred flesh lingering in the air as Lieutenant Dausch crouched beside a twisted heap of what had once been a Yeti tank. His pulse quickened as Colonel Thomas's orders echoed in his mind: "Check the bridge, quietly. Report back." The request was straightforward, but nothing about this war had been straightforward.

"Corporal Chow, grab your squad," Dausch ordered, his voice steady despite the tension gnawing at him. "We need to recon that bridge. Stay low and stay sharp."

Chow gave a sharp nod, motioning to his squad to move out. They advanced carefully, sticking close to the remains of vehicles, buildings, and smoldering ruins of the battlefield, using whatever cover they could find. Dausch watched them move, feeling a sense of pride in their discipline. These weren't fresh-faced recruits anymore; they had been hardened by the hell of Eurysa. Every movement was deliberate, precise—Chow and his team had become an extension of the war machine.

Dausch, however, was still adjusting to the feel of the lieutenant's bars weighing on his shoulders.

This wasn't supposed to happen, he thought, glancing at his men. *I wasn't supposed to be here, not like this.* He had fought hard to remain an NCO, fighting on the front lines with his brothers, but after the losses they'd taken, the responsibility had been thrust upon him. He had no choice. At least now I can make sure these guys get through this war alive.

They approached the remains of a Linebacker that had been reduced to a blackened husk, its turret blown clear off. Chow signaled for the squad to spread out and take up defensive positions, eyes scanning the area. The bridge loomed ahead, its once proud structure now marred by battle. Dausch could see the craters and jagged edges where artillery shells and missiles had torn through the rail lines and vehicle lanes.

"Lieutenant, I've got eyes on the bridge," Chow's voice crackled over the comms, soft but steady. "One of the two rail lines are missing. The remaining one looks intact, but I wouldn't trust it until engineers confirm."

"Copy that, Chow. What about the vehicle bridge?" Dausch replied, creeping up to where Chow had set up his position.

"Two of the three eastbound lanes are gone. Looks like a twenty-five meter gap. Westbound lanes look intact, but there's craters—two meters wide at about forty meters in. Another one two hundred meters down the road." As he spoke, the video feed streamed to Dausch's HUD, showing the damage in real time.

Dausch grimaced. The bridge was critical to the next phase of their push toward Vrahk'tol, and it was hanging by a thread. He rolled onto his side and quickly opened a chat window to Colonel Thomas back at the TOC. "Eyes on the bridge established," he dictated quietly, his speech converted to text. "No sign of enemy forces. Structural integrity questionable—request engineering support for further assessment."

He was about to hit send when Chow's voice came through again, this time tinged with confusion. "Uh... sir, are you seeing this?"

Dausch minimized the chat window and froze. Through the cracked lenses of his visor, he could saw it—a strange vehicle slowly making its way toward them from the other side of the bridge. It was unlike any Pharaonis vehicle they had encountered before. Its segmented hull gleamed under the alien sky, but it wasn't armed—or if it was, it wasn't pointing anything at them. The vehicle slowed, then stopped.

"What the hell is that?" Dausch whispered to himself. Then, to his astonishment, a hatch opened on the roof of the vehicle, and a long, slender rod began to rise. Unfurling at the top of the rod was what looked like a flag—this was something he had never seen the Pharaonis do.

Dausch's heart pounded in his chest. "Chow, open a channel to the TOC. They need to see this." He quickly routed the video feed to Colonel Thomas's command center. "Longhorn Six, this is Mustang One. I've got visual on an unknown Pharaonis vehicle displaying what appears to be a flag. Stand by for more information."

Then the sound started. Low, almost imperceptible at first, but it grew louder. "Do you hear that?" Chow asked, his voice tinged with disbelief. Dausch strained his ears, trying to make sense of the strange noise. It was rhythmic, almost musical, but distorted.

Then it hit him. They were trying to communicate.

"I'll be damned," Dausch muttered. "They're trying to talk to us." He quickly activated the translation software in his HUD, routing the audio feed through the Republic's best guess at deciphering the Pharaonis language.

The translation was rough—just fragments of words, disjointed and unclear—but the message was unmistakable.

"Lieutenant..." Chow's voice was low, his tone a mixture of disbelief and cautious hope. "Did they just say what I think they said?"

Dausch swallowed, his mouth dry. "Yeah, Chow. They did." He blinked, eyes wide as saucers beneath his visor. "They're asking to surrender."

The realization hit him like a punch to the gut. After all this—after the months of bloodshed and destruction—could it really be over?

"Get me Colonel Thomas," Dausch ordered, his voice tight with urgency. "Now."

****

11th Spartacus Regiment
Tactical Operation Center

The door to the room they had turned into their map room swung open, and Captain Fordham barged in on Colonel Thomas's planning session.

"Colonel, you've got to come with me. You have to hear this." The young captain was practically bursting with excitement. His enthusiasm caught them all off guard.

"Whoa, slow down, Eli, what's going on?" asked Thomas in a more controlled, restrained tone.

"Sir, it's the Pharaonis—you've got to hear this," Fordham replied, then guided the group to another room that had been turned into a comms center.

When Thomas entered the room, one of the sergeants handed him a pair of headphones to put on and played an audio recording. At first, he didn't believe it. He ordered his comms soldiers to double-check the audio and the translation software. They verified the specific word he had been questioning—it was accurate.

That was when it hit him: *they're surrendering.*

Chapter Forty

Seven Hours Later
Wardroom, RNS *Draco*
Zanthea System

Admiral Rosentreter smiled in amusement at Lieutenant General Jayden Hopper's awestruck facial expression. "I must say, Willie, this ship is a beauty, a truly amazing-looking warship," complimented General Hopper after the stewards had removed everyone's dishes, leaving only a fresh cup of coffee. "When I stayed aboard one of those New Eden class heavy orbital assault ships, RNS *Eisenhower*, I thought the amenities were impressive for a warship—I was wrong. The *Draco* takes the cake," praised General Hopper again as he reached for his coffee.

"Thank you, Jayden. I'm still getting used to it myself," replied Admiral Rosentreter. "The closest thing I can compare it against would be the *Freedom*, but it's been a long time since I last served on her. The *Draco* still doesn't have quite the elaborate MWR setups the *Freedom* does, but this is far better than even the *Victory*-class battleships."

"Yes, well, I suppose we should get down to business," General Hopper said as his tone turned serious. "For the past several weeks, I've had our signal intelligence people listening in on Pharaonis communications while our AI continues to try and piece together their words and phrases to create a more accurate translation of their language. We're translating roughly sixty-two to sixty-seven percent of what they're saying. Even while we only understand a little more than half of what they are saying, it's enough for us to start piecing things together."

"Is any of it proving to be helpful?" Rosentreter asked.

"Yes and no," Hopper replied. "Yesterday we intercepted some comms traffic within the capital that was later transmitted to the other cities and industrial centers we haven't destroyed from space yet. It was a little hard to decipher it, but the best we've been able to figure out is their queen appears very concerned with the level of destruction we've wrought upon the planet and their cities. We're viewing this as a positive indicator that the queen might be open to ending the war soon."

The general had barely finished his sentence when Rosentreter's comms device chirped. "Hang on a second, Jayden. Let me find out what's going on," he explained, connecting the call to his neurolink.

This is the admiral. What's going on, Lieutenant Willard? he asked through the neurolink connection.

Admiral, sorry for the intrusion. We received a priority message from the battleship Gladiator. *They're relaying a message to us from Major General Kim Chaek, the Fifth Corps commander—he said a representative of the Pharaonis Queen made contact with one of his units...sir, the Pharaonis have requested to speak with our leader. They wish to discuss terms to end the war. General Chaek is asking how you would like the unit they made contact with to respond,* explained Lieutenant Willard.

Rosentreter turned to Hopper. "I'll be damned. One of your commanders—General Chaek—he said a Pharaonis emissary made contact with one of his units and is asking to discuss terms to end the war."

Hopper smiled brightly. "Hallelujah. Miracles still do happen! Well, Willie, I suppose we should send them the terms of surrender and take it from there."

"Besides ending what has been a brutal war, you know what else this means?" Rosentreter asked with a grin.

Jayden laughed sarcastically before his face turned into that of a cold-blooded killer. "Yeah, this war is ending—now it's time to finish what the Zodark started."

****

Void Harbinger-7
Zanthea Star System

The *Void Harbinger-7* drifted silently in the cold darkness of space, a speck in the abyss, hidden by advanced technologies that made it invisible even to the most sophisticated enemy sensors. Its mission: to observe, to gather, and to report back to the Collective Nexus. For weeks, this Legion stealth corvette had silently observed the Pharaonis homeworld, watching the Republic and its allies rain fire down upon the planet's surface. When they had detected a signal the Pharaonis had asked for terms of surrender, they had seen enough.

Inside the cramped command deck, Commander Dyrann-09 stood motionless before the central console, the cold eyes of his Cyborg body fixed on the holographic display that flickered with the lines of data. The others—Zephak-222, the ship's engineer, Torrak-349, the tactical officer, and Gryllar-179, the sensor operator—worked silently around him, each attuned to their specific duties.

"Transmission decrypted." Gryllar's metallic voice cut through the silence, his slender fingers manipulating the console to bring the data into full view. "Final report from the ship they call *Draco* confirms energy signature matching Gallentine technology."

Dyrann's dark eyes narrowed. The Treaty of Yarmouth had been the Collective's one assurance that the Gallentines would remain neutral in this war, allowing the Milky Way's factions to determine their own fate. And yet here they were, in direct violation of the treaty.

"Their intervention is undeniable," Torrak-349 added, his tone as cold and indifferent as the void surrounding them. "The Orbots were right. The Gallentines are putting their hands on the scales."

"The treaty was always fragile," Dyrann replied, his voice calm yet laced with an edge of calculation. "That ship, *Draco*—it's energy readings are consistent with those used by the Gallentines. This adds further validity to the Orbots' account of a Gallentine fleet smashing their forces on the verge of victory against this faction they refer to as the Republic."

Gryllar-179 chimed in, "The Republic itself appears to be comprised of Humtars—but how? They were killed off long ago."

When the Orbots had reported their demise to the Collective, the Nexus had directed Legion to investigate. Their directive was to determine the validity of the Orbots' accounts. For a mission of this magnitude, Dyrann and the *Void Harbinger-7* had been chosen. His crew was relentless in their efficiency—no emotion, no hesitation. They delivered results, time and time again.

"This intelligence will shift the Nexus's entire strategy," Torrak-349 observed. "The Collective will have to make a move. Beyond the Gallentine betrayal, the discovery of Humtars…" His voice trailed off, an uncharacteristic display of uncertainty.

Dyrann's face remained stoic, his thoughts guarded. He had seen a great many things in his long service to Legion, but even he knew that if the Collective responded to this violation, it would expand the war into one more galaxy.

"*Void Harbinger-7* will return to the Nexus," Dyrann announced, breaking the silence. "We'll report directly to Primus-Kharak-001. The Nexus will decide our next move. Until then, we remain silent and not speak of what we have seen with anyone."

Zephak nodded sharply. "Understood. Preparing for pocket jump."

Dyrann's eyes lingered on the holographic display, the discovery of Humtars and the evidence Gallentine treachery clear before him. The Collective had remained patient, watching as the Milky Way tore itself apart, content to guide the outcome from afar. But now, with the Gallentine Empire's hand exposed, a resurrection of Humtars—the time for restraint was ending.

As their ship activated its wormhole generator and they prepared to disappear into the void once more, Dyrann allowed himself a single moment of contemplation.

The galaxy is on the edge of a storm, and we just lit the fuse.

****

From the Authors

Miranda and I hope that you've enjoyed this book. It's hard to believe that this is the eleventh book in the Rise of the Republic series, isn't it? Well, book twelve will be just around the corner. The preorder for *Into the Schism* is live—simply visit Amazon to sign up. Due to several personal factors, we've put the date for this book farther out. However, as always, we do aim to try and release it well before the date that we currently have on Amazon.

Although this portion of the series will be wrapping up with the twelfth book, we do have an exciting announcement for you. A new spinoff series, spearheaded by our friend and successful science fiction author, Brandon Ellis, will be debuting soon. Battles of the Republic will deep dive into some of the campaigns you've already read about in our main series, adding to the richness of the universe you've come to love. To sign up for the preorder of the first book in the new series, *The Intus Invasion*, Amazon is your destination.

On other fronts, if you are a fan of our military thrillers, we will be releasing a follow-up book to our Monroe Doctrine series, *A Post-War Novel*. This book will set up our Surrogate Wars series, which will describe the often alluded to AI war that you've read about in the Rise of the Republic. Even if you haven't read the entire Monroe Doctrine series, this book will help to understand some of the background of our sci-fi universe. To preorder—you guessed it—just visit Amazon.

As always, we appreciate each and every one of you that take the time to read our books. We definitely couldn't do this without you. If you've enjoyed *Into the Inferno*, we would love it if you could take a moment and write up a review on Amazon and Goodreads. Early reviews really make a huge difference in new readers discovering our books, and that in turn helps us to continue writing full-time and bringing you the stories you love.

All our best,

James Rosone and Miranda Watson

Abbreviation Key

1MC	Shipwide Communication System
AMP	Advanced Multipurpose
APM	Anti-Personnel Munitions
AO	Area of Operations
AOR	Area of Responsibility
AP	Armor Piercing
APC	Armored PersonnelCarrier
ASAP	As soon as possible
AT	Anti-Tank
ATAC	Armored Transport Assault Craft
CAC	Combat Air Coordinator
CAS	Close-Air Support
CIC	Combat Information Center
CO	Commanding Officer
COB	Chief of the Boat
CQ	Charge of Quarters (guard duty)
CSB	Combat Support Base
CSW	Carrier Strike Wing
DEAD	Destruction of Enemy Air Defense
DM	Direct Message
ECM	Electronic Countermeasures
FAE	Fuel-Air Explosive
ENVG-B	Enhanced Night Vision Goggle—Binocular
ETA	Estimated Time of Arrival
FITREP	Fitness Report
FRAGO	Fragmentary Order
FTL	Faster Than Light
GDF	Gurista Defense Force
HQ	Headquarters
HUD	Heads-Up Display
IED	Improvised Explosive Device
IFV	Infantry Fighting Vehicle
INTSUM	Intelligence Summary
IRW	Intergalactic Rules of War
JATM	Joint Advanced Tactical Missile
JSOC	Joint Special Operations Command

KBR	Keller, Booth, and Root
KIA	Killed in Action
KPS	Kilometers Per Second
LMG	Light Machine Gun
LTV	Light Tactical Vehicle
LZ	Landing Zone
MW	Megawatt
NCO	Noncommissioned Officer
NOS	Zodark Officer
OAD	Orbital Assault Division
OAR	Orbital Assault Regiment
OAT	Orbital Assault Troop
ODA	Operational Delta Attachment (Special Forces)
OP	Observation Post
OSA	Omni-Spectral Array
P2	Priority Pad
PACT	Pilot Adaptive Combat Training
PDG	Point-Defense Gun
PELS	Pulsar Echo Location System
PFC	Private First Class
PTP	Pallas Training Protocol
QB	Quantum Beam
QF	Quantum Fusion
QFR	Quantum Fusion Reactor
QRF	Quick Reaction Force
R & R	Rest and Recreation
RNS	Republic Naval Service
RP	Rally Point
SAM	Surface-to-Air Missile
SITREP	Situation Report
SNA	State of Northeast Africa
SOF	Special Operations Forces
TAO	Tactical Action Officer
TOC	Tactical Operation Center
TRADOC	Training and Doctrine Command
UAV	Unmanned Aerial Vehicle
VSR	Void Scientific Research

XO   Executive Officer

THE END

Printed in Great Britain
by Amazon